THE BUSH CLINIC

BOOK I OF THE TRIBAL WARS

STELLA ATRIUM

ARRIVI DUCHY

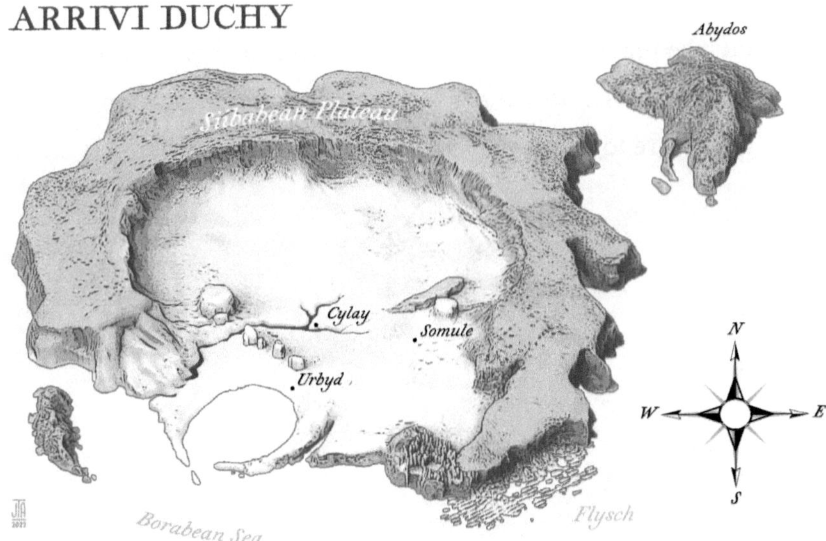

For the reader's convenience, a glossary of character names
with relationships, and a separate glossary of locations and
terms, are found at the end of this book.

ONE

from Dr. Edna Edwina Greensboro

"THE WHITE SKY OVER MEKUCOO LAND IS SO DIFFERENT FROM the golden savannah," Hakulupe Le said as we walked together in the humid afternoon. This local medical work slowed my research. I was looking for an exit, any excuse to call the duty complete. I had a lorry full of supplies waiting for the drive to my bush clinic.

We skirted the empty refugee camp. The stench was nauseating; not of death since morgue crews had passed this way, but of human and animal offal. Black insects buzzed near tent poles in the haze of heat. I saw discarded gallon containers of molded plastic, mismatched hemp-soled shoes, and damaged guns.

We saw him sitting on a stump by the road. Perhaps age fourteen, he wore ripped dungarees and a ragged tunic. Deep-set eyes watched us while he shooed insects by swishing a makeshift grass fan over a long gash on his leg. A sheen of sweat made his dark skin glisten. A karkar waited nearby; boy soldiers were never without their automatics even when ammunition was scarce.

Hakulupe Le approached him speaking in his dialect. She was age twenty, hair coiled at her neck and a linen skirt hanging to her ankles. I caught a few words of their exchange. She turned back, fixing me with forest-green eyes.

"Dr. Greensboro, can you look at his wound?"

"He should come with us to the hospital."

"He must wait."

"He cannot stay here. He'll be dead in two days."

Hakulupe Le came back to me. "His name is Karlyhi. His mother sat him here to wait until she returns. So he waits."

I took a disposable camera from my backpack and clicked Karlyhi's photo before he could object. The square print rolled from the camera's front. "Leave this photo with a note," I instructed. "If his mother returns, which she won't, she can find him at the hospital."

Karlyhi frowned at the photo that Hakulupe Le showed him.

"This is Edna Edwina Greensboro, a Softcheeks doctor," she began. Then I lost her meaning in the stream of strange words.

While Hakulupe Le talked, Karlyhi considered me. His steady gaze caused me to take stock. My jacket and skirt were caked with road dirt. My canvas shoes had lost their shape from the needed walking. Wisps of sandy hair had come loose from the binding cord.

Karlyhi calmly shook his head in the negative. Against my will, I admired his resolve. I took an energy bar from my pack, broke it in half, and bit into one section. I extended the other part to Karlyhi. His expression changed, but he saw my smile and looked away.

I gave the food to Hakulupe Le. Karlyhi accepted it from her hand.

He glanced over my backpack while he chewed and looked at the photo. He would make his own decision. He stood to place a hand-made crutch under his arm, and slung the karkar over his shoulder. He held out his other hand in a curt gesture, indicating that I should give him the backpack.

"You must," Hakulupe Le said, "so he saves face."

Hakulupe Le scribbled a note and fastened it with the photo onto the stump that had been his station. We walked past him for several yards. With determined strength, Karlyhi hobbled behind us. I was glad my backpack held only the day's necessities and was not a burden for him.

We heard sounds ahead, shouted commands and vehicle engines. We rounded a corner and came upon the remains site, older than the deserted camp. All Siibabean males, the grouping of bodies spoke to a massacre. It appeared that they had been made to stand on the rim of a pit and were eliminated by a barrage of automatic gunfire.

Investigators from the Westend Consortium of Planets had fashioned a matrix of sorts, partitioning the area with thin wood slats and string. They wore surgical masks, and their arms and hands were covered against the stench and filth. A lieutenant spoke into the low-fic of his headgear and directed a backhoe operator where to dig among the decomposing bodies.

Acrylic remains cases were stacked nearby. Only three had been filled by the backhoe's robotic arm. The driver of the anchored machine, seated in an enclosed cockpit, measured a certain length of grave material, slicing through the jumbled mass like a cookie cutter to lift and gently drop that section into the amber-colored container.

Karlyhi spat into the dirt. He hobbled back to the road where he stoically waited.

Dr. Leslie Abercrombie approached, removing his surgical mask and gloves. We had served a race-diversity residency in the same hospital at Two Forks on Cicero. He had pushed his idea of combining grant funds with mine to better serve the tribes, and had disembarked in a cycle ahead of me. I recently had spent the rainy season serving on his hospital staff and, when the billabongs finally receded, I opened my own clinic in the foothills of Mekucoo land.

"You're late," he told me. "You have thrown us completely off schedule."

"Nobody cares about your schedule, Leslie."

"You can walk back to the hospital," he said. "You wouldn't last twenty minutes on the open savannah."

I stuck out my chin; an unattractive gesture, or so I had been told. "I could make it."

"You're too valuable for—"

"Yeah, yeah," I said. "What did you find?"

Dr. Abercrombie paused, leaning slightly forward with one hand on his hip. "An impossible situation," he said in quieter tones. "When news spreads about this massacre site, the Siibabean will mount a new offensive. Your bush clinic is not safe."

"I decide when my work is in jeopardy."

"You cannot just—"

"Will you stop? You manage the hospital. I run the clinic."

"Look, Edna—"

"I'm Dr. Greensboro. In front of all these, I'm a doctor. Equal to you."

"You just called me Leslie!"

I stared into his face, a gesture Hakulupe Le had called evil-eye. Dr. Abercrombie looked around at the questioning faces of tribesmen and technicians. Hakulupe Le stared at the ground. "Well, then. I must remain here to make a record," he said, "and notify the local authorities. You can grab a ride on the airbus."

The airbus was a new addition to the savannah's travel options, imported with Consortium funds. A cushion of forced air levitated the wide-bodied chamber eighteen inches off the ground. Only four of the original seven were still in service. Their engines ran hot while the swirling dust clogged their moving parts. Three airbuses were abandoned metal frames left on the red desert providing shade for snakes and pincher scarabs.

In the cooler and grassy Mekucoo region leading to a low mesa where the hospital was established, the sectioned buses were still in service. The rear flatbed was crowded with starving stragglers. I climbed into the air-conditioned patient section behind the cab, signaling for Hakulupe Le and Karlyhi to join me. The Consortium driver stared hard at the boy's karkar while I pulled the heavy door closed.

The airbus powered up. Soon we were gliding over uneven terrain. Seated across from me, Hakulupe Le and Karlyhi were silent. Hakulupe Le was from the olive-skinned Arrivi tribe, serving as nurse and interpreter at my clinic. She was ostracized by the Arrivi, a shame they called goulep, but I had not yet learned her true history. Her special gift was to easily pick up languages. She was indispensable to me, and a good friend.

I had heard old stories told in chants across family campfires outside my clinic entrance. Each telling was different. Certain heroes grew in stature whenever tribespeople steeled themselves for some impending fight. One short tale was about the ghost Spindel who wandered the savannah as a giant ketiwhelp. I had heard chants about the Mekucoo warrior Cyrus who rivaled legends of Oria for bravery. I had asked which were real and how much was embellished, but Hakulupe Le only shrugged. "Who can see with the eyes of Dolvia?" she said.

"Tell Karlyhi I'll look at his leg now," I instructed.

While Hakulupe Le explained in his dialect, I prepared an anesthetic wash and searched through the drawers for an abrasion maser. Karlyhi braced himself and stared as I placed his foot in a hospital bucket and poured the wash along his wound. The liquid bubbled with a white froth and ran into the bucket, turning yellow and gelatinous.

I held up the elegant maser, shaped like a stun gun with a row of indicator lights near the concave head. "This will make him slightly nauseated. A current runs through his body."

Hakulupe Le spoke a few words in his dialect. Karlyhi's eyes skirted left and then right, but he made no protest. I passed the maser over his wound and watched the flesh pull together to form a healing pink shape.

"Tell him to favor it for a few days. I can look at the mark again tomorrow."

She nodded and they both stared. Modern medicine held the allure of magic for them.

Situated on a low bluff overlooking the parched savannah, the hospital was a three-story red brick building with wide hallways that allowed a breeze. The airbus stopped in front. An orderly approached the crowded flatbed to direct new arrivals.

"Keep Karlyhi apart from the others," I directed Hakulupe Le as we stepped down.

The orderly stuck his head into the patient chamber, showing a bloated and ruddy face. "What were they doing in there?"

"He's a patient," I said. "That's a patient chamber."

"Which pieces did you use? I'll need to sterilize everything."

"So I should leave him bleeding on the side of the road to save you some work?"

"You cannot just—"

"Oh, get off it, Reggie," I said.

We guided Karlyhi around the building's side to the employee entrance. In the supply room, Hakulupe Le instructed Karlyhi to bathe, find something to eat, and get a good night's sleep. She explained that we would travel to my clinic at dawn, and added that he was responsible to me now. Karlyhi said nothing, but the next morning he waited by the lorry loaded with my supplies. He still carried the black karkar.

For the occasional drive from my clinic, I preferred the diesel-powered lorry. My thinking was that when the engine broke down, tribesmen could figure a quick fix. Most Dolviet machines were unreliable Consortium issue or scrounged Chinese-made army surplus quality, vehicles included. Only the hospital wards and Dr. Abercrombie's branch offices had computers and high-tech surgical equipment. At the bush clinic, I maintained a low-tech presence in all concerns except research.

We left early to make the most of the cool morning hours. I drove the lorry with Hakulupe Le at my side and Karlyhi seated on the canvas top. The gears were grinding as we drove up the steep grade. A winding road led around the many knolls of Mekucoo land. Long grass flopped left and then right in the unruly wind, a metaphor for the struggle to maintain my clinic. I rolled my shoulders against the tension.

Once we were on higher ground, a steady twenty-mile-an-hour wind troubled the canvas cover of the truck bed. We stopped and Karlyhi crowded into the cab with us. Trees bowed their heads and snapped back, and their branches swung as if cheering at a sporting event. When wind gusts pushed us onto the shoulder of the road, I glanced out the side window at the danger.

Hakulupe Le was sanguine. "We have many windy days before the rainy season begins in earnest. A blessing of Dolvia."

By the time we were stopped by Consortium soldiers, I was ready to stretch my back. The officer who approached our vehicle stood in a wide stance against the blowing wind, a chinstrap securing his hat. He looked over my travel papers, holding them tight in a meaty hand.

"Edna Edwina? Did your parents stutter?"

I was accustomed to jibes about my name, but this lieutenant irritated me more than most. A burly Hardhand from Cicero, the closest inhabited planet, he had dark eyes and dark hair. I was certain he smoked kari root and forced native women for sport. His men pulled Karlyhi out of the cab and confiscated the karkar.

"You have a orphan soldier," the officer accused.

"My assistant."

"Where are his papers?"

I shrugged slightly without meeting his look. "What's one tribal kid, more or less?"

"Did you issue him this gun?"

"Lieutenant Shaw," another soldier called, pointing at the hill-crest where Siibabean tribesmen stood in a long line silhouetted against the white sky. Siibabean were easily identified by large head-dresses made of black Murmurey feathers forming a mock halo from shoulder to shoulder. The winds seemed calm at their position, maybe an illusion caused by distance.

"You'll have the pleasure of our company at your clinic, I'm afraid," Lt. Shaw said.

"I won't be cover for your reconnoiter."

"Stop me," he said with a dark smile.

They pulled an open jeep in front of the lorry, and their two trucks fell in behind. Karlyhi scrambled to his high seat, still favoring his raw leg. We completed the long drive without incident.

My clinic was an adobe and thatch building with a secure storeroom, set back from the slope and less exposed to gusting winds. The grant funds had seemed generous when I first committed to this project. But as Dr. Abercrombie explained, the costs to ship equipment through a region with no infrastructure had forced some difficult choices concerning comfort. There was fresh water, however, and edible local produce, grains and olives mostly. We had excellent herbs for tea and fresh erriv meat for strength.

Usually I treated patients on the verandah while family members watched. Laundry was on the left, the fire and kettle shaded by the spreading catalpa tree. The remnants of tribal campfires, individual and communal, littered the yard. Traveling family groups sometimes rested overnight before the long trek back to their erriv herds.

The military trucks pulled around back. I stopped the lorry at the entrance. Many tribespeople waited, but they were not desperate and crowding like in the refugee camps.

Hakulupe Le greeted the women with reassurances that I would see patients the following morning. She spoke to Karlyhi concerning the laying-in of supplies. Two tribesmen joined Karlyhi and, surprisingly, took his instructions for the unloading.

Lieutenant Shaw and two soldiers came around the building. The women backed away. "We will camp behind," he said to me. "We can throw up a perimeter. My detail will be gone by morning."

"There's a stream down the way."

"We saw it." He curtly nodded to Hakulupe Le and joined his men.

Inside the clinic were three patient cots and a desk from where I dispensed medication. On the side and behind a decorated Chinese screen were a closet and bed as well as a table and a small stove. My servants had laid out a formal Arrivi tea there.

My research room was in the back, a twelve-by-twelve sterile space lined with Cicero acrylic, light and cheap. A generator kept the room cool and well lit. My test equipment and monitors were Earth-engineered and manufactured in Westend, but certain pieces had been imported through the wormhole.

I stepped behind the screen that was a gift from Leslie Abercrombie, something he had scrounged from a Company fire sale. I removed my jacket and billed hat. I soaked a cloth in a gourd of water that hung from a spike, and used it to refresh my face and arms. My blouse was soaked through. I put on a fresh one from the closet and peeked around the screen.

Hakulupe Le waited near the cots. "Please join me at the table," I murmured.

She held a palm high in the greeting of her tribe and came around the screen. She poured tea and waited. I must be the first to taste the dried fish on salty flatbread. I sat at the table and tried to look appreciative concerning the tea service. After I took a bite, Hakulupe Le also sat, and she sliced some fruit that we shared.

"Lupe, do you know those soldiers?"

"Lieutenant Shaw trains Dolviet recruits. A man of some restraint." In their culture, her phrase meant sexual restraint.

"You don't mind if I don't believe you."

"My words are not law," she whispered. I saw a flash of those green-green eyes.

"I can see patients for an hour or so if you will select them," I said.

She made the motions to end our tea and return to work. "After a while," I quickly added. "After you have rested."

"We sat all day in the lorry. The activity will do me good."

I opened each of the French-style windows beside the empty cots and looked out at the misty sunset. I was glad to be home. My clinic was less than one season established but I felt I was home within my function, in my correct place.

My servants entered and bustled about with importance. I put on a smock and plastic gloves before I stepped out onto the veranda where tribal women with sick children stood in a line. It overwhelmed me sometimes, the degree of their need, the endless stream. But just then the service felt righteous, the way I had imagined the work while I was still in medical school.

In the refugee camps, parasites and complications from malnutrition had been foremost until the outbreak of typhus. Some wounded tribesmen—mostly warriors from roadside ambushes—were brought to me in a rush but were beyond help. Here in the rural outback broken bones, snakebite, virulent infection, and hemorrhoids were the daily fare. I set bones, inoculated children, and advised mothers concerning hygiene and thoroughly cooked food.

It was deep night when I returned to my private place. My servants had set out water and clean clothes. I lay back on the bed and was instantly asleep.

Usually I rose at dawn, but that morning I overslept. I pulled on clean clothes and followed my nose to the still-warm tea left at a native campfire. I sat by the fire and yawned over a steaming mug. My Putuki servants were doing laundry while Hakulupe Le counseled some newly arrived patients.

True to Lieutenant Shaw's word, the soldiers were gone. I knew without investigating because the tribespeople were relaxed and friendly. Children gathered around me with shy smiles and offered gifts of glassy stones and spring slugs. I pretended to play their game, a native version of ball and jacks, tickling one toddler who giggled and squirmed.

Karlyhi stepped onto the roadway and cleared his throat. He was carrying the karkar again, returned to him or re-stolen. I knew male gestures well enough. I nodded to Hakulupe Le before I followed him up the way a piece. Two Mekucoo warriors waited in a stand of ferns. Mekucoo were lean and brown, and stoic in the presence of foreign women. Their weapon barrels were caked with concealing mud, a precaution taken when danger lurked.

One spoke in Arrivi, the only dialect I had mastered. "The soldiers attached to you will remain how many days?"

"They are not assigned. I assume a sweep of the area."

"What armaments?"

I shrugged. Karlyhi made several gestures indicating the inventory of their ordnance. Of course, I thought, the good boy soldier.

"Can you keep the soldiers at the clinic?" the Mekucoo asked. I shook my head no.

They curtly nodded and turned to melt into the bush. Karlyhi followed a few steps. One warrior showed him a resistant gesture and spoke in his dialect. He was not to join their work.

Karlyhi shot an angry glance my way, but I only chuckled. I returned to the clinic with the sure knowledge that, however sourly, Karlyhi would remain in my service.

His tribe was the Cylahi, landless poor who got by with day work plus some artisan skills. The men gained status through militia service. Karlyhi must have hated the idea of clinic work while others died fighting the Siibabean and were lauded in tribal chants.

We fell into a daily routine. Karlyhi took over some of Hakulupe Le's burden and installed insect traps that were our line of defense against the threat of dengue fever and river blindness. Tribal men were seen more frequently at the clinic. Where once they lost face by entering the women's camp, now they could stand in groups and talk with this boy soldier. We learned about the movements of tribal factions, of nearby conflicts, and of the rush of incoming patients. Karlyhi became as important to my operation as Hakulupe Le.

And Karlyhi delighted in troubling me. I asked him to remove a salamander that had made its home in the cool earth under the clinic's platform floor. I had stumbled over its fleshy tail the night before when it claimed the space between desk and cots. It had a wide mouth with whiskers like a catfish. The beady eyes were nearly blind, but its flesh provided enough sensory information to hunt. Salamanders tended to live in groups, or so Hakulupe Le said, meaning three more probably nested under the research room.

"He ate last night, a banded rat," Karlyhi claimed as though that made me safe. "He may crawl into your bed for warmth, Sheeks-Cylom."

My Putuki servants giggled. Hakulupe Le turned a shoulder to me. To hide her smile, I was certain. Karlyhi walked away with extra bounce in his step.

Later at tea, Lupe explained. "The salamanders wait for the rainy season. Then they will hunt in the billabongs and forget about the clinic."

"What did Karlyhi call me before?"

"Sheeks is short for Softcheeks. Cylom points to a degree, between cylay and om."

"A degree of what?"

I had struggled to master their standard of measure, something about placement on a continuum between netta and om. The lesson went netta, kari, cylay, and finally om; a series of stages from desert dry to fruition of events. The four tribes used these designations for everything. Karkar was the native term for automatic weapons, by way of example. Lupe had explained that the weapon was stuck in kari and had nothing of either netta or cylay. Hence, the term karkar.

"You think of your skin as one color," Lupe said. "But Karlyhi's nickname refers to the full range of color, as though one can see deep into your body." She gently took my hand, turned it over, and touched my wrist where the blue veins ran up my arm. "Karlyhi's words are a compliment."

I didn't believe her.

One hot night before the rains, Hakulupe Le and the servants came into the clinic. They opened the windows and tensely stared out. I dressed and joined them while Karlyhi distributed karkars from the storeroom. I checked the load and grabbed an extra box of shells.

We waited, sitting between the French windows with our backs against the wall. Dolvia's two moons, one much larger than the other, hung overhead in the clouded night sky as though winking at us. I jolted when the salamander nudged my leg with his massive head.

The women rested their weapons against the wall. Hakulupe Le dozed a little. Karlyhi stood guard at the door. And then we heard them, the staccato trampling of feet. A tight detachment of Siibabean warriors traveled the road with their dancing quickstep, looking neither left nor right. We crouched at the windows with our weapons poised. I took Karlyhi's place and asked him to hide in the storeroom. Many stories circulated about the scouting parties taking boy soldiers as slaves.

A scout darkened our doorway. A circular headdress of luscious Murmurey feathers framed his plaited hair. Siibabean were tall and lean and blue-black. They had regular features with high cheekbones and perfect teeth. This one carried a decorated shield and a karkar. With a glance into the moonlit night, he learned all that was important about these women living alone and off the road. Then he saw the salamander's sidling motions as it serenely joined me by the desk like a house pet.

The creature lifted its head. A feathery tongue shot out with rapid motions. Moonlight reflected blue in its unblinking eyes. The staring warrior gingerly backed out of the doorway. As he sauntered off, I saw a glint of waning light on the gun barrel that Karlyhi held.

"Small prey, us," Hakulupe Le postulated. "Not worth interrupting their march. What honor in killing women and docile carrion eaters?"

I instructed Karlyhi, "Tomorrow cover all the guns with soot."

"But—" He was proud of our firepower and had kept the many pieces in working condition. We stared each other down. I realized that a day would come when the clinic would be too small for us both.

We stored the weapons and went back to bed, but I could not sleep. I began planning our return to Abercrombie's hospital to wait out the rains. The bush held too many dangers for four unprotected women and a self-indulgent boy. At dawn I dressed and opened the French windows to gain a breeze before the humid day began. I pulled on a work smock, gray with many faint bloodstains, and switched on the desk lamp.

I heard an angry whisper. "Are you alone?"

Lieutenant Shaw glanced in the doorway before he looked around the yard. The Siibabean were long absent, but perhaps his men had not found the evidence.

"You endanger the clinic by returning here," I said.

There was a slight noise, a twig breaking in the underbrush. Lt. Shaw quickly entered and grabbed my arm. He led me back between the French windows and pressed me against the wall there, all as one motion.

"What the hell?" I complained. "That noise is your men mucking about."

He put a knee firmly between my legs and pressed his chest against mine. He smelled of freshly turned earth and vaguely of eucalyptus. "Release me this instant!" I insisted.

Lieutenant Shaw pinned my arms behind my back and covered my mouth with a grimy hand. All the while, he stared out the window as if searching for someone. I struggled against his strength and opened my mouth to bite his finger.

"Go ahead," he whispered into my ear. "It would pleasure me to hurt you back."

I relaxed under his grip, and he removed his hand from my mouth. His dark eyes ran over my face and chest. "Why don't you do something with your hair? And why hide this body in those god-awful clothes?"

I tried to jerk away, but he tightened his hold and chuckled.

There was a sound outside. Lt. Shaw released the safety strap on his holster. He pulled away a fraction to better see out the window in the gathering light. I saw chest hair and his pulse racing through corded neck veins. I felt his taut stomach pressed against me and the round muscle of his arm. He surrounded me with lethal intent.

We waited a long moment until Lt. Shaw received a signal from his men concealed in the underbrush. He relaxed and released me. I brushed his tracked-in grit from my clothes. "The Siibabean passed by here in the night."

He watched each of my gestures. "They may return."

"The clinic is off-limits."

"Is that from the Geneva rules of warfare?" I stared at him but saw no smirk. "Gather your things," he said. "We can take you back to the hospital."

"I'm not going." I lifted my chin with a resolve I had not felt an hour before. "Get your men out of here. Their presence puts us in danger."

"Do you always talk so much, Edna Edwina?"

Karlyhi silently showed himself at the doorway. A karkar rested across his forearm as if he was an aristocrat out hunting quail, except he was barefoot. When he had reassured himself that I was unmolested, he passed on.

"You armed him again?" Lieutenant Shaw asked.

"Out here, one must select one's danger."

Lt. Shaw had a jarring laugh. "'One must select one's danger,'" he mimicked. He left when my servants entered with anxious questions.

The hospital was a day's trip from the clinic. The lieutenant's men commandeered my lorry, ending the debate about remaining behind, and packed in our weapons and supplies. Hakulupe Le and the servants were helped into the back of a military truck that already held some waiting tribespeople.

I headed for the lorry intending to drive, but Lieutenant Shaw grabbed my wrist. I quickly raised my arm with a doubled fist, pulling against his gesture, but he held me fast. "My corporal will handle the lorry," he said, ignoring my angry move. "You ride with me."

Karlyhi passed us with a wide grin and shimmied onto the lorry's canvas cover.

Two soldiers climbed into the truck's cab with us, crowding me against Lieutenant Shaw's side. We drove for hours in that cramped position, and I dozed a little, lulled by the truck's motion and my sleepless night.

I awoke with a start, aware that I had rested against Lieutenant Shaw's back while he leaned forward over the steering wheel. His uniform's rough cotton concealed rounded sinew and a long backbone. I had learned more about his body that day than I cared to know. I was certain that he had imagined mine.

The two soldiers slept, slumped together against the window. We were no longer going downhill but followed the road around the knolls that led to the hospital. Entering the savannah from the cool highlands was like going down into a basement with a furnace and no ventilation. On one curve, a vista opened over the vast flatlands still brightly lit in the late afternoon. A gray and apricot haze hung low like city smog. I knew that ultrafine dust filled the air during the dry season. I was ready for the rains to start.

I stretched my spine and pulled the skirt hem over my knees. Lt. Shaw glanced back at me. "Do you need to stop?"

"Not unless you do."

"It's best to drive straight through."

The hospital yard was in chaos, filled with desperately wounded warriors of all tribes. Family members went from litter to litter to find loved ones. The lorry nosed its way toward the entrance where Reggie was in charge. "I'm taking your supplies," he curtly claimed. Karlyhi and Lt. Shaw both faced him off. Reggie stepped back with saucer eyes.

Hakulupe Le stepped down near where two Arrivi men waited. Tribespeople scrambled down from the truck. They each bowed slightly to her, and she held a palm high. The passengers entered the crowd to help where they could.

Reggie called to them. "Where are you going? Get back here!"

"What harm, Reggie, if they distribute water and offer a kind word?" I asked.

He glanced at Lt. Shaw. "There's no time for this posturing. We have dying here."

"Then I will speak to the living first," I said.

I turned to make my farewells with Hakulupe Le. Reggie shrugged with a big gesture and returned to his triage duties. Hakulupe Le took my hand in her intimate manner. "I can return to the clinic after the rains," she said. "Karlyhi may come with us now, if you want."

I had not thought about where he should sleep. My plans had been rushed by Lt. Shaw's gruff insistence. I glanced at Karlyhi who moved a fraction closer to Lt. Shaw.

"We have plenty of work for him here at the hospital," I said.

Hakulupe Le nodded with humor in her eyes. "I can send someone for him before the Feast of Oria. He must not neglect tradition."

"How generous."

"Dolvia has blessed you." She walked away, and the Arrivi men trailed her steps.

"Karlyhi can stay at the barracks," Lt. Shaw said.

"He has no loyalty to you."

"Would you like to learn how to drive the airbus?" he asked the boy. Pleasure registered on Karlyhi's dark and implacable face. "Anything else?" Lt. Shaw asked me.

"That's quite enough, thank you." I took my case from his hand and walked into the needful crowd.

In the hospital hallway, the crowd of wounded and crying family members made my stomach twist. Cylahi nurses moved among patients, securing bandages and offering words of comfort but no real assistance. I didn't know their dialect. I could not direct them to the supply of antiseptic washes or demonstrate the value of butterfly sutures.

"Where is Dr. Abercrombie?" I asked. "The Softcheeks doctor?"

An exhausted nurse pointed right. I made my way through the crowd to the surgical theater. Under hot lights in a less-than-sterile room, two trained nurses assisted Dr. Abercrombie while he furiously labored over a dying warrior. Leslie looked up, his weary eyes over the white mask filled with resignation.

I put on an operating gown, scrubbed in and labored at his side. Moving to a second table, I cleaned wounds and knitted together abrasions with the maser, constantly giving instructions to the nurses. Leslie bent over the serious cases, my specialty not being surgery.

The work pulled at my heart. In the past, hospital assignments had exhilarated me. Highly engineered instruments were used to save lives and monitor stabilized life signs. Leslie's nonintrusive microscopic surgery could remove tumors without laying open internal organs. Even with my limited knowledge of cutting, under controlled conditions I could feel confident in each lifesaving gesture based on learned procedure. It was not messy.

But on Dolvia our training was inadequate. There were too many, and they were too mangled from the fighting. For hours we barely spoke except for instructions and calls for more supplies. Finally the stream of wounded lessened, and we could cease our work under the hot lights.

Leslie turned to me. "You need to remain here until the fighting eases."

"I can train the nurses for triage."

"Just the basics."

So I settled in at the hospital. I had the hallways cleaned and showed Karlyhi how to whitewash them. I showed a nurse named Nellie how to inventory the supply room using a checklist on a clipboard. We ordered additional goods from Stargate Junction. I gave regular lessons about triage and surgery prep, my words translated by Reggie. Leslie and I quarreled about my open instructions on the uses of certain equipment, especially the abrasion maser. He claimed that closing an unclean wound caused more harm than good. I assured him that the nurses would not be trusted until their skill level was raised.

I spent my little free time with Leslie's medical books. He had a sterling collection.

A two-story patient dorm and a staff dorm were under construction using Arrivi red sandstone bricks. A section of the patient dorm had been roofed in a hurry anticipating the rains. Arrivi men labored to finish its many rooms. A long colonnade banked an interior grassy yard where Leslie had plans for a fountain and sunny walk for convalescing patients. A facing building of similar design housed the Consortium peacekeeping detachment, including their offices and motor pool. Every hour of the day, I heard the buzz saw and the constant pounding of hammers. Workmen gruffly answered shouted orders. I pined for my quiet clinic.

That rainy season was mostly a blur to me. Truckloads and chopper loads of wounded arrived from the northern conflict. I labored in a separate operating room, and my newly trained nurses assisted. I addressed one desperately wounded warrior after another, sometimes standing for hours under the hot lights on a floor made slippery with blood. Shrapnel, knife cuts, and the multiple wounds of automatic weapon fire. I became numb to the carnage. Remove the foreign object, stop the bleeding, clean the wound, pull the muscles together, and suture the flesh. Bring in the next one.

One night during the hardest downpour, there was a break in the fighting. I sat at dinner with Leslie and several Softcheeks guests. They were journalists and investors who, like us, were waiting out the rains. I was tired; I remember thinking that. Leslie put his hand over mine as he related some recent incident to the smiling off-worlders.

Leslie's hand was cool and skeletal.

How often I had seen his hands flitting across a gaping wound to save a warrior's life, directed by Leslie's sane intellect. But just then his hand seemed to carry the touch of death. Perhaps he had been laboring too long in the morgue.

I looked around at the rosy faces. I was surprised to see Lieutenant Shaw seated at the table's end, moody and silent. He darkly stared at Leslie's hand over mine.

I remembered Lt. Shaw's touch and the smell of him, the aroma of earth and crushed leaves. It might have been my exhaustion playing tricks on me that night, but Lt. Shaw represented life and strength. Leslie was cold as the tomb.

After dinner, I carried my coffee out onto the verandah. The long dormitory buildings, finished and occupied, stretched away from my view, partly obscured by the dark downpour. The interior yard was one big puddle.

I felt Lt. Shaw behind me. He removed the cup and saucer from my hand and led me to the stairs on the right. We quickly walked along the colonnade away from the lighted party. Our footsteps on the red brick walk were muffled by the noisy rain. His hand still grasping my wrist, we entered the dormitory.

Lt. Shaw paused outside my rooms. "Go on," he said.

I saw only the turned-down bed. I crossed the narrow space and was asleep before my head hit the pillow.

When I awoke, it was late afternoon the following day. The servants from my clinic were setting out tea in the front room. I murmured hello and allowed them to help me dress, an honor I had always refused. Lush orchids floated in a bowl on the table. Pelting rain streamed down the overhang.

The servants were from the Putuki tribe. We spoke little because I had not mastered their dialect. I knew tribal differences because patients from so many tribes had crossed my operating table. Putuki were heavyset with bowed legs and barrel chests. The women were subservient and easily frightened. I had little contact with the Putuki businessmen who were merchants and government officials in the capital city of Cylay.

Arrivi were olive-skinned and gained weight easily. They were prone to bone disease and colon cancer, I assumed from diet deficiencies. Older Arrivi were often blind.

Mekucoo were small and lean, chocolate brown with various skin diseases. Their immune systems were tested from their wide-ranging hunting habits. The men came into contact with more foreign influences than village-bound Arrivi.

I had treated few Cylahi men on my operating table, but the nurses had chronic ailments peculiar to their tribe. They had poor eyesight and weak bones from long years of malnutrition. They carried no extra weight even when prosperous, and displayed a nervous energy that made them seem uncertain.

Siibabean, at least the few I had operated on, were healthy to the extreme. I surmised that their diet staples must be vegetables and roots, especially taro which was high in fluoride needed for well-formed bones and perfect teeth.

There was a noise in the hall. I went to my door and saw Karlyhi stationed in the corridor with his karkar and an oversized Mekucoo shield.

"Is there a costume party?"

From down the way Lieutenant Shaw approached, carrying something square with a big kerchief draped over it. He also led a leashed gualarep, a valued reptile sometimes bred in captivity on Cicero, the lieutenant's home planet. The Putuki women squealed at the sight of the big reptile and scurried some distance up the corridor where they turned and stared.

The gualarep was a beautiful creature, truly, but at the same time grotesque. Muscled flanks led to bowed and pigeon-toed legs. Nails clicked against the polished floor. Its lumbering gait included swinging its body and long tail from side to side. A fleshy tongue with a forked tip continuously flicked from a noble head.

Its hide resembled a child's collection of marbles lined up in tight rows. Faint ridges, like those on a crocodile, ran down both sides of its back and tail, rounded as if extra rows of larger marbles had been stacked on top. The gualarep's hide was rich green with swirling patches of red and yellow. It seemed that God had painted him with colors freshly poured onto the palette and then, still feeling creative, had added the marbled texture as an afterthought.

"Lieutenant Shaw," I said with formality, aware that we were being watched.

He indicated the yellow bars on his uniform sleeve. "That's First Lieutenant now. I have something for you."

I reached to touch the reptile's head. The marbled gualarep hissed and snarled. I jerked back my hand and heard Karlyhi chuckle.

"You're giving me that?"

"I raised him. He's loyal only to me. I wanted to give you these."

Lieutenant Shaw handed the package to Karlyhi and pulled back the kerchief, revealing two infant gualareps in a small chicken cage. He poked his finger through the wire mesh. One lifted its head and he stroked its lighter-colored neck.

"They're only female," he said. "You will need to feed them at first, insects and young rodents. But after a certain day, they can find their own meals." Both men smiled. "You must handle them for twenty minutes each day so they imprint on you. Later they can learn a battery of hand signals."

"And they'll grow into that?"

"Ralph is only age twenty, not yet fully grown."

"And you taught him to bite everybody?" I asked.

"I taught him to bite nobody. He dislikes you." Lieutenant Shaw met my gaze. "You smell of death."

Perhaps I had been too long laboring in surgery. The skin of my hands was dry to the point of cracking. My complexion was extra pale, and my skin smelled of medicine. My hair had grown, falling onto my shoulders when I removed the operating cap.

"Won't you come in?" I asked, stepping back.

"I have a duty shift now. But take these." He handed me the cage. "And Karlyhi will see that you're not disturbed."

The women whispered together, so I quickly took stock. "Look, this isn't necessary."

"No?" Lt. Shaw asked in a stern voice. "Tell me this; what day is it?"

"I don't know. Tuesday, perhaps."

"And how much time has passed since we came down from the clinic?"

I stuck out my chin. "My help was needed. They were all dying."

"Since you refuse to care for yourself, Sheeks-Cylom, you force us to look after you."

"And do you intend to run my life forever?"

"I have work." Lt. Shaw indicated Karlyhi. "That's why I am leaving this boy." He moved his hand in sign language. The guala-rep turned as though he understood, and walked with Lt. Shaw up the way they had come.

The women whispered again. Dwarfed by the Mekucoo shield, Karlyhi stoically stared past my head to the doorjamb. I retreated into my rooms and remained there for three days, resting and regaining my strength.

The infant reps were a joy. Or rather, they created joy in me. Each the length of my forearm, lighter than their grown cousin and only partly marbled, they held their chins high and watched every movement. I remember that first day I set the cage on the nightstand and opened its door. They cautiously poked out their heads.

I held out a hand for one to walk onto. They ran their tongues across my fingers and pulled back with displeasure. So Lt. Shaw's claim was true. I smelled of death.

I took a long shower without soap, possibly another offensive odor to them, and rubbed on a natural linseed oil. I combed my wet hair and went back to the nightstand. The cage was empty. The gualareps were nestled together on my bed just below the pillow. One raised her head and made a soft clicking noise, their version of cooing.

After that, I never worried for their whereabouts. They clung to the folds of my bedspread or my skirt but easily avoided being crushed. Once I drew one from a big pocket of my skirt. She looked up at me with always-open eyes and a false grin.

Their cool detachment seemed to calm my anxiety. I breathed in rhythm with their cooing while I petted them or when they were tangled in my clothes. My Putuki servants, however, refused to enter my rooms to clean. Only after I gathered the girls, one on each forearm, did the women deliver tea service. My laundry collected in a big pile until Leslie cursed the servants for their superstitions.

The whole countryside was in bloom. Newly green trees were hung with exotic flowers and unripe fruit. The infant reps ate anything, including the orchids in the bowl on my morning table. During my duty shifts, which were severely curtailed for a time, Karlyhi fed them with insects and spiders.

Soon he brought chicks and small rodents that the infant reps killed with a single lightning strike and ripped apart with glee. After the rain had stopped and the floods receded, Karlyhi walked the gualareps on the hospital grounds where they scurried into stands of tall razor grass and found their own meals.

One night I stirred in the dark to the sound of their rapid clicking. I was aware of the gualareps on the bed with me, tense and prancing. I saw the image of Leslie's blanched face floating above me, but the face drew back into darkness. I saw his bony chest under the open shirt. His belt and trouser buttons were undone. The images folded into my dream then, and I was uncertain of them the following morning.

Leslie had a mole under his left nipple. I did not make the connection until days later, when he was changing from a soiled hospital gown. He stripped off his sleeveless t-shirt that was soaked with blood and quickly splashed water onto his chest before he donned a fresh green pullover.

I caught my breath and just stared. He frowned, but returned to the press of work.

While I labored under the hot lights, I tried to tell myself I had seen that mole before. Our work meant close quarters and casual modesty. But I knew I had not, except for late one night in my room when the presence of the gualarep infants had interrupted Leslie's intentions.

The question faded though, lost in the days of needful pain and death.

TWO

ONE BRIGHT DAY WHEN THE RAINS WERE LESS, I JOINED KARLYHI alongside the barracks. A patch of razor grass that could lacerate the flesh on our arms had sprung up there. We heard the chase and then the pounce. One section of the wicked growth shimmied for a moment.

"Why do the girls like it in there?" I asked.

"Rodents nest below the sharp spines," Karlyhi said. "Also, Ralph goes in there."

"Ralph?"

"Mike's gualarep. They can smell him. Or so Mike explained."

"Mike?"

"Ralph is the barracks' mascot."

"Mascot?"

"Why do you repeat what I say?"

"Sorry. What else did First Lieutenant Shaw explain?"

"That gualareps have a calming quality, thera . . . thera-poll—"

"Therapeutic," I corrected. "They make you feel better."

"It must work only with females."

I frowned at his tone. "You have been living in the barracks for too long. The Feast of Oria is soon. Have you thought about what you will do?"

Karlyhi shrugged.

"You can stay with Arrivi," I said. "You won't be taken for the fighting. Or you can return with me to labor at the clinic."

"I have no fear to fight."

"I would hate to find you one day on my operating table."

"I will die on the savannah. It is seen."

I stopped, taken aback by his certainty. I had not realized he held with tribal prophecy or the gift of second sight. "And death will come at what age?"

"I will outlive you."

"That's a comfort."

The gualareps, now thrice their original length, came in a nail-clicking scurry out of the grass and jumped onto my skirt, nearly knocking me down. "It's time they were broken of that."

More wounded warriors, Arrivi and Siibabean, arrived at the clinic. I completed many shifts at the operating table and began to discern patterns in the wounds: an upward thrust under the ribs, then a deep slash across the throat. Ankle tendons were sometimes severed from behind, crippling a man for life. Those were the graceful wounds, less messy than incendiary bombs that exploded in the chest and automatic weapon projectiles that shattered bone.

Then a short break came.

The Feast of Oria was planned for two days that week. Except for convalescing warriors, the hospital was mostly deserted even by staff. I had no plans to attend the event on Arrivi land, but I was glad for the quiet. I carried an open medical book and walked along the hall, my footsteps echoing in the deserted expanse.

I looked up when a Cylahi nurse emerged from a supply room. Her uniform was disheveled and her cap askew. I glanced into the room and saw Dr. Abercrombie conducting a supply inventory with clipboard in hand. He only smiled and nodded.

That evening in the apricot sunset, I walked with the gualarep girls to the edge of the bluff that overlooked the green and wet savannah where hoards of nesting birds nested by the many billabongs. In the near distance were several bonfires. I assumed that was the feast's location.

A gaggle of white herons with black-tipped wings glided nearby, gently landing in the bluff's tall grass. The gualareps cooed with question and sidled off into the underbrush. I was not worried. They often hunted together, returning after dark to the dormitory.

I heard a step behind me. It was Dr. Abercrombie. "This is a favorite spot," he said. "Perhaps I will build a residence here one day."

"Assuming the tribal fighting ends."

"Either way. The hospital is protected from tribal law."

I thought that was a strange phrase: protected from tribal law. Why not protected by tribal law? Why did Leslie make me uneasy? Since childhood, I had resisted figures of authority. I chose to hold onto that frustration and not seek another answer.

"I'm sorry, what did you say?" I hedged.

"Nothing important. Come on, I'll walk you back."

We went to Leslie's office where he locked the door behind us. I had been in this room many times and immediately went to the bookshelf.

"Would you like a drink?" he asked behind me.

"Oh, I don't drink much."

"You don't do much at all, except work and read." He poured two glasses of red wine and held one out to me. "You will like this. Sweet but not strong."

"Thank you." The dark liquid was both sweet and biting, with a bitter aftertaste. I stood by the window and watched the waning sunlight. Leslie joined me.

"I don't suppose I could get you," he said, "to remain at the hospital year-round. Abandon the bush clinic and collaborate with me here?"

I sighed softly. This was a repeated pattern. Not just Leslie, but all men I had met in my profession wanted me to work for them. None asked what were my goals, my aspirations. "I should be close to the people for field study and testing."

"Do you often communicate with the grant committee?"

"Why? Is there a problem?"

Leslie chuckled and drew closer. He gently brushed a strand of hair from my forehead. "You're very focused. I admire that."

I moved away. "Focus allows me to get some work done."

"How do you like the wine?"

"Very nice," I lied.

"Drink up."

I reluctantly took another sip and sat on the couch. Leslie switched on his desk lamp in the gathering gloom.

"This wine is strong," I complained. "It makes me lightheaded."

He sat next to me. "You're just not accustomed to drinking."

There came a knock at the door. Leslie did not move. I heard a second knock. "It could be important," I said. "Few staff are here now."

I set down my wineglass and walked to the door. I twisted the lock and opened it. Lieutenant Shaw filled the doorway, his big frame dark against the lighted hall. His face was grim as he looked past me at Leslie, still sitting on the couch.

"We were just—"

"You will come," Lt. Shaw interrupted. "There are wounded in the lorry."

I looked back at Leslie with a vague smile and left with Lt. Mike Shaw. Our footfalls sounded in the empty corridor. I grabbed a hospital smock on the way out and held it over my head to block the drizzle. When we reached the nearby truck, I peered into the back and saw only stacked supplies.

"There are no wounded."

"Get in," Lt. Shaw said. "You cannot stay here with your precious Leslie."

"And I should leave with you?"

"Must everything be a negotiation?" He roughly grasped my elbow to help me into the truck bed. I jerked away.

"You are not the boss of me!" I pressed a hand against my forehead, resisting a sudden pain across my eyes.

Lieutenant Shaw glanced over my shoulder to where Dr. Abercrombie stood watching from the dry verandah. "Is there a problem?" Leslie called out.

Lt. Shaw called back, "No, no. No problem here." He sighed shortly and turned to me. "Hakulupe Le says you are to attend the Feast of Oria. They need a virgin to sacrifice."

"Why, of all the insuff—"

He pulled me around to the driver's side, pushed me into the cab, and climbed in beside me. I scooted over to the passenger seat and sat scrunched against the door.

"And who the hell told you I was a virgin?"

Lt. Shaw stared for a moment. Smile lines appeared near his eyes. He said nothing more while we barreled into the moonless night with only the lorry's misaligned headlamps beaming on the wet and narrow road.

It was late morning when I woke with a pounding headache. I identified nearby kitchen sounds of women chatting while they pounded barley meal. I was in a sparse and cool adobe bedroom with a west window. I lay on top of the covers, still fully dressed.

I sat up but regretted the move as my head throbbed. When I could finally focus, I stumbled to the doorway, an opening covered with simple burlap. I stepped onto a long verandah with a red tile roof. The sunlight made my eyes ache.

Several women worked at a table in the yard, assembling goods to sell during the feast day. Hakulupe Le stood among them. She saw me and spoke to a young girl there who left.

Hakulupe Le came to the verandah edge. "Would you like tea?"

I nodded. "What place is this?"

"The home of my aunt Karima Le."

"I thought your aunt was Kyle Le."

"They are sisters. Karima Le's husband Haku rabbe Murd has left for the feast, but you may thank him there."

"Thank him?"

"You were talking too much," Lupe said evenly. "You kept insisting to Lt. Shaw that it was none of his business if you were or were not a virgin."

"Oh, man." I sat on a cane chair. Hakulupe Le chuckled. I'd had romances with classmates in college, and even was engaged for a short time with a medical student who turned out to be a momma's boy. Moving among schools and internships had worked against finding a domestic relation, though.

I was jealous of the lovely hacienda where I found myself. Karima Le's home had a spacious main room with a high ceiling, banked by a kitchen and several bedrooms along an east verandah. Outbuildings were in the front, forming a semicircle around a big and dry yard. A spreading thorn tree in the yard's center lent shade even during the dry season.

I walked along the verandah and peered into the remaining rooms. The girl Hakulupe Le had been talking to earlier shyly followed my steps. At the building's end was a small classroom for perhaps twelve students. The room had two benches and four old school desks as well as a blackboard and a pathetic bookshelf that was half filled.

"Do you take lessons here?" I asked in Arrivi.

She shook her head. "Only the boys."

"What is your name?"

"Brianna."

"Not Brianna Le?" I asked.

She sadly looked away.

Hakulupe Le approached with an older woman who was obese with thinning steel-gray hair bound in a tight bun. "This is Karima Le, wife of Haku rabbe Murd."

"Hiki, Dr. Greensboro," she said holding an open palm at elbow height. Her voice was full of honey and gravel. "It is good that you should visit at last."

"Hiki, Karima Le," I said, also showing a palm.

Karima Le was helped by herdsmen who I assumed were family into a covered jeep. A high two-wheeled cart pulled by an erriv heifer carried the many homemade goods prepared for the feast. Hakulupe Le, Brianna, and I walked behind.

"We are walking to the feast?" I asked. "In this heat?"

"A show of respect," Lupe said.

At the feast site was situated next to a tall and shattered butte, but above the flooded plain. An extensive bazaar had been assembled between two large pole tents where family groups took their meals together. Tribespeople milled about in the butte's shadow, speaking mostly Arrivi that I understood. Well, sometimes understood.

Women wore finely embroidered long skirts and sleeveless tunics with extra panels that crossed the bodice and tied behind. There were many burkas carried as shawls, but no woman covered herself as the Muslim women on Earth did.

There were Mekucoo without weapons, Cylahi in bright body paint and shorts, and western-dressed, black-skinned Putuki men who bartered in loud tones using many English words. I was impressed with the quality of the overflowing artisan goods, especially the garments made of Mekucoo leather intricately decorated with beads and colorful feathers. I saw olive oil and herbs for cooking, snakeskin bands for forehead and wrist, and a certain style of shoulder garment made from ketiwhelp fur.

For all the camaraderie, this was a segregated event; men on one side, women on the other. Only Putuki bazaari swaggered between them with importance, proprietors of the best bartering tables.

At one booth, a Putuki man displayed an assortment of black stones with binding cords for use as a necklace piece. Semiprecious stones and quartz crystals were regular fare at bazaar booths, so I thought it was strange that he hovered to protect his treasure.

Behind me, Brianna spoke. "Tektite, stones from the sky."

I stared at her, trying to understand. "Oh, meteor fragments," I said in English. I reached to pick up one misshapen stone.

The bazaari cleared his throat. "Are you going to buy?" he said in English. His manner really made me bristle, so I smirked and moved away.

Warriors with freshly plaited hair congregated at the bazaar's edge, an area the women studiously avoided. Only the young men, perhaps not yet initiated as warriors, violated the parameters of female activity. Some boldly walked through the center aisle, laughing together and signaling to the matrons with jokes and big gestures. The married women blushed and giggled.

All the women greeted Lupe's aunt Karima Le while she managed the laying out of their goods on a long table. Two Mekucoo youths, perhaps ages twelve and fourteen and apparent favorites among the older women's cohort, strolled through the center as though that was their right. They nodded to Karima Le and began some running joke they repeated in Mekucoo to her delight.

"Who are they?" I asked Hakulupe Le.

"The sons of Cyrus the ketiwhelp killer by Kyle Le."

"Would that be the Cyrus who eats the beating hearts of his enemies?" I asked, modulating my voice in whole tones. "And where is he?"

"Cyrus walks with his ancestors now."

"Oh, sorry. And will Kyle Le attend the feast?"

"Of course. She's very curious to see you."

"Me? But why?"

Hakulupe Le considered me with those lambent-green eyes. "Softcheeks remain a curiosity for some."

"And this young girl, she is not called Brianna Le?"

"She has a Softcheeks father."

Lieutenant Shaw stood with two Putuki men just beyond the bazaar tables. "I need a few moments with him," I said to Hakulupe Le and walked up the aisle. Brianna quickly followed.

"Lieutenant Shaw," I said. "If I may have a word."

Mike Shaw slowly turned while the Putuki men stared with saucer eyes. I stood in the midst of the men's group. I noticed Brianna shyly waiting at my elbow.

"May I help you?" I asked her in Arrivi. She only shook her head with downcast eyes.

"She is helping you," Lt. Shaw said. "At this Arrivi event, it's unseemly for you and me to talk without a chaperon."

Just then a woman passed, accompanied by two others. She was fully veiled in sky blue with a lace facial panel. Tribespeople bowed as she walked among them, headed for the long tables and the women's group. She nodded slightly to Lt. Shaw and passed on. I saw dark eyes through the thin lace.

"Who is that?"

"Kyle Rula of Arim," Mike Shaw said, a measure of gentleness in his voice.

"Look, I care nothing for this," I said to him. "Men on one side and the women over there. You think women are all the same, huh?"

Lt. Shaw squinted but did not answer. Following his cue, Brianna also squinted.

"I'm no rural housewife," I added. "I'm not the same as them!"

"Look again, Edna Edwina," he said in low tones. "A warrior can be lost on any day. The women make the tribes stable. They run everything."

I pointed at the suited Putuki bazaari. "Then who are they? Don't try to justify this … servitude to me. I cannot be controlled."

Brianna murmured something in what must have been Mekucoo. Smile lines appeared on Lieutenant Shaw's face.

"What did she say?" I demanded.

"Nothing."

"What?"

His voice was suddenly stern. "She said, 'Softcheeks are something.' Look, Edna Edwina—"

"Stop calling me that!"

"Look, you. Nobody is trying to control you here. Warriors keep their distance from respect. And you cannot tell the difference between respect and your precious Leslie who—"

"He's not my Leslie."

Lt. Shaw's color was suddenly high. He looked around but chose to speak anyway. He bit out the words. "The Right Honorable Dr. Abercrombie sells your drug shipments on the black market and treats the wounded in pain."

"He saved many lives!"

"Many more were lost!"

"We cannot do everything!"

"If you set aside the books and looked around—"

"How dare you lecture me! Who the Sam Hill do you think you are?" Suddenly my headache was back, but I did not waver.

Lt. Shaw tried to cover his laugh. "Sam Hill? Is that an Earth phrase?"

"I don't have to listen to this."

I walked away. Behind me, I heard Brianna repeat her phrase, "Softcheeks are something."

My headache was extreme. I sought some tea to take an aspirin. Hakulupe Le included me for their family lunch in one of the big tents. I was made to sit with the women's group and wait while the herdsmen were served fish on a salted patty with olives and fruit.

An older blind man, obese with one side of his face scarred from an old napalm burn, sat at the tent entrance. He was Haku rabbe Murd, and each warrior spoke to him when entering and before exiting the tent. The Mekucoo youths who were sons of Cyrus attended his needs. Karima Le never acknowledged him. I did not see the veiled woman, Kyle Le, again.

After the Arrivi herdsmen had finished their meal and left, Brianna brought an earthen pitcher filled with tea, as well as soft bread purchased from a Putuki bazaari. The women thought the pastry was a delicious treat.

Hakulupe Le, Brianna, and I sat a piece apart from the others. We three were the only ones to drink tea from that pitcher. I was beginning to feel that the aunts and cousins did not like me. But then Karima Le casually joined us, crowding her massive self onto the bench seat and yammering with Hakulupe Le about who was born and who had married. Her voice was a delight with its mixed soothing and grating texture.

At the tent entrance, Karlyhi spoke to Haku rabbe Murd and then waited. The younger Mekucoo brother, who had earlier shown so much bravado, came inside and whispered something to Karima Le. She nodded and he left.

Karima Le turned to me. "We regret you cannot stay for our evening celebration, Sheeks-Cylom," she said in a grainy voice. "We are glad to see the spirit in your face on this feast day. You must go with Karlyhi now."

I looked at Hakulupe Le but, of course, she would not counter her aunt's words.

"I appreciate your hospitality, Karima Le," I said. "I only hope I was not a burden. Thank you again." I stood and formally held an open palm above my shoulder before I walked to the tent entrance.

I did not know if it was my place to thank Haku rabbe Murd with my exit. I considered what to say. But Karlyhi moved to stand between me and the blind man. He indicated I should hurry, thus nullifying the question.

Karlyhi and I approached the lorry where Lieutenant Shaw stood talking with three Mekucoo. Karlyhi led me to the lorry's cab. I was beginning to resent being shipped around like a sack of potatoes. I made a move to speak to Lt. Shaw. With a definite strong-arm gesture, Karlyhi blocked my way. Lt. Shaw ignored my presence.

I stomped to the lorry's rear and climbed into the truck bed. I stacked some supplies to make a place for myself and waited. I was resolved to never again travel on the savannah at Lt. Shaw's behest.

After a short time, I felt the motor engage. I bounced around in the unlit and stuffy truck bed for more than an hour, ruing my rejection of the cab's padded seat. We stopped several times and started up again. The engine would grind and the lorry's wheels spun without traction. It was my impression we were not moving along a well-used road.

We stopped again. I was at the end of my patience. I moved to the tailgate and threw back the canvas flap. Lieutenant Shaw stood perhaps four meters away with two Putuki men dressed in Arrivi pantaloons and flak jackets. A small stash of medical supplies waited on a tarp by the muddy road. Three Cylahi crouched nearby. All carried karkars and were waiting for instructions to carry the supplies into the night, I assumed.

One Putuki nodded to them. The Cylahi quickly grabbed the branded crates and carried them to the lorry. I moved back into the truck bed when they dropped the tailgate. They saw me and stepped back.

"Nu delaya!" Lt. Shaw called out.

He came forward and peered into where I waited. "Enough pouting? Will you please ride in the front now? Please."

"These are hospital supplies."

"These are recovered hospital supplies," he said. "They won't be returned to your precious Leslie so he can resell them." He impatiently sighed. "Just get out."

I dropped down from the tailgate and picked my way through the mud to the cab door. I heard him add behind me, "It must be something to be so damned rich you don't even bother to keep track."

Karlyhi was leaning against the lorry's hood smoking kari root. He looked back at me seated in the cab's center, but his implacable face betrayed nothing.

Presently Lt. Shaw took the driver's seat and Karlyhi the passenger seat. Lt. Shaw drove along the moonlit road, swerving to avoid the deepest ruts. Dolvia's larger moon hovered overhead, while the smaller one was partly concealed by horizon-level clouds. I leaned forward to better watch them.

"The best part of Dolvia is the moonlight," I said.

"Mekucoo call the male moon Nettom," Lt. Shaw said. "The one overhead. He proudly reveals himself and lights the terrain. The lazy female moon never rises into his portion of the sky. The Mekucoo call her Nettki, meaning she holds her treasure close, not allowing it to ascend."

"That's lovely."

"I'm surprised your precious Leslie didn't explain about them."

"Don't start. I am too tired to fight."

"You're still sluggish from that sedative he gave you."

"What do you know?"

"Your precious Leslie has a reputation among the nurses."

"Are you saying he tried to . . . Look, we were just having drinks." I did not mention my suspicions about the night Leslie had entered my room.

"No opportunity," Mike Shaw said.

Oh, which was the more irritating man? "Because of you?"

"That's right. Because of me." Lt. Shaw waited a moment, allowing reality to sink into my muddled head.

"And he abuses the Cylahi nurses?" I asked in a quieter tone.

Lt. Shaw nodded. "Then makes them abort. Karlyhi has sworn to kill him."

I stared wide-eyed at Karlyhi who barely glanced my way. Neither Lt. Shaw nor I spoke again during the remainder of the trip. I was too tired to fight, and he was probably too disgusted.

I looked up from the operating table as they removed the body of a young Mekucoo whom I had not been able to save. I looked at my arms. The gloves and smock sleeves were soaked with blood and flecks of flesh. The conflict was well advanced and loyalties had shifted, including my loyalty for working at Dr. Abercrombie's hospital. At the doorway, Karlyhi held a Mekucoo shield and made a soft clicking noise indicating I should come with him.

I pulled off the gloves and smock and my soaked shirt. Modesty was secondary to hygiene. I grabbed a clean pullover in the hall and followed him out into the bright day. He looked down at my hospital shoes, red and brown from my work. I kicked them off and dropped them on the overflowing dumpster.

Loitering outside the hospital entrance were tall warriors with perfect white teeth and the formal headdresses of jet-black Murmurey tail feathers. They were Siibabean ambassadors sent to negotiate a truce. I hated them involuntarily, bile rising in my throat.

They seemed nonhuman to me, able to carry out such carnage and to command massacres on these young men and boys.

We threaded our way through the crowd of bleeding warriors and desperate women with small children who searched among the wounded. With poised weapons, Lt. Shaw's men stood by two military trucks and two lorries. Mike Shaw argued with Dr. Abercrombie who was tense and flushed.

"I will have you court marshaled for this," Leslie sputtered. "These supplies are needed!"

Karlyhi helped me into the truck and secured the shield, which he seemed inordinately attached to, against the exterior hood. He climbed in next to me.

"Don't think your acts will go unreported," Mike Shaw returned to Leslie. "Consortium officials will learn about your profiteering, col-la-bo-ra-tor." He spat out the last word in hateful, measured syllables that caused gooseflesh to rise on my arms.

Lt. Shaw drove the convoy's lead truck off hospital grounds and along the muddy road. Lush new growth hung over the narrow lanes. Karlyhi leaned out the cab window and grabbed a fern branch that easily broke. He sat again and handed the feathery leaves to me, then stoically stared out the windshield.

I crushed the stem and smelled the fresh pulp. I rubbed the shiny oil against my arms and legs. I reached under my pullover to place the scent on my chest, as well as I could. I glanced at Lieutenant Shaw, but he was concentrating on his driving.

Karlyhi offered me an eight-ounce canister. I screwed off the top and smelled the liquid, but drew back with a sour face. "Drink it," Lt. Shaw commanded. "It will help you rest."

I held my nose with one hand and managed to swallow a mouthful, although I wanted to gag. The effect was immediate. My arms felt weighted with pleasant warmth. I saw the outside foliage in shimmering colors. I turned to Mike Shaw with a silly grin and cooed my thanks. He shrugged me off.

Later, I woke and found myself stretched across the seat of the closed and stifling cab. The female gualareps had been put in with me. One stood on her hind legs and stretched across the steering wheel. The other had crowded onto the narrow dashboard, tense and watchful.

I sat up and yawned, and then rolled down each window a mite to get some air. The girls came to me and nuzzled their noses under my chin. I glanced into the side mirrors and saw only foliage. The lorry was parked in a stand of tall prairie grass, perched on a mound so the wheels didn't sink into the saturated earth of the floodplain. I looked out the windows, trying to see over the new growth, but only saw waving tassels heavy with seed, the same in all directions. I sat back, unwilling to roll down the windows so the girls could escape.

"At least it is not razor grass," I muttered.

I rolled down one window further and pulled in some tender grass blades. I put them on the cab floor for snacks. The girls climbed down onto them and sniffed and circled, but did not eat. I pulled in more tassels to provide nesting materials and a fresh odor.

There was gunfire off to the left. The girls pranced on the nest with quick and tense motions, but somehow I was not worried. Barefoot and unarmed, what could I accomplish?

I was cold and hungry, though. My soiled surgical shirt was inadequate. I searched around for something to eat. I found a loaded handgun in the glove compartment next to the drink canister. There were men's clothes, but no shoes, behind the seat. I changed into the trousers, rolling up the cuffs and threading my belt through the pant loops to pull them tight. I pulled the roomy shirt over my shoulders and tied up the long ends at my waist.

The girls cocked their heads and considered me with question. "I know they are Mike Shaw's clothes. I'm confident he will forgive me."

In the side mirrors, I saw the men coming through the brush. The members of his detachment scrambled into concealed trucks and quietly latched the doors. Lieutenant Shaw and Karlyhi, with karkars, joined me from each side, pulling the doors closed without a sound.

"You look ridiculous," Lieutenant Shaw claimed in a gruff voice.

"Is there something to eat?"

"Be quiet," he whispered while they tensely watched out the side mirrors. Lieutenant Shaw grudgingly pulled out some jerky from his jacket and handed it to me. I broke off a small piece and reached toward the gualareps.

"Don't waste it. They can eat greens for now." He looked at me with a scowl. "You're too indulgent with them."

I sighed and chewed the jerky.

"What are their names?" he asked. I hesitated, looking at Karlyhi's implacable face. "Great," Lt. Shaw complained. "You let them sleep with you, but you have not named them."

I only shrugged.

After a long moment, he said, "Edna." The lighter-colored gualarep with an underbelly the color of fine porcelain with flecks of blood red, held up her chin and regarded him with question.

"Edwina," he said. The second one came to attention with an identical motion. Both men laughed. The gualareps changed places, tensely prancing as though the sound of the men's laughter was as strange as the earlier gunfire.

"When will they get darker?" I asked.

"They take on the colors of their familiar."

I drew in my breath with sudden realization. The gualarep Ralph was not the color of grass, but of Lieutenant Shaw's motley uniform. Its yellow was the same as Mike Shaw's insignia, and its red was the hue of the lieutenant's ruddy face when he came in from the hot sun.

My two reps were girly despite their grotesque shapes, showing the many colors of flesh. Their increasingly marbled backsides displayed vein-blue with infrequent blood-red freckles. Their undersides were a uniform transparent cream.

"I don't look like that," I lamely insisted.

Both men laughed again.

Rain had washed out the road. The trickling stream where we drew water for the clinic had become a raging torrent. Our convoy edged north, seeking a reasonable river ford. The men got out to stretch their legs and conferred about the best route.

We drove into the water, and the cab floor was soon soaked. Once the lead truck reached the far side, Lt. Shaw and I waited in its cab while other trucks attempted the crossing.

Karlyhi frolicked on the muddy bank with Ralph. The female gualareps raptly watched out the window on my side. Hoards of birds, several varieties, flew overhead in tight packs. They were a transient population that benefited from the seasonal rains.

Never chatty, Lieutenant Shaw began with accusations. "You have no head for business, do you?"

"I'm a research doctor, not that I have done much research. My discipline is the study of local viruses so that disembarking colonists don't die from epidemics."

"One-third of the hospital provisions were yours through a separate grant."

"And you brought along two lorries' worth."

He sighed with impatience. "That's a fraction of your entitlement. Your precious Leslie has been profiteering. He had the topaz and peridot gems gained in trade sent offworld so they are impossible to trace."

"Stop calling him that. And he built the hospital."

"Your grant funds must be used for the clinic so there's no confusion when the prosecutors arrive. I secured affidavits concerning your lack of involvement with the provisions or about his … personal business with the hospital nurses."

We watched the second lorry drive into the stream.

"Not to make excuses," I shrugged, "but those nurses are the only native women Leslie has the right to test. The only ones he knows are clean."

Mike Shaw gave me a long look. "Is that part of your 'selecting one's danger' philosophy?"

We finally arrived at the clinic, and I could not believe my eyes. The thatch had been replaced with tin, and a verandah had a screen on all sides against insects. Two additional buildings had been constructed, a clapboard patient dormitory and a second structure for staff and supplies. I stepped down from the truck and stared into Lt. Shaw's face.

"We needed the room to store your rightful share," he said.

Soldiers released Ralph from the truck bed. He commandeered the small yard, planting himself in the center and facing off any who approached.

"What's he doing?"

"They can be territorial."

While we watched, Ralph lumbered up the verandah steps and nosed his way into the refurbished clinic. We heard some thumping and the sound of furniture crashing.

"The salamander! I forgot!" I said with sudden realization.

Karlyhi rushed to the doorway but backed out slowly. Ralph appeared with the limp creature in his mouth. He curtly swung his head, flopping the long body around as though he was angry at the quick kill instead of a contest between equals.

Karlyhi called out, "It is better to have fangs!"

The female gualareps climbed down from the truck cab. They waited near me and made barking calls I had not heard before. They cautiously approached Ralph, each less than a third his size, and tried to snatch the kill from his jowls.

"He could devour them," I whispered.

Lt. Shaw slapped his trouser leg with four fingers, front then back. Ralph scowled and hunched down, resentful but immobile.

"You think he's more loyal to your hand signal than to blood-lust?" I asked.

"He had better be."

The girls quickly gobbled the salamander pieces in whole chunks. They seemingly chortled and then went to Ralph who nipped at them.

Lt. Shaw again slapped his leg. Ralph resentfully returned to his muscles-down posture. The girls jumped over his back in acrobatic twists. They strongly rubbed his flanks back and forth, rolling over in front of him exposing their creamy bellies.

Lt. Shaw opened his palm outward and Ralph relaxed, raising his noble head, allowing the girls' lascivious display. "Now that is how females should act," Mike Shaw said.

"They are only little girls," I said.

"And virgins like you."

I roundly slapped him. The soldiers tensed, quickly hiding their smiles. I turned on my heel and walked into the clinic. I made a low clicking noise in my throat. Edna and Edwina deserted Ralph's side and followed me into their new home.

What I saw there stole my breath. The fallen bookshelf had crashed against a long metal table lined with new research equipment and many additional pieces. How had they arrived there? In the back, a second acrylic-lined room had wide shelves, ready to hold my specimens and instruments. There were switched-off halogen lights for growing herbs and cultures, plus the needed spectrograph and monitors; all the basic requirements for effective fieldwork.

The girls sniffed around in corners, seeking more denizen no doubt.

I picked up a hardbound book from the floor, a tome on anatomy. A second fallen book delved into airborne microbe research.

"Lieutenant Shaw!" I called out. "First Lieutenant Michael Peter Shaw!"

He came to the doorway, entered cautiously, and reached to replace the bookshelf.

"About before—" I began.

"It's all right," he whispered. "Not a thing to be said out loud."

"You never let me finish. I'm trying to say that I'm not without experience. I've known many men. Well, not many. When I was in med school, and colleagues on a project."

"So, three men?"

I looked at him with a squint. "A person of my education … the things I have seen on the operating table—"

"Well," he said without meeting my gaze. He touched the closest piece of medical equipment. "Most of this stuff is second hand. And this one, whatever is does, I don't think it's working. The motor is probably burned out."

Not knowing what to say, I opened a rectangular case on the table. Inside was a powerful three-lens microscope. Tears came to my eyes. "Oh, man."

"There's more," Lt. Shaw quietly offered. "I mean, I know where to get it. Whatever pieces are missing. And you have the funds."

"Will you join me for a formal tea?" I asked as I brushed away a tear. "On the verandah in an hour's time?"

He nodded and left.

The soldiers unloaded the supplies under Karlyhi's direction. Two Putuki women, who I had not realized had traveled in our company, set out tea. They gave me quick hugs and congratulations on my increased wealth, and then left to explore the staff dormitory. It was my impression that they did not care for cohabitation with the gualarep girls.

I changed clothes, choosing a dusty dress from the closet behind the Chinese screen. I brushed out my hair and sat in a chair before the metal table. I heard someone prime a motor and try the ignition several times. The motor kicked in finally, and the generator began humming. I reached to switch on a lamp. The girls were impressed and made rapid clicking noises.

Edwina rested her head on my lap. Edna nuzzled my chin with her nose, her long tongue exploring my features. I thought Mike Shaw must be right that I had been too indulgent.

Basically, they made me uneasy. I mean, they were adolescents with no experience with copulation. Yet they emitted a new fragrance, a different energy. I tried to tell myself it was the new home in a lush jungle and a better scent arena, but I knew it was their proximity to Ralph. They wanted to play with Ralph.

I heard Lieutenant Shaw's step on the verandah. I went to the doorway and saw him place orchids in a shallow bowl on the table. "I suppose the orchids in my room at the hospital were from you."

"We don't have orchids at Two Forks on Cicero," he said. "We have poppies and sunflowers and ragweed, but no orchids. Here they are common."

I served the tea along with dried fish on a wafer and sliced fruit. We watched the sunset while Edna and Edwina catnapped on the porch.

"Hakulupe Le will arrive this week," Lieutenant Shaw said. "She will have more supplies."

"You have engineered everything, then?"

"The Arrivi came to me asking if you were with your precious . .
. with Abercrombie. If you were part of his black market activities.
Hakulupe Le claimed collusion was not possible, citing your work
here. I thought perhaps you did prefer the good doctor, so I poked
around a little. Contracts, shipment records, income stream; things
like that. Then it came to me that you were blithely unaware, always
with a patient or with your nose stuck in a book.

"Plus, how could a person with your philosophy be . . . nefarious?"
he continued. "One must select one's danger. Finally, I accepted
that you just allowed Abercrombie to work you into the ground and
steal your fortune. That was when we stepped in, Karlyhi and me."

"That was when you brought the girls."

"Then more shipments came," he continued in his studious way.
"Medicine that never arrived at the hospital. I enlisted some higher-
ups and engineered a sting operation on Abercrombie's profiteering. We made them sign affidavits."

"And you were promoted. You saved face and money for the Consortium."

"That was not my primary goal. My unit is reassigned now."

"You're leaving?"

"I cannot spend all my time ferrying you back and forth. We'll
be gone by morning."

There was a commotion in the yard. The truck rocked from interior pounding. Edna and Edwina came instantly alert. "It's Ralph,"
Lieutenant Shaw said. "I locked him up. He's not happy about it."

The infant reps moved to the verandah's edge and stared across
the yard. Each looked back at me and then pranced and stared.

"There are few of Ralph's kind here," Lt. Shaw added. "He does not know when he may have another opportunity."

"They are only little girls."

"They're animals. It's not the same as with us." Karlyhi came around the truck's end, waiting for Mike Shaw's signal. The girls anxiously cooed and pranced.

Petulantly, I asked, "Did you ask the girls what they want?"

He smirked. "You already know."

"Fine! Release the monster." I stood and signaled Karlyhi. "If Ralph eats them, at least somebody will get what he wants out of this."

Karlyhi dropped the tailgate. Ralph poured out onto the yard and lumbered to the place where he had first claimed territory. He made several quick turns as if to check his flanks, and then jumped six inches into the air. I could not be sure in the gathering darkness, but it seemed that his marbled hide was uniformly black. With several angry false starts, he sidled toward the porch.

Meanwhile, Edna and Edwina called and pranced from the top of the steps. They were staring and appeared to be sweating. Gualareps don't sweat, of course, but the girls were giving off serious pheromones. Each lifted one front and back foot, rocking on opposing feet. Then they switched to the other feet, rocking as if the surface of the porch was too hot.

"You must signal your permission," Lt. Shaw probed.

"I never taught them hand signals."

He just waited. I turned, undecided. The girls ignored me, intent on Ralph's movements. "Go on, then," I said, and they were in the yard in a flash.

The moons had not risen. Night in the bush was darker than dark. I stared hard, but the girls were the same color as the yard. I could discern them only by their movements. Ralph was the jet-black of Murmurey feathers on a Siibabean headdress.

I heard a scurrying and a couple nips and yelps. The girls raced toward the bush, past the catalpa tree. Edwina turned back, calling to Ralph with barks. In the weak halo of clinic light, Ralph looked up at Lt. Shaw as if to ask, "Is this necessary?"

Mike made a long waving motion, and Ralph lumbered after the girls.

Karlyhi sat on the verandah steps. For twenty minutes or so we heard the gualareps thrashing about, then complete silence. I searched for a safe topic.

"How did you come by Michael Peter as your name?"

The Lieutenant gave me a level look. "My grandfather worked for Softcheeks on Cicero, and most of the local men took to soldiering. The guilds filled with Softcheeks technicians who spoke only English, and our skills were discounted. My father was posted off-world when I was born, and the attending doctor was a man Softcheeks call Irish Catholic."

"And his last name was Shaw?"

"My father's name was Shananinni. It was common to shorten names for advancement."

"You're from the ninni tribe?"

"People were designated by occupation. Ninni only means farmer."

"And these other soldiers have fake names?"

"Names refined for advancement," he corrected.

We heard a ruckus among the macaws. Hyrax and addax came streaming out of the bush.

"So . . . Ralph has devoured the girls and now he traumatizes the wildlife."

"Look on the bright side," Lieutenant Shaw said. "The clinic area will no longer be plagued with bottom feeders like the salamander."

Later, after everybody had retired to new quarters, I caught the odor of kari root smoke. Unable to sleep, I rose from my bed and lit a tallow. The generator had switched off, but the tallow's yellow light was adequate to guide me.

The gualarep girls were still absent. In my thigh-length night-shirt, I stepped onto the verandah and held the tallow high. Its fluttering candlelight barely reached the porch's edge.

Lieutenant Shaw was sitting on the wooden steps. He snubbed out the cigarette. "Dowse the light," he whispered. I blew out the tallow and set it on the railing. Intermittent blue moonlight penetrated the rolling clouds.

"I wanted to say," I said, "and let me finish this time. I don't know when I will have another opportunity. Just . . . just thanks for what you have done."

I crossed my arms and sighed, not aware that I had pulled the shirtfront taut over my stiff nipples. Lt. Shaw just stared.

"I should go in," I said.

He stood and came to the doorway. I backed inside. With my heart palpitating and a furtive gesture, I retraced my steps. "The tallow—"

He put his hand on the doorjamb to block my steps. I waited, staring at the floor. "I don't know what is needed here," I said in a small voice.

He placed his hand on my neck and fumbled with the tiny buttons on the ruffled bodice of my shirt. Oh, why had I worn that stupid, stupid shirt?

"Please say something."

"This may hurt a little," he whispered.

I awoke the following morning to the fragrance of turned-over earth and crushed leaves. But the body next to me was not Mike Shaw. I sat up and yawned. "You girls are too big now to sleep in my bed."

Ralph is gone, Edwina accused.

"He will come back," I answered, but then frowned and shrugged it off. Edna and Edwina never climbed into my bed after that.

THREE

BEFORE HAKULUPE LE RETURNED, WE HAD OTHER COMPANY. IT was late, and I was in bed reading a medical book by tallow light. I heard a step on the verandah and assumed it was Karlyhi, the only one among our company who never wore shoes.

But the shadow that darkened my doorway included the feathered circle of a Siibabean headdress. I drew in my breath in fear. Edwina scurried out from under the metal table and faced off the warrior with a hissing sound. She was jet black and positioned in the center of the floor.

Just as I extinguished the tallow, Edna jumped out next to her sibling, modulating her color from porcelain to floorboard brown. She seemed to flash across the room and then disappear. The startled warrior cried out in his language and backed away. I heard him trot across the yard.

I grabbed my bedside karkar and crept to the doorway, but could discern nothing in the deep night. I resolved to read under cover. I lowered the gun and turned back. The watchful girls had resumed their transparent cream color with vein-blue and freckle-red hues. I sat on the floor and allowed them to snuggle next to me. Edna was trembling. I decided they could maintain the darker color transformation only when frightened or aroused.

Hakulupe Le arrived in late morning the following day. She had with her some Arrivi men, all wearing pantaloons and the sleeveless tunic of their tribe, and an erriv-drawn cart. The erriv had fleshy snouts and ridges of horns on their skulls like a roster's comb, only bony and pointed.

We exchanged greetings, and she stepped onto the verandah, glancing around with those lambent eyes. "Are you pleased with the buildings?" I asked. "Lieutenant Shaw had them built."

"Arrivi men did the construction," she returned. "Although they failed to understand about Cicero acrylic, how the pieces fitted together. Or why Sheeks-Cylom needed an acrylic-lined room. Lieutenant Shaw had to visit once during the rains to make a demonstration."

"I see."

"This area is above flood level," she continued. "The additions mean you can remain year-round." Hakulupe Le saw the gualarep girls, who cautiously poked their heads from the doorway.

"Oh, these are my—"

"I heard," she said with delight. "It was my impression that they were smaller."

"They have grown some. They're shy just now, though. We had quite a scare last night. A Siibabean warrior."

"Not a group? Not carrying weapons?"

I shook my head. It was the tribal way to ask rapid-fire questions concerning enemy sightings. But Hakulupe Le did not seem unduly alarmed.

The men had led the cart to the staff dormitory. They were unloading supplies under Karlyhi's direction. "He has also grown some," Lupe noted.

My servants brought tea. They paused at the verandah steps. "Go inside," I said to the gualareps. The women placed the tea service on the verandah table and formally bowed to Hakulupe Le, who greeted them with warm hugs. The servants began some long story in their dialect, both chattering at the same time. Hakulupe Le frowned and glanced my way. I blushed.

I retreated inside to where the girls languished under the metal table. Edna looked up with question and then lowered her head over Edwina's back for a catnap. They could not be expected to spend their lives cooped up in the clinic. I needed to make peace with the tribespeople and find acceptance for Edna and Edwina.

Hakulupe Le was in the yard, talking quietly with the men. I was anxious to speak with her. While the Arrivi made preparations to depart, I came out onto the verandah and loitered by the steps. The two men and a young boy faced my way and showed palms at elbow level. This was a new gesture for me, one of high honor. I bowed slightly and sat at the table, wondering if I had precipitated their action by interrupting their farewell.

They moved off with the cart, and Hakulupe Le joined me at the table. She reached to pour tea and uncovered the laid-out meal.

"So," she began, "three buildings. Tribespeople have a policy that perhaps you have heard. No equipment is allowed on Dolvia that

Dolviets cannot operate. Karlyhi will need to be instructed. And you should order an EAM."

"That's too extravagant." An EAM was an extra-atmosphere modem, a high-function computer linked by satellite to Stargate Junction. The connection was a valued tool and a wonder among tribespeople.

Hakulupe Le fixed me with gimlet-like eyes. "You are the only woman on Dolvia, you know, who has three houses."

"Dormitories like at the hospital."

"The hospital has a bureaucracy and a garrison of soldiers. You have only these reptiles."

"We arrived ahead of you. That is all."

Lupe smiled slightly. "The men believe you trust your spirit, the Sheeks-Cylom, to protect you. They believe Dolvia tolerates this spirit in these reptiles. They believe you require two because they are only female."

"And you dispelled such nonsense, I trust."

"I encouraged it. The larger your reputation, the more secure your actions."

"So I am living large, am I?"

"And now you must choose an assistant."

I had many times considered getting an assistant. I needed to re-engage with research, my purpose for coming to Dolvia. "If I selected Karlyhi as an assistant, would that be incorrect?"

"He has a certain gift, you know. With animals."

"Yes, I have seen it." I waited, then ventured, "Karlyhi spoke of things that are seen. Is he meant for some other path?"

"How thoughtful of you to ask," Lupe said. "Karlyhi will keep your accounts for a time. Lieutenant Shaw showed him how. He can travel to the hospital with the Arrivi men and bring your EAM."

"Which is already ordered."

She shrugged.

Edna and Edwina waited at the doorway. With caution, they came onto the verandah. Edwina went to the other side, but Edna hesitated. She hiked a front leg and the opposing back leg, tense and watchful, then switched to the other two and rocked a little.

"Edna wants to meet you," I whispered.

"It is not healthy living with these reptiles. One day they will outweigh you."

"They are no longer allowed in my bed."

"In the bed?" Lupe asked. "And what about the other one?"

"Edwina is sulking."

From her place on the side, Edwina shallowly coughed. "Ka," she said, and coughed twice more. "Ka, ka."

Lupe shyly smiled. "Perhaps we should hold classes here," she continued without acknowledging Edna. "Reading, math, and anatomy." Edna turned and flicked her tail. She clicked in agreement.

"She likes you," I claimed. Lupe looked at her, but only sipped some tea.

"We could teach here, I suppose," I said, considering her proposal. "Some students might graduate into internships. The studious ones could assist me with patients."

Edna again cooed.

"Male students only?" Lupe asked.

"Open enrollment, I should think. Advancement for those who won't be taken to fight. Education is an investment in the future."

Edna pranced and cooed.

"We shall call it an academy," Lupe agreed, "for research." She watched Edna's display. "I believe that one wants to teach."

"We could get additional funding, perhaps."

"From the clinic grant?"

"An education grant. A different committee, but a similar structure."

"Softcheeks are the most wondrous people," Lupe said. "You are unconcerned with the tribal wars, but you lavish money on the study of microbes."

Edna came to her side, friendly but cautious. "Just open your hand," I said. Edna's long tongue flicked across Hakulupe Le's palm. "Now stroke her neck." While Lupe leaned down to comply, I added, "So now you are friends. Edna can find you from forty kilometers away, or so claims Lieutenant Shaw."

"No crawling into my bed," Lupe admonished.

Hakulupe Le's presence at the clinic brought back the patients; women with children mostly, but also some curious tribesmen who questioned Karlyhi about the girls. Karlyhi ran the clinic's operation and traveled often to the hospital for supplies. He returned with erriv-drawn carts, as the incline to the clinic was too steep for the airbus.

The gualareps never entered the patient dorm or the staff dorm. We established regular hours when Karlyhi took them out to hunt and play using their own path away from the buildings so visitors were not frightened.

Not that the girls cared. They allowed only Hakulupe Le into the clinic that housed my research equipment, and engaged in an ongoing battle with the servants. Edwina delighted in frightening them. She did no real harm and bit no one. She just played on their fears.

Hakulupe Le managed the preparations to establish the academy. Another building was constructed for classrooms, this one in Mekucoo style with a thatch roof and rounded pole sides like a wattle fence. Boarding students took over the former classrooms which were partitioned for privacy.

Hakulupe Le greeted the families who brought their young children to be placed under our care. To increase my legend, she insisted that I must be seen in the yard with the gualareps trailing behind me. When Karlyhi had the girls out hunting, however, I was required to greet the families and learn the children's names, all part of native protocol.

Hakulupe Le hired teachers from the Arrivi and Putuki tribes. There was also a Mekucoo woman named Kecouroo who taught three afternoons a week. She was bright and stately and very good with children. Edwina liked her.

Mekucoo women seldom left their land. They wore decorated single-garment leather with sheathed belt knives. Their nappy hair was short over high foreheads and beaded earrings. Kecouroo wore a necklace that sported several pieces of the black tektite that, legend had it, boosted a natural gift of intuition. I asked if Kecouroo could take on more classes. It was explained that she could not be absent from her nearby village for longer periods.

We set up the EAM, or extra-atmosphere modem, on the clinic's front desk. Hakulupe Le spent one evening teaching me how to access the transport library and use the tool bars. I even communicated with colleagues on Cicero.

Soon the clinic operations all hummed along smoothly. I saw patients for two hours each morning and two more before sunset, depending on the volume. I spent the remainder of my time bent over the books and microscope, recording notes in the daily logbook.

Finding answers was slow work. My research grant stipulated that I should seek vaccination possibilities for native diseases, and then add the compounds to genetically engineered vegetables as was common on Earth. After field tests, if sick children received rations of the augmented vegetables, malnutrition complications due to rapid dehydration could be mitigated.

The compounds we had imported by way of Stargate Junction worked only sometimes. Plants I tested seeking new substances were structurally different. Potency could not be gauged. The battery of tests I routinely employed needed standardization for a different climate.

I submitted several EAM requests for current papers on the local flora and possible cures taken from the many flowering plants. Little information was forthcoming. One doctor, a Henry Beecham, posted a formal letter implying that I must complete the encyclopedia myself. Hakulupe Le thought he was being haughty.

"Be careful how you reply," I said. "He manages the grant committee for the academy."

The committee replied once to our academy proposal with a request for more information, and then there was a stony silence. Hakulupe Le went forward with her school, using tribal gifts proffered for relief from suffering. A small operation with a restricted budget was our best effort, but we could apply again during the next grant cycle.

I treated one girl, not yet six years old, who had benign tumors in her throat that threatened to close her windpipe. She was emaciated because she could not swallow, but had a bright face and was eager and incongruously happy.

Hakulupe Le explained to her Arrivi family that I could operate to remove the lumps, but they would grow back. She questioned them for family history and diet, and about what regions they had passed through and the girl's activity there. We found no apparent reason why she should suffer while others did not.

After surgery, the girl left with her family who promised to return before the rains for a follow-up exam. I did a biopsy on the removed tumors and noted my observations. Hakulupe Le encouraged me to enter the paragraphs in the EAM's data processing program. I only shrugged. My work was at the research table, not the front desk.

Soon she brought in two male Cylahi students to meet me, both about age fourteen. One would transcribe my notes onto the EAM, and the other, who could render, would make drawings of the herbs and succulents I grew under lights in the back.

The gangly, sandy-colored boys wore only dungarees, and mostly entered the clinic when Karlyhi had the girls out hunting. They were no bother, so I tolerated the activity while they fooled around with the EAM and scanned some drawings to be manipulated on screen.

I looked up from my work one day and saw Hakulupe Le seated at the EAM. Edna waited at her side, cooing with each of Lupe's sighs. I felt a twinge of jealousy. The gualareps were not allowed to enter my acrylic-lined research rooms, so I spent many hours separate from their company. They had made friends elsewhere.

"Dr. Greensboro," Hakulupe Le said, "you should see this." I put down my work and joined her at the EAM. On the screen was idling an official note from Stargate Junction.

Leslie Abercrombie, M.D., MBA, Ph.D., Director of Research at the Consortium's Dolvia Outreach Hospital, had been assassinated. A Siibabean spearhead was thrust under his ribs, piercing the heart. His remains were scheduled for shipping to the orbiting transport, and from there would travel back to Earth. The Westend Consortium was set to conduct an investigation under a civil mandate led by Mr. Frank Duerr of Somule, a populous Arrivi town nearby.

I sat down next to Hakulupe Le. "Assassinated," I said. "I mean, I know his activities were not altogether upright. But assassinated? That is for . . . that's for politicals." After a moment I added, "Do you know anything about this?"

Lupe blinked twice. "Siibabean don't share their plans with me."

"It could have been anybody," I said, "using that spearhead to throw off investigators. Do you know this Frank Duerr?"

"He's a Hardhand with cartel connections. But tell me, why ship the remains back to the Softcheeks' world?"

I shrugged slightly. "Leslie may have a family burial place there. Perhaps he wants to be remembered by someone."

"But his spirit lingers here."

"Have you seen it?" I asked with a grin.

"Of what significance is the body?"

"Softcheeks have trouble letting go."

While Hakulupe Le was off visiting the neighbors one day, I sat at the front desk, holding a failed experiment under the light while I compared the growth to an onscreen image. Edna lingered at my side. "You like Lupe, huh?" I asked. Edna looked up with question. "Do you like her better than me?"

Better? came her question.

I thought about the query for a moment. I took two small rocks from the collection on the windowsill and sat on the floor with Edna. She was bigger; I remember thinking that. And her richly marbled hide was the color of the sandy compound yard.

I held up the red sandstone paperweight that Edna fingered with her tongue. "This is Hakulupe Le," I said. I held up the other rock of speckled granite. "This is Dr. Greensboro. Me." I set them both on the floor and pointed to each. "Hakulupe Le, Dr. Greensboro. Now you must choose. If one of us must go away, which should remain?"

Edna cooed with question, a low clicking in her throat. "Ah . . . go away," I said. "Like Ralph is gone. Go away."

I picked up one rock and held it behind my back, then replaced it. I repeated the motion with the other, and placed them both before Edna. "Which do you choose? Which can go away?"

Edna made a rapid series of coughs. "Ka. Ka, ka, ka." She twisted and gingerly picked up both stones in her jaws. She threw back her head to place them under her tongue and scurried out into the yard.

"Edna, wait! It was just a question."

I heard visitors squeal and someone's dinner pot was overturned by Edna's tail. I followed her to the catalpa tree where she scrambled up the wide trunk to the branching fork. She climbed higher and clawed at another fork to dig out a hole. Arrivi visitors clamored to each other and gathered in a wide circle. Karlyhi and Edwina joined me while I watched Edna's activity.

"I didn't know they climbed trees," I told Karlyhi.

After she had secured the rocks together in the hollow she had forced, Edna pulled some branches over the fresh scars on the bark. She climbed down with difficulty, her nails leaving long marks while her weight pulled her to the ground. Edwina joined her at the trunk's base, where they made the same guarded jerky motions Ralph had used to claim territory.

"Let it be known," I said to Karlyhi. "Nobody climbs the tree for a while. And remind me to not use metaphors with the girls."

"What is met-a-phor?" he asked.

When I related the story to Hakulupe Le over tea, she could not stop laughing. "Your soul and mine are planted together," she claimed when she could catch her breath. "Resident forever in the catalpa tree."

In truth, I should have posed more questions to the girls, or so we learned when the mandate investigators visited. One Hardhand in a suit and tie, with a pile of credentials, poked his nose into my clinic. Like all Hardhands, he was from Cicero, Lt. Shaw's home planet.

Edna hissed, and I quickly led Mr. Duerr into the yard. His ECCAV, enclosed cross-country air-conditioned vehicle, was parked there. I was surprised that the graceless Cicero-engineered car had conquered the steep incline to my clinic. The doors stood open, hinged upward like a Murmurey fledgling exercising its wings.

Another white man, standing near the classroom entrance, was blocked by Karlyhi with his Mekucoo shield. A third with a shoulder camcorder lurked around the open windows of the patient dorm. They had gone to some trouble for this visit.

"We're just tying up loose ends," Mr. Duerr claimed, "concerning Dr. Abercrombie's estate."

"His estate?"

"You were notified. We are just following up on certain facts."

With skittish eyes, Karlyhi led the second man toward us. Edwina herded down the cameraman. He recorded her turns and jerks while he backed into his compatriot.

"Shut that thing off," I said.

I had grown accustomed to my instructions being obeyed without hesitation. So had the girls. Edwina grabbed the camcorder's long strap in her teeth and jerked the black box to the ground. The suited man reached for the strap as Edwina pulled the still-operating case through the dirt. Edna, hissing and barking, got between them and he stopped short.

Edwina stepped over the camcorder and urinated to place her scent on it. "Oh, man," the technician complained. "It's ruined for sure."

Mr. Duerr drew a laser pistol, the elegant Tzu that Company men carried, from his suit and aimed at Edwina. I threw myself against his arm. The discharge went off into the air, a bright flash and buzz. An entire city of birds nesting in the surrounding bush took to wing.

From behind, Karlyhi placed his belt knife against Mr. Duerr's throat and took the gun. "Nu delaya," I said, and Karlyhi hesitated. I held out my hands, fingers widespread to indicate everybody must slow down. I quickly took stock.

"Now that I have your attention," I told Mr. Duerr, and I nodded to Karlyhi who released him. Mr. Duerr felt his throat for blood.

"This is my clinic," I said sternly. "My instructions are followed here. You have caused me to lose face in front of these ones." I played to Hakulupe Le and the staring tribeswomen who kept their distance and held their children close. "You would kill such a beautiful creature over a camcorder?" I loudly asked. "Or because she is loyal to me? Or because it's just in your nature to destroy everything?"

"I am the law in this region," Mr. Duerr said.

"Then what need to settle questions with your weapon?" Karlyhi chuckled.

"It's a long drive back to the hospital," I added. "And dangerous. I suggest you start now before the sun sets."

"But … but nobody travels the bush at night," Mr. Duerr said.

"Then you will have a heroic story when you return," I said without empathy. "Tell about how you exercised your lawful authority over the savannah. Oh, and leave the guns. All the guns." Karlyhi quickly searched them and their ECCAV for weapons. The two technicians collected the gummy camcorder and threw it in the back of the vehicle.

"I won't leave without the Tzu," Mr. Duerr said. Karlyhi reluctantly handed it to him.

"We hope the weapon protects you on the savannah," I said.

The hissing girls followed him to the wide car. After they drove away, Edwina turned her back to the road and threw up her hind feet, first one then the other, as if to say good riddance. The tribeswomen grinned and went back to work.

"You have not seen the last of them," Hakulupe Le said.

"Let's store the weapons, Karlyhi."

In the storeroom that I admit I had not visited, I saw stacks of automatics all exactly the same, plus crates of ammunition. "Not yours," Karlyhi quickly claimed. "Just resting here."

"Resting?" I asked.

Among the tribesmen weapons were a motley collection of outdated models, mostly Cicero-made. They were useless raid trophies since it was difficult to make bullets of the correct gauge. But this cache of weapons was a militia arsenal, associated in my mind with uniforms and jackboots and intel maps.

"Bring a karkar and one of those," I said, indicating a pistol. "We're going out with the girls."

We walked along the gualarep path, over the hill and down to the stream on the other side. Many flowering plants had dropped petals and green fruit. It was already late in their cycle that followed the rains. The waterline on the bank was littered with tough berries that squished underfoot. Spiders scurried to harvest the treat scattered at our arrival. "Now pay attention," I told the girls. I handled the pistol. I aimed at a tree nest and fired. Two dozen birds rose from the tree with irritated calls and flapping wings. One bird fell to the ground.

Edna cooed. "Ka, ka, ka, ka." She and Edwina lumbered over to the dead bird.

"Bring it back," I called out too late, for the morsel was gone. The girls returned with appreciative clicking noises.

"Look," I claimed. "I am trying to make a lesson here. That Hardhand could have killed you." I knelt next to them, trying to find a place where my skirt would not be stained by the fermenting berries. I opened the pistol's cylinder, allowing each gualarep to flick her tongue over the spent shell.

Edwina drew back with displeasure. "Ka."

"Take something down with the karkar," I said to Karlyhi, "then show them the shell." I turned back to Edna. "Bring the prey here."

The automatic's report startled more bush denizen that took to flight. I was surprised at the density of their population. The girls returned with the dead bird. Edna flickered her tongue over the large shell and fingered the bird the same way.

"Give me that." I indicated the karkar.

"I can do it," Karlyhi said.

I took the automatic from his hand. "I passed proficiency tests before I disembarked." I secured the strap on my arm and held the gun against my side. New and heavy, it was a practical weapon ideal for bush fighting. "And we need to have a talk about the arsenal that's just resting in my storeroom."

Karlyhi rolled his eyes.

I pulled the trigger to fire at the far bank, but nothing happened. "The safety," Karlyhi whispered. I searched both sides for the switch. He gingerly pointed past the pin assembly. "There."

"Fine," I said, handing him the gun. "You do it. Just fire into the bank."

Karlyhi took the heavy gun and spread out some shot. Spent shells flowed in an arch from the carriage and dropped to the ground. The girls scurried behind me. "Now go across and sniff it out," I instructed.

"They can smell it from here," Karlyhi corrected. He met my squint with a steady gaze.

"Take down a lower branch," I said. "Across the way."

Karlyhi shrugged and fired into the opposite thorn tree. A brittle branch fell.

"Ka, ka, ka, ka," Edna cooed. I stared at her.

I knelt near them and displayed the pistol. "Let's review. When the Hardhand pointed this weapon at you, what did that mean?"

In a flash, Edwina knocked the gun from my hand. She kicked it into the dust and urinated to place her scent on it. Karlyhi burst out laughing.

"That does not work with everything, you know."

Felt good, she shot back and flicked her tail. I looked at Karlyhi, wondering if he could hear her thoughts, but I shrugged it off. "And if you draw human blood, they will hunt you down and kill you."

Catch me first, Edwina claimed.

"You won't see the ambush coming."

I sighed. Was the lesson even worthwhile? I joined Karlyhi, giving the girls time to digest the difficult concepts. "Take the pistol back for cleaning."

"You pick it up," he said.

I gingerly collected the gummy pistol with my skirt hem and dropped it into my wide pocket. We walked back together. "And no talking in front of strangers," I added as a coda. "Or thinking. Ralph doesn't talk to strangers."

Not to you, Edwina chortled with a tail flick.

Later while I worked at the front desk EAM, Edwina brought an orchid, its lush petals a bluish-white tinged with pink. "Are you trying to make up?" I asked. "This is beautiful. Lieutenant Shaw used to leave orchids. Which you devoured, as I recall."

Edwina entered the research room. "Don't go in there!" I followed her trying to get to the table first. She rose on her hind legs and supported herself on the table with one bow-legged arm. She nudged the petri dishes that contained tissue from the throat tumors I had removed from the Arrivi girl. Edwina flicked her tongue across the assembled equipment.

"Don't do that. You may impact the experiment."

Edwina passed her tongue over the orchid. "Ka," she articulated.

"Are you saying the orchid and the throat culture are the same?" Edwina dropped to the floor, no longer able to support her considerable weight in the upright position. "Which part?" I eagerly asked. "The petals? The stamen? The pollen?"

She just stared at me with those unblinking eyes.

"Never mind. I can test them all. And Edwina, if this pans out, all is forgiven."

She tossed her head with a lightning quick jerk, as if asking a question.

"Forgiven?" I asked. "You forget the things I did to you, like sending away Ralph. I forget the things you did to me. A clean slate between us."

She lumbered out onto the verandah. *No forgiven*, she insisted.

FOUR

SOON AFTER MR. DUERR'S VISIT, EVERYTHING CHANGED, COL-
lapsing in a single day. The natives called the time following the
rains that year the season of kari. I did learn more about the words
of power taken from the Mekucoo dialect. They included netta, or
desert dry; kari for the stirring of new life; cylay for strong growth;
and om, which meant an ending of sorts. By tribal reckoning, we
had emerged from a season of netta into a season of kari.

Hakulupe Le shrugged when I later complained to her. "Who
can see with the eyes of Dolvia?" she asked.

Anyhow, that day began simply enough. I had wanted to compile
my observations concerning the incomplete orchid tests. I sat at
the EAM and saw idling on the screen the needed flora encyclopedia. A battery of plants was listed with drawings and specifications,
preparation methods, and ailments they might alleviate.

I realized that the students had transcribed a substantial body of
study. The plants were not tested, however, and the portions were
imprecise. Also, the recommendations were not mine.

"Hakulupe Le, what is this?" I asked when she entered, ready for patient rounds.

"Just a beginning," she shrugged.

"This must not be published. The experiments are inconclusive."

"Something to keep the students busy."

"Where did you get the template? And the scientific names for the plants?"

"Dr. Beecham supplied a list, along with a few recommendations for structure."

"Beecham? Are you using my name? This is my professional reputation on the line."

"It's just a beginning," she repeated.

Just then, we heard a ruckus in the yard outside the classrooms. Hakulupe Le and I rushed toward the noise. Karlyhi held a female student by her upper arm and was beating her with a thick switch. She was Brianna, the girl I had met at the Feast of Oria.

"What's going on here?" I demanded.

Karlyhi stared me down, his blood still high from whatever insult she had made. I quickly took stock. Karlyhi stood tall and said nothing. Brianna, not fourteen, stared at the ground and controlled her sobs. Kecouroo stood in the doorway but made no gesture of explanation. The other students just stared.

Wants her, I heard Edwina say behind me.

"This is a little girl," I told Karlyhi.

"Then what are these?" He roughly handled her small breasts under the linen gown. Brianna pushed away his hands and stood with her arms across her body.

"Go wait on the verandah," I told her. Brianna frowned and stepped back a fraction. "The gualareps won't bother you." She sourly walked down the path with Hakulupe Le.

I turned to Kecouroo with a curt nod. "Would you have a few minutes to spare before you leave today?" She nodded and took the other students back into class.

"May I speak with you?" I asked Karlyhi in a stern voice. We walked away to where our conversation would be private. Edwina tagged along. "What is Brianna to you?"

"Just a thing."

"Why did you beat her?"

"She refused."

I smirked. "You know that makes you the same as Leslie Abercrombie." He drew in his breath. I had struck home.

"Karlyhi," I added, "you have been valuable to the clinic, and I have trusted your strength. But you and I must go our separate ways now."

With his jaw set, he stared across the horizon. I began again. "You have spoken of things that are seen. Perhaps you should travel that path. Think of the macaw chick in the nest. First it's in the egg, then grows too large and breaks free. The clinic is the egg, and you are the chick. The chick never returns to the egg."

Emotion flashed across his implacable face, but was quickly vanquished.

"I will talk with Hakulupe Le," I continued. "You may take a few days to consult with the Arrivi men. Oh, and remove the arsenal resting in my storeroom. Am I clear?"

"Yes, Sheeks-Cylom."

"You and I are done." Seized with a fear that I would say more, I walked down the path toward the clinic. Edwina followed.

Forgiven? she wanted to know.

"There is no forgiving."

Before I could further dispose of the matter, we had company. Two Arrivi men in pantaloons and paneled tunics stood near a family fire. They approached when I came down the rise. They stopped, staring at Edwina. She became agitated, I assumed because of the one stranger's looks. There was something odd about him; I could not place it. Then the difference came to me. This stranger, although dressed like Arrivi, was Softcheeks under his rich tan, possibly offworld-born like me.

Edwina jerkily turned around several times and actually hopped in the air. Edna came down the clinic steps, also aroused. "Ka, ka, ka, ka, ka," she called. The gualareps gathered together near the steps and anxiously waited.

Hakulupe Le and I held palms high to the wondering men, and Lupe made the introductions. "This is Orin rabbe Murd, a cousin. And I need to present Joseph Osborn."

"Hiki, gentlemen. Melinga," I said. Orin rabbe Murd was a stout and deeply tanned Arrivi of some authority and Karima Le's son, perhaps her oldest. It was difficult for me to keep the family ties straight in my head.

"Joey has a letter," Lupe added.

It was from First Lieutenant Shaw. Each gualarep stood on two legs and impatiently rocked. Perhaps they could smell Ralph on Lt.

Shaw's letter. "Would you step up on the verandah, please?" I asked the men. They frowned but complied.

I opened the envelope and drew out the letter. While I followed our guests onto the porch, I allowed the envelope to flutter to the ground. The girls fingered it with their tongues, sniffing and rocking, and joyously tossed it into the air with a circling dance. They left their scent all around, unable to contain their excitement.

"Edna, please," I called. "You are piddling all over the yard."

Edna gently took the envelope into her mouth, and they scurried off toward the bush.

Brianna sat on the verandah floor rubbing some paste on her leg welts. "Brianna," Hakulupe Le said, "would you ask the servants to bring tea, please?" She nodded and left.

Joseph Osborn got right down to business. "The prosecutor you disarmed, Mr. Duerr, has lodged a complaint. You are to appear before the magistrate in Somule."

"I have no time for Somule. I have work."

Orin rabbe Murd's eyes grew wide. He drew back slightly. "You are summoned," Joey explained into the tense silence.

"You can take my deposition here."

"Mr. Duerr says you threatened to kill him."

I slapped my palm on the table. "He was going to shoot Edwina!" Orin stared with question at Hakulupe Le. "I could not allow murder in my yard," I added. "Besides, we returned the weapons."

"Perhaps you can relate your side of the story while we travel," Joey suggested.

"I am telling you now; it was nothing."

"A trip to Somule," Lupe interrupted in whole tones, "would be a welcome diversion. Think of this as an opportunity to consult with the grant committee and reunite with some friends." She looked down at the letter I still held.

"Excuse me for a moment," I said. I went into the clinic to read Lt. Shaw's letter under the table lamp. I glanced out to the verandah where Hakulupe Le tried to calm Orin rabbe Murd as the servants brought tea service.

"Sheeks-Cylom," the letter began. "I am writing to put in my request for an hour of your time when you visit Somule. Be forewarned, your legend has spread. No hiding behind a medical textbook. Bring the girls."

What an odd note, composed as though Lt. Shaw thought more than one person might read it. I returned to the verandah but did not sit. I handed the single page to Hakulupe Le.

"We can visit my aunt, Karima Le," she said. "You remember her from the Feast of Oria."

"Of course I remember," I said. "Orin rabbe Murd's mother." He relaxed somewhat, calmed by my newfound ingratiating gestures. "We could travel in the lorry," I suggested.

Orin squinted. Apparently, I was not to make travel decisions either. "We can pack the truck bed with dirt," I doggedly continued. "High enough so the gualareps can see out the back. How many days?"

"Two," Mr. Osborn said.

"And two to come back," I calculated, "plus a few days layover. We should close the clinic and academy." Orin rabbe Murd stared, and nobody added their ideas to mine. I sighed heavily. I was getting this all wrong. I excused myself and walked up the path to the classroom. Behind me, Hakulupe Le began the logistics discussion with her cousin.

Damn, I thought. A whole week lost with this trip. And what about my experiments? Just trash them and begin again.

Kecouroo joined me at the classroom doorway while the students pretended to study and sneaked glances our way. She wore a finely brushed suede garment and Mekucoo leggings. Her only decoration was the necklace that was a binding cord with misshapen black stones, which seemed odd compared to how other Mekucoo adorned their garments with rows of beads and gems.

"I have been busy," I began in Arrivi, "and have not visited your land. I apologize for the oversight."

"Edwina visits often as your eyes and ears."

"She does?" I quickly recovered. "Well, I wanted to ask. Has Karlyhi troubled the female students before?"

Kecouroo blinked twice. "You have acted on the matter. Why tell stories now?"

I was not sure what she meant. I began a third time. "Ah, Hakulupe Le and I will travel to Somule for a time. We need to close the clinic and the classrooms. I was wondering, would you look in on the buildings when you can? Just so they don't go downhill in our absence."

She frowned and glanced at the clinic below.

"Go downhill is just a phrase," I quickly added. "So the buildings are the same when we return."

Kecouroo coolly considered my face and looked around as though taking mental inventory. "I accept the clinic and the academy under my protection." Her words were formal as though we were setting a contract.

"Nothing official is needed here. Just so the place does not burn down."

Kecouroo nodded and returned to the classroom with her stately stride. That seemed to be the end of that.

When I returned to the clinic, the men had left to fuel the lorries from the underground diesel tanks. "You put Karlyhi out?" Haku-lupe Le said with accusation. Her green-green eyes seemed to flash darker.

I was suddenly bone-tired. "So much trouble all of a sudden."

"These matters were always here," she returned. "Today you looked up."

I felt my energy flow away. "I acted wrongly?"

She thought about it for a minute, not that anything could be reversed. "You were guardian to Karlyhi when his Cylahi mother failed to return. You allowed him many privileges: weapons, accounting, and airbus driving. He grew in stature with the tribes-men while under your care. Very unusual for Cylahi.

"His pride is wounded," she continued, "because of the swift-ness of your action. But this act seems harsh only in comparison to your former generosity. When his anger subsides, Karlyhi will see that he has no complaints."

"He's so young to be alone in the world."

Lupe considered that. "Karlyhi had aged when we found him on the road that day. Now he must prove himself without the aid of Sheeks-Cylom and the gualarep spirit."

"So I am redeemed?"

"Dolvia blesses you," Lupe said while she shook her head. "I have seen the evidence. But it's truly a wonder, sometimes, how you survive your day."

The following morning, while we packed the lorries in the dawn light, Karlyhi showed himself on the road beyond the compound. He was naked but brightly painted after the customs of his tribe. The long scar on his leg was outlined with yellow pigment. With both hands he held a karkar over his head. Karlyhi called out some Cylahi words I did not know before he turned on his heel and sauntered up the road.

Edwina opened wide her mouth and rolled that fleshy tongue away from me, a most indiscreet gesture. "Ka," she said. "Ka, ka."

"Oh, shut up," I complained. "And what is this about you being my eyes and ears with Kecouroo?"

Somebody had to, she shot back. Edwina's thoughts were strongest in disagreement.

I was later told that Karlyhi had pronounced, "None shall harm Sheeks-Cylom on the road. I, Karlyhi who Dolvia embraces, declare this before all men." And indeed, we arrived in Somule without incident.

Hakulupe Le rode in the first lorry with Orin rabbe Murd driving. Brianna rode in the back since we were returning her to her family,. I rode in the second lorry with Joey Osborn driving. The gualareps were gathered in the dirt-packed rear.

We emerged from the lush northern foothills and entered the savannah. It had been a big-wet year, but the flooding had passed. Tall grasses concealed fauna of all kinds, particularly transient birds. Blue herons, red-breasted grouse, and yellow-billed pelicans had staked out nesting and rutting territory. We saw brilliantly colored parrots of all shapes and sizes. In great flocks, they chattered and strutted on the steamy plain.

The gualareps loved the savannah, but they hated the lorry. We stopped during the heat of the day, and the girls scurried off into the grass. We had to blow the car horns and frighten thousands of birds to call them back. I remember the thrill of seeing the denizens lift off the ground as one body, multi-colored flapping wings in the bright sun.

The girls were silent before strangers. It felt odd not to be privy to their thoughts, as though I was rejected. Edna cooed with a soft clicking noise as if to reassure me that I was not forgotten.

Joey told many stories about the Arrivi and past events in Somule. He was not particularly chatty; it was just a long drive. He spoke about the former prison where tribespeople suffered and the toxic dump that had been removed. There was a Company refinery, formerly run by a Chinese mining corporation, which Dolvia Herself had swallowed to save the tribes. Dolvia then slumbered for many seasons, but the big-wet had brought Her back to life.

Sometimes I tuned out his words and just stared at the passing grassy marshes.

I did learn why Hakulupe Le was considered a goulep, or somehow tainted, within Arrivi hierarchy. She was born from a union between Haku rabbe Murd and his wife's sister, Katelupe the martyr, forced on them in prison during the Company occupation. Incest was taboo among Arrivi. Hakulupe Le could never live down her shame, but she served and was honored for her work at the clinic's academy.

We stayed overnight at the hospital that was mostly deserted with a break in the fighting. Early on the second morning, we traversed the land of Haku rabbe Murd and arrived at the complex of buildings I had visited before the Feast of Oria. The hacienda's wide verandah with red tile overhang was welcoming and, as before, the thorn tree provided hospitable shade. The place swarmed with children playing stickball and tormenting chained mongooses. Girls had their skirts tied up like blousy pantaloons and played just as hard as the boys around the center tree.

As our vehicle approached, young people ran after the lorry and gathered in a wide circle, staring into the truck bed. The gualareps flicked their long and forked tongues at casual intervals. Children ran to Karima Le standing in the yard with her gray hair tightly coiled at her neck, and they pointed at the gualarep girls.

Karima Le embraced Hakulupe Le. That seemed odd since I had learned Lupe's origins. I shrugged, assuming I would never get it all straight, how these people were related.

Karima Le held an open palm at elbow height, signifying on me. "Hiki, Sheeks-Cylom," she said in her gravel and honey voice. "An honor to know the spirit in your face." The arcane Arrivi phrases excluded me even while she seemed to accept me.

"Hiki, Karima Le," I returned with an open palm. "Melinga."

"I regret that we have no time for a formal tea," she said. "Perhaps on your return."

Some Arrivi men came around from the back of the house. Haku rabbe Murd, obese with milky cataracts in both eyes, hoisted himself from the chair on the verandah. Orin helped him down the steps, and Haku bowed to the leader, a Putuki with round-rimmed glasses.

"Rabbenu Ely," Joey told me. The men saw us staring and moved away. In the sunlight I clearly saw the left side of Haku's face that was disfigured from an old napalm burn.

"I can take you into Somule now," Joey added. "Lieutenant Shaw has made arrangements for the gualareps."

I hugged Hakulupe Le who chose to remain with her aunt. "I hope I make it through the coming days without your care."

"Your soul and mine," she said, "are planted forever in the clinic's catalpa tree. I can visit Somule during your stay."

Joseph Osborn and I got back into the lorry and drove around the yard. The children ran after us, calling to the gualareps. Brianna stepped out and Joey stopped the vehicle. She handed me a bundle of fruit through the cab window before she jumped back and ran after us for several yards, waving good-bye. I was sorry I did not have a return gift.

"Has Haku rabbe Murd considered a cataract operation?" I asked. Joey glanced at me and shook his head. "With the proper equipment," I added, "I could relieve his blindness, at least in part. Will you make the overtures?"

"My wife is Arrivi," Joey said. "I can mention it to her. You will be staying with us, by the way. There's plenty of room."

We saw the town in the distance: a group of low adobe buildings with two hotel towers standing together like abandoned twins.

The railroad ran through the stockyards, and there was an electric power station north of town.

We stopped at a blank and square building west of Somule. Its modern design was incongruous with the landscape, and the yard was trashed and overgrown. In the lorry's rear, the girls became agitated. "This building was Company," Joey explained, "before they were forced off the savannah. Lieutenant Shaw has made a place here for Ralph."

He released the girls from the back of the lorry. We followed them up the steps and past an unused security area, traversing a long corridor with many slat and paper Chinese-style doors on each side. Through some torn paper, I saw a blank studio. We followed the girls around a sharp corner to another deserted corridor. They turned right and poured into an overgrown Chinese garden. Ralph was waiting and called to them, a frightful barking sound. They scurried into the unkempt vegetation.

We could not see where they got off to, but we heard them for maybe twenty minutes, thrashing about and calling to each other with barks.

Joey and I decided to look around. We entered one apartment that was lavishly furnished with bureaus with intricate inlaid ivory and cloisonné. There was a massive teak bed with rotting covers. "This stuff is valuable," I said.

"The Company left suddenly, some time ago now," Joey said. "Tribespeople have a special hatred of this place."

We entered a spacious dining room with many long tables and layers of dust. In the front were two thrones with Luduan statues, prey animals with toothy grins, on each side. And by them waited

First Lieutenant Michael Peter Shaw, inspecting a Luduan head as though he was spending the afternoon at a museum.

"First Lieutenant Shaw," I said.

"Edna Edwina," he said.

"Perhaps I will just move the lorry out of the sun," Joey offered and left.

"You must appear before the magistrate later today," Lt. Shaw said. "And sleep over with Joey's family." We heard some thrashing about from the garden. Something fell with a loud crash. "And don't worry about the girls," he slyly added. "Ralph has plans for them."

"Can you read Ralph's thoughts?"

"No, and he doesn't come into the bed with me either."

I laughed at the image of that. "You should have warned me from the beginning."

"Who needs to be told to not sleep with reptiles?"

"Or with first lieutenants," I added.

He gave me a long but not accusative look. "Come along, then." His voice was gruff. He cleared his throat. "There's a great deal to straighten out concerning your legend." We walked up the narrow corridor together. Lt. Shaw was careful to not touch me.

"Hakulupe Le has been working overtime to increase my reputation," I offered to have something to say.

"There's a story among the Siibabean about the Sheeks-Cylom. How she gives fangs to salamanders and her spirit enters the monster's body at night."

"A series of simple misunderstandings."

"And now you have joined forces with Kecouroo. Do you even know who she is?"

I shrugged. "A school teacher."

He shook his head. "It's true what they say. Dolvia has blessed you."

Before we reached the security area by the door, Mike Shaw pulled me farther back into the corridor. He drew me to him, cradling me against his big chest. Then he kissed me with hunger.

"I'm glad you came," he whispered.

"I was summoned."

Mike Shaw thought about that for a moment. He walked me to the lorry and shortly waved as Joey and I drove away.

Joey Osborn's sprawling woodframe house on a busy Somule street had the usual verandah with a red tile overhang. His wife was an olive-skinned Arrivi named Karen. "Karima Le lived in this house during the Company occupation," she shyly offered.

I tried to keep the cynical edge out of my voice. "You mean, before Dolvia swallowed the refinery?"

I was shown to a separate apartment next to the big kitchen and with its own back entrance. The sitting area looked out on the wide backyard that included a clothesline and a rough-hewn table. Karen laid out linens for me while her auburn-haired son and daughter, Patrick and Kelly, lingered at the doorway and stared.

Karen considered me with level hazel eyes.

"What is it?" I asked.

"You are whiter than white."

"Perhaps I can work on getting a tan and put that issue to rest."

"There was a Softcheeks before you with light-colored hair, Brian Miller. He wore a native paste as insect repellent that stained his skin."

"I know this paste. Most effective, but gummy."

"You must hurry now," Karen said. "Your appointment is soon."

Joey and I walked to the courthouse. Somule was a quaint place with an elevated wooden sidewalk on both sides of the single main street, probably maintained against the muddy rainy season. It put me in mind of a western town from old cowboy movies, but I didn't say that. Joey wouldn't get the reference, anyhow. There was a clapboard church with a steepled bell tower. That seemed odd in this native setting. The local bazaar for purchasing staples was down one dusty alley, and the main street ended at a bank building where the sign read Tri-City Corp. The real business, of course, took place in the stockyards at the railhead.

Joey carried a brief and the summons paper. In a stuffy courtroom with a slowly rotating overhead fan, we sat before a Putuki judge with brown-black skin and a wide nose. Mr. Duerr, the complaining civil authority, sat across from us with a battery of cronies and witnesses.

I whispered to Joey. "None of those people were at the clinic."

We had devised a strategy during our drive to Somule. We would argue that Mr. Duerr was, in effect, my guest at the clinic and had threatened to destroy my property. Edwina was a valuable research creature and could not be replaced. She had posed no physical harm and had only damaged the camcorder. The camcorder's value was insignificant in comparison to her value. Also, the weapons had been returned.

The petitioner was allowed to speak first. The lawyer called as witness one of my Putuki servants, who I hadn't realized had also traveled to Somule. She hated Edwina who often played on her fears. She began a long stream of complaints in her dialect with the judge nodding in agreement. My heart sank. I would have to pay the fine, or even go to jail.

I whispered again to Joey. "What is she saying?"

"You need to hire different servants."

During the break, I waited in the hall and mopped my brow. Two Softcheeks men spoke to Joey who pointed my way. They approached me, and one offered a page taken from an EAM printer. It was a study page from Hakulupe Le's flora encyclopedia.

"Did you create this?" He demanded.

"Where did you get that?" I asked. "It's not for publication. The tests are incomplete."

"And this one?" He showed me a second page that held a drawing and the specifics of my orchid tests, notes compiled while I searched for the tumor cure.

"I am still working on that," I complained. "If I may ask, who are you?"

"Dr. Henry Beecham. This is my associate, Dr. Mitterand." The second man was younger and a Frenchman. "I was wondering," Dr. Beecham asked, "would you be open to having dinner with us tonight? At the hotel. It could be worth your time."

"If I'm not in jail by then."

"This civil complaint?" Dr. Beecham said. "It's nothing. I can get the charges dropped."

"Excuse me?"

"Duerr's a pompous ass," he said without hesitation. "Many wish your gualarep had bitten him."

Joey chuckled. I hoped nobody voiced that sentiment in Edwina's presence. She might take it as an open door. Dr. Beecham gestured left, and I walked out with them. "We so admire your pioneer work here on Dolvia," he said.

"Pioneer work?" I glanced back at Joey Osborn. He only frowned.

"Your clinic," Dr. Beecham said. "In this climate."

"Actually, the clinic is north of here in the grasslands."

"Don't be so modest," Dr. Beecham said. "Your reputation has spread offworld."

Living large again, I thought.

Joey Osborn accompanied me to the Softcheeks dinner. We met the doctors in a hotel restaurant with Chinese decor where we were served rice dishes and pressed duck à l'orange. I thought the establishment stuck out like a sore thumb in this rural town.

The two Softcheeks were engaged in a doctors' rotation in Westend. Dr. Mitterand was a viral specialist fulfilling his surgical residency on Dolvia. Dr. Beecham had recently agreed to assume management of Dr. Abercrombie's hospital. He was reassessing the humanitarian aid structure for the Consortium. He had little contact with the managers of my research grant, though.

"We received the renewed grant request for the academy from Hakulupe Le," Dr. Beecham explained. "As support material concerning the students' good work, she sent along these pages. Imagine our surprise to find the orchid cure was accomplished by Arrivi and Putuki junior high students."

"She meant only that they did the inputting," I explained. "One student can render. They all love the EAM."

"So the academy would benefit from additional EAM stations? And what other support?"

"Our intent was to allow advanced students," I said, "to assist in the clinic, but all the students are at first level now. There is no . . . um, fruition of goals."

"Your standards are too high," Dr. Beecham said. "We barely achieved daily attendance in classrooms at the hospital."

"You must treat attendance and good marks as a matter of honor," I said. "Hakulupe Le speaks to their families. Failure in the classroom shames the parents. Here in Somule, I would first contact Karima Le on the land of Murd. Mr. Osborn knows her."

Later, when the conversation turned to research, Joey sat back with glassy eyes. Ours had been a busy day after a long drive. Dr. Mitterand saw the change in mood. An ordinary looking man, he seemed restrained and well bred. "Perhaps we can agree on an appointment at the doctor's office tomorrow," he said. "Early, before it gets hot. We can discuss your progress on the orchid cure."

We shook hands and stood to walk out together. We followed Dr. Beecham through the bar area where he crossed to greet Lieutenant Shaw having a drink with some officers there. With Dr. Mitternd and Joey Osborn, I joined them. "Lieutenant Shaw may take a post in Cylay," Dr. Beecham said, "as Director of Natural Disasters Control."

"That should keep him busy," I said.

"He has not yet accepted," Dr. Beecham said. "I suppose we must promote him to captain first and provide a helicopter."

"A helicopter?"

"A two-passenger stinger," Dr. Beecham said with a grin. Smile lines appeared on Lt. Shaw's face. Dr. Beecham's voice was full of humor. "Tribesmen have dubbed it the Murmurey because the stinger is black and fast."

I turned to Lt. Shaw. "You will become the envy of the entire garrison."

"We shall see." His attitude seemed sanguine, maybe influenced by hours of drinking. Mike Shaw shook hands with the two doctors again and rejoined his friends.

The following day I kept my appointment with Dr. Mitterand at the empty space that had been Dr. Abercrombie's branch office, a junky storefront near the native bazaar. Two patient examination rooms held second-hand equipment. A doctor's study with book-lined walls had a private backyard verandah.

In the study, Dr. Mitterand had already piled some furniture and files on the side and installed a holographic EAM, or HGEAM, that Westenders called a hay-gee-am. "Dr. Beecham must have secured serious funding to afford one of these."

"Actually, there are three. This one is yours, for the clinic."

"My funds are budgeted for more immediate needs. I cannot justify—"

"The cost is absorbed by the Consortium."

"Who snookered them into that?"

"Henry did." Dr. Mitterand booted the HGEAM and initiated contact with the orbiting Consortium transport. A cycling holographic cube appeared four inches above the base, filling the room with yellow-blue light. Within the holograph, a technician's head and shoulders came online. "Voice confirmation," the young man said.

"Dr. Mitterand, code ER2031 dash WE87."

There was a two-second lag time. Communication was instantaneous, so the pause was for a security check. "Dr. Mitterand, how may I direct your call?"

"Transport library, please." Vivid yellow-blue light filled the room while the trunk call was transferred.

"Concerning the orchid cure," Dr. Mitterand offered during the wait. "We examined each section of the orchid's corymb, even the epicalyx. The enzyme was in the petal."

A librarian's image entered the cycling cube. She was a young woman, perhaps a crewman's daughter who worked there to pass the time. "Dr. Mitterand," she said with a wide grin. "We talk more now than when you were on-station."

"Mary Ann, this is Dr. Greensboro." He pulled my arm to sit beside him within range of the three synchronized cameras. "After today she will run this unit, but under a new code."

"So good to meet you at last, Dr. Greensboro," Mary Ann said. "Leave it to Pierre to search you out so quickly."

"Mary Ann," Dr. Mitterand said, "could you call up the diagrams we looked at earlier, please."

"They should be in your memory cache."

"Yes, but without hyperlinks."

"Anything you say." Mary Ann looked down, I presumed to work the console. Her image vanished, and we were presented with digital 3-D element depictions from the library archives. I stared while the represented molecules combined into useful compounds.

"Yes, this is the structure of the little girl's tumors," I said. "Can we make a serum?"

"Much more than that," Dr. Mitterand said with restrained excitement. He used the arrow keys on the HGEAM's numeric keypad to select a separate diagram. It displayed a similar growth, but one that was more virulent.

I stared into the cycling blue cube. "What is it?"

"Catarrh, a cattle disease that causes boils," he said lightly. "It can be lethal. Your patient may have contracted the tumors from ingesting tainted meat."

I looked at him with a squint. "A cattle disease? And the cure is effective for all varieties of the bovine family?"

He shrugged. "I'm told that during the tribal unrest, many people were hungry."

I considered the possibility. "Family members," I postulated, "would not confess starvation and eating carrion to Softcheeks, so Hakulupe Le would not have learned the truth of the girl's medical history. Can we develop an erriv vaccine?"

"Yes, on Cicero," Dr. Mitterand said. "Perhaps ready in a few months. But we cannot produce the vaccine in volume. The compound is not stable for storage for more than a season. I wanted to ask, what led you to study this particular orchid?"

"Ah, it was a hunch."

"A brilliant hunch."

I would have to thank Edwina. "Connections become clear," I said, "when you work closer to the problem. Perhaps you would like to visit the clinic one day, after we reopen."

"When I have the vaccine."

"Fair enough," I said.

"Will you upload your flora encyclopedia pages to the transport library?"

"Ha, the recommended cures are untested," I hedged. "There is enough work here for years of field study."

We talked about the value of folk cures, and I explained about Hakulupe Le's sources. We agreed on a professional contract wherein I would send samples and suggestions to the hospital along with my hunches. Dr. Mitterand would run tests and further compile the encyclopedia pages for later publication. Through the Consortium, the academy would receive the needed funds to expand.

"This new grant must include similar schools in Somule and other savannah towns," I insisted, pressing my advantage.

"If all this pans out, Henry will have you knighted."

"I thought only men were knighted."

"You should take this hay-gee-am back to the clinic," Dr. Mitterand offered. "There's a new feature recently added, a Westend media feed." He accessed a separate modem call wherein a Chinese-descent announcer, perhaps seated in a Stargate Junction studio, recited censored Consortium news.

"Not interested," I said and switched off the HGEAM. My eyes hurt for a moment in the relative darkness. "The single greatest blessing of Dolviet field study is that I'm not bothered by offworld white noise."

Dr. Mitterand only grinned.

We talked through the day. We ordered tea and lunch. We sat in the cane chairs by the French doors that looked out on the brightly lit backyard, reminiscing about the rigors of our medical educations. I suddenly missed Earth and my family. I had not thought about the past since, well, since I had been so exhausted at Leslie's hospital. My homesick yearnings were excited by the presence of this thoughtful Frenchman and his fresh arrival from Earth.

Later, we sat again in the HGEAM's yellow-blue light discussing database research options. There was a ruckus in the outer office. Hakulupe Le entered, speaking in Mekucoo. I thought that was very strange. "Softcheeks are all the same," she complained. "Sit in the dark and talk offworld while you ignore the life outside your window."

She hustled me through the office to the street verandah. "Do you know how unseemly it is to spend the day without chaperons?" she hissed in Mekucoo.

"I have no chaperons at the clinic."

"There are no Frenchmen at the clinic."

In the street, Lieutenant Shaw was demonstrating a magic trick to some kids, pulling a coin from behind somebody's ear. Hakulupe Le pinched the back of my upper arm.

"Oohhh!" I complained.

"Go invite Lieutenant Shaw to dinner at Joey's place."

I rubbed the smarting spot and nodded to Dr. Mitterand who watched with raised eyebrows. I joined Lieutenant Shaw in the cooling sunlight. "I was just ordered to invite you to dinner. I hope you have the time."

"I could work it in."

"Nod to Hakulupe Le so I don't receive more bruises."

At Lt. Shaw's signal, Hakulupe Le gave Dr. Mitterand a haughty look and left. The young doctor went back inside the office.

"So, tonight," I added. "I don't know what time."

"The Osborns sit down at seven," Mike Shaw said.

"I see."

"Would you like to visit the girls tomorrow?"

"Very much."

"I can get a jeep." He walked away then, leaving me alone on the street. I retreated to Joey's house where Brianna waited on the verandah.

"Hiki, Brianna."

"Hiki, Sheeks-Cylom. I have been assigned to serve you."

"My chaperon? Then join me for tea in my rooms."

"I will bring tea."

"Bring an extra cup."

Within the hour we sat at my table ignoring the nearby kitchen bustle, and looked out on the backyard. I was glad for the rest. I fingered the orchids in a bowl on the table. "Tell me, Brianna, where did you get your name?"

"My father was Brian Miller, but he died before I was born."

"And your mother?"

"Klistina Le of Arim. She died when I was six. I was raised by my aunt, Karima Le."

"And why did you come to the academy?"

"Many students came," she said in defense. "Many girls."

"You have every right to attend. I only meant, what did you hope to learn?" Brianna was silent. "What is your ambition?" I added. "What do you want to be when you grow up?"

"I want to visit my father's world."

"Well, that is a big ambition. Have other Arrivi traveled through the wormhole?"

"Nobody," she murmured. "And I am mulatto, not Arrivi."

"Where did you get that word?"

"It is wrong?"

"So, being mulatto, you had no defense against Karlyhi's advances?" She ducked her head with shame and moved to the window. "On my world," I offered, "any woman may refuse any man. It's her choice who she accepts."

"The Softcheeks' world must be wonderful."

"But with freedom comes responsibility," I added wondering at my bent for teaching. "I must accept the consequences of my actions."

"Dolvia blesses you."

"People of mixed blood are not so blessed on Earth," I said. "You must study and arm yourself for travel." She shyly turned to me, hope playing on her features. "It will be a difficult road," I added. "Not for the faint of heart."

"My heart is strong."

Dinner at the Osborns was a family affair with dishes passed around the table, instructions to the children, and meandering conversation. Brianna sat with us and shyly smiled at the melee.

Lieutenant Shaw sat next to Joseph Osborn at the other end of the table. He was not smiling about anything.

"So you had a good meeting today?" Joey asked between bites.

"Yes, um," I shrugged. "Dr. Mitterand favors the academy grant and the orchid research. He was most helpful. We can even establish an academy in Somule."

Lieutenant Shaw stared ahead and munched with measured motions.

"And did you speak with him about the cataract surgery?" Joey asked.

"It slipped my mind," I said. "Perhaps tomorrow."

"Weren't you going out tomorrow with Lieutenant Shaw?" Karen asked.

"I cannot do both?"

Joey glanced at Mike Shaw. Brianna shyly looked up at me. I was doing something wrong; I just didn't know what. Karen ventured, "Is Dr. Mitterand a married man?"

It finally came to me, the insult I had offered. But I could not lie; Lieutenant Shaw would know the truth. "No, he's not married," I admitted. "He's younger than me, though. The surgical residency will keep him busy. Our shared interest is research," I added. "The study of viruses. Only that." My voice trailed off.

Nobody believed me.

After dinner, I spoke to Lt. Shaw. "Thank you for the orchids today."

He only shook Joey Osborn's hand and left.

"What did I do?" I asked Karen.

"In Arrivi tradition he must leave the house before ten o'clock."

The following morning, I wrote thank you notes to Drs. Beecham and Mitterand who were both leaving that day. I pleaded exhaustion and asked that they excuse my absence at the farewell. I asked them to please take the HGEAM to the hospital because I had no need for it at the clinic.

I sent Brianna to deliver my notes at the hotel, and then I dressed and waited. If Lt. Shaw wanted to keep our date, he knew where to find me. Presently Karen poked her head into my room. "There is a jeep outside."

Like a high school sophomore, I raced through the house and bounded down the verandah steps to take my seat next to Mike Shaw. Karen waved from the porch while we drove away, stirring a cloud of red dust.

Lt. Shaw drove west on the savannah toward a giant butte. "Aren't we going to see the girls?" I asked. He glanced my way but kept silent. I was not forgiven.

I stared at the passing savannah. Oleastra bushes were weighted with clusters of green fruit. A desert vine spread its tendrils among clumps of dune grass and displayed trembling bellflowers that turned their faces to the sun. The shadow from the butte slowly climbed the face of the companion plateau. Like an old married couple, they shared the day in comfortable silence. One immense section of the butte lay shattered on the ground and caused the stream there to divert its path. We drove north following the rushing water and came to freshwater flats that gave off an artesian odor with a gurgling rumble.

I saw geyserite formations like terraced palace gardens of all colors, and mud pools that popped and spat. A sudden geyser appeared where the plateau's edge began to rise from the flatlands. The tall column of heated water sprayed a fountain and mist over several yards.

Lieutenant Shaw stopped near a big rock in the middle of the flats. Made of smooth granite and taller than a man, it seemed placed there by some omniscient hand, not formed by underground pressure.

"It is lovely here," I said as we stepped around the big rock.

"This whole area is geothermal. Ralph likes the hot springs."

"Are the girls in danger?"

"They know better than us what to avoid. There's a holy woman who lives here, in a fortress in the basin wall. You saw her at the Feast of Oria. Kyle Rula of Arim."

"You mean Kyle Le? Karima Le's sister? She may put a hex on us for trespassing."

"Nah, she likes Ralph."

"You mean Ralph likes her, whereas he has no use for me."

He finally looked at me. "The girls . . . the girls have grown. You can be proud."

"I was neglectful. Others nurtured them."

They came to us then, the gualareps. I sat on the ground and the girls fingered me with their tongues. "Edna, you have been with Hakulupe Le. And Edwina, you are golden brown and . . . and warm."

"Ka, ka, ka, ka, ka," she cooed.

Bigger than her, Edna added.

I stroked their necks. "You finally found something bigger than yourself, huh, Edwina?" I looked over at the waiting male guala-rep. "And Ralph, can we begin again?"

He raised that noble head. Ralph deferred only to Mike Shaw who never stroked him.

"Well, just a thought." I stood and brushed grit from the back of my skirt. "So show me around, huh?"

The girls led me down to the stream flowing through some reeds. They slid into the water, gliding into the current, and strongly stroked their tails. I waded in knee deep and splashed at them. The water was cool, maybe a runoff stream from a billabong rather than fed by underground springs. Each girl flicked her tail and got me soaking wet. I stripped off my long-sleeved blouse and slung it over my shoulder. I wore a thin camisole of pink and beige.

We splashed around a bit. The girls swam out to deep water and chased each other's tails. I started wading back. Lt. Shaw and Ralph were seated on the bank. I waved to them. They both looked away, so I shot them raspberries. Sour old men.

Without warning I was surrounded by a school of carp in breeding pandemonium, the males pursuing the females who sprayed thick clouds of eggs into the water. They pushed past me and around me and flopped against me with strength. I called out, thrown off balance among the thrashing bodies. I landed hard in the water, and my hands sank into the mucky bottom. One carp placed an angry sucker mark on my leg.

"Hey! Give me a chance."

Lt. Shaw reached to pull me out of the muck. "What the hell?" I asked.

"Breeding kariom. You got in their way."

"One put a mark on my leg."

"Using your sliding scale of philosophy, Sheeks-Cylom, you should select this danger." He noticed the blue bruise on the back of my upper arm.

"Hakulupe Le gave me that for spending time with a Softcheeks."

"Remind me to send her flowers."

I was tired of his reproachful manner. My blouse was gone and my skirt soiled. I brushed the muck off my arms as best I could. "I was thinking about a tan anyhow," I lamely offered. "To stop the talk about my skin color."

Lt. Shaw turned away. I was sure he was hiding a grin. "What?" I insisted.

Without turning back, he asked, "Will that be an all-over tan?"

He walked up the bank with chortling Ralph in tow. Both males must have surmised what I looked like from the girls' color display as infant reps. I shot them raspberries again.

Lt. Shaw gave me his shirt, and we climbed using some footholds to sit on the big rock while the reps stalked prey on the flats. Mike wore a sleeveless T-shirt over his tanned and hairy chest. He leaned back on one elbow with the round muscle of his arm bulging.

I blushed and looked away. "What will you do with Ralph when you move to Cylay?"

"I'm not going."

"Not even for a helicopter?"

He smiled and shrugged. "It is tempting."

"What's Cylay like?"

"Mostly a slum," Lt. Shaw said. "Dolviets migrated there during the drought, and then another wave of herders were displaced by the tribal conflict. Many are moving out now, returning to the savannah to make a fresh start in the season of kari. Keeping the tribal ways."

"A positive move."

"Less urban crowding means less violence," he said. "The tribes each have their boundaries again. But the renewed savannah will draw more outsiders. The water table is too shallow to sustain boom-towns like Somule. Then a new drought and new wars."

"You are certainly being cheery."

"And what about you?" he asked. "Your reputation is made with this cure. You could take up lecturing."

"Did you get that from Dr. Mitterand?"

"I heard them talking."

I waited for a long moment. He was too well informed. "I'm returning to the clinic."

His gaze wandered to the horizon. "Haven't you burned enough people with your snap decisions, Edna Edwina?"

He meant Karlyhi, of course. None of my actions were private. I sighed. Perhaps I was being too assertive. "Come to dinner tonight at Joey's. Please."

"If you insist."

When we returned to Somule and Joey's house, Karen hid her smile at my disheveled looks. Brianna followed me into my rooms, carrying a shallow bowl of water. As I stripped my ruined clothes, I could not control my irritation. Brianna encouraged me to sit with my feet in the water and wrapped my ankles with a hot cloth. That was helpful, very relaxing. I showed her the mark on my leg.

"Goddamned carp," I complained.

"This is a mark of high honor," she said. "Kariom were once revered as godlike because they were the first transients to come with the rain. This was before people knew they burrowed into the body of Dolvia. It is said the warrior Oria went out during the wet season one time and returned with marks like this. It is said that only those who Dolvia honors are so kissed."

"I stumbled into a school of them while they were breeding. That is all."

I was irritated during dinner as well. And sunburned; my nose and forehead were flaming red. Patrick and Kelly stared at my face until Karen admonished them to look at their plates. Lieutenant Shaw and Joey discussed barracks politics and the new construction in Somule.

Lassitude made my arms heavy. I ate very little. Before ten o'clock Mike Shaw nodded and left. What a bust.

When I was finally alone, I could not sleep, mostly because I was not accustomed to city noise. I tossed and turned until the house and street grew quiet. I caught the scent of kari root smoke, so I pulled on a thin robe and looked out onto the back porch. Lieutenant Shaw stood there with his back to me.

I opened the door, so he quickly turned and snubbed out the cigarette. "I wasn't going to come to you like this. I promised myself. Never again."

We heard someone turn over on a squeaky bed. I gestured that he should step inside.

"I always felt bad," he whispered. "You know, about the other time. When I left before you woke. I didn't know what you were thinking." He loitered by the doorway and sighed, unwilling to look at me. "But you came to Somule. And that first day, you made light of . . . all that. You seemed . . . friendly enough. Then you took up with that Softcheeks doctor."

I put my hand on his arm. "You are the only man who has ever touched me. And the only one who ever will." Lieutenant Shaw reached out for me then. He held me tight, nearly forcing the air out of me. He kissed my face all over.

Much later, Mike Shaw dressed to leave. He sat on the bed and pulled on his boots.

"Don't go," I said.

He looked back at me and touched my sunburned nose. "Come to church services today. Joey's family attends. Come with them."

"Won't God strike me dead or something?"

"That's a danger you must select."

Lieutenant Shaw was gone by first light. I napped a little before I rose to dress for church. I could still smell him on my skin.

FIVE

THE LUTHERAN CHURCH WAS A CLAPBOARD BUILDING WITH A white steeple. The high-ceiling sanctuary was whiteboard with a prefab stained-glass window behind the choir pews. The pastor was an older man with a full head of white hair and a ruddy complexion. Hardhand families who had converted to Christianity on Cicero and other Consortium planets gathered there in their Sunday best, which included hats for women and white gloves. A few Putuki women attended.

Lieutenant Shaw, as it turned out, was a deacon. Wearing a dress uniform with many medals, he ushered us to a middle pew and winked before he walked away. The Osborn kids left for Sunday school. I sat with Joey and Karen while morning sunlight fell across my shoulders from the colorful window. I just hoped I could keep from dozing off.

Three barracks officers sat in the back row. Before services began, Mike Shaw slid into the pew next to me, staring ahead in his studious way. His fellow officers cleared their throats noisily. Many church members glanced over and whispered. Lt. Shaw took my hand in his big paw and casually held it on his lap. The whole event had a strange feel to it, warm and fuzzy.

Later Karen introduced me to some church members whose names I quickly forgot. Hardhands accepted Karen even though she was Arrivi. As Joey's wife, she had status. While we were walking out, the pastor shook my hand and invited me to join them every Sunday. I thought Sunday was an abused concept here in Westend, but I just smiled and shrugged. We went back to the Osborn house and I took a long and delicious nap. After all, God had not struck me dead.

When I woke, there were fresh orchids in a bowl on the table. I brushed back my hair and wandered into the kitchen. Joey was in the backyard, standing head to head with Lt. Shaw in an intense discussion. I joined them with a big yawn. Joey made an excuse and went into the house.

"What is going on?" I asked.

"Nothing. Look, I need to ask . . . Will you marry me?"

"Excuse me?"

"Well, I need to make the offer before that Softcheeks doctor returns."

"We never talked about this. And I am not moving to Cylay."

"Yeah, but the thing is," he hedged not looking at me. "The Sheeks-Cylom who expelled her Cylahi son for molesting a goulep cannot be seen sneaking around with a barracks officer. You can see how that doesn't fit the legend."

"People are talking?"

"It is just a matter of time."

I squinted at him. "You planned all this, didn't you? Come to Somule, bring the girls, dinner at Joey's house. And church. It was all orchestrated so I cannot say no. I would lose face."

He looked at me leaning back like I might slap him. "You said there was nobody else. You said that." He waited a long moment. "I sent flowers."

"We can talk about this later. Tonight maybe."

"I won't come to you like that again," he claimed in a resolute voice.

"Sneaking around, as you call it, didn't bother you last night."

"That was before."

"Before what?"

"Before I thought about it," he said. "So what's your answer, yes or no?"

I held up my chin in a defiant smirk. "No."

He caught me around the waist and held me close. "I can get Ralph to follow you around. You will have no clinic patients."

"Bully."

"Say it."

I leaned back in his arms. "I suppose you have the preacher lined up and everything planned."

"So it's yes?"

"Bully."

We were married later that week at the Lutheran church. Joey and Karen Osborn stood up with us. Hakulupe Le and Brianna attended, as well as the barracks officers. When the preacher asked,

I said, "Yes, I select this danger." Mike Shaw did not look at me, but he was grinning.

The following morning, I awoke to find Mike beside me in the bed. It was broad daylight and he peacefully slumbered with his back to me. So this was marriage; waking up together, facing the day together. It had a certain feel about it, a warm and fuzzy glaze.

I returned to the clinic with much more than I had possessed at my departure. Ralph had taken up with Karlyhi, I was told, and roamed the veld with the warriors' peer group. The girls mourned Ralph's absence, and Karlyhi's, dragging themselves around the clinic without interest in anything. Mike took them hunting and visited Kecouroo's land without me.

My husband remained several weeks and oversaw the construction of more buildings with tin roofs. "This place resembles a roadside brothel," I teased.

Joey Osborn visited and brought four EAMs for the classroom. He and Mike installed them and spent the afternoon counseling the teachers on menu choices. The students, especially the boys, took to the keyboards like murmurey fledglings to a fresh kill. Kecouroo drew up a schedule that included specific hours when girls only had access to the equipment.

Then, as he had planned the whole time—such a methodical man—First Lieutenant Michael Peter Shaw accepted the Cylay directorship and the promotion to captain. He wanted that helicopter. So he was gone, and once again I was sleeping alone.

Hakulupe Le made arrangements to manage the upstart Somule school and also packed to leave, even though I argued that she must stay. Wasn't her soul planted with mine in the catalpa tree? How would I survive my day without her? She brought forward a Putuki woman to replace the discharged servants and manage my clinic. "This is Lula," Hakulupe Le said. "My first mother."

They were all related. It made my head ache. "Lula and Lupe? I'll never keep it straight."

"You may call her Martina. Many do."

She had a slight scar over her eyelid, and a second one by her ear—old marks caused by a healed fungal growth. I returned her deep bow. "Hiki, Martina. Welcome to the clinic."

This one spoke little; no long discussions over tea as I had enjoyed with Hakulupe Le. She managed the staff dorm, the patient scheduling, and the classrooms with competence, though, leaving me to work only with patients and the teachers.

Brianna had returned to the clinic school and usually brought in my tea. One day when I came down from patient rounds, I found Brianna by the catalpa tree with a warrior who was maybe twelve years older than her. Kecouroo silently waited on the side. The warrior sat leaning back over a laundry tub while Brianna washed and rinsed his long hair.

It was all so very strange. He dressed Mekucoo and wore amulets of honor, yet his orange hair streamed down his back in a way that Mekucoo hair does not grow. He stood and coiled the wet hair over his shoulder. He was muscular with stained skin and many scars. He carried extra weight that Mekucoo men usually did not maintain. Plus he had red chest hair.

Brianna held a hand high at my approach. "Dr. Greensboro, this is Dacupitte my adopted brother, sometimes called Pete."

"Hiki, Dacupitte. Melinga."

"Melinga, Sheeks-Cylom."

Brianna and Kecouroo were beaming. He was obviously their favorite. "Pete was raised with Kecouroo," Brianna explained. "His mother was my father's wife before—"

"Don't explain it to me," I interrupted. "I can never get the family ties straight in my head. Stay, and enjoy your visit. I will get my own tea."

Once inside the clinic building, however, I could not stop myself from directing hidden glances at the adoptive siblings who still lingered by the catalpa tree. Pete allowed Brianna to comb out his rich hair while he talked and laughed with Kecouroo. What was it that held my attention? Perhaps the exotic view of a white man in the Mekucoo leggings.

"Ka," I heard behind me. I jolted and grabbed my cup so it would not fall and clatter. Edna cooed with delight. She had caught me spying on Pete.

Later that week, I traveled to the hospital where Dr. Mitterand was finishing his surgical residency. We consulted, made preparations, and undertook Haku rabbe Murd's cataract operation. His condition was advanced, a common form of cataracts on Dolvia caused by a long-term parasite infection that could be easily avoided by a better diet.

Haku was wheeled into the recovery room, and Dr. Mitterand, satisfied with the work, left to complete doctor rounds.

Dr. Beecham invited me into his office. The room had been Leslie's office and still sported a collection of medical books and other books imported from Earth. "Has the Cicero laboratory completed tests on the erriv vaccine?" I asked.

"Animal tests are encouraging," Henry said. "There's still the question of keeping the serum fresh in this climate. Arrivi won't understand if erriv sicken after receiving the hypo."

"And Dr. Mitterand's paper for the medical journal?"

"Well, I wanted to ask … A battery of specialists want access to your folk cures, but the pages are compiled in Arrivi. The translation program is outdated with nonsensical phrases and poor syntax. Could you, or one of your students, undertake an English version of the pages?"

"Why don't your specialists visit and do the translation themselves?"

"Dolvia is a disease-ridden desert overrun by tribal wars."

"No pioneers among them?" I asked. "No living large?"

Henry only frowned at my attempts at humor. "You could delimit the study for Arrivi to English." He waited a moment, and then added, "A big service like this means an increase in grant funding. Your tribal friends could afford to maintain a secondary school in Cylay."

Dr. Beecham certainly knew which carrot to dangle. "I can look into it."

When I returned to the clinic that week, the patient dorm was empty. Martina was teaching a class, as was Kecouroo. I entered

my research clinic and found Brianna seated alone at the front desk
EAM. "Where is Edna?" I asked.

"She visits Hakulupe Le on the flats of Arim."

"Where is Edwina?"

"On Kecouroo's land with Karlyhi."

Everybody hung out with Karlyhi, even the redheaded warrior
Pete. But it was wrong for me to complain. I had acted on the matter;
I could not renege. The imperative did nothing to lessen my irritation. "Did I say the girls could leave? And what about you? Are
you leaving?"

"I am assigned," she murmured with downcast eyes.

"I see. That's why you attend here rather than the Somule classroom. And that's why Pete must come to you for . . . personal groom-
ing." I sighed, trying to manage my irritation. "Well, since you're the
one who is assigned, then you're the one who gets to learn English.
Would you like to know the language of your father?"

"My father was American."

"Americans speak English," I said in that teacher's voice, "as do
Canadians and the Irish. And Australians. Well, a form of English,
anyhow. We can start today," I added. "We need to discuss the different word substitutes, just you and me. When you can make sense
of the syntax, that is sentence structure, you can translate the encyclopedia pages into English and Dr. Mitterand's paper to Arrivi.
What do you say? Are you interested?"

"Dr. Mitterand will return to Earth one day? Through the wormhole?"

"Yes, I imagine so."

"Then I will learn."

Dolviets were compliant when it served their goals, this fourteen-year-old orphan included. "I'm glad I can be of service," I said.

All during the dry season, Brianna and I learned English and Arrivi. We ate together and even visited Kecouroo's land. I was surprised when we walked into the extensive village. Mekucoo were wealthy compared to other tribes, more affluent even than Haku rabbe Murd. There were grain silos and public wells, along with many agrarian activities. Women were busy grinding barley meal, dressing hides for the warriors' shields, and brushing suede. But few men were there.

The women wore supple leather or suede fashioned into a single garment with a brief skirt. In the cool evenings, they pulled on a tunic decorated with beads or bright parrot feathers, which came just past the waist. The women seldom wore leggings, but sometimes sandals. Their jewelry consisted of strands of bright beads, as well as beaded earrings and arm amulets. Many women in this group displayed their wealth by adding semiprecious gems to the lengths of necklace. I saw opals, amethysts, and garnets. Some matrons included long silicide crystals that resembled quartz and were said to amplify light. I saw none of the native peridot stones that Arrivi women seemed to favor.

"I have come to visit at last," I said to Kecouroo. "I apologize for the long delay."

"We welcome your step upon the land of our ancestors," she said, slowly articulating the formal phrases. Even in her own household, Kecouroo sported only the necklace of black tektite stones held in place by a simple leather cord. "These are the homes of my aunts and cousins. The men are on the land."

Dacupitte emerged from a richly decorated thatch-roofed building. He bowed to me and led Brianna away like a daughter.

"May I ask, what is the feeling between Dacupitte and Brianna?"

"Their fathers were both Softcheeks, so there's a recognition," Kecouroo said. "When my father returned Pete to Somule, as a child, Brian Miller became his guardian."

"And your father was Cyrus? The Cyrus who ate the beating hearts of his enemies?"

She smiled. "You know how the stories grow."

Outside a rounded pole hut decorated with painted rawhide, Edwina sunned herself with her mouth open. She looked at me with lassitude. "Ka," she said.

"Edwina is just up from the grotto," Kecouroo said. "Her blood is still cold from swimming there."

We agreed to stay overnight and walk back to the clinic when Kecouroo came down for her afternoon classes. The men returned at dusk. We sat through a communal dinner, followed by group dancing in the compound's center. Forty people or more were gathered there. "What is the occasion?" I asked Kecouroo.

"The season of cylay is upon us."

"Cylay?"

"Forces strongly spread out independent of their roots."

"Of course," I returned with a frown. "I saw it coming." Kecouroo only smiled.

Brianna danced with the adolescent girls wearing borrowed jewelry. The young men danced opposite them in a long row, preening and strutting with a vivid display of feathers and ketiwhelp claws. It was beautiful and frightening; the huge fire, the shields and weapons, the chanting songs. The communal energy was most sexual in its display.

Even Edwina got into the act. Young girls squealed and backed away when she came to the dance center and threw around her weight with a series of twists and short hops. Edwina was the color of the savannah, and modulated her markings to jet-black as though aroused. I grew alarmed, but Kecouroo only smiled. The dancing men feigned honor with irreverent bows to the gualarep. One Mekucoo mooned her, showing his bony and brown buttocks. Edwina haughtily walked away.

I was an early riser, but the men were already gone when I came out of Kecouroo's building the next morning. Edwina was waiting. *Grotto?* she asked. I walked with her into the bush, assuming she would not lead me into an unselected danger.

We came upon the loveliest waterfall, maybe twenty feet high, surrounded by flowering vines and hanging moss. A blue macaw sounded the warning at our arrival, and many denizens scurried away. Edwina hunted there, I assumed.

She splashed into the water and glided along the bank. "The last time I went swimming with you, I was attacked by killer carp," I said. But there was no bush creature larger than Edwina or more lethal. Her color in the water was the same as when they had been infant reps—creamy with vein-blue accents.

I eased myself into the crystal-clear pool. We splashed around a while and she came alongside me. I grabbed her shoulder and held on for dear life while she strongly undulated toward the waterfall. Edwina dove deep, dragging me into the white spray. I heard the crashing water above and felt the rising bubbles, most invigorating. I was ready to come up for air long before Edwina flicked her tail and propelled us toward the surface.

We rose in the grotto, a high cavern of water-carved granite that held a pool of glimmering cold water. Shards of sunlight streamed in through roof vaults. I felt nurtured by the exercise of swimming there. I pulled myself out and sat on the bank, shivering while I looked around the narrow water-polished ledge that was much like any cave. The wonder was in the pool.

Edwina swam to me, her considerable weight buoyant in the water. The cream of her marbled hide was lovely against the transparent water. "Ka, ka, ka, ka," she called.

"You are right, of course," I said, hearing my voice reverberate against the walls. "This pool is much better than the clinic," I whispered. "I should have visited long ago."

I dove in and grabbed Edwina's shoulder. She dragged me down through the narrow passageway and past the waterfall. When we breached the surface, I inhaled in great gasps, fighting for warmth as much as air. We climbed out where we had first entered the water, and Edwina sought a patch of sunlight. Being a reptile, she needed the regulating warmth to restore balance. But the grotto was worth it.

Later we walked down to the clinic in time for Kecouroo's classes. That is, Brianna, Kecouroo, and I did. Edwina came along later. She required no company on the trail.

When we arrived at my compound, there was a veritable delegation waiting; tribesmen and soldiers, as well as two transport helicopters. Hakulupe Le was there with Joey Osborn and Rabbenu Ely. Dr. Beecham stood with my husband. I walked to Mike Shaw and waited for a kiss.

He shook his head. "You are being unseemly."

"What?" I asked. "You prefer to sneak in the back door tonight?"

"You may invite me to a formal tea."

"Fine, in an hour on the verandah."

"I'll just see to the soldiers' bivouac," Captain Shaw said to Dr. Beecham before he walked away.

While the tribesmen greeted Kecouroo, I shook Dr. Beecham's hand. "The vaccine is ready," he explained. "This group decides how to administer it."

I joined Hakulupe Le who introduced me to a lovely Cylahi woman of some status. "This is Marcy, Rabbenu Ely's wife. She has arrived to greet the Sheeks-Cylom."

"Hiki, Marcy," I said with an open palm gesture. Then I whispered to Lupe, "Now what have I done?"

She shook her head and knowingly glanced at Marcy. "Sheeks-Cylom is blessed by Dolvia. More than any have seen, you are the agent for spreading forces in the season of cylay."

Being blessed by the benign planet had always felt gratuitous. But nurturing was often accomplished for a future task beyond what others must perform. This season of cylay demanded more of me and of the plans I had implemented than I cared to sacrifice.

The Arrivi, along with Joey Osborn, gathered around family fires in the yard. They all seemed to be waiting for something, or maybe someone, who was tardy. Dr. Beecham loitered at the verandah table where I joined him. From his pack, Henry drew the HGEAM and assembled it on the table.

"I don't want that here," I complained. "I already said."

"This is important."

Dr. Beecham set out three cameras, each small enough to fit into the palm of my hand, at appropriate angles and booted up the HGEAM. A glowing and cycling cube appeared just four inches above the base. At the flood of yellow-blue light, the tribespeople looked over with curiosity. With wide eyes and her mouth dropped open, Brianna came to the verandah's railing.

The image of a security officer came online. "Voice confirmation, please," he said in English.

"Dr. Henry Beecham. Code ER3271 dash WE86."

There was a brief lag, then, "Dr. Beecham, how may I direct your call?"

"Colonel Hartley, please. He is expecting this call." The screen went to vivid yellow-blue. I looked around and saw that Captain Shaw and the Consortium soldiers had joined the staring crowd. Rabbenu Ely stood somewhat apart, with his arms crossed over his chest. Joey Osborn whispered into his ear.

On the verandah, the three-dimensional image of a Hardhand man in a blue Consortium uniform came online. He was seated at a transport operations station. "Dr. Beecham," he said, also using English. "Punctual as ever."

"Gene, we are transmitting here from the bush clinic. This is Dr. Greensboro." He signaled that I should come into camera range. I stepped behind him and shortly waved at the cycling cube image.

"Dr. Greensboro." Colonel Hartley's image nodded. "Many at Stargate Junction have petitioned to speak with you."

Brianna turned to the crowding faces and explained in Arrivi, "The floating head honors Sheeks-Cylom!" The tribespeople whispered together.

I sighed. I did not need this. "Questions should be directed to Dr. Mitterand," I said. "And to Dr. Beecham here."

"Please," Colonel Hartley said. "Humor us."

"This hay-gee-am represents a drain on my generator."

"We can send a new generator. You must not refuse us."

"Yes, well," I reluctantly said. "Just now I have tribal guests. Perhaps tomorrow."

"Tomorrow early. I will send along security codes and notify the trunk call operator."

Brianna called out to the crowd, "The floating head returns tomorrow!"

Dr. Beecham looked around. "We should go," he told the colonel. "Keep in touch."

"Tomorrow, then. Beecham endit." The cycling cube went to vivid yellow-blue again, and disappeared. The verandah seemed dark in the middle of the day while our eyes readjusted.

The wondering tribespeople talked together and returned to their places near the cooking fires. Captain Shaw spoke to Kecouroo and Marcy. Many people were loitering in my yard, and I felt an impending doom.

I did not need this, whatever was coming. "Brianna," I said, "help me store the hay-gee-am." She came onto the verandah while I packed the three flimsy cameras in the case. Brianna gingerly carried the HGEAM into my clinic. "It won't bite you," I said with a grin and followed her. We placed it on the desk.

"Later, I can show you the assembly," I told her. Her eyes glowed with eagerness. But then Rabbenu Ely stomped through the doorway and glowered at Brianna. He was leader of all Arrivi, a war hero and Softcheeks liaison, like a provincial governor.

"You taught this one the Softcheeks language?" Ely demanded.

"I have been teaching her English," I said in even tones, "so she can translate some study pages." Hakulupe Le and Ely's wife Marcy lingered just outside the door.

Ely spat out his words. "So she can migrate to the transport and become a Company whore like her mother. Forget the tribal ways and pretend to be Softcheeks."

"I am Softcheeks," Brianna petulantly claimed.

"Your father was Softcheeks. Your mother was a Company whore."

Why did he repeat that, I wondered.

"I was sent as a student to the Company transport," Ely pointedly told me. His face was twisted into an angry mask behind the round glasses. "I lived in conscript quarters and was beaten and spat on. They would have killed us in the night except for the fair trade with Oriika."

I wondered who Oriika was.

He stepped closer. "I know Softcheeks ways. Brianna must be taken from this no-good place."

"She was assigned to me," I lamely asserted. I looked to Hakulupe Le for reinforcement, but neither woman moved from the doorway.

Ely stared into my face, his barrel chest heaving with anger. "Brian Miller provided no covering for her mother. He provided no covering for this mulatto. She stands naked before the evil wind, and Softcheeks don't care."

So . . . I learned where Brianna had picked up the cruel label. I waited a long moment, quietly taking stock. "I meant no harm," I murmured holding an open palm at elbow height.

Brianna was dragged out into the yard by the angry leader. Marcy handed him a switch, and Ely raised welts on Brianna's legs and back. I could not believe it. The women related to Brianna, Kecouroo and Hakulupe Le, made no protest while Rabbenu Ely brought down the switch across Brianna's legs several more times.

I stepped forward to stop the beating, but my husband grabbed my arm and sadly shook his head. Finally Ely released her, winded and sweating. With tears and a set jaw, Brianna limped to Kecouroo who led her toward the classroom.

I glared at Dr. Beecham. "See what your technology brings?"

Rabbenu Ely trashed the switch he had used on Brianna, and my husband led me back to the verandah. "Will you settle down?" he whispered harshly.

"Lupe is Brianna's aunt," I whispered. "Not a murmur of protest came from her. Or from Kecouroo."

"Nobody counters the actions of rabbenu." He gestured that Dr. Beecham should join us, and we passed a few moment of tense silence.

I was not going to be the one to apologize. I regretted nothing. Apology was not part of my quotient. "What are they all waiting around for? What do they want?"

"Please, if we can focus on the project," Dr. Beecham said, unwilling to meet my look. "We have negotiated what the tribes call a fair trade. We plan to send two teams for the erriv vaccination process, led by myself and by Dr. Mitterand. Because of native protocol, this trip is my introduction to the Arrivi power structure."

Captain Shaw was not listening. "The linchpin here is Brianna." I saw his jaw move as if he was grinding his teeth.

"How so?" Dr. Beecham asked.

"Ely did not notice her," Mike postulated, "until the Sheeks-Cylom here taught her English. Beating her before the gathering will prove to be a grave mistake."

After a moment's thought, Dr. Beecham sighed. "The situation is fluid." I suspected he did not lend the same importance to the cruel beating. "Rabbenu Ely wants his handpicked ministers, Orin rabbe Murd and Joey Osborn, to travel the savannah. He has asked them to compile a family register, like a census, of the Southeast Arrivi families."

"For what?" I asked.

Dr. Beecham shrugged. "For better governing. Their rabbenu structure is shaky."

Before we could regroup for the negotiation, Dacupitte entered the camp accompanied by Edwina. Pete must have been the missing committee member who had caused a delay. He joined the men, and the gualarep came to me. "Ka, ka, ka, ka."

"Oh, shut up," I said. "And go inside."

She rolled back her tongue with disdain and lumbered through the clinic doorway. I wondered how events would have been shaped if Edwina had been present when Rabbenu Ely had burst in while Brianna and I stored the HGEAM.

It was growing dark, and the central fire was stacked and lit. Kecouroo returned with Brianna whose eyes were red-rimmed. We offworlders stepped down into the yard where I joined Hakulupe Le. "The entire power structure is here," I whispered. "Except Karlyhi."

"He's close by," Lupe said.

Since Hakulupe Le was goulep and could not serve there, I was led by Marcy to the communal fire. Dr. Beecham was led forward by Joey Osborn. Pete and Kecouroo stood together, but Captain Shaw hung back. His men, however, established a formidable Consortium presence within the clinic compound.

We stood in a circle. When all protocol was satisfied, the discussion got underway.

"We have developed an erriv vaccine which may alleviate—" Dr. Beecham began.

Rabbenu Ely interrupted. "We have set a task for the Sheeks-Cylom. The one who is blessed by Dolvia will travel the savannah and vaccinate erriv. Not these … offworld doctors. This task must be accomplished before the rains."

Dr. Beecham glanced around at the leaders in disbelief. Pete and Marcy exchanged glances but said nothing.

"Several teams should go out," Dr. Beecham said. "The serum is volatile. The rains are soon."

"No Softcheeks men will visit the families," Ely said. "Only the one Dolvia blesses." He spat out the last words as a challenge.

I held up a hand to caution Dr. Beecham, attempting to honor Ely. "I cannot travel the savannah alone. May I select my companions?"

"Two only," he insisted with his jaw set.

My choices were limited. Choosing my husband built no bridges. Hakulupe Le was goulep, so the tribes would not allow her to minister to the erriv. The Softcheeks doctors were banned from the effort. Traveling with a tribesman was unseemly, even for a married woman like me. Joey Osborn, married to an Arrivi, was the obvious choice.

"I select Dacupitte and Marcy."

"My wife is not available," Ely said.

"You said two of her choosing," Pete claimed. "Why do you withhold honor from the tribes that rabbenu's wife should visit?" The formal Arrivi phrases from his mouth sounded stilted.

"A difficult journey," Ely said.

"More difficult for Marcy than for Sheeks-Cylom?"

"This is not agreed!"

Pete answered with steel in his voice. "Sheeks-Cylom will complete your task, imposed in addition to the fair trade, with the ones she has selected. Also I choose as my second my sister Brianna."

"Your mother was not Brianna's mother," Rabbenu Ely said. "Your father was not Brianna's father."

"Nor am I related by blood to Kecouroo. Try to separate us."

Rabbenu Ely glared at me. "You will travel with Orin rabbe Murd and Joey Osborn."

"But—" Dr. Beecham said.

Hakulupe Le called from the side. "I will speak before the group."

"Be quiet, goulep," Rabbenu Ely said.

"I will hear from the goulep," Pete countered. "Her soul and that of Sheeks-Cylom are forever planted in the clinic's catalpa tree. She has knowledge of Dr. Greensboro's mind and what to expect." Again, Pete seemed to use the language of diplomacy rather than speaking directly to the situation.

Hakulupe Le stepped forward, just beyond the fire's bright circle of light. As goulep, she could come no closer. "The Putuki Ely," she began, "has long led the tribes with honor and just rulings. Ely's wisdom puts us in mind of his tribesman Martin Sumuki who was once worthy of an assassin's plot. But the rabbenu is scarred by his treatment at Company hands. The Company no longer troubles Dolvia. Rabbenu Ely continues to fight the earlier battle, and reads into Dr. Greensboro's gestures intent she does not know."

This was recent history I had not studied, elements separate from the chanted legends about Oria and Cyrus. The participants were still living and ruling.

"As goulep," Lupe continued, "I cannot argue against the rabbenu's ruling. I appeal instead to Marcy, one of Lucy's kids and once in service to Brian Miller. Think back for a moment, Marcy. The tribes did not come to your aid at the time of your Cylahi mother's death. As one of Lucy's kids, you received no honor from Putuki or Arrivi. Lucy's kids made their own way and gained honor through valor only."

More long-dead tribespeople, I thought. Why not just act from logic? Why bring up these tales about events from twenty years ago?

"You would not have survived," Lupe said to Marcy before the company, "except for Softcheeks generosity. You had no education except at Brian Miller's behest. Yet you greatly served Dolvia during the trial of Katelupe the Martyr by your presence, along with Dacupitte, at Brian Miller's side."

Marcy and Pete exchanged glances. So they shared past experiences, big surprise. Could we just get on with it?

"If this orphan Brianna," Lupe continued, "who has no covering among the tribes, is nurtured by Sheeks-Cylom, where is the harm? Sheeks-Cylom has set Brianna above Karlyhi, who would use Brianna even before she bleeds. Does not that show that Sheeks-Cylom's generosity is similar to the generous acts of Brian Miller?"

"This Softcheeks is not Brian Miller," Ely said. "This is not the season of om."

Lupe made an expansive gesture to show she meant no harm. "I appeal to Rabbenu's wife. What about these uncovered women on the land?"

There was a long silence. Ely crossed his arms and stood with feet planted wide apart. Pete stared at the ground but could not hide the humor in his face.

"Rabbenu Ely," Marcy began, "has led since the time of resistance to the Company. Ely stopped uranium mining. Ely stopped Hardhand immigration onto the savannah. Rabbenu is his rightful office. This orphan mulatto female is an insignificant thing, not a question to trouble rabbenu."

There was a shuffling of feet.

Marcy glanced at Dr. Beecham. "This vaccine will be given to erriv according to the fair trade that the rabbenu has accomplished. Ely need not be concerned with who travels the savannah, so long as Sheeks-Cylom guarantees completion before the rains."

They all looked at me. I shrugged and nodded, an act I would later regret.

Our conference was ended. The logs of the center fire collapsed with a swirling display of sparks, causing Brianna and two others to scramble to contain the embers. Tribespeople mixed and mingled around the cooking fires, and Dr. Beecham joined my husband and me on the clinic verandah.

My irritation had evaporated. "Dr. Beecham, I am sorry for my harsh words earlier. We lead a quiet life here. So many events all of a sudden."

"I should have sent word before our arrival," he said. "None of this is working out the way we planned."

"Pete agreed to the task to reprimand Ely for Brianna's beating," Mike said. "It has been seen in tribal prophecy that Pete will lead during a cycle after Ely. Rabbenu now views this vaccine effort as a threat."

I shrugged. "He should not have countermanded Dr. Beecham."

"He had his reasons," Henry said. "The question now is, can we finish the vaccination process before the rains?"

Dr. Beecham unfolded a topographical map of the savannah and the north foothills, and pointed at the clinic's location on high ground. "We are here. Southeast are Somule and the flats of Arim. East of there, we have the Canyon of Buttes, and south is Cylay.

Arrivi family groups are spread all over this area. We have two jeeps, but some family farms are beyond the roads. You will do some walking.

"The original plan," he continued, "was for me to take the southeast group and work my way up to families near the canyon. Dr. Mitterand was to administer to the family groups who are west and north, and then we would meet up in the middle. When the herds mingle for the drive to high ground, we will not know which have been inoculated. Erriv may sicken from a second hypo. So this needs to be competed, especially in the southeast, weeks before the rain."

"How much time do we have?"

"Less than a turn of Nettom for this area. Then a race to stay ahead of the herds."

"Six weeks on the open savannah," I said, quickly taking stock. "At the height of the dry season."

"Your other concern is the serum itself," Henry added. "We can pack a quantity in dry ice, and more can be delivered at regular intervals. We devised a simple litmus test for stability. Use the test each morning and after the siesta period. Compromised serum can be lethal."

"Delivered by whom?"

"By the Director of Natural Disasters Control, of course."

"I was wondering how long before you got into the act," I told my husband.

"You will come to like helicopter rides," Mike said.

"The task will not be easy," Henry said. "So many erriv."

I shrugged, "If I fail, then Marcy has failed. Also the next rabbenu, Dacupitte. They will not allow that."

"You should take along the hay-gee-am," Henry suggested.

"I don't want that damned thing around here," I said. "You saw what happened."

Dr. Beecham gestured and opened his mouth to argue before he dropped his hand. "Dolvia blesses you, Sheeks-Cylom. We must learn to trust that."

I retired with my husband into the clinic, as was our right. Later we lay together in bed and listened to the Arrivi chants sung around cooking fires outside my clinic's window. Rabbenu Ely's name was often heard amid lists of exploits, as well as Cyrus, the Mekucoo warrior of legend. We heard new verses about Sheeks-Cylom and the floating head, but nothing of Captain Shaw. "Do you frighten them?"

"They believe my status is gained through marriage."

"Truly?"

"First to separate your wealth from Leslie's, and then to start the school system. Also to serve in Cylay with the other married officers."

"You're lucky Ralph doesn't like me."

"And now my wife," he said with an arm around me, "will be introduced to each Arrivi family by rabbenu's wife. That carries more weight than chanted stories."

"You have become an equal to Rabbenu Ely?"

"You are the Sheeks-Cylom, agent of the season of cylay."

"That's silly."

"No matter. The savannah will humble you soon enough."

SIX

MARCY PROVIDED LIGHTWEIGHT ARRIVI SKIRT AND A CHADOR FOR me, along with wide sandals meant for walking. Mike gave instructions to Marcy concerning my stamina level and loaded me with insect repellent and sunscreen. He packed a canister of that nasty syrup that puts you right out and bought a wide-brimmed straw hat he claimed looked lovely on me. I was eager to set out and escape his nagging care.

The ride to the southeast in the open and wide-bodied transport chopper took nearly an hour. Marcy and Pete braced themselves with white knuckles when we took off, but soon relaxed. They pointed and stared at passing landmarks that were holy places to them.

I didn't know Pete except for his time spent with Brianna, and I had met Marcy only a few days before. Although she wore an Arrivi skirt and wide sandals similar to mine, her hands were soft and her arms unscarred. Life in Rabbenu's house must be easy duty. Marcy and Pete had embraced this adventure not for the erriv vaccinations so much, but from the need to maintain balance among the tribes. Relative tribal status was not my bailiwick, and I expected little help from them with the actual task of working with the herd animals.

South of Cylay, the loaded jeeps were waiting. We drove to the first Arrivi family herd; right away, I was glad I had included my doctor's bag and daily logbook. I had long known that patients made the trek to my clinic seeking relief from inflammations that curtailed their ability to work. Serious afflictions or chronic conditions were stoically tolerated by Dolviets until they worsened to incurable. With simple penicillin, tetracycline, and streptomycin, I could relieve the ailments of many village-bound Arrivi.

Medical care for people and erriv was possible only after all protocol was met. The village was laid out in a circular pattern with circular animal pens behind. An ancient stand of acacias shaded afternoon labor, and water meandered in a nearby stream. Children gathered in a tight gaggle, pointing and giggling. Overhead on the tree branches sat a brace of colorful parrots, also in a tight gaggle, adding their raucous talk to the general clamor.

The men sought an afternoon hour with Pete to deliver the compiled census papers and discuss tribal matters. No payment was accepted for our services, which were part of a larger fair trade. And anyway, they had no money. Even the poorest families offered hospitality to rabbenu's wife, though. Some women who greeted Marcy wore burkas with facial panels.

Erriv heifers provided a beige and runny milk, but for calves only. Arrivi were known to drink milk and draw erriv blood under duress in times of drought. It was otherwise considered unseemly to rob the heifer's bounty.

We spent tiring hours with the restless floppy-eared erriv. The corrals had a series of braces where compliant heifers were moved through in single file and later released to graze. The curious erriv nuzzled me with fleshy snouts and grew dizzy and feverish with the hypo, but were clear-eyed the following morning. I was happy with our results on this test group.

After a couple of flash burns, I grew tan on my face and arms. I wore the hat only during the afternoon heat. I learned to tie up the Arrivi skirt into blousy pantaloons as young girls did, so that my feet and calves were also exposed to the sun.

My hair was greased back with the insect paste and my daily sweat. When I washed it in the occasional stream, the length was silver-blond against my tanned skin causing the staring children to whisper and giggle. Matrons sometimes offered me white flour for my face, indicating that my former pale looks were more desirable than being tan. I had become Arrivi, more golden from time spent on the savannah than even Edwina.

The heat and insects, the smelly beasts, and dust-filled air made me wheeze during the hot hours. Marcy was alarmed at my response. "You may use the acclimation pill for comfort," she suggested.

"It's just wheezing," I shrugged while I refilled the hypo gun. "My husband sent a battery of medicines."

"They don't work if you don't take them. Perhaps Pete and I can join in for some duties with erriv."

"You would do that? As rabbenu's wife."

She chuckled. "I am one of Lucy's kids before my marriage. I saw Heather's fire." I didn't know what either of those boasts meant, or how they recommended her for the vaccine job. My wheezing while I considered the re-sorting of duties decided the matter, though. By the second week, we were using three injection guns, one for each of us. We cleaned the equipment and drove on to the next village's elaborate receiving ceremony. It was often deep night before we could steal some rest.

Dacupitte wore his hair in unkempt dreadlocks down his back. Brianna had twisted them with a rich oil, and they were caked with desert dust, obscuring the orange color. He wore loose dungarees and a Mekucoo belt-knife. He sometimes pulled on a tunic, especially in the cool night, but mostly exposed his skin to the raging sun.

Each morning and again after siesta he rubbed on aloe, allowing it to mix with the grit clinging to red chest hair. I repented often of the need to watch him during this twice-daily routine. I turned away but sometimes turned back with my hand supposedly over my eyes. He was dark and sinewy; the only betrayal of his fair skin were the boyish freckles across his nose. When he bent to cover the defined muscles of his legs with the oil, I walked away, unable to bear the indiscreet view. Strangely, I had no such sinful thoughts about the nearly naked tribesmen we greeted each day.

Mostly I remember punishing jeep rides across open terrain and long walks in the burning heat, my moist legs tangled in the skirt's many folds. I remember the sounds of lowing erriv and cracking whips.

In each village I was stationed near the neck braces, with aching muscles from repeated motions. Each heifer was trapped to receive the hypo in the shoulder, staring with too-wide eyes exposing glassy whites. Then a tribesman, usually a young boy, released her and herded in the next struggling yearling.

Macaws of the most shocking colors mixed together following the herds: blue ones, red and yellow ones, some with iridescent features that glistened like oil slicks. When a group of yellow parrots arrived, they seemed unfriendly or even territorial. The birds chattered and jostled for position on the corral fence. Marcy explained one day that erriv in that area ate a hard nut that grew on a ground vine, but the cattle expelled the nut core undigested. Parrots gleaned their droppings for the softened treat, a lazy bird's diet.

"Usually there were few of these pests," Marcy said while we worked. "Two big-wet seasons in a row have increased their numbers." The parrots raised long tail feathers and gingerly walked the railing on big claws in a charming display, almost companionable. But after a while, the ruckus they raised and their aggressive curiosity drove me batty.

While we traveled, I cut desert succulent samples and put Brianna in charge of keeping the collection and my notes in order. Before long, she brought in dry stems that responded to water and quickly produced seedlings. She managed the drawings and the simple tests we had devised. We named more than one new sample after her suggestions.

Brianna was everywhere, anticipating my needs and suggesting solutions to travel questions. Proud of her good service, Pete and Marcy were seen sharing their jerky with her.

I became proficient in the dialects and came to understand the tribal fire chants.

> Dacupitte sets foot upon our land
> And brings with him the Sheeks-Cylom
> Who speaks to women the same as a man
> And who Dolvia embraces as one
> She and the gualareps also

Or something to that effect. With Brianna translating and taking notes, some mornings I discussed with the tribeswomen the plants' medicinal uses. We discovered a different spice and herbal philosophy than Hakulupe Le used. Although they lived within a hundred miles of each other, the families held widely varying culinary and home-remedy traditions.

I gained some of Pete's time one hot afternoon. "I requested more medicine to be delivered with the vaccine."

"Sheeks-Cylom," he said with irritation. "We can live on jerky and vegetables while we minister to erriv. You can return later for tea with the old women."

"You find the time," I countered, "to count the families and sign off on their census papers."

So Brianna and I limited our talks with the tribeswomen to the heat of the day when the erriv were irritable, and also after dark. Brianna watched with concern while I wheezed out some instructions for the alleviation of common ailments, and waited until I told her to get started.

Marcy watched me closely. "You attempt too much. You put our mission at risk."

"The need is so great, and the solutions simple," I said. "How can I not reach out?"

Pete made a couple generous gestures toward me, mostly to ease my physical discomfort. One day he offered a pulpy aloe stem. "Break it," he said, "and rub it on your skin."

"Don't I have enough sunscreen ointments?"

"This one is for dryness."

"Thanks for the thought," I refused. "You need not serve me."

"You serve me at every turn," he countered with a shrug. "You saved my sister from Karlyhi's advances. You arranged this tour for census taking, and put me into competition with Rabbenu Ely."

"You don't find me demanding?"

"Ah," Pete shamefacedly grinned. "Like the rutting sand grouse." He stood and imitated the common bird. With his chest puffed out and his elbows back, he strutted first left then right while he bobbed his head.

"I don't do that!" I called out. "Stop it!"

"'I don't do that,'" he mimicked in exact tones, still bobbing his head and strutting. "I am the Sheeks-Cylom."

"Cut it out!" I insisted with laughter. I followed him with doubled fists, a true threat. Pete caught my arms to avoid the laughter-weakened blows and held me close.

"Release me. I'm a married woman."

"So?"

I struggled free and slapped his arm, still playing. His expression changed, and I felt a cold chill on my neck. Pete caught my arm with an iron grip and turned me around, pinning my arms behind me. The cool edge of his Mekucoo knife was at my throat.

"Nobody strikes Mekucoo," he whispered into my ear. He pushed me so that I fell, and he sheathed his belt knife. "If you were not the Sheeks-Cylom, you would be dead where you stood." He turned on his heel and walked away.

I felt my throat for blood. I believed him.

Captain Shaw met us at agreed rendezvous points, replenishing our supply of diesel fuel and serum from the transport helicopter. He always brought food, bread and pasta and sticky rice. He sat next to me and glowered while I forced down the carbo-fare and named the prescriptions I needed for the village we had just passed through.

"Oh, and bring along another abrasion maser next time," I instructed. "Plus a fresh supply of antiseptic washes."

"Why are you doing this?" he asked slowly.

"Did you know their diet in this area is substantially—"

"Will you stop?"

"Why should I stop?" I asked. "Listen, contact Dr. Beecham. See if he knows a dietician who is interested in fieldwork. He could do some follow-up. You know, enter the village after we're gone, dispense the ordered drugs, and study their cooking habits."

"This is not part of the fair trade negotiated with Rabbenu Ely," my husband complained.

"The pharmacist need not travel with us. The follow-up could be separate."

"There's just no end to you, is there?"

"What?"

"What day is it? How much do you weigh?"

"We do quite well without your nagging, thank you very much."

Mike provided an inhaler to alleviate my bronchial trauma. The acrid spray made me high and jittery, but it opened my lungs. He lectured Marcy concerning my changed looks and work burden. She, in turn, glowered at me. But my samples cases were filled, and my notes for native cures had become voluminous.

On another day, we walked through a rock and stick field to reach one family group. Pete pointed to a swirling dust column that danced just above the sandy trail. "Tunanin," he named it. "Ancestral spirits survey the land in advance of the rains."

Later, he drew me aside. "You can rest now. Perhaps four hours."

"I'm fine. Don't stop for me."

"Look there," he said, pointing west. "Cooler air blows in. We must find cover."

The sand storm came suddenly out of a clear blue sky. We crowded into the jeeps, securing the canvas roof and plastic window covers. Whole dunes of sand and sage blew past, punishing the vehicles with blustery winds.

I reached around to grab my notes to study.

"You can sleep now," Pete insisted. "I'll give you the syrup if I must."

I dropped the book and glanced at grinning Brianna who sat scrunched in the back. I settled into my seat and closed my eyes, pretending to sleep on command. And of course, I was out in two minutes.

Later I heard a calming heartbeat, and felt warm arms around me. I woke to the odor of heated oils and realized I was cradled in

Pete's arms while his legs were stretched across my seat. Heavy dreadlocks rested on my shoulders while he slumbered as if alone.

I glanced into the back where Brianna was curled in a siesta with her back to us. I snuggled against Pete's oily-gritty chest with the red chest hair and relished the quiet moment, delicious because it could not last and could never come again. Pete was not like my husband. Even in repose, he was nothing like Mike Shaw.

When I woke again, I gasped at the strange sight. Eerie and clustered yellow faces crowded the plastic window. Pete stirred and shrugged me off his lap.

"What is it?" he groggily asked. I pointed at the new arrivals crowding the window. "There must have been rain in the dust storm," Pete claimed while he shook Brianna's shoulder. "The succulents can grow within a few hours."

Brianna yawned and stretched. Pete climbed over me to push the door open and exit from my side. His dreadlocks and knees and elbows were all over me. I saw only red chest hair. "We're being attacked by killer hyacinth," he told his adoptive sister.

Fresh air, cool and moist, filled the jeep. Pete exited and poked his head back into the cab. "Hyacinth is a favorite breeding place for wasps and pincher scarabs, so don't go poking your nose into the flower bells."

"Yes, Kee-mo-sa-bee," I mocked while I bobbed my head.

He frowned, grouchy after his nap.

"Whatever you say, Dacupitte," I corrected. Pete left. I turned to Brianna. "Get my samples case."

The succulents had indeed grown as tall as a preteen in a quarter day. The tight flower clusters, bright yellow with teasingly white interiors, seemed to wither before they reached full bloom. The buzzing insects arrived as predicted.

Clouds rolled overhead for many days, and heat lightning set off dramatic thunder. One afternoon it actually rained. Heavy drops left perfect imprints on the parched ground, absorbed as soon as they landed. Pete talked with the tribesmen and recommended a new itinerary, citing the need to stay ahead of the southeast roundup.

At our rendezvous place, two wide-bodied choppers touched down in a whirl of dust. Captain Shaw waited there with a big German woman named Louise Bilesketchum, a trained pharmacist and dietician, who was as tall as him and dressed in khaki dungarees that defined her round bottom. The tribesmen averted their eyes and walked away. Marcy spoke with some Arrivi women, going from one family to another until finally an appropriate skirt was procured, long and hand stitched.

I shook hands with this new field pioneer. "I'm Dr. Greensboro. I can show you how to tie up the skirt as pantaloons."

We packed into the helicopter my many samples to be delivered to Dr. Mitterand for further tests. I tried to thank my husband for meeting my needs. "If I had not," he sourly returned, "you would have found a way to be in two places at the same time."

"I'm fine," I reassured him. "I am having the time of my life."

"You're two days behind schedule. You're sick and underweight."

"I'm not sick."

"Then what's that wheezing sound?" Mike graced me with a hard stare. "There's no time margin now for a setback. How will you complete the task?"

"This is preventative medicine. Not an epidemic."

"Have you forgotten Rabbenu Ely's challenge?"

"Surely he would not punish me for greeting the people. For giving them aspirin."

"Get your succulents," he sourly instructed.

I went to our crates that contained the last of the seedlings. Mike and Louise talked with the pilot. Brianna watched them while she was supposed to be lending a hand. "You allow that?" she asked. "I mean, in front of your face?"

I glanced over at their conversation. Louise laughed and lightly slapped Mike's arm. Her gesture reminded me of when I had slapped Pete's arm and his reaction.

"They are colleagues," I said. "Louise Bilesketchum has her own professional reputation. Within that discipline, her opinions cannot be countermanded by any man. They are equals."

"So," Brianna extrapolated, "I can talk to Dr. Mitterand."

"Well, as an apprentice," I shrugged while I struggled with the last carton. "You must study and gain entrance into the closed professional group."

"This equal thing," Brianna said with a downturned mouth. "I think maybe it's false. A false attitude that Softcheeks women like to claim for themselves. Arrivi know that all men desire all women. That is why one must be covered."

"But I travel without covering."

"You are covered by the Sheeks-Cylom reputation," she said simply, like reciting the facts. "But even so, you are exposed to Dacupitte."

"What do you mean?" I asked, trying to sound casual.

"A Mekucoo leader may have any woman. Not as an equal, but as a thing."

"My husband would kill him."

"And touch off civil war?"

"Does Pete exercise this right?"

"A great honor for the woman, and more so with Pete because the children are sometimes redheaded."

I had seen these off-color children present in all four tribes. "And what do the husbands say?" I asked.

"It means the warrior has a desirable wife who is otherwise covered."

"Do the husbands really feel that? Are the women eager?"

"Do Softcheeks women truly feel equal to the men?"

When the helicopter was packed, I kissed my husband. He looked at me with surprise. I received no hug, no hungry questions concerning my return. The blades began to rotate. "Complete the task!" He climbed onboard. "That's all that matters!"

I tried to shout my good-byes over the chopper noise, but could only lean against the disturbance and back away.

For two days Louise and I talked when we could; it felt so good to discuss medical concerns and to speak in English. I described tribal taboos, including Arrivi bluntness and no trousers for women. Louise looked through my sample case and recent notes that Brianna proudly displayed. Brianna was frustrated with Louise's German accent, but soon understood our words. Pete and Marcy stood aside and shrugged. It was always the same with Dolviets. One Softcheeks was a curiosity, but two were an invasion.

We separated when our vaccine work in that area was finished. Marcy, Pete, and I were set to drive past the Canyon of Buttes and begin the second round of inoculations on the lands of Murd and Arim. Louise returned to the most recent village with her Putuki guides. Brianna joined Louise as interpreter and helpmate. That was a prudent move, but it left me with a cold chill, Brianna being so young and uncovered.

Pete drove the jeep along a dirt road with deep ruts. "So you are done now with this female talk?" he pointedly asked. "We can concentrate on the matter at hand?"

"I was only trying to help."

"We must complete the task before the rains. There's no more time."

"Yes, Da-cu-pit-tee," I pronounced, bobbing my head.

He sighed and relaxed. "My real name is Hamish."

"Hamish?"

"I was taken as a newborn and raised by Kecouroo's mother, Cyrus's first wife."

"Taken?"

"It is a long story."

"And Kecouroo's mother, she was a woman of some importance?"

"She was Cara's sister. The current Mekucoo leader."

"I can never get the family ties straight," I said shaking my head. "So genetically, you are in no way Dolviet?"

Pete chuckled. "Scots-Irish."

"The Sheeks-Dacupitte?"

"Dacupitte is a Mekucoo word and loosely translates to 'waits with angry eyes'. I was a difficult child."

"I bet that part is true."

"You know how a child hates to be different," he said while he watched the sandy road. "So I set out to prove myself each day and refused extra rations or soft duty. I was determined to be a better warrior than even Cyrus."

"And you are a warrior."

"None can be better than Cyrus; that was a young boy's fantasy."

"But you will lead one day?"

"So it is seen," he sighed. "Perhaps by default when all the real warriors die in battle."

"Then war is coming?"

"A great red stain of blood-guilt on the land, or so our prophecy says."

For the time being, Dolvia provided. The northwest Arrivi were considerably richer than the southeast group. They were family to Haku rabbe Murd, and thereby to Brianna. The elaborate ceremonies were set aside for herd work. Even the repeated motions of the vaccine task seemed easier perhaps due to cooler weather.

After the few brief showers, hibernating animals came to life, mostly insects. Rapacious and aggressive, they must complete their growth and breeding cycles within a few weeks. The swarms of dragonflies were quickly decimated by parrots. Tiny termites had papery white wings held high like a sailboat that caught the sunlight. They hovered together in a morning puddle like a miniature regalia. They were devoured by chattering birds before the heat of the day. Parrots sometimes returned to the corral railing with layers of termite wings showing in their beaks.

I received a spider bite on my arm, an innocent-looking lump that I showed to Marcy. She grew alarmed and called Pete.

"Are you trying to rob the desert of one?"

"I don't know what that means."

To my astonishment, Pete drew his knife and slashed across the bite area, then strongly sucked the blood and puss from there. He spat with a big, liquid spray. He ordered me to drink fresh water all day, until I became dizzy, then handed me a bowl brought forward by a tribeswoman.

"Yuck!" I complained. "It's urine."

"Human urine is a common antidote for poisonous bites."

"Venom," I murmured. "I have not studied venom yet."

And then I fainted.

When I came around, my husband hovered over me. I saw his face through a fuzzy haze, and realized it was mosquito netting over the cot. "How long was I out?"

"It does not matter," he said.

I realized we were moving. The cot was rigged in the back of a military truck. The vaccine task had become a convoy. "Rabbenu Ely won't be pleased that I have more helpers."

"Only Marcy and Pete work with the injection guns. The rest of us are just visiting."

"How many?"

"Practically everybody."

I looked at my throbbing arm, which was tightly wrapped to past the elbow. A compact battery-driven IV gently delivered liquid into my other arm. "The bandage reduces the swelling," my husband explained. His look was accusative. "Spider venom can cause the spot to swell until the skin splits open."

"Don't bully me," I whined. "Please don't yell. How was I supposed to know about the spider? A cute green thing with stilt legs, like from a child's fairy tale."

"Here, drink this." He separated the netting and offered me the syrup canister.

"I don't want that."

"I can hold your nose and pour it down your throat."

I took the canister and managed to swallow a little. Under his harsh gaze, I forced a second mouthful. My arms went limp, and I was soon dozing again.

When I woke, we were parked and it was raining. Heavy drops pelted the truck's canvas cover. I could smell freshly turned earth and crushed leaves. My husband must be nearby. I heard nails against wood and quiet cooing. It was Edwina beside me, crowding the cot with her bulk. I separated the mosquito netting and she fingered me, her fleshy tongue wetting my face and arm.

"Oh, quit now," I said. "I'm fine."

I felt strangely at peace. "That comes from you, huh? You give off that calm feeling." Edwina flashed her tongue across my face again.

I looked out at the dark rain. Rivulets had formed on the denuded desert terrain. We had missed our goal. We were days late. I had let them down by admiring a green spider. With the swollen fingers of my wrapped arm and hand, I searched through the first-aid kit my husband had left there. I gingerly removed the IV from my other arm. I swabbed the tender place and added a simple bandage.

The rain stopped suddenly, although the truck's cover continued to drip. I stretched and opened the tailgate. Edwina lumbered onto the soggy ground. I struggled out after her and looked around. Daylight was creeping over the horizon. The truck was parked several feet from another truck, two lorries, and the covered jeeps.

Edwina's tongue flicked against my legs. We walked up the rise a short way and saw the refreshed savannah gently lighted by a false dawn. Crescent moons seemed about to dip below the horizon. Where desert had reigned not five days ago, all was green and sprouting. The air was clear with rolling pink clouds. The wet ground smelled verdant.

A parcel of blue macaws glided nearby and landed with flapping wings. They raised their long tail feathers just above the wet dirt. They kept their distance because of Edwina. They did not peck the ground but seemed to stare out at the vista, sharing a quiet moment in our company.

Edwina turned at a noise behind us. It was my husband checking the truck. "Ka, ka, ka, ka," she articulated, and he looked our way. We turned back to the glowing sunrise while Mike Shaw came up the rise.

"Blue macaws for the Sheeks-Cylom," he whispered. I leaned back against his chest, and he encircled me with his warm presence, careful to put no pressure on my swollen arm. We lingered there until the sun broke over the horizon.

"I need to get you a cowbell," my husband said, "since you won't stay put."

"Bully. I am sorry we missed the task deadline."

"Who said we missed it?" he asked. "A little rearranging. One cattle herd goes north while others are mustered here. Orin was not pleased with the prospect of arriving last in the north grazeland, with the choicest pasture already taken and all that. But they want the inoculation. They want Sheeks-Cylom to visit."

"So I am redeemed."

"One family group south of Orin's land is plagued with a sickness. The tribesmen won't go there and risk the pox. But we made arrangements to access that herd as well."

"Running my life for me again?"

"You overextend. Besides, this was Pete's deal, once he was selected." Mike emphasized the word selected. "Pete deftly managed the tribal negotiations and the census taking. He should run for political office in Cylay."

Perhaps it was because we approached the end of our project. Perhaps it was simple exhaustion. Perhaps it was the tribesmen's need to manage an erriv group not their own. But the whole thing ended badly. I was still somewhat unsteady; I admitted that to myself. I removed the arm bandage and flexed my stiff hand. There was a wicked scar across my forearm from Dacupitte's knife, but the swelling had mostly subsided.

Rabbenu Ely was waiting. He saw me and started to move my way. Marcy walked past him nearly pushing him aside. She looked back; I didn't see her face. But Ely sure did. Sometimes you just don't cross a wife.

We prepared the injection guns. I labored alongside Marcy as well as I could. Rabbenu Ely stood glowering with two Putuki men who were his ministers. We finished with Orin rabbe Murd's sleek herd and retested our hypo provisions while the floppy-eared erriv were led away by Arrivi herdsmen who waved to Pete. They cracked whips overhead encouraging the erriv to move along and started the trek to claim high grazing land.

Hakulupe Le joined our group bringing tea and fruit. I realized that it was already afternoon. I was so glad to see her. It seemed we were separated for so long. Edna had traveled with Lupe and now fingered my exposed calves with a moist tongue.

"Will you quit now? I'm fine. I will be fine."

Edna and Edwina greeted each other with open mouths and flicking tails. They indulged in long body rubs while they kicked up dust near the corral.

"Look on the rise," Marcy said. Through the hazy day, we saw the last erriv brought in from the feral group belonging to the families stricken with pox. On the ridge a young warrior and a gualarep were backlit by the late afternoon sun. Karlyhi and Ralph herded erriv from the family groups where no other tribesmen would enter. Ralph called to the slow-moving herd with an authoritative bark. Karlyhi swung the long whip over his head and snapped it with a reverberating crack. Together the warrior and gualarep directed an alpha bull toward the corral circle.

The emaciated and unkempt erriv docilely entered the pens and crowded together. Young boys from Orin's group herded them into the neck braces so Marcy, Pete, and I could administer the hypo. The sons of Cyrus who I had seen at the Feast of Oria, named Lynus and Rufus, labored near me. We bent over the work, releasing the struggling heifers one after another to graze and regroup.

Karlyhi sent more erriv over the rise; they crowded the holding pens. These were from several family groups; the mane braids were distinctly different. They had not traveled far together, so dominance was still in question. While I bent next to a glassy-eyed heifer with scarred legs, I heard a ruckus by the corral opening, an angry barking noise and a high-pitched squeal. We dropped our tools and rushed to find out the trouble. Two bulls traded blows and faced off with tense flanks and wildly bobbing heads to display their horns.

Wielding the long whips, Pete and the Mekucoo wranglers separated the combatants and shooed them out of range. The heifers lowed and stomped their hooves in an uncertain moment. Edwina faced off the waiting heifers, but they only turned away with indifference.

When the dust settled near the gate, we found Edna on her back and bleeding from the chest. "No!" I cried out with a wheeze. "This cannot happen!" Barely able to draw breath in the heat and dust, I dropped to my knees on the ground next to her. I quickly took stock.

Edna had been gored during the struggle. The bull's horn must have caught her under the front leg. When he'd jerked back his head, a deep gash was torn across her muscles and ribs. The bull had flipped her over to pull his horns free and face his true opponent. I needed to work fast to stop the bleeding and irrigate the wound.

Fix her? Edwina asked while she kept a keen eye on the herd.

You know better that to mingle with erriv, I answered without speaking. *What were you thinking?*

Edwina lifted her sizable head. The unblinking eyes held my attention for a long moment. Then she sauntered off, her body and tail swinging laterally while she ambled up the rise to where Ralph and Karlyhi had shown themselves.

My husband came to my side. "Bring some bandages," I instructed. "Can we get her into the truck? And get the maser!" I grabbed the offered Arrivi skirt. My hands flew over her body, desperate to stop the bleeding and keep sensation in the flesh.

Edna struggled when we tried to lift her, displacing my hastily wrapped cover. Mike brought the syrup canister. I looked at him with alarm, but he only shrugged.

"Edna," I said. "You must swallow this. I know it tastes nasty. You will go soft inside and perhaps fall asleep. When you wake, all fixed. Swallow a little for me, huh?"

I poured some onto her tongue. It had the consistency of honey, but with dark flecks and a shocking odor. She made a gagging noise. Mike nodded and I doused her open mouth with a second swallow.

"Ka, ka, ka, ka," she complained and tossed her head. We jumped back while she jerked and flicked her tail. But her movements grew sluggish, and soon she was passed out.

I deserted the vaccination task. I did not care whose erriv received the catarrh inoculation. The men struggled to hoist Edna's weight into the covered truck bed. I climbed in alongside her. Lynus and Rufus threw in freshly cut bulrushes as bedding. Rufus showed his face at the tailgate. His features were so fine he could easily pass for white. He blinked at my stare and offered me a long sliver of bone. He made a quick sewing motion when I frowned.

"Melinga," I whispered.

I irrigated the wound and used the abrasion maser at pinpoint intensity to close off exposed veins. I continuously brushed the raw flesh to keep sensation present, and bathed the area with an antiseptic wash. The liquid bubbled before it ran off into a greenish-yellow residue. I did not care for the look of that.

My husband climbed into the stuffy enclosure next to me. "Can you stop the bleeding?"

"I'm not sure how effective the antiseptic was. I cannot close the wound using the maser without knowing it's clean."

"Their blood is different from ours; that is all."

"I cannot be sure," I whined.

"Then we shall have to close the wound the old-fashioned way," he reasoned. Mike fashioned a slit on the bone needle and threaded it with a strand as thick as hair. After I had repaired as much internal damage as I could, he expertly sewed up Edna's wound, pulling her thick hide together with his paw-like hands, and forcing the needle between bumps on the marbled texture.

"Her leg is broken," I wheezed. "We need a splint."

Mike showed me a compassionate look. He poured water from his canteen onto a clean cloth. He caught my arm and firmly washed my face as if I was a toddler. "The others must not catch sight of your tear streaks." He handed me the cloth and climbed out of the truck to find suitable branches for splints. I sat back and wheezed. I soaked the cloth again and placed it on the back of my neck for the cooling effect.

Mike was right as usual. I had overextended and put everyone at risk with my broad goals. My faith in imported technology had not proven so valuable with fieldwork. The native drink was probably what had saved Edna's life. I decided it was better to think like a man, better to be single-minded.

"This is why women don't rule the world," I told slumbering Edna.

Mike returned and fashioned the leg splint. That was all we could accomplish without clinic equipment. "Can we take her back to the clinic?" I asked in a small voice.

"We should head out now before the sedative wears off. You must say good-bye to Marcy and Pete."

We climbed down and joined the worried tribespeople. I held an open palm high and murmured good-bye. "Sorry," I told Pete. "I am so sorry. All this trouble. I meant no trouble, just relief from sickness. Sorry."

I rode in the truck's cab while Mike drove. As we left the flatlands behind and climbed the grade to the clinic, the stiff winds buffeted the truck, so I braced my arms against the seat and door. Many erriv groups were already stationed along the roadway and warriors wore extra garments against the wind. This was the season the families spent on Mekucoo land in seasonal structures near the herds.

"I think I hurt Edwina's feelings," I said, and wiped salt tears from my face. "She will never forgive me." My husband drew me close while he drove with one hand on the steering wheel. I curled up in his warm presence, lulled into restless sleep by his warmth and the regular heartbeat.

At the clinic, we struggled to get Edna's bulk out of the truck bed. Finally, Mike loaded her sleeping form onto two planks and lashed her down with ropes. He rigged a pulley over the verandah rail, cutting through the screens, and strung the ropes to the truck's trailer hitch. He drove the truck away from the building until Edna's rig was dragged up the steps onto the verandah. We moved her, still lashed to the planks, inside the clinic building.

I gave her shots in her tongue for tetanus and rabies prevention and also a second sedative. We had accomplished little more than to make her comfortable when Ralph came onto the verandah.

"He cannot come in here," I whispered.

Ralph waited for Mike who joined him outside. I just could not decide what more to do. Edna stirred in her slumber, and her legs mimicked running as if to escape night terrors.

Mike sat on the verandah chair. I came out and climbed onto his lap, seeking the comfort I had felt during the ride to the clinic. I sank into Mike's presence and listened to the heartbeat in his big chest like a gentle metronome.

Then I heard the question. *Heartbeat?* Edna asked.

Of course! What an idiot I was. Mike had provided comfort so I could rest and heal.

"Ralph," I said. "Go on in." He entered the clinic and raked about, toppling the bed stand; a carafe and glasses scattered. "Let's stack the furniture," I whispered to my husband.

We moved the Chinese screen and the table and cot. Mike cut fresh bulrushes out by the catalpa tree. I drew fresh water and poured it into the foot bowl. I knelt next to Edna, but Ralph hissed and faced me off.

"I just need to remove the bandage," I whispered in a calming tone. "So you can get to the wound for licking. But I won't cut the stitches, and I am leaving the splint." I gently reached out, waiting for a signal that he would not attack. Ralph assumed the muscles-down posture, and I quickly cut away the smelly cloth.

I stood and backed away. Ralph fingered the wicked gash with his fleshy tongue. He nestled long-ways against Edna, who moaned and relaxed, perhaps lulled by his heartbeat.

"What else?" I asked.

Lights, came to me in a masculine voice.

So Ralph could throw his thoughts to me. He had selected to ignore me all this time. I flipped off the lights. Moonlight flooded the room with a bluish glow.

Mike and I went back to the verandah. "You said Ralph doesn't read your thoughts."

Mike shrugged. "Language is not his strong suit. We played a game when he was growing wherein I could see through his eyes."

"Can Ralph see my thoughts?"

My husband waited a long moment. "Consider it from his point of view. What do you study all day long? Microbes and printed text in medical books."

"But he can see my thoughts?"

"Exams for pregnant women. Ralph thinks that's disgusting." He grinned. "The gualarep girls' ability with language was a big surprise. We decided it was because you had allowed them to sleep with you as infants. Some serious bonding there."

"Who is we?"

"Me and Karlyhi."

"Damn! Ralph talks to Karlyhi?"

"They were initiated together as warriors. They experience the savannah together. It's more than sharing. It's ... it's more."

"And Karlyhi talks to the girls."

"The girls are limited," Mike said, "with the pictures thing, maybe dependent on language now. But Edwina especially will grow in ability."

"And you were not ever going to tell me?"

"So you could dissect Ralph to search for special microbes in his brain? Besides, I figured what he wanted you to know, he would tell you."

For days we all slept and ate and then slept again. At dusk, I sat on the verandah wondering how we had become so exhausted. Two blue macaws took up residence in the catalpa tree and often rested on the verandah railing. They were truly beautiful with lush feathers. I figured they would desert their place as soon as Edna could get around again. This was her home.

They flew to the catalpa tree when Ralph returned from hunting. He dropped at my feet a fibrous stalk called okiioc, a common underbrush plant on Mekucoo and Siibabean land. "Ralph, are you becoming a vegetarian?"

Haku, he said.

"Haku, rabbe Murd? Who had the cataract operation?"

Si … Siiba …

"Siibabean? Known as tuber-eaters?"

No milky eye, came the thought.

"Siibabean don't get cataracts?" I said. "None of them live long enough."

I handled the stalk that had the weight and feel of sugar cane. "Cataracts are the result of a long-term viral infection and are easily controlled by correct diet. Are you saying the tuber-eaters are safe from cataracts? Made safe by eating okiioc?"

Ralph turned with a quick jerk. I leaned back. His speed was frightening. I never got past the knowledge that he was wild, not a domestic creature at all. He entered the clinic and took his station next to Edna.

"Your secret is out," I called after him. "You can talk to me."

Only females need words, Ralph shot back.

Later that week I sent the okiioc to Dr. Mitterand at the hospital, along with the hunch that its inclusion in a native diet could prevent cataracts.

SEVEN

AFTERNOON SHOWERS PELTED THE TIN ROOFS AND INTERRUPTED Edna's naps. So Mike had the Arrivi cut catalpa leaves and ferns to fashion a wide thatch covering for the crenelated roof. After that, the noise was muffled and strangely comforting.

Mike showed me plans for a second student dormitory including private rooms for the older girls. During the rains enrollment actually increased since tribal kids could not work the farms or herds for several weeks. "They live better here than within their family circles," I complained. "And whatever happened to directing natural disasters?"

"Arrivi don't consider the rain a disaster," he grinned. "They are more concerned with the trouble Sheeks-Cylom brings them."

Hakulupe Le visited early that season, and carried several udder bags filled with water slung over her shoulder. With her came an Arrivi woman of great status and wealth. It was Kyle Rula who lived on the flats of Arim. She wore a hand-stitched gown and many pieces of peridot jewelry. She carried as a shawl the Arrivi burka that was mostly obsolete. Martina, who she called Lula, held an open palm high. Kecouroo warmly embraced her.

Then, of all things, Ralph came down the verandah steps and sidled up to Kyle Le. She sat on the ground while he fingered her with his tongue and stepped over her lap, strongly rubbing her with his flanks. I felt a hot flash of unreasonable jealousy. Ralph barely acknowledged my existence, and I was Mike Shaw's wife. Me, not her. Not this old tribal woman.

Ralph looked back at me as though he knew what I was thinking. With his mouth wide open, he rolled back his tongue in the gesture Edwina used when she was fed up with me. How insolent, I thought. What gave him the right to make judgments about me?

Ralph lumbered off to hunt. Kyle Le stood and brushed her skirt. Martina brought a moist towel so Kyle Le could freshen herself after Ralph's greeting. They giggled together. I had about decided to make my way to the patient dorm when Hakulupe Le approached. "Dr. Greensboro, may I present Kyle Rula of Arim?"

"Hiki, Kyle Rula," I murmured with an open palm at elbow height. "Melinga."

"Melinga, Sheeks-Cylom. You must excuse Ralph. We were separated for the time of the vaccine task."

"I am glad Ralph has many tribal friends," I said evenly. "Won't you join us for tea?"

"Perhaps on another day. I must greet my Mekucoo sisters."

"Yes, of course. Another time."

She graced me with another moment of her time. "I don't know if people have said, Sheeks-Cylom. Arrivi much appreciate what you have did for the herds. We regret that needless harm came to Edna. We hope she is recovering."

"She's in here."

Hakulupe Le mounted the clinic steps. She turned back with a farewell, and cautiously entered the room of convalescence. Kyle Rula and Kecouroo walked away as though I was of no importance, so I joined Lupe. The clinic smelled of bulrushes, a crisp and acrid mown-grass odor. My neglected experiments gathered dust on the table in the acrylic enclosure. Across the way, Edna idled on the matted nesting and lifted her head at Lupe's entrance. "Ka."

Hakulupe Le hung the udder bags on a peg and soaked a cloth in the water. She sank to her knees beside the patient who was the same color as the nest, and gently placed the wet cloth over Edna's long gash. Glassy-eyed, Edna flicked her tongue to finger Lupe's face and arms.

Orin north? came the question.

"They all safely arrived," Lupe said, "in the north grazeland before the rain. Well, in time, anyhow. No mishaps."

As though her head was too heavy to support, Edna rested it on the greenery. Lupe soaked the cloth again and laid it across Edna's wound before she joined me by the door. "I had no idea her injury was so serious. I mean, there was no complaint."

"She's stronger now. Ralph brings part of the daily kill. We can only wait and see."

"I had no idea," Lupe repeated.

"What's that medicine?"

"Spring water," she shrugged. And while the water lasted, we kept Edna's scar moist with it. Even Ralph slopped his tongue in the water and wetted Edna's side as well as he could.

One cloudy afternoon, Dr. Beecham visited by helicopter and brought Brianna with him. She could not stop chattering about chopper rides and Dr. Mitterand's promise to take her to Earth. I tried to explain, "Softcheeks men can make casual promises they quickly forget."

"Pierre says you are controlling and too focused," she accused sharply.

"Pierre?"

"You did not even know his name. Pierre Arnold Mitterand. And he's going to take me to Earth one day."

"He didn't . . . You did not let him—"

"I am just a little girl, remember?" she angrily shot back.

What was this new attitude? Here was an enemy I had not made. I sent her off to Kecouroo's classroom. Dr. Beecham handed over my samples case that was in shambles.

"It got wet."

"Where was Brianna?"

"Actually, Louise carried it. Fieldwork did not agree with her."

Henry Beecham and I went up to the clinic building where he looked over some patients and asked about new treatments. We passed a classroom on our way to see the new student dorm. Brianna sat in front of the class, relating a story she had learned from Softcheeks. Kecouroo and the students raptly listened. We stopped and eavesdropped a little.

"There was once a young woman," Brianna said, "who suffered under the curse of an angry witch, who felt an affront because of the girl's gentle manner. Although the girl was very beautiful, she had to spend one-half of her day as an ugly old hag. Only at night, separated from the community, could she bathe and dress in her finery and live to her true potential.

"One night a young man happened by and fell in love at first sight with the beautiful girl. He was crestfallen when he learned the following day that she was also an old hag scorned by others and persecuted by schoolchildren. But he loved her and contrived to be with her when he could, day or night. So great was his love that the old witch was moved to forgiveness and lifted part of the curse. The ardent suitor was allowed to choose which half of the day the girl could be herself—either during the daytime when she could interact with her family and his friends, or at night when he would have her to himself."

"I wonder who the young man in this story is," I whispered to Dr. Beecham. "Perhaps Pierre Mitterand."

"I wonder who is the witch," he whispered back.

"The young man," Brianna continued, unaware of us, "thought about the choice and about his chiv-ral-lous love. He selected that she should be beautiful during the day so she could know his friends. The old witch was so moved by his chi-val-ry that she lifted the curse and allowed the young woman to be herself both day and night. So they married and lived happily ever after."

Henry and I moved away from the window. "Perhaps we should have left the Arrivi in their ignorance."

"Too late," he said. "We offered the fruit of the tree of the knowledge of good and evil. Eden will never be the same."

Dr. Beecham sat with Mike and me for tea that we still enjoyed on the clinic verandah. The blue macaws waited on the railing. "Braaadt," one called. They spread their wings and turned their backs as if to allow the sun to spotlight their lush feathers.

"Surely you're not feeding them?" Henry Beecham asked.

"They only visit when Ralph is out hunting," I said. "Has Louise Bilesketchum returned to Cicero?"

He glanced at Mike before he looked away. "To Cylay."

"We can arrange for samples to be sent there," I said, "along with our recorded discussions about culinary use. Perhaps Louise can complete some simple tests. Data could be captured without the need for a walkabout."

"You could move to Cylay," Mike suggested.

"I cannot desert the school or my clinic patients." I turned back to Henry. "That was my lesson from the vaccine trip. Only ambulatory patients come to the clinic. Disabled or chronic patients just tolerate their afflictions until they die. We need to take preventative medicine to the family farms."

"We could not guarantee security."

"Security from what? I experienced no trouble."

"Others are not so self-willed."

"So where is your battery of doctors who sought grant status?" I asked, only a little chiding.

Henry showed me a level look. "Dr. Abercrombie angered the tribes and got himself murdered. Dr. Mitterand suspects he has contracted a native virus. Louise Bilesketchum dislikes the climate."

"Climate, disease, spider bites," I said.

"No glory," Mike added.

"Nobody will commit?"

"You are the only one, Edna Edwina," Mike concluded. "And Henry."

"I'm an old man with few other options," Henry said, his thin hair moving in the breeze. "This is my final professional position."

"Well then, we shall have to put Dolviets on the project," I said. "I can set Brianna to entering the pages in English. We will need fresh samples for tests, though. Oh, I almost forgot. Did any of your hospital researchers take up the study of venom?" Henry shook his head. "How do they treat snakebite at the hospital? Did they wonder about native cures? Did they ask about the custom of drinking urine?"

"The hospital doctors," he tiredly claimed, "have no time for scholarly papers."

I turned to my husband. "Perhaps the Arrivi will agree to gather local snakes and spiders during this season. I could study the venom properties while there are fewer patients."

I turned back to Henry. "Now, about the pox—"

"Well," Mike said as if to close the conversation. He stood and held a hand past the overhang, testing the moist air. "You should go before it rains again."

I walked with Henry Beecham to the waiting chopper. "I am sorry," I offered. "Was I being assertive? You have been a great friend, and I value your guidance."

"The secondary school Hakulupe Le started will be the source of your future assistants, not the hospital. Also, grant funds may dry up, perhaps soon. I hope your Arrivi friends are prepared to take the baton when it's time."

"What is the impediment? Consortium politics?"

"Ask Mike. I have to go."

"Thanks for everything, Henry. Truly, I appreciate all you have done." The chopper blades began rotating. "And visit us often!" I called and backed away. "Whenever you can!"

He only waved as they lifted off and banked left into the mist.

My husband was installing a screen door when I returned to the clinic building. He was like that, always finding new chores, especially when harsh words hung between us.

"What?" I asked at his dark look. "What did I say?"

"You shame him with your energy. Besides, he knows Edwina found the orchid cure. It was Edwina."

I met his level gaze. "To give her credit, I would need to expose her abilities."

"Just the same. Others who follow your path won't make shocking discoveries."

"Is Edwina still angry at me for yelling?"

"You taught her there is no forgiving. She feels as exiled as Karlyhi."

I sighed and moved my shoulder to relax. "I did not mean it. How can I get her back? What do I have that she wants?"

"Just be aware, you make as many enemies as friends."

Dr. Beecham's visit had included the lumber delivery Mike had ordered to complete the new construction. I watched him walk up the path to where workmen waited for instructions. I wondered why he was still here. It was great to have his company, of course, but the helicopter had just left without him. Why did he linger?

Later that day, while Mike worked alongside Arrivi carpenters constructing a brace for the roof of the student dormitory, I sat alone on the clinic verandah. Ralph flashed his tongue and pushed open the new screen door. He paused and considered me with a long stare.

"Hey, Ralph. Perhaps you know how I can make it up to Edwina, huh? You see, sometimes people speak out in anger, but . . . Well, you know." I sighed and sat back with closed eyes. As many enemies as friends, Mike had said. I felt my enemies were former friends.

I began thinking about the grotto, how Edwina and I had gone swimming there one day. How in celebration she had displayed her infant rep colors, cream and vein-blue against the transparent blue water.

But my daydream seemed to include more than my memory. I saw the grotto wall, below and above water, in clear detail. Oxygenated bubbles rose past my face. Then I was swimming through tunneling passageways and viewing underwater structures I could not have known, cave walls populated with long opaque crystals, places I could not have explored because they were too deep. I discerned shapes and distance in blue and red just as though I could see in the dark. Without pressure in my lungs or the cold water on my skin, I soared deeper and farther, gliding through an aquifer alight with silicide crystals and luminous algae.

With a start, I sat up and looked at Ralph. He had sent me the remote viewing, pictures planted in my mind. He tossed that noble head and left to hunt in the sunset hours.

"You are a scoundrel, Ralph," I called after him. "Don't think I did not notice."

The clinic smelled musky and was piled with tracked-in dirt. I sat next to Edna and showed her the scar on my forearm. "Dr. Greensboro has a scar. Edna has a scar. But my other arm is good. My legs are good." I tapped the flat part of my fist against my forehead. "My mind is good. Huh?"

"Ka, ka, ka, ka."

"Edna's hind legs are good, huh? Your tail is good." She flicked her tongue across my face. "Your tongue is just fine," I added.

"Come on, Edna. Let's go outside. The sun is on the verandah. Bask in the sun awhile. Besides, I am tired now of this green color. We need a little variety on your hide. Come on, girl. Come on."

Edna looked at the entrance, and she moved with caution toward the sunlight. When she emerged from the building, the blue macaws cried, "Braaadt," and flew to the catalpa. Soon Edna was basking in the sun with her mouth gaped open and asked, *Edwina?*

"Where is Edwina?" I said. "Is that what you asked? I hurt her feelings on the day you were gored. She won't come in here."

No forgiving? came the thought.

"It was momentary anger. What were you girls doing by the corral, anyway?"

Still angry?

"No, Edna, I just feel bad. It pains me, like a stone on my heart, that you were cut up like that. I feel guilty that Edwina does not understand. Our ways are not your ways. Situations are not black and white with us."

What is black?

"I give up. It's just . . . different for us. We can speak in anger and still love."

Mike had assembled a new sterile research room in the staff dorm and had the dismantled acrylic pieces steamed cleaned. Brianna and I scoured the clinic floor and walls and piled in fresh bedding for Edna. I even fashioned new school wear for Brianna because she was outgrowing her shabby gown. Martina sat in the evening and embellished the bodice and skirt hem with embroidery. I told her that was not necessary, but Martina said she didn't mind. She suggested we order more garments of similar cut so the female students had a school uniform. All tasks were completed, and the damage from the vaccine effort was made right, as best we could manage. I was gripped with the urge to start with research again.

After patient rounds the next day I walked up the path to the staff dorm, just dropping by to see when the new accommodations would be ready. Mike was whitewashing the building side, working quickly to stay in the shade. "The Director of Natural Disaster Control should find a better use for his time."

He ignored me and kept stroking with the big brush. I took a step closer.

"Why are you still here?"

"Nearly finished."

"You know what I mean," I said, maybe a little petulant. "Why are you at the clinic instead of the barracks in Cylay?"

"Cylay is a slum that stinks during the rains."

"It stinks there all the time, I imagine. Aren't you needed for disastrous control?"

He dumped the brush into the bucket and nearly splashed my skirt with his curt gesture. "You're picking a fight. You know that, don't you?"

"I was just wondering … You used all the lumber, and the screens are mounted now. The paint will soon run out. Will you go to Kecouroo's village and whitewash it too?"

Brianna came around the side of the building carrying a heavy bucket of freshly mixed whitewash. She stopped short, perhaps wary of the tension between my husband and me. I met Mike's level gaze for a full minute, then turned on my heel and walked away. Maybe I was picking a fight, but he was hiding something; I just knew it.

Later we sat together on the verandah while Dolvia's two moons hung low in the sky. We had not spoken ten words since tea. Members of a few Arrivi families had gathered around a cooking fire in the yard. Two men sang of their erriv, naming each and listing the heifer's virtues. Then a woman brought laughter when she began with a new ditty.

> Sheeks-Cylom and Dacupitte
> Vaccinate erriv and number Arrivi
> Rabbenu Ely struts and frowns
> But Edna is gored before the rains.
> So much hurt, and mores the pity.

"Should we expect new gualareps soon?" I asked my husband to have something to say.

"Ralph is too young for musk."

"But he is more than age twenty. How long do they live?"

"Nobody knows. Perhaps to a hundred and twenty."

"And Edna is too young for laying eggs?"

"Females can breed any time. The males have a life cycle."

I squinted, trying to understand gualarep behavior. "So he's celibate?"

"He's not in musk. It's like shooting blanks."

"But they're mated?"

"To the exclusion of Edwina, you mean? I doubt it."

After a long moment, I asked, "Why does Ralph like the one Kyle Rula?"

"She lives on the flats of Arim. They share the geysers and pools and the great view."

"You mean they trade mental pictures?" I licked my lips and tasted sage. "Something more interesting than microbes and textbooks."

"You're jealous," he said. "You're never jealous with me, Sheeks-Cylom."

"I'm just surprised Ralph goes to Kyle Rula like a . . . like a student."

Mike considered that for a moment. "He is her student, I guess. A student of seeing."

"I thought Ralph was the gifted one."

"His gift is remote viewing, and the ability seems to grow over this rainy season," Mike said. "But Kyle Rula sees the future."

"Well, I have nothing that competes with seeing the future." I ran my tongue over my teeth and tasted sage again.

When the heaviest of the rains abated, there were no more excuses. Captain Michael Peter Shaw needed to return to his work in Cylay. But first, he solved one last problem for me. I had asked what I possessed to offer Edwina as a peace offering.

The big helicopter waited in the yard. We scrambled on board and secured safety straps. The pilot lifted off and we journeyed over the wet savannah to the south. The chopper sides were open and the blades provided a constant swoop-swoop-swoop rhythm.

"Are you sure this will work?" I asked Mike over the engine noise.

"Just relax and open your mind. The gualarep does all the work."

Beyond the flats of Arim, we approached the shattered butte and facing plateau. The pilot flew over geysers and crystal-clear mineral pools. We buzzed geyserite formations and disturbed the hot springs' steaming mist.

Mike looked out the right side, and I stared out the left. We saw the shallow marshland that was the savannah, with sunlight reflecting on the water under the reeds and wavy grass. We saw below us the transient birds, great flocks of them, their wings spread wide as they effortlessly rode the thermals.

A city of pink flamingoes banked left as a single body. There were yellow herons with black-tipped wings and stark-white egrets. Tiny shimmering blue kikis resembling an oily cloud erratically bobbed after insect swarms.

And parrots! Green and blue parrots, yellow ones with orange breasts. Bright red parrots that lined high branches like stiff tulip buds. Above them all with his daily majestic view, the black Murmurey soared and dipped as though his body followed his thoughts without resistance.

I hoped Edwina was getting all this. I stared and stared. And then came my answer.

Sa-a-a-va-a-a-a-a-na-a-a-a-ah, Edwina sang in my head.

I sat in on Kecouroo's class one day. She wrote algebra equations on the blackboard and encouraged the older barefoot boys and girls to find the value of x. She accepted a crayon drawing from a young Putuki and praised her creativity.

She asked a Cylahi to sit with a younger Arrivi boy and show him how to access the learning menus on the EAM monitor. Once the luminous screen was booted, students turned away from their math exercises. "When you have completed that," Kecouroo said, indicating the equations, "you may investigate the flora and geography EAM choices." The boys frowned and agreed to work on the problems together, excluding the girls who smirked.

On the side blackboard, the week's homilies were lettered by an older girl with good penmanship, part of the curriculum that Hakulupe Le had standardized. They included several well-known Earth sayings:

"A stitch in time saves nine."

"Nothing is good or bad, but thinking makes it so."

"A fool and his money are soon parted."

"The child is father to the man."

"Liberty, fraternity, equality."

"Sufficient onto the day is the evil thereof."

Kecouroo joined me in the back. She wore the necklace of black meteor pieces against a garment of rich suede. "What are those stones?" I asked.

Her hand went to the necklace. "Each person is gifted as Dolvia would have it. Some are limited in areas needed to serve the tribes."

"The necklace says you're limited?"

"These stones boost mental ability for knowing the minds of others."

"For reading minds? You can read Edwina's thoughts?"

"Ah, if only I was as gifted as her."

"Yes, well. For today's problem—" I seldom felt Kecouroo and I communicated freely, not from language differences or from lack of trying, but we were always talking past each other.

"The accounting class schedule," she reported, "has arrived from Dr. Beecham. I fear these lessons are beyond my ability. Perhaps you should find a Softcheeks teacher."

"For a beginning, lessons can be translated into quantities the students can grasp."

"There is no Mekucoo quantity for compound interest."

We smiled together. "I can speak with my husband. Thanks for the suggestion, Kecouroo. Perhaps there's a barracks officer who has been a Dolviet resident long enough to figure out how to transpose the concepts. But I wanted to discuss something more. During this fruitful season, I was hoping to undertake the study of venom. I need a certain number of the most troublesome snakes and spiders. Living specimens."

"Not to bring in here?"

"Well, that's another problem. Perhaps we could have a separate and secure building, something built after Mekucoo tradition."

"Soon you will have a village that rivals Somule."

"Can you get the warriors to help?"

"There is one who some years ago learned much about snakes." She smiled as if she told a private joke. "I can speak with him."

As was the norm with Mekucoo, my request turned into an extended production. One misty morning, Kecouroo and her aunts and female cousins came down the trail carrying loads of cut branches and poles. School was ended for the day. The boys went out to hunt. Girls of all tribes joined the women who used machetes to clear a place about a quarter kilometer up from the clinic buildings. More women arrived, bent under impossibly heavy bundles of handwoven hemp and dry limbs. The sticks tore at their garments. I reached to help an older Mekucoo drop her bundle, but she strong-armed me aside. I stepped back and looked at Kecouroo with question.

"Each must carry her own. It's a statement of place."

"I see. And my place?"

"You are the Sheeks-Cylom."

"But I want to help."

"Your offer diminishes these ones as if they are not competent."

"Fine," I sighed. "Call me when you are ready."

I tried to stay away. During the hot afternoon, while the women sat together and shared their food provisions, I strolled into the clearing. They intently eyed me, even turning to watch me pass. None offered a greeting. Kecouroo left two aunts who appeared to be in charge and joined me.

"Am I being a snoop?" I asked.

"If you were a man, they would have shamed you out of camp." She led me aside to where poles had been secured into the ground to shape a roomy and round enclosure. "Today we will erect the ritual building here."

"Ritual? But I only need a small—"

"Your needs are secondary to a warrior's needs."

"What needs?"

She gestured widely. "A spacious room to display themselves."

"Uh-huh. And when is it no longer unseemly for me to visit?"

"I will send someone."

It was four days. I communicated via EAM with Captain Shaw and Dr. Beecham about my needs and future goals. I received no answers. I was being ignored, an unpleasant sensation. I sorely missed Hakulupe Le who had once shared with me the workings of Arrivi ritual. Kecouroo's few instructions were two-dimensional by comparison.

Each dawn, with bows and murmured hellos, the female students greeted the Mekucoo women when they arrived laden with more building materials. Throughout the day, the women whispered and the young girls giggled while they learned new chants and new skills. Tribal girls valued this time as more precious than their studies, the honor of working alongside Mekucoo.

Finally, I could no longer stand it. One evening, after the aunts and cousins had left, I walked up the rise to where I found a nearly completed round and tall ritual building constructed of branches lashed to vertical poles. The sides were carefully twined to not reach the ground in wattle fence style. It was a substantial structure topped with a thatch roof. An eighteen-inch screened-in gap was under the overhang for ventilation from the interior fires. Two decorated ketiwhelp hides hung near the wide entrance.

I guiltily looked around before I poked my head into the entrance. The interior was quiet with a sanctuary's stillness. Three tiers were dug in a circular communal arena with a central fire. And along the walls were stacks of smallish chicken cages and woven baskets, presumably to hold the captured specimens.

I was about to step inside to further investigate when behind me someone cleared her throat. I quickly turned. Kecouroo stood on the trail with an armload of Mekucoo shields. She dropped them with a clatter and quickly joined me.

"You must not enter."

"But this is for—"

"This is for the men. You will work over there." She led me aside to view a covered arbor that joined a smaller and more open building set off from the trail.

"But … but—"

"You are provided with all that is required. Cara arrives tomorrow."

"But why can't I enter?"

"Your presence spoils the purity."

"Because I am Softcheeks?"

"Because you are female."

"But women built this place. This is impossible, Kecouroo." I heard the whine in my voice, very unbecoming. "I must have access to the specimens."

"You will show Cara. Cara will show the warriors. You will handle no snakes and no spiders."

"But … but—"

"All will be accomplished. It is seen."

I stopped short. "Seen? What is seen?"

Kecouroo thought for a long moment, maybe how to manage this willful student. "There is a place in your religion," she said tolerantly. "Kyle Rula told me. You call it mercy seat."

"Well, yes," I hedged. I felt like a sprig of sage was stuck in my teeth. Kyle Le discussed religion with Kecouroo but not with me. She seldom accepted an invitation from me or extended one. "In Jewish tradition," I said slowly, "mercy seat is a place to commune with God. Very holy and unapproachable."

"And women are not allowed."

"Most people are not allowed. Only the rabbis."

"Who are men."

"Well, yes."

"It is seen; this milking of snakes is a mercy seat for communing between warriors and Softcheeks. Very holy, anticipating om."

"But this is the fruitful season. How can there be an ending?"

"An ending before a new beginning."

I hated riddles. Why couldn't she just say what she wanted like the Arrivi did. "Kecouroo, I know I have not been that studious concerning Dolviet tradition. But I feel I must ask for a better understanding of what will take place here."

"Only what Sheeks-Cylom has requested."

"And what is that?" I pointedly asked.

"A fair trade. Cara will manage the snakes and spiders. You will provide a Softcheeks teacher for accounting courses."

"And what is seen?"

"That Dolvia blesses you."

"Can you be more specific?"

"You ask many questions," she said thinly. "I recommend silence with Cara." She waited with a sly smile and offered, "Kyle Rula gives only the images. We don't add to them."

"What images?"

"This ritual house is the agent of cylay. Many will gather here. We shall gain insight concerning om and how to prepare for the next cycle."

"I still don't understand."

"Who can see with the eyes of Dolvia, huh?"

The next day, I was just completing afternoon patient rounds when Brianna showed herself at the dorm entrance. Martina cleared her throat so I would look up. There was tension in the air. Or rather, a tense anticipation. I took off my plastic gloves and wrote on the patient chart. Martina offered me a shallow dish of oil, indicating I must rub it onto my hands and arms. Brianna placed a laurel twist on my head.

"Should I put on some lip gloss?" I asked, but they only frowned.

Brianna led me up the trail to the ritual hut. She gestured to Kecouroo and stepped back. I reached for Brianna's arm thinking she should remain beside me, but she sidled away. Those of mixed blood must not stand forward on this auspicious day.

Mekucoo shields were displayed in staked rows at the building's entrance. The women stood in groups perhaps twenty paces removed. Each had freshly twisted her hair and wore her best suede garment decorated with beads and gemstones. Young Mekucoo women wore a light dusting of flour on their faces and arms.

The men came walking down the trail just as though it was Monday. They stopped before they reached the women. Each in turn stepped forward with his shield held out. The colorful designs matched the shields by the entrance. The warriors joined the women who were their wives and sisters and aunts and daughters.

An older Mekucoo, wearing a suede tunic similar to Kecouroo's but elegantly decorated, stepped forward from a group of four men. He was tall and striking with golden skin and high cheekbones. His arms and legs bore many scars that were surely battle wounds. He sported a long necklace of polished ketiwhelp claws.

With her head and shoulders bowed and her hand held high with palm upward, Kecouroo met him in the yard. "Siccamawbe, Cara," she said. "Bororfulna."

"Melinga, Kecouroo," he returned.

She led him to me. "Sheeks-Cylom, this is Cara, second to Cyrus."

I had not been schooled in the appropriate greeting. I offered my hand to shake. "Hiki, Cara," I said. "Melinga."

Smile lines showed on his leathery face. His nappy hair was white at the temples. He graciously took my hand for a moment.

"Melinga Sheeks-Cylom," he claimed. "We are glad to know the spirit in your face."

I smiled, but could think of nothing more to say.

"We ask that you sanctify this poor dwelling," Kecouroo added, indicating the ritual building. Cara took a step toward the entrance but turned and looked back at me. His eyes wandered to the scar on my forearm where Pete had sucked out the spider venom. He seemed entertained by something. He strode to the entrance followed by the three elders.

Kecouroo joined me. "Now what?" I asked.

"Now we wait."

We stood in the gathering twilight for perhaps forty minutes. Nobody talked or broke ranks. Finally, one elder stepped out and made a wide gesture in the air. "Hai," the men called. "Hai, hai." The Mekucoo turned away, walking up the trail in jubilant family groups.

"That's it?" I asked Kecouroo.

"We did well. No adjustment is needed."

"A blessing," I dryly added.

She turned to her aunts, ready for the stroll back to their village. "Tomorrow," she said to me as an afterthought, "Cara will arrive at dawn. You should wait there." She pointed at the smaller enclosure.

"Thank you, Kecouroo. And thanks to your aunts."

"This was not done for you."

"Thank you anyhow."

When I returned to my rooms in the staff dorm, I booted the EAM to see if Dr. Beecham or my husband had responded to my messages. Nothing. I was being ignored in all sectors. I was preparing for bed when I realized that I still wore the laurel twist in my hair.

At dawn, I entered the small enclosure. Under the connecting arbor, Cara stood alone without shield, karkar, or necklace of ketiwhelp claws.

"Hiki, Cara," I said with an open palm held high.

He only frowned.

"What is our correct greeting?" I asked. "I know few Mekucoo words."

"Arrivi is adequate."

"And should I bow?"

"I am only an old man, past worrying about."

"A warrior, second to Cyrus."

Cara looked over my head. I turned to see if someone was coming, but there were just the two of us. "Cyrus has robbed the desert of one," Cara said. "Many are gone while I linger here. Dolvia punishes me with Her neglect."

"You mean, that She does not allow you to die?"

"To join my ancestors," he said without expression.

"But you are no older than Haku rabbe Murd."

"Haku too much loves his erriv. He refuses to leave."

I nodded to show I took his words seriously. "Perhaps Dolvia has some great deed in store for you."

"Only this task."

"You would not cause some … slip-up with the snakes to … uh, join your ancestors?"

"What honor in that?"

"Yes, well." I sighed shortly, ready to being. "I have a need for a supply of snakes. Actually, for snake venom taken in sterile conditions for testing to find an anti-venom."

He squinted slightly. "I was told a vaccine."

"Vaccine and anti-venom are different."

"Start with vaccine."

"Ah, by injecting a small quantity of diluted virus with the hypo, we give the body a chance to produce the combatant cells for immunity. So when the real infection comes, the body is prepared to recognize and defeat it."

Cara only stared over my head again.

"Okay," I slowly continued. "Now with anti-venom, we must study the properties of the snake's venom. There are two kinds—hemotoxins and neurotoxins. We must find natural complements that quickly neutralize the toxic effects. Or, at the very least, help the patient recover from the debilitating results."

"Explain neu-ro-tox-ins."

"If I had a specimen, I could cut it open and show you muscles and nerves."

"No specimens."

"Are illustrations adequate?"

"Explain il-lu-stra-tions."

And so went our day. We spent the time seeking dialect equivalents for English technical terms. I showed him the assembled equipment and described each step for milking snake fangs. I cited the need for sterile utensils, controlled conditions, repeated tests, and expected results.

We talked and talked. The men came and went in the yard. Many held up burlap sacks filled with writhing snakes. But Cara was not prepared to begin a procedure until he had a complete understanding of the end results. So we talked.

"For instance," I claimed, "the Southeast Arrivi have a folk remedy for snakebite."

"Their words are not true."

"Their herbs for food and medicine are different," I said. "But they cope with the savannah just like the others."

"They have no true drought. What can they know?"

I nodded again, trying to be collegial.

That afternoon I brought to our discussions a medical book I had inherited from Leslie Abercrombie. I turned the pages to anatomy illustrations. When Cara saw the diagram of muscles in the body, he groaned and stared, grasping their meaning without effort. As a warrior, he must have seen many gaping wounds open to the bone.

I turned to the page that illustrated the alimentary canal and organs for excretion. Cara took the volume from my hand and then fingered his own abdomen while he studied the drawing. With the book in hand, he crossed to the ritual building and did not come back.

What was the solution? I walked down to the classroom building and consulted with Kecouroo. After a short greeting, I asked. "Can your students dissect frogs and render drawings of their organ? Eighth-grade science stuff?"

"Frogs on Dolvia have no venom," she said.

"We are not even at the venom part," I complained.

We walked among the desks to identify which students were prepared for new tasks. One Cylahi boy, the same one who had illustrated the flora encyclopedia, had a talent for rendering. When I looked to Kecouroo for confirmation that he should participate, Brianna glowered at me.

He and two more students soon left the classroom walked up the rise to join the men. They seemed jubilant, maybe to avoid lessons for today. Brianna was still sending me daggers with her eyes.

"What?" I asked Brianna.

"His name is Tom," Brianna said in an angry whisper. "Son of the oldest of Lucy's kids and nephew to Marcy. You did not even know his name."

"I'm not his teacher," I defended. "I'm excluded from the work of the men."

The task was set. Schoolboys labored in the ritual building, making drawings while elders sliced open snakes and frogs for classes on discovery. I loitered in the female enclosure with nothing to do, waiting for Cara to acknowledge my presence. I was told that when Cara saw the drawings the students offered, he only grunted.

One morning, Cara entered the female enclosure with a disagreeable frown. "Why do you refuse?"

"Refuse what?"

"Explain neu-ro-tox-in."

"If I could just have access to a spider specimen."

Cara thought about it and then left. This was getting me nowhere. I went down to the clinic and sat on the verandah near where Edna basked in the early sun. The blue macaws tensely waited on the other railing.

"Edna, would you like to see Hakulupe Le?"

"Ka," she said without closing her mouth to the sun's warming rays.

"I would like to see Lupe," I wistfully claimed.

In my mind's eye, I glimpsed Hakulupe Le teaching a class of eight-year-olds in Somule. Behind her on the blackboard was written the day's homily, "A bird in the hand is worth two in the bush." With reading glasses perched on her nose, Lupe read from a textbook and pointed at an equation written on the chalkboard. I smiled at the image of her daily endeavors.

But then I sat up. "Edna, does Hakulupe Le know you invade her privacy?"

What is pri-va-cy? came the thought.

I was tired of explanations, of remedial lessons on anatomy, of the warriors' exclusion of my female self. "Edna, we are going to Somule. I'll tell Martina."

Lorry? came the question.

"Yes, we can take the lorry. Can you tell Hakulupe Le to expect us?"

"Ka," she said.

I was not sure what that meant. I was too tired for more questions.

On the spur of the moment, Brianna joined us. While I threw some dirt and bulrushes into the truck bed, she put fruit and the canteen on the bench seat. I backed up close to the verandah, and Edna gingerly made the jump across the tailgate, still favoring her scarred side.

Once we got on the road, Brianna seemed excited at the prospect of our spontaneous trip, but she had little to say. I was glad for the break in lessons. In the afternoon, we stopped on the verdant savannah's edge, mostly to keep the lorry from overheating. Edna lumbered out of the dirt-packed truck bed and sidled off into the underbrush.

When she returned, Edwina was with her. I sat on the ground, and Edwina climbed over my lap, rubbing me with her flanks. She wet my face and arms with her tongue.

"I am glad to see you, too," I said with truth.

Forgiven? Edna wanted to know.

Clean slate, Edwina returned.

I was thankful she could be so generous. I stroked her neck while she cooed, giving off that rich calming sensation. "How did you girls find each other in the razor grass?"

They cocked their heads and stared with those unblinking eyes. What did it matter, huh? I stood and brushed the back of my skirt. Brianna gestured that my face was streaked from Edwina's tongue. She wet a cloth from the canteen, and I washed my face and arms.

"Can you both crowd into the back?" I asked the girls. "Ka, ka, ka, ka," Edna said.

"That's not the answer to everything, you know."

Meet you there, Edwina said.

"Thank you, Edwina." I climbed behind the steering wheel while Brianna secured the tailgate. "We'll see you at Haku rabbe Murd's house."

And with that the girls were gone. The underbrush trembled for a few moments. With angry cries, a gaggle of startled egrets rose into the air. The cranes rose next, followed by hundreds of flamingoes, and so forth. We knew the exact route the girls were taking, moving fast. Brianna laughed until her sides hurt.

In late afternoon we approached Somule, but the drive was rough going. The deeply rutted road was packed with military trucks and jeeps hemmed in by vegetation and laboring men. Consortium soldiers wore green and brown fatigues and blue tams that designated they were peacekeeping. Recruited from many Westend planets, they were mostly olive-skinned men of stocky build, competent and intent on the task. They only glanced at the lorry. Some noticed Brianna and stared.

I called out to an officer to inquire. He explained that the Consortium undertook routine maneuvers called war games, except there was nothing routine nor entertaining about the melee. I pulled the lorry into line with a column of trucks. We inched along. Brianna offered to go ahead on foot, or show me a nearby turn-off to Haku rabbe Murd's land. I was uncertain how soggy the cross-country adventure would be, or if the lorry would become a shooting target.

The column veered right before it reached town. I drove on the road's shoulder for a couple hundred meters and then broke free and sped into Somule that was full of soldiers. Some were loading provisions, and some stood guard. Others looked to be on furlough.

I drove to the unused doctor's office that was an extension of the hospital, thinking we could have some peace there. But the rooms had been opened by the landlord and served as a makeshift office by supply officers. I parked in the back.

When we entered the office bustle, a Lieutenant Manenowski recognized me. "Dr. Greensboro?" he said. "You should have notified us you were coming."

"I did not know you were coming."

"Captain Shaw has a room at the hotel, if you want to use that."

"And where is the captain now?"

"I have been expecting him for—" Lt. Manenowski looked at his wristwatch. "Maybe two hours." The watch was an affectation since nothing got done on Dolvia according to a timetable.

"You can tell him we're at the hotel," I said. "Oh, and I parked the lorry in the back. I expect to find it there."

"I can post a guard."

"Thank you, Lieutenant Manenowski."

Brianna and I struggled through the street crowd. "I will join Hakulupe Le at the school," she offered.

"Come by the hotel later for tea. See you there."

She waved and headed off the other way. I ducked into the tall hotel where many squads of soldiers crowded the lobby and hotel bar. I approached the desk to request a room key. The Putuki attendant was harried and uncaring. When I said I did not know which room it was, he scowled, irritated that he had to look up Captain Shaw's room number.

I took the elevator to the seventh floor, looking forward to a shower and some quiet. I put the key into the lock, and the door swung open. I was greeted with a musty odor.

The curtains were drawn, and the lights were down. The bedcovers were rumpled, and clothes were strewn on the floor. Seated on the bed and dressed only in a cotton slip was Louise Bilesketchum, her unkempt hair down to her shoulders. Her bare feet under the fleshy white legs were placed wide apart on the floor.

Nonplused, she stared at me.

"I am sorry," I murmured. "I must have the wrong key." I started to back out and close the door.

Behind Louise, someone sat up in the bed, groggily running a hand through his hair. It was my husband, bare-chested and squinting at the light from the hallway. He saw me, and that it was me. Mike's shoulders slumped, and he looked away.

I gently closed the door and went down the service stairs. They led to a building exit and into an alley connected to the doctor's office alley. I breathed in big gulps tasting almonds and the dust-filled air. I walked quickly with my head down, not wanting to draw attention. No contact with others was my greatest wish. Just … just nothing.

I scurried to the lorry and took the driver's seat. With an image in my head of Brianna's confusion when she found that the lorry was gone, I drove out of town without regard to roads and crowds and angry shouts.

I drove toward the flats of Arim, skirting the guard barricades and splashing mud from the shoulder of the road. Consortium soldiers shouted and waved their arms that I must stay out of the area. I broke free of the military congestion, gunned the lorry's engine, and sped into the underbrush. The wheels caught on some encumbrance. The lorry flipped over. I was thrown free of the vehicle and onto the wet ground, banging my knees and shoulder. I hit my head hard, and a strange aching sensation filled my sinuses before all went black.

PART TWO

Siibabean are tall and mad
And murder without qualms
Against their number a warrior fights
And thus a man becomes
Their only good: they die.

EIGHT

from Dr. Henry Beecham

HENRY BEECHAM HERE. I KNEW LT. MIKE SHAW AS THE CONSOR-
tium officer who had invited us to Somule for a fact-finding tour.
The drug trafficking charges warranted the trip. Our travel preparations were in place when we heard about Abercrombie's assassination. Dr. Mitterand and I had papers for inoculation and steroids
needed to build stamina, so we decided to take an earlier shuttle
that went first to the transport that orbited Dolvia. Carrying our
luggage, we followed the crowd of passengers into midship. "Dr.
Beecham," Colonel Hartley said while we shook hands. "If you can
spare a few moments."

"We're just making connections," I said. "The shuttle leaves for
Dolvia in the next watch." In Westend even a senior citizen like
myself found executive duty. I was first stationed at the biosphere

on Cicero as a general practitioner giving seminars on race diversity, but opportunities had developed from there.

"We know," Hartley said and glanced around the open concourse. "Just a briefing on what to expect in Somule." Hartley was a big fellow with a square jaw. As part of the old guard, he had a working knowledge of Arrivi politics from way back, albeit an outsider's.

"This Dr. Pierre Mitterand," I said indicating my companion. "He will complete a doctor's rotation at the hospital." A delightful fellow, full of humor and energy, Pierre had recently come through the wormhole and had not shed his Earth ways. At the Cicero biosphere he had assisted with a virus-barrier project. His quick insights contrasted to local leaders who were still learning skills for bulk purchasing, just-in-time delivery, and accrual accounting.

They shook hands, and Colonel Hartley led us into the Consortium section of the three-part transport and to a crew lunchroom. He motioned to offer refreshments. I shook my head slightly and sat in one of the molded chairs. Dr. Mitterand went to the coffee dispenser and looked at its operation before he made a selection.

"What are we to think?" I said. "Lt. Shaw is a demoted Consortium officer, and his complaint against the hospital included native claims worded in angry rhetoric."

Hartley crossed his arms and rested his bum on the table. "I believe Mike Shaw," he said, "if that is what you're wondering. He has a black mark on his record from Cicero. But read his dossier and consider who charged him."

Dr. Mitterand joined us but didn't sit, slurping hot liquid from a plastic cup.

"Shaw is a straight talker," Hartley added. "I would be glad to find him at my back in a firefight."

"I read the academy application's executive review, but not much more," I said. "Dr. Mitterand noticed the cure."

"What cure?" Colonel Hartley said.

"The orchid cure," Pierre Mitterand said. "It was like being punched in the chest. I sat up and read it over and over. Teenage students had tested a common orchid for a cure to throat rash and stumbled across a compound effective against erriv catarrh boils."

Hartley squinted with his mouth open.

"Pierre's specialty is infectious diseases," I said. "Another doctor may not have recognized what he saw on the page."

"But it was Dr. Greensboro's research, right?" Hartley said.

Mitterand shrugged. "We assume so." He sipped again making a slurping sound.

Colonel Hartley nodded with a knowing look and switched to the matter at hand. "Now, on Dolvia you will find Frank Duerr, the Somule magistrate. I can send letters of introduction. The ones to watch are the colonists' kids and their businesses. Joey Osborn's sister Carline and that whole bunch. They muscled in to turn a buck using their import/export licenses. There's nothing wrong with turning a profit, except they don't respect tribal rights."

We talked about expectations until Pierre's wristwatch made a beeping sound. The shuttle was accepting passengers. Colonel Hartley stayed with us while we queued up for the shuttle connection. Dr. Mitterand was rifling through his case for some missing item. "Mike Shaw knew Cyrus, you know," Hartley said as if filling the idle time with chatter. "The famous Mekucoo warrior. Mike claimed that he saw Cyrus die. He had piloted a chopper evacuating some Arrivi families. Women and children were struggling toward the landing place, but the Siibabean were about to overtake them. On the ground, Cyrus shouted a challenge and held his karkar over his head.

"Any Siibabean who killed him," Hartley said, warming to his story, "would get the tribal glory. Cyrus fought the Siibabean hand-to-hand with knives. Munitions must have been depleted."

He showed me a friendly smile. Maybe this was daily fare for military talk.

"After the families were loaded, Mike Shaw circled back in the chopper. He had to see." Hartley continued. "Cyrus was crumpled on the exposed rise. Eight dead Siibabean were around him, and more were limping away. The rescued Arrivi families were crying, but they had survived."

"Why are you telling me this story?"

"You will encounter tribal logic soon. Be prepared for how they reason."

Tribal logic. Huh, an interesting phrase. "I wish we had more time together," I said. "Our schedule is rushed. Maybe another time."

Pierre waved to Hartley's family who stood behind the loading barrier.

The shuttle landed in Cylay, and we were slated to take the train to Somule the following day. The oppressive air turned my legs to water. The short walk to the Cylay hotel was a struggle. Mitterand mopped his brow and tried to remain upbeat. We didn't bother to meet in the hotel bar, taking our meals separately. I sat before the room's blower in my shorts, just hoping I wouldn't embarrass myself the next day.

For the train ride to Somule, from a private compartment I watched the dry savannah pass our view. The red sand rich in iron was punctuated by clusters of oleastra in the shade of tall thorn trees. Pierre ignored the natural beauty and smoked a slender cigarette, which appeared wicked. Most Consortium officers did not smoke, and Dolviets preferred kari root cigarettes. "From Cicero," Pierre claimed when he saw me staring. I could easily see the long and uniform white stems were a contraband Earth brand.

Pierre smiled with eyes twinkling. "A young man's wife was experiencing chest pains, so he took her to the doctor who did a thorough exam. The doctor joined him for consultation and said, 'Your wife has acute angina.' The man said, 'I know, doc, but what's wrong with her?'"

Heh, heh, that's a good one, huh?

Joey Osborn was waiting at the Somule hotel, and was invited into my suite where the blower was turned on high. "How are your land legs, Dr. Beecham?" he asked while I grabbed my breath. "Dr. Greensboro is at the courthouse."

Frank Duerr had filed a complaint against Dr. Greensboro, something about how she had made him lose face. Pierre and I each took an acclimation pill before we crossed to the courthouse, eager to avoid a day trip into the oppressive bush to interview Dr. Greensboro. She waited in the torrid courthouse like an immigrant, submissive and uncertain. She used native greetings with an open palm held high.

When Pierre confronted her with the application pages, she only shrugged. "The students were fooling around with the EAM. I should discipline them." She saw our blank stares and added in an assertive tone, "The orchid drawing is eye catching, that's all."

Pierre and I looked at each other. Finally, I was able to speak. "Would you care to have dinner with us at the hotel? It could prove worth your time."

We agreed hastily before she was called back into the courtroom.

That afternoon I also met with Hakulupe Le who had submitted the grant proposal for the Dolviet academy. She arrived at the hotel wearing an Arrivi skirt and paneled tunic, but without adornment and without escort. I was immediately taken with her forest-green eyes against olive skin. "We are interested in grant funds for the academy," she said straight out after we sat in the lobby, "which you are empowered to release, Dr. Beecham."

Arrivi seemed brusque and grasping at first encounter. Their system of indebtedness meant that it was better to say what was needed than to describe what was offered in barter, as part of tribal logic. "You have begun a study of local plants that interests my associate," I returned, also trying to be gracious.

We discussed plans for an academy curriculum. Hakulupe Le struggled with my poor Arrivi, and many technical terms did not translate. I sat back wondering how to find common ground. "Don't your storytellers," I asked gently, "repeat old stories during tribal chants at family campfires?"

"The warrior adds his experience with new verses," she agreed.

"Perhaps he changes the verses. Events get lost from poor memory or from jealousy."

"The telling by this man on this night delights the young people."

"But for information separate from tribal history," I said, "such as the position of the lungs and heart in the chest. These facts never change, and can be taught by anybody."

"Nothing is separate. Only Softcheeks see these separations."

"A quantified matrix allows for standardized repetition."

Hakulupe Le frowned and lowered her eyes. I stopped, frustrated with the pompous-sounding English phrases. "Each student," I said more slowly, "will receive the same lesson on the same day. In Somule and Cylay as well as at the bush clinic. You can feel confident about what they learn."

"Students will embrace Softcheeks ideas and talk back to warriors."

"Did you get this from Dr. Greensboro?"

"What does Sheeks-Cylom know about children?"

We agreed on elementary-level competency standards, in principle at least. Each lesson Kecouroo and Martina taught was to be recorded and printed in textbooks for the Somule classroom. We wanted lessons in math, horticulture, and hygiene. We talked about including campfire chants so that the tales of Oria and Cyrus became tribal canon.

After an hour we stood and she waited with those bright eyes downcast. I only hoped she was competent to implement our goals. Just then Lt. Shaw joined us wearing a brown work uniform that was open at his collar. "Hiki, Hakulupe Le," he said.

"Melinga," she said with a palm held high.

"Where is your escort?"

"No need for you to worry," she said.

"I can provide some–"

"No need, Lieutenant Shaw. Melinga."

Hakulupe Le left and I went into the hotel bar with Lt. Shaw who I took to be a drinker. We had Kiam gin with ice. The drink was harsh and probably interacted with the effects of the acclimation pill. "Soldiers here avoid blue," Mike Shaw said when he caught me staring. "Dolvia's personal color. Blue tams for the peacekeepers are objects of tribal scorn, for example.

"It was Karlyhi who killed Leslie Abercrombie," he added as his report. "I don't think Dr. Greensboro knows. He lives at her bush clinic."

"A tribal kid? We should start an inquiry."

"Abercrombie was abusing Cylahi nurses," Shaw hedged. "A public inquiry may bring media attention and elevate the smuggling to a Consortium incident. Do you want that, Dr. Beecham?"

I wondered if he was threatening me. Lt. Shaw tended to see corruption everywhere, though. His family on Cicero had been sacrificed to events from a government corruption investigation. A house fire caused by a leaky gas line was the report. His wife and daughter were lost. What faith could Mike Shaw have in a Consortium decision secured among officers who undercut their own?

The hospital site where Abercrombie had once ruled was pleasant enough, situated on a bluff looking toward the sunset. Dolvia's two moons hovered over the savannah like uneven headlights. Clouds moved down from the high Siibabean forest to form a thick mist most mornings, but the rains were not anticipated until another turn of Nettom, as the Arrivi said. Most of the hospital construction was completed. Abercrombie's vanity had been indulged by way of his office and private rooms there. Pierre moved into the apartment, and I took over the book-lined administrative office just down the hall from reception.

There was a learning curve for patient rounds, of course. Mothers held no trust for Softcheeks cures, and my attempts to explain positive outcomes were hampered by dialect differences. I shook my head often when I watched the tension. I had to wait for patients to accept my touch. I had to give instructions to the Cylahi nurses instead of addressing the patient's fears. I had to step back with using medical terms. "Give me that curved one," was a better instruction during surgery. My lectures for new arrivals on sensitivity to native methods, from my time on Cicero, now felt like I had been chewing dung.

Dr. Mitterand had an easier time of it for working through the tribal differences. The women especially seemed eager to meet his needs. I didn't begrudge him that appeal, though. We used the tools at hand.

Dr. Greensboro visited the hospital to arrange a cataract operation for Haku rabbe Murd, an aging Arrivi of some property. She was unconcerned with events beyond her clinic and academy. She was one of those intellectuals who pursued an idea until a stable process was implemented, then abandoned the project for the next interesting concept. She was disinterested in discussing academy curriculum refinements, pushing that task onto her clinic school teachers Kecouroo and Martina.

We spent time in my hospital office. Dr. Mitterand poured brandy from a flask into his teacup. He offered Dr. Greensboro a taste, but she only smiled and shook her head. "I talked with Hakulupe Le," I said. "I was able to secure some curriculum standards, but she misunderstood my ideas about small business accounting."

"Why don't you download secondary textbooks and translate them into the dialects?" Dr. Greensboro asked. "I mean, two plus two still equals four, even in Westend. The sum of the square of the triangle's two sides still equals the . . . whatever it is. The long side."

"The hypotenuse," Pierre said.

"That must be a French word."

"You know it's Greek."

"But that's the crux of it," I said. "There is no term in Arrivi for hypotenuse. Perhaps you could undertake to develop an Arrivi-to-English dictionary, and then add English technical terms with no Arrivi equivalents. I could get extra funding for Cylay classrooms."

"For you, Dr. Beecham, anything."

"How did the cataract operation go?" Pierre asked.

"So hard to get the Arrivi to agree to treatment," she complained. "We should test their solutions for ailments."

"They have no remedy for cataracts," Pierre said.

"They have netta and a native insect repellent. I'm confident we can learn from them." And then she was onto something else.

Later Dr. Greensboro spoke kindly to the recovering cataract patient and showed an open palm to his wife. "If you return on another day," she said, "we can fix the right eye."

"My husband has said he is content with the current blessing," the stout woman said. "We thank the Sheeks-Cylom."

Dr. Greensboro returned to her clinic then, accompanied by two lorries loaded with supplies. While we watched her drive away, Pierre said, "Siibabean tell a story about how Sheeks-Cylom gave fangs to salamanders and entered the monster's body in the deep night."

"How did that story get started?"

Pierre smiled. "Does she suspect what her new husband has become in Cylay?"

"Perhaps she holds onto what she would like him to become."

"Pity," Pierre said and returned to his hospital rounds.

Pierre found time to prepare the tests that Dr. Greensboro had ordered and listed his name along with hers on the title page for the growing journal of native remedies. Pierre came from a famous professional family on Earth. He had his reputation in mind.

I made several trips to Cylay to shore up Consortium support for the hospital and the academy. Perhaps the old quarter of Cylay had been a pleasant burg once, with three or five-story brick houses with square walls. The red brick streets were barely wide enough for two passing pedestrians. The business district had amber streetlights and musky hotels with Earth-replica saloons.

Surrounding that eight-block warehouse sector by the Iamida River was a squalid slum with no electric lights and no sewer. Displaced tribespeople, uncounted and untaxed, put pressure on the local government's limited resources. Residents in Cylay resisted the concept of revenue collected for social services. And personal income tax was widely regarded as a Softcheeks evil. The city was a slum, and would not grow into a business center for many more seasons.

So one day I visited the Consortium military compound laid out in orderly fashion that was the same as on Cicero. I joined Mike Shaw in the wide and noisy hangar that served as a motor pool. After testimony about his role in exposing the smuggling operation, he had been promoted to captain and a new position as Director of Natural Disaster Control.

"I have been invited to dinner tonight," I began. "Care to join me?"

"At Carline Bryant's place?"

"Ah, yes. You know about it?"

"Duerr and Gotskind will be there," he said. "There's no other game in town."

Captain Shaw used an open jeep, probably Company surplus, to pick me up at the hotel for a ride to dinner at Carline's house. Carline Bryant was Joey Osborn's sister and the social center of the cartel that Colonel Hartley disliked. Carline had married a colonist's son, Sean Bryant, and was on good terms with his four brothers. They comprised a formidable commerce block, the cartel's core. The Bryant families lived in clapboard row houses stuffed with imported goods of all kinds: ornate furniture and anomalous statuary, some crystal and flatware, and Earth gallery paintings of a different tradition.

Three Consortium Hardhands held power in the provisional government established during the tribal wars. One was Frank Duerr, who had lodged the complaint against Dr. Greensboro. His associate Brent Gotskind displayed a classical education and a penchant for balance. Gotskind was balding and not remarkable by any measure, and was concerned about substandard Dolviet skills for industry jobs. Steve Swanweil was younger, dark and brooding. An adventurer. I did not expect to find him in this same line of work five years hence.

Sean Bryant greeted us at the door with congratulations to Captain Shaw about his marriage to Dr. Greensboro. I castigated myself for ignoring that social duty, not that I had been invited to the wedding. Mike grinned a lot with this group, eager to hear about their business triumphs. To me, it felt odd to dine with Cylay's civil authorities and business leaders and see no tribal faces at the table.

Sean Bryant was a little guy and tended to stay in the background while Carline managed the social events. After we were seated, I asked, "Will Steve Swanweil be joining us tonight?"

"Oh, he is out on the savannah," Carline Bryant said. "Richer pickings." I was unsure of her meaning, but I detected a certain bitterness. Carline was not a beauty, but she was queen bee. She had a couple too many that night and put it to me directly.

"We were held as conscript, Joey and me," Carline said while we were all seated, "after Company Blackshirts gang-raped and murdered my father. Us kids were nothing to them, just meat. Things were done. I swore my life would never be like that again. I swore that when I got out of that hellhole, I would make it so I was beholden to nobody. Never again." She sipped from her cordial glass, her face flushed in the amber light.

"The very worst is to be uncovered," she said with a slur. "That's the worst."

"The Company has no savannah investment," I said.

"You think the tribes are so much better? Ha!" Carline waited for a servant to fill her glass again. "They don't even save their own. Rabbenu Ely's wife, Marcy? She was abandoned along with seventeen other toddlers when their mothers died of dysentery. Did the tribes come to her aid? No. It was a Softcheeks, Lucy Kempler. Then when Lucy died, those Cylahi kids were no more than age twelve. Who helped them then? They gained a place through suicide missions for Mula."

She drank deeply and licked her lips. "You think the tribes would fight alongside colonists in a crisis? Ha! You have to secure your own way in Westend. That's just how it is. Don't expect nothing, 'cause it won't be there when you need it."

Coffee was poured by Putuki servants. "Dr. Beecham," Mr. Gotskind said, "while you are in Cylay, perhaps you can review our rice farming venture with the Southeast Arrivi."

"Rice is a water-intensive crop," Mike Shaw said.

"A fast-growing crop," Gotskind agreed, "ideal for their rain-flooded fields and length of season. We have one village engaged now, waiting for the rains to start."

"The savannah has cycles as a desert," Mike nearly whispered, "perhaps in less than seven years. What will Dolviets do when your cash crop fails?"

"What did they ever do?" Frank Duerr replied.

"I worked with relief organizations in the sub-Sahara," I said. "The few permanent improvements were the ones suggested by people who lived on the land."

"We're offering Arrivi a way to get ahead," Brent buoyantly insisted. "To store a little something extra. What's wrong with that?"

"You're offering them," Mike returned, "an untested alternate farming method that reshapes the land's contour."

Frank Duerr sipped from his cup, careful to hide his true opinion of Captain Shaw.

"The rabbenu structure," I offered, "could create an farming fund to subsidize tribal suggestions that pay real dividends like clearing obstructions from a ruined well."

"We don't have time to hear their small complaints," Frank said.

"At least put Dolviets in charge of administration," Mike said.

"That only leads to graft."

"The graft I have seen has not been from the tribes," Mike countered. Frank Duerr considered him with an arched eyebrow.

"You could create small loan groups," I added, "wherein each borrower is a guarantor for the others. They would lose face within the tribe by defaulting. That becomes their incentive."

Gotskind nodded, glad to expound his pet project. "I have discussed these very concepts with Putuki tribesmen. But they have little understanding of delayed returns or repayment with interest. We would never see that money again."

"They don't even market erriv," Frank added. "Or sell the milk."

"On the land of Murd," Mike claimed, "erriv are like family members. It's considered unmanly to exploit the birthing heifers by stealing their bounty."

"They don't have a proper slaughterhouse," Frank said. "Or a set rate of exchange."

"A man's wealth," Mike explained in whole tones, "is measured by the erriv he has, not by those he has just sold."

After we returned to the hotel, I was astonished a second time at Lieutenant Shaw's duplicity. We were greeted in the lobby by Louise Bilesketchum, a grant recipient and author of a poorly worded thesis on native diet strategies for gathering wild fruits, olives, and nuts. Louise was a big German woman with pleasing features that tended toward plump. She had a disconcerting laugh. But then, I'm an old man. These adventuring women made me uncomfortable. They were unmarriageable back home and immigrated to Westend where the men-to-women ratio tilted in their favor.

Mike Shaw liked Louise. They entered the hotel bar and sat with their heads together. She put a hand on Mike's arm while he intently listened to her words. It was none of my business, of course. I shrugged and went to my suite. I did not want to know what happened next.

I worried again about Captain Shaw's motives when we toured the Southeast Arrivi and their new cash crop venture with Brent Gotskind. Tribal kids gathered around the landed helicopter and stared. Some touched Captain Shaw's brown uniform. Mike was teasing with the kids. He performed that trick where you pull a coin from behind somebody's ear.

In anticipation of the rainy season, several fertile fields had been converted to rice paddies with ridged embankments and managed irrigation. The local rabbenu bowed and proudly indicated his assembled family labor force, eager for the benefits of Hardhand farming methods. The shy women pulled their shawls in front of their chins and whispered together. A few wore full body burkas.

Captain Shaw waited by the helicopter, ready to ferry Brent Gotskind and me back to Cylay. While Gotskind conducted his goodbyes, Mike frowned. "I hate to see this. Why do they turn over their futures to this misguided man?"

"It could work out," I said hopefully. "The season's length, the volume of rainfall."

"By the next season of om, this whole clan will be working in Cylay factories for slave wages. Mark my words."

"You could speak out to prevent that."

"And risk a house fire?" He met my look. "Gotskind and Duerr are not exceptional men. Their kind lives everywhere."

Dr. Mitterand, consulting with a biosphere clinical laboratory on Cicero, succeeded in manufacturing a quantity of the catarrh vaccine. Our plans were set. As administrator of the Consortium mandate, my intent was to travel with the tribal group. Dr. Mitterand would travel with the second detachment to inoculate erriv before the herd drive to higher grazing land.

Time was short. Pierre and I took the train to Somule where, to my surprise, Steve Swanweil was already sitting in the Executive Club with Joey Osborn. "Mr. Swanweil," I said and shook hands. "We met in Cylay." He wore a business suit with his hair slicked back, a younger man who I took for an opportunist.

"Dr. Beecham. Dr. Mitterand. A pleasure."

After we ordered drinks, Joey offered, "Steve and I were just discussing the market possibilities for the new vaccine. With Consortium health code approval, we could penetrate markets on Cicero, on—"

"Who is we?"

"The Westend division of a pharmaceutical concern," Swanweil said through his apparent apathy.

"The vaccine is not approved," I said. "Field tests are not completed."

"Not today, perhaps," Swanweil added.

"So you want access to our test results," I postulated, "after the erriv are vaccinated?"

"The Consortium," Swanweil said, "does not have the deep pockets needed for medical advances. The tribes don't have the distribution channels. My people can secure the capital and guarantee the end-use market."

"You and the Bryants?" Dr. Mitterand asked, just to be sure.

Swanweil leaned forward, his dark eyes flashing. "Think of the potential for return. You will receive points. A good deal all around."

Dr. Mitterand nudged my arm while he showed Swanweil an urbane smile matching his own. "We can give it some thought," I said dryly.

It seemed that everybody wanted a bite out of the vaccine apple. The following day, I traveled with Joey Osborn and Swanweil to the butte below the flats of Arim, my first venture onto the plain. The dry expanse seemed unfruitful in all ways. We did see one geyser shoot up near a stand of bare acacia trees. "The holy woman said we'll have a big-wet season," Joey said while he managed the ECCAV. "They can tell by monitoring the geyser activity."

In the shadow of the butte, an open tent had been erected for no apparent purpose. Rabbenu Ely met with us there in the sweltering heat. Joey sat at my elbow to translate any terms I didn't catch. While the formal meeting dragged on, I admitted to myself that I disliked being point man for any endeavor backed by the Bryants, rice farming included.

These former colonists claimed to improve Dolviet living standards, when in fact they intended profiteering from uneven offworld exchange rates. While we sat in the torrid tent, for example, Steve Swanweil made no offer to Rabbenu Ely for points on the deal. His stated appeal centered on humanitarian goals.

"We can be instrumental," Swanweil said with an expansive gesture, "in providing the vaccine serum during the next cycle, after these Softcheeks doctors have returned to their families on Earth."

Seated in a cane chair under the tent's shade, Ely stoically listened. I knew his reputation as a leader in a former conflict where a refinery had collapsed during an earthquake. Ely wore a business suit, which felt in conflict with the staged native setting. His seconds stood behind, all dressed in Arrivi pantaloons and tunics. Rabbenu Ely did not seek their counsel. Instead he addressed me. "Is Sheeks-Cylom involved?"

"I'm going next to the clinic," I said. "But I'm confident that Dr. Greensboro is agreeable. Dr. Mitterand and I will each take a team to visit savannah families and inoculate erriv. All must be accomplished before the rains."

"I will go to the clinic also," Rabbenu Ely said.

"That's not necessary."

"Your field tests are for erriv. That is true?"

"Well, yes. Of course, you are welcome."

Rabbenu Ely stood, so we all stood and shook hands. I was surprised at his use of the Softcheeks gesture. "I know transport protocol," Ely claimed. "I was an exchange student there."

Dr. Mitterand and Steve Swanweil remained at the Somule hotel. Joey Osborn and I, along with Rabbenu Ely and his wife Marcy, caught a chopper ride to the bush clinic with Captain Shaw. A second chopper with a peacekeeping detachment accompanied us.

What a painful event that was. Captain Shaw took a passive role with his Consortium group. Anyone watching wouldn't even know he was married to the bush clinic doctor. The event started with a beating in the yard of a young Arrivi who had learned some English phrases. Rabbenu Ely held an ad hoc tribal meeting by the communal campfire. Each person spoke, even Hakulupe Le. But Ely's word was law. I would not travel to meet Arrivi families. Dr. Mitterand would not take a second group onto the savannah in a race against time. Only Sheeks-Cylom would be honored to know savannah families and their erriv.

Dr. Greensboro's grant was Earth-based and independent of the Consortium mandate. Her field test results were not for Westend publication, nor available to the Bryant cartel. Steve Swanweil's group would have to pay a premium for use of the eventual patented rights to gain the distribution monopoly for Westend. As I puzzled them out, all the undercurrents, I came to realize that Rabbenu Ely's move to place responsibility on Sheeks-Cylom had stopped the Hardhand cartel cold in their tracks.

But then! Amazingly, Captain Shaw claimed that the linchpin for erriv drive was the Arrivi orphan who had just been beaten. How could that be? Dr. Greensboro seemed to agree.

What did I know? I was mostly saddened that she would need to travel the heated savannah to fulfill a grueling task that I had wondered if Dr. Mitterand and I could accomplish by working together.

Back in Cylay, I kept an appointment with Sean Bryant at his business. Situated in a low adobe building that fronted their brick warehouses, the Bryant Inc. offices were cool and bright with overhead fans and blowing air conditioners. Sean Bryant greeted me in the spacious lobby and introduced his two brothers, carbon copies of himself, Daniel and Patrick. He ushered me into his spacious office, and we sat in cane chairs with overstuffed cushions.

Sean got right down to business. "Is there a way to leverage the brand name and distribution of the erriv vaccine?"

I drew in my breath. His naked avarice was forthright. "You're in talks with Steven Swanweil?"

"We have interests with Swanweil," Sean Bryant said, "and some offworld financiers to improve conditions for the tribes."

I nodded, choosing to keep my words neutral. "Bush clinic funds originate with a Softcheeks grant that's separate from the Consortium mandate," I said. "There's no exposure for the patent. I'm afraid her work and published results are untouchable."

"Dr. Mitterand's name is on the research paper."

"But the research funds, and therefore the patent, belong to her." I sat back with a wide grin. Dolvia blessed the Sheeks-Cylom, with a little help from Rabbenu Ely.

The Bryants did not pause to lick their wounds. Sean was onto something new. "We have been in touch with Colonel Hartley on the transport," he said. "He reports that the Company has reopened trade relations with the Consortium. New personnel will arrive through the wormhole."

"The Company?"

"They never relinquished trade route advantages at Stargate Junction, perhaps you knew. They want to consolidate trade at this end. They're sending an advance guard under the command of a Tuang Cho. They have plans for high-tech satellites connected through our EAM system. One array to orbit Cicero and one to orbit Dolvia."

"Why Dolvia?"

"The Company has been in negotiations with some city-states beyond the savannah. Basically, the Company is back."

"And what do you want from me?" I asked.

"We must present a united front. They will use any opening."

"I have no businesses here, just a professional position."

"You think your executive position is secure?" Sean Bryant said with sudden anger. "Nothing is secure. Men from the Company are not above using prison and torture, any method to consolidate their position."

"I will take extra precautions at the hospital. Thanks for the heads-up."

He leaned across the desk, his dark eyes flashing with anger. "Ship nothing except through a secure channel. We can help." He paused, holding his avarice in check for the moment. "You will return for our help," he added with a turned-down mouth.

"I trust I will be welcome on that day." I stood and offered to shake hands.

I went directly to the Consortium base in Cylay and asked around for Captain Shaw. A young lieutenant directed me to the hangars used to protect the helicopters. He saw my uncertainty and offered a ride in his jeep, holding up two manila envelopes. "I need to deliver these out that way. Hop in."

His name was Lt. Manenowski, a burly little guy with big paws for hands and a quick grin. He parked the jeep and accompanied me into a hangar where polished helicopters were maintained by Putuki noncoms.

Captain Shaw had his sleeves rolled up and his arms deep in the engine of a military truck. Another soldier was flat on his back under the chassis. They called instructions to each other. This was a common endeavor in the absence of spare parts. Captain Shaw turned at our arrival. He lightly kicked the soldier's foot, wiping his hands on an oily cloth.

Lt. Manenowski snapped to attention and saluted. "Sir, this civilian was on the grounds and requested to talk with you."

"At ease, Billy. This is Dr. Beecham who runs the bush hospital."

Lt. Manenowski turned sharply and offered his hand to shake. "Dr. Beecham."

Manenowski actually stepped back when the Putuki soldier with grease-stained coveralls rolled out from under the truck and stood to join us.

"Thank you, Billy," Captain Shaw said. "If you will just wait to give Dr. Beecham a ride back?" The lieutenant saluted and turned on his heel to wait by the jeep. The mechanic, his black skin glistening with sweat, watched Billy with a scowl. "I will be just a short while," Captain Shaw told him. "Next we can look at that lorry."

"Yes, sir."

Captain Shaw rolled down his sleeves while he walked with me into the bright sunlight. "I would have met you at the Officers' Club if you had sent word."

"It's always good to see where mandate resources are invested."

"Do you have a question concerning my quarterly report?"

I grinned at him. "Not at all. I wanted to discuss … I just came from a meeting with Sean Bryant. He claims the Company will return to Dolvia."

"It's official then."

"I cannot say."

"We can no longer trust the EAMs," Mike Shaw sanely explained, as though this was just another logistics problem. "The Company's taste for eavesdropping is legendary. We must find an informal system not dependent on their networks."

"What does the Company want?"

Captain Shaw shrugged. "What Sean Bryant wants. What the Consortium wants. Dr. Beecham, do you have a reason to visit the transport any day soon?"

"I have Consortium business."

"Let me know when you will board the shuttle, and I'll come along. Perhaps we can capture an hour of Colonel Hartley's time while we're there."

"So it's true?"

"The sand grouse that squabble among themselves are about to be devoured by a murmurey bird."

NINE

I JOINED CAPTAIN SHAW AT THE SHUTTLE LAUNCHPAD WEST OF Cylay. The holding area was a rounded quanza hut left over from Company rule. A wide roll-up door led to a busy freight area that managed the real volume of offworld traffic. Captain Shaw wore a dress uniform and carried a small rucksack. We stepped outside where Mike lit a kari root cigarette. "Last chance," he grinned behind the aromatic smoke.

The launch pad was situated on a rise from where we viewed the shantytown's meandering alleyways. The upright shuttle was gleaming within the scaffolding and spewing white steam while a ready-check was completed. The contrast was difficult to ignore. "Just think," I said, "once all this was a desert."

Smile lines appeared on Mike's face.

"How is the vaccine task coming along?" I asked.

"Behind schedule. My wife is sunburned and wheezing."

"I'm sorry that I put her in—"

He exhaled and the rich aroma enveloped us. "It's not your fault. I did send Louise Bilesketchum to join them."

"Louise?"

"She's doing follow-up with the villages. And she took over the samples collection."

"Louise," I repeated.

Mike met my incredulous look with a scowl. "What choice did I have? My wife attempts the labor of three people."

"She often succeeds."

Mike deeply inhaled cigarette smoke. "Will you settle here on Dolvia, then?"

"Habit is a great equalizer. What about you?"

"You trapped me here with salary and rank. Besides, you couldn't blast my wife out of that bush clinic."

"She does good work. She has a pure heart."

Mike snubbed the cigarette against the metal wall. "I know you have a special feeling for her. Who doesn't, huh?" It must have been the kari root's calming effect. Mike was more open on that day than I had ever seen him. "She accepted me because I boxed her in. I know she preferred Pierre. And before him, the other good doctor. You know, the rapist."

His look was hard, features set like granite. "I'm aware that whenever I touch her, that it somehow … diminishes her. But tribal law being what it is, and her position being so exposed. What solution, huh? I did what I figured was best for everybody. Call it opportunism, if you want, or profiteering off my wife's fortune.

"But I can tell you this," he added. "Nothing will be allowed to harm her. Others won't get that close, and I don't care who. And I don't care about the consequences. Dr. Greensboro is mine now, and that is how it is. I protect what's mine."

"And when she finds out about you and Louise?"

"She won't find out," he spat out as phlegm.

"Why do you even—"

"Why does any man?" Mike waited a long moment and then added, "My wife is so … fragile, you know? She's so … I guess it hurts, being with her. Our time together makes me ache, day and night. In a way, spending time with Louise only causes me to treasure my wife more, to appreciate how transparent and special she is. How … well, I don't expect you to understand. I don't make excuses. That's just how it is."

Mike shrugged and kicked the dirt with the toe of his boot. "Let's go inside."

In service now for a quarter century, the orbiting transport showed patchwork repairs and scars from solar wind. The exterior Panda decal was battered and badly needed a replacement. The shuttle ride was two hours, followed by a customs check where inoculation papers were inspected. From customs we entered the midship concourse. Hardhand shops lined the promenade, advertising repair and resale services in blue and red neon.

A transport officer led us past a security check and thick pneumatic doors to a well-maintained Consortium section with gleaming edges and bright directional icons.

Colonel Hartley labored in a crew operations room that held several wall screens and desk monitors. He saw us pass in the hall and curtly nodded to our escort. We were led down the corridor to a conference room where presently Hartley joined us. He thanked the officer who saluted and left. "This room is secure," Colonel Hartley said, indicating that we should sit at the conference table.

"What news?" Captain Shaw asked. Hartley pulled a manila envelope from under his uniform tunic and handed it to Mike Shaw. It contained security camera photos taken at the biosphere and on Company transports. One was of Steve Swanweil talking with two Company executives. I was mostly impressed that Hartley used hard copies instead of images on the table monitor.

"That's Tuang Cho, the Westend commander," Hartley explained, indicating a small Chinese man in an impeccable dark-blue suit with a round mandarin collar.

"Commander?"

"Don't let the business suits distract you. They're officers. This is war."

"And this other Han Chinese?" Captain Shaw asked, indicating an older man with flat planes to his face.

"Daniel Chin," Colonel Hartley said. "He was the Company prosecutor at the famous trial involving Brian Miller. His solicitor's office has maintained a presence at the biosphere for fifteen years. Business dealings are difficult to track, but he's listed in Earth's financial magazines among their hundred richest entrepreneurs. By Earth standards."

"So this is where Steve Swanweil secured his R&D capital?" I asked.

"There's something else," Colonel Hartley added. He searched through the photos and displayed one of Joey Osborn wearing a business suit. He was sitting in a dark hotel lobby on Cicero, talking with Steve Swanweil and Tuang Cho.

"My god," I said. "I mean, Carline Bryant had shown her colors, but this—"

"The Company is busy displacing Uburu families from the mesas," Colonel Hartley said. "The groups who agree to grow coffee exclusively are allowed to return."

"Coffee?" Captain Shaw said. "Only mature plants yield a crop. There's no return for seasons. How are they expected to live?"

"They can borrow against future harvests."

"Oxygen-suckers," Captain Shaw said.

I looked at the worried faces. "These tactics have been used by the Company to manage agriculture in China, in Kurdistan, and in the Islam regions. The population is indentured to some five-year plan to increase crop yield. Displaced Uburu families will enter the savannah to pressure the rabbenu structure."

"There are fewer than 60,000 Uburu altogether," Colonel said.

"And if all of the Uburu," I said, "enter the savannah in the same season, what conflict do you see? Stressed services and local con-flicts. Destabilize the whole region."

"We had reports of Uburu in the Siibabean forest," Captain Shaw said. "Full of predators, the forest is. One tribal clan wanted us to remove the Uburu since it was families and not invaders. The forest has no roads or river for transportation, just trails among the trees."

"What did you do?" the colonel asked.

"We sent Karlyhi." The captain chuckled. "He could travel fast with Ralph and locate the camps. The canopy is dense without an opening for choppers. We finally evacuated the families using rescue gurneys lowered by a wince. We made six trips."

"Ralph too?" I asked. I couldn't imagine the big gualarep strapped in and swinging in the chopper disturbance.

"He wouldn't get on the gurney," Shaw said. "Karlyhi has returned now, helping to finish the erriv drive."

"The savannah will be more inviting to refugees," Colonel Hartley said. "We can monitor these Company players we have identified. But they will spy on us just the same."

"What precautions can we take?" Mike Shaw asked.

"There's no EAM security from eavesdropping," Hartley said. "They can break any code. We need a shadow system."

"I might have an idea," Mike said, "for ground talk. But the transport would be out of range of a shadow network."

"Well, if we keep it casual," Hartley said. "We need a backdoor that Company men don't suspect. I mean, they're not overlords, just snoops."

"What do you suggest?" I asked.

"The major open channels," Hartley said, "are the Bryants' business licenses and supply orders for the savannah hospital. The Company will monitor these upfront. Bryant has already lodged a complaint. The other avenue is Dr. Greensboro's downloads. She receives data in chunks, and translates from there. We can take advantage of the minutiae needed for the academy textbooks in four dialects."

"Actually, that is Hakulupe Le's area," I said. "She just uses Dr. Greensboro's codes."

"Let's get individual codes for each location. Spread out some shot." Colonel Hartley watched me for a moment. "Also at the hospital, Dr. Mitterand uses a specialized language based on Greek and Latin."

"Medical terms," I agreed.

"Perhaps we could imbed certain phrases in bulk orders and the white papers that get circulated. Is Dr. Mitterand trustworthy?"

"To a point," I shrugged.

"One other possibility," Hartley added. "My teenagers want to visit Dolvia. You could organize a greeting party at the Officers' Club. Set a standard for exchange of students so their baggage won't be suspect, at least at first. Later, more graduates could undertake similar excursions."

"Your daughter too?" I asked.

Colonel Hartley grinned. "You try excluding Heather."

"You would put them in harm's way?" Mike asked.

"I'm seeking reassurances from you."

Mike grinned. "Who can manage teenagers, huh?"

On the walk back to midship, we greeted Hartley's wife Billie, a plump woman and the picture of health. She doted on the younger daughter Jesse who was born to them later in life. Billie's two teenagers, Carl and Heather, were nearly finished with Junction courses and looking forward to a college term at the Cicero biosphere. They were big like their parents, trim and dark haired with blanched white skin. But they were cultured, their rough edges smoothed from being nurtured in the transport's cosmopolitan environment.

"May we drop by the hospital when we visit Dolvia?" Carl asked.

"We're doing the senior trip thing," Heather added, "before Carl leaves for university."

"Of course," I said. "I'll send my EAM codes so we can plan ahead." Such fine kids.

On our return to Dolvia, Captain Shaw learned that his wife had received a venomous spider bite during the erriv drive. He ordered a military escort to meet them on Orin rabbe Murd's land and boarded a chopper, rushing to her side. I learned via EAM that Dacupitte had saved her life by slicing her arm and sucking out the fresh poison.

The vaccine task ended badly, with Mrs. Shaw exhausted and wounded, and her gualarep gored. The erriv were all in the northern grazing land, and the tribes were at peace for once. But at what price, I wondered.

It was raining most afternoons by the time Louise Bilesketchum joined us at the hospital from her savannah excursion. She dropped her soiled luggage in the outer waiting room and shook hands. Her grip was strong and rough skinned. She offered the ruined samples case with the notes nearly illegible.

"Village women are intractable," Louise complained. "They cannot follow simple instructions."

While she talked with Dr. Mitterand concerning the primitive conditions she was forced to endure, I went out onto the verandah where Brianna, the orphan who Mike Shaw had claimed was the linchpin to the tribal rivalry, waited on the steps. I felt a sudden protective urge. Trouble was coming. How would these young people survive?

"Brianna, what will Dr. Greensboro say about the condition of her notes?"

The sixteen-year-old sourly shrugged. "Dolvia blesses Sheeks-Cylom. Dolvia does not bless Louise Bilesketchum."

That was succinct. "Won't you join us?" I asked with an open gesture. Brianna glanced inside. "Dr. Mitterand waits to congratulate you on your good work."

She stood and squinted at me. She wiped her hands on the gritty Arrivi gown and hesitantly entered the hospital waiting area. Pierre turned to her. "Hiki, Brianna Miller."

"I am not a sister of Arim," she whispered. "No honor is due."

"Beauty demands its own honor," he said. She frowned, ever suspicious, but then slowly smiled.

"You can ride with us to the bush clinic," I added.

Brianna's face was suddenly bright with eagerness. "In a helicopter?"

"During a break in the rain," I agreed. "But for now, won't you join us for tea?"

Brianna glanced at Louise and shook her head no.

"Louise," Dr. Mitterand said. "Surely you are eager now to wash off the road dust. Join me later for dinner. I can have it catered. Say, seven o'clock?" Louise flirtatiously smiled before she hoisted the heavy bags and left. Brianna's hooded look lightened somewhat.

"Tell us what happened, Brianna," I said.

"People invited us into their homes. They offered their best."

"And Louise was rude?"

"The people have honor." She glanced around, while hospital staff noted her stained gown and dirt-caked hair.

"So," Pierre asked, "how about that tea?"

Brianna nodded and walked across the lobby.

"She's underage," I whispered into Pierre's ear while we walked behind her. He only smiled. Brianna turned with question. "Over here," I said, and led her into my office.

With a furtive gesture that proclaimed his innocence, Pierre joined us for tea.

I found a room for Brianna in the women's dormitory. During the following days, she worked to salvage Dr. Greensboro's notes. Some mornings before Pierre's rounds, she lingered with him in the laboratory, describing where she had found certain succulents and what to expect during their flowering stages. She searched the tattered notes for needed data and shyly smiled when Dr. Mitterand praised her resourcefulness.

Brianna brought tea and sandwiches to my office each afternoon, after I insisted. She claimed the hour we spent together was a great honor. We swapped English taglines, and I allowed her to investigate my many books there. I was called away; it was on the third afternoon, I think. I returned to find her in tears, curled up in a deep chair under a single lamp. She cradled a ragged illustrated volume of fairy tales and Irish myths. The book was open to a sentimental illustration of a long-haired princess leaning from a white steed to accept a bright flower from a suitor's hand.

"The Softcheeks' world must be wonderful," she whispered.

"It's just a drawing, a fantasy."

But she only smiled and wiped away her tears. My heart pulled down in my chest. I felt old. "Well, let's put away fantasy and look at reality." I pulled out some National Geographic magazines, their worn yellow covers distinctive on any world.

"These will introduce you to Earth." I gently removed the book on myths.

She thumbed through the magazines while we sat at tea. They contained photographs of schools of stingrays in the ocean, of iguanas on island preserves, of open-mouth snakes that angrily struck at the camera. There were painted Africans and South Americans dressed for Carnival. There were Tibetan monks seated in front of elaborate prayer wheels and Siberian Eskimos herding reindeer.

Brianna held up an open page that displayed brightly colored fish swimming by a coral reef. "They live in a grotto?"

"In the ocean. Dolvia has oceans."

"Dolvia has the savannah."

I booted up the EAM. "Allow me to show you." I called up a photo of Dolvia from the transport library.

"I have seen this at the academy," she said.

"Arrivi live here." I pointed at the vast golden savannah. "Siibabean live north above the cliff. If you follow the Iamida River east past Cylay and past the city called Urbyd, you come to an ocean called the Borabean."

She frowned while staring at the image. "Dolvia has an ocean?"

"Yes, deep and wide and teeming with fish. The birds that arrive here for the wet season fly over the Uburu mesas from the ocean. After their young are hatched and grown, they fly back to ocean-side nests and hunt fish there."

"Arrivi don't know the ocean."

"Another tribe lives there, the Abydian."

"A-by-di-an," she repeated.

"And in the mesa region between the Arrivi and Abydian live the Uburu."

"Many Dolviet tribes?" She held up the magazine. "Like the many tribes in here?"

"Yes, many more than we know."

Brianna digested the new ideas. I wondered how she would sort them out. Later, I was to wonder which volume she had seen that day did more damage to her willingness to serve.

Hakulupe Le was present the day we loaded the helicopter to visit the bush clinic. The vaccine task was finally completed. The guala-rep Edna was recovering at the clinic, where Captain Shaw was spending the rainy season with Mrs. Shaw.

Lupe offered certain packages for Sheeks-Cylom and small remembrances for Martina and Kecouroo. Lupe had her own EAM codes by then, and was in daily contact with the clinic. We loaded boxes of spiral-bound textbooks for the clinic school, and lumber ordered by Captain Shaw for additional construction at the clinic. Karlyhi arrived with the lumber shipment that day. He was nineteen or thereabouts, a warrior wearing dungarees but with Cylahi body paint and a shoulder-slung karkar.

Karlyhi stood aside while I talked with Hakulupe Le. Red and green parrots, transients during the rainy season, landed on the ground and tucked in their wings. They seemed to group themselves at Karlyhi's feet. Arrivi took note of how certain people were accepted by savannah denizen. A tribal chant, for example, named Katelupe Le, a sister to Kyle Rula, who was killed by Company guards at a prison. Her spirit walked the savannah in the company of a big ketiwhelp, seeking the ghost of her dead lover Spindel.

At any rate, Karlyhi was certainly good with the gualareps. He and Ralph had rescued Uburu families lost in the forest. He and Ralph had herded some feral erriv during the final days of the vaccine task. Brianna also noticed Karlyhi's parrots when she joined us with the last of the packages. "They fly in from the ocean beyond the mesas."

"O-cean?" Karlyhi asked. "What is ocean?"

"Like the grotto, only bigger. And with salt water."

"There is no such water."

"There is so, and I can prove it," she said with her chin stuck out. "The ocean has fish more brightly colored than the parrots."

"What does a goulep know?" Karlyhi asked as a taunt.

Brianna shook her fist at him. "What do you know? I'm telling you, there's an ocean called the Borabean."

He reached for her. "You need a good beating."

I saw flashes of red and blue while the parrots took to wing, blocking the space between them. Brianna scurried to the helicopter and climbed onboard, calling back, "Ha! They came here to shield me. Not you at all! Only me!"

Karlyhi turned on his heel and walked away, perhaps twenty paces. The birds landed and folded back their big wings, nonchalantly strolling to his same position.

Hakulupe Le shook her head. "And so it begins. Students talk back to the warriors."

"I am afraid this was my fault," I said. "I was showing Brianna some—"

"It is seen," Lupe interrupted. "Soon all the students will talk back. We discussed this; how the presence of the academy changes the balance."

I nodded slowly. "I don't think I realized we were discussing tribal prophecy."

"Hasn't it been so for tribes on your world?" Lupe asked sanguinely. "Students challenge the old order? Isn't it true everywhere?" She showed me the open palm gesture and stepped back near Karlyhi while the chopper blades began rotating. The parrots flew away.

By the time we arrived at the bush clinic that day, the weather had clouded. The helicopters were a great addition to travel options, but often grounded during the rains. Some Arrivi men came down to unload the supplies. Dr. Greensboro and Brianna had an altercation in the yard, something about how Dr. Mitterand had made a thoughtless promise he did not intend to keep. With so many angry words all of a sudden, I wondered at Brianna's willful rebellion. Her increased knowledge only caused her to chafe against authority.

Anyhow, Brianna went up to the classroom to greet Kecouroo. I joined Captain Shaw where Edna was recovering in the old clinic building. Her nest filled the room, but we took tea on the verandah there. While Dr. Greensboro poured for us, I noticed the wicked scar on her forearm. Mrs. Shaw, I mean. I needed to get used to using her preferred title.

Mrs. Shaw talked about her clinic patients and the need for more research. She wanted to study venom. She also took considerable interest in the outbreak of pox among some Arrivi families and wondered if the hospital had received many pox-suffering patients.

It was quickly apparent to me that Captain Shaw had not taken her into his confidence concerning the Company's return or about Louise Bilesketchum. Mike seemed to be hiding out at his wife's compound, ignoring his Cylay duties and his future worries. Perhaps he only wanted happy memories with his wife, to rest and recuperate a short time. Perhaps he was trying to assuage his guilt for his relationship with Louise.

I was completing hospital rounds that day. The rain was mostly in the afternoon, but the floodplain was quickly filling with runoff from the high forest. Hospital patients arrived plagued with fungus and mites, and infected broken legs from falls taken when they had ventured out to hunt in the uneven and soggy terrain. Dengue fever and river blindness were on the increase.

Dr. Mitterand had been called away to serve the Consortium troops that were completing three days of maneuvers west of Somule. As the colonel in charge had explained, this was their opportunity to shake out equipment and test rescue procedures. Dr. Mitterand was required by the mandate to provide triage in the event of injury and to prepare the wounded for evacuation to the hospital. Of course, we expected no wounded. These were war games only.

The increase of Consortium presence had been arranged, in fact, by Colonel Hartley on the transport to deliver a message to the snooping Company advance men. The savannah was settled and protected by Consortium might. The Company must keep out.

At any rate, I was doing hospital rounds in Pierre's absence when Karlyhi showed himself at the doorway and cleared his throat. I handed the chart to the Cylahi nurse and joined him. "You must come," he said with native succinctness.

I peeled off the plastic gloves and grabbed my doctor's bag. "What is it?"

"Come," he repeated.

We hurried to a waiting lorry that Karlyhi recklessly drove over swamped roads and toward the high butte. I looked in the back to spy on our escort, but the truck bed was piled with automatics and ammo crates. Karlyhi saw me staring and just grinned, showing his uneven teeth against the black skin.

Several sonic booms were followed by overhead phosphorous bursts. The chattering birds were in constant turmoil, rising in great flocks with each boom. Three parrots fell together onto the hood of the lorry and slammed into the windshield before they slid onto the side of the road. I twisted to see, then looked into the side-view mirror. Two of the birds regained their feet and ruffled feathers, hunching together on the roadside. The other one didn't move. I looked at Karlyhi's face, but he didn't slow or swerve.

Finally, we passed the butte and entered the flats of Arim. This sacred area seemed off-limits to Consortium maneuvers. The flats were on high ground and less overrun by the water-nesting birds. Karlyhi stopped in front of a shallow escarpment cave known as the fortress of Arim. Kyle Rula lived there, a tribal holy woman who I had met twice in formal settings.

I grabbed my doctor's bag and entered the low doorway. The interior was lighted with tallow. A big table had several cane chairs. Roughly chiseled walls were lined with free-standing bookshelves all piled with spiral-bound transport library translations.

"This way," Karlyhi said. He led me to a second chamber with a high ceiling, cool and moist as it was dug deeper into the escarpment wall. I saw a kitchen area with an EAM on the table, a rudimentary laundry facility, and a few handmade beds with thin mattresses. Kyle Rula sat by one bed, leaning over a patient.

Mrs. Shaw was passed out on the cot.

"Sheeks-Cylom's lorry turned over on the savannah," Kyle Rula explained as I took her seat. "Karlyhi brought her here. Her injuries are more than I know."

Sheeks-Cylom was out cold. Her superficial abrasions had been bathed with spring water. An ugly black bruise was just showing on her swollen jaw. I lifted each eyelid and checked her pupils. I felt her arms and shoulders for broken bones.

"She has a dislocated shoulder," I summarized, "a concussion, and maybe a broken jaw. I can give her a hypo and set the bones. I will need something for splints."

Kyle Rula nodded to Karlyhi who left.

"We must immobilize her jaw," I instructed. "A couple straps of leather or cloth."

Kyle Rula brought two long strips of thin leather used for making furniture. I crisscrossed the strips under and over Dr. Greensboro's jaw and tightened them behind her cranium. She looked to be wearing a mask of torture accentuated by the black eye.

Karlyhi returned with some thin slats used to reinforce home-made furniture. I got behind her torso and snapped the shoulder into place. Karlyhi pulled back at the sound of the bone snap, and actually showed emotion on his face. We immobilized the shoulder and set the wrist in splints. The patient moaned and stirred, but did not come around.

"That is all we can do for now."

Karlyhi left. Kyle Rula and I went to the kitchen area where she brewed tea. "So what happened?" I asked, seated at the table.

"Sheeks-Cylom was driving too fast from Somule and crashed through the military barricades. The soldiers seem afraid of their own ordnance, so Karlyhi reached the overturned lorry first and brought her here.

"After I got her situated," Kyle Le continued, "I talked on the EAM with Hakulupe Le." "Brianna said they drove down from the clinic on the spur of the moment. Sheeks-Cylom went to the Somule hotel and apparently interrupted her husband with Louise Bilesketchum."

"Oh, man," I complained. "I told him."

An oversized sky-blue macaw flew in from the other room, perhaps attracted by the cooking odors. He landed on the table and tucked his long tail feathers behind him. He walked toward me on clawed feet while he cocked his head from side to side. Kyle Le shooed him off the table. He flew to a high perch and stared down at us.

"Gonna rain today," the macaw said in Arrivi, then repeated, "gonna rain today," with exactly the same inflections.

"It rains every day," Kyle Le told him. She joined me at the table.

"A friend of yours?" I asked.

"He was here when we first came to the fortress, what, twenty years ago. Parrots and macaws can live to be old." She leaned forward and confidentially added, as if out of his hearing, "An ancestor who loves to trouble me. Also, he poops on the books."

"Gonna rain tomorrow. Gonna rain then, too," the macaw said.

"Does he speak Mekucoo?" I asked.

"Don't encourage him."

"Ralph will come," the macaw claimed. "Braaadt. Ralph will come."

Kyle Le glanced at me, suddenly serious. "I have been expecting Ralph for a while now. Perhaps he hesitates because of your presence."

"Why me?"

Kyle Le stared for a long moment, but shrugged. "You will need to stay overnight, I fear. Karlyhi's driving is scary enough during the daytime."

"The circumstances are awkward," I said, "but a visit is pleasant. I meant to ask, though. The lorry is loaded with—"

She quickly interrupted. "Karlyhi picked up some stored goods at the hospital. How often does he have access to a vehicle?"

"Whose weapons are they? Who said they could be stored at the hospital?"

"Perhaps he believes the storerooms are for anybody's use." She showed me a smile, lovely and engaging. "A method he may have learned from Dr. Abercrombie."

After our refreshments, Kyle Rula and I made a tour of some low adobe buildings about half a kilometer down from the fortress. Consortium maneuvers must have ended for the day. We heard no ord-nance reports. Wildlife had settled somewhat.

The buildings contained a cottage industry. Women sat at rows of manual sewing machines, some assembling Arrivi skirts and burkas, while others hand stitched elaborate designs onto the skirt hems. In the second building several older men, both Arrivi and Putuki, constructed cane chairs as well as some tables and bed frames.

They stopped working and waited while Kyle Le described the processes. "These ones come every day during the rainy season," she explained. "The women, especially new mothers, take home piecework.

"We are interested in developing more small businesses," she added. "Maybe Arrivi and Cylahi artisan skills. We have not explored the export market, though. We want to avoid the Bryant cartel."

"The offworld market may soon contract rather than expand," I said.

"We own some licenses," Kyle Le said while we moved away from the worktables. "Perhaps you did not know that. We want to use our rights, but we need a trusted Softcheeks, um . . . front man, I believe is the term. Someone who will return to Earth one day and develop more markets."

"Have you spoken to Dr. Mitterand?"

"Hakulupe Le suspects him."

"Perhaps Colonel Hartley on the transport."

"The colonel is not Softcheeks."

While we walked back to the fortress, Karlyhi and the gualarep Ralph came up from the flats. I had not seen Ralph since my first visit to Somule some time ago. He stirred conflicting emotions in me. On the one hand, Ralph was majestic. He could change his color for the season and location. On that day, his marbled hide was the golden of the savannah with swirls of brown-black, the same as Karlyhi's skin color. His jutting jaw was regal and the unblinking eyes soulful.

But Ralph was a reptile, resembling an oversized iguana with marbled crocodile ridges running down his back. His waddling gait and lightning-quick jerks classified him as wilder and more lethal than most.

Kyle Rula showed no fear when she sat cross-legged on the ground. Ralph fingered her face with his fleshy tongue forked on the tip. He walked over her lap, strongly rubbing her with his flanks. Captain Shaw had explained once that gualareps imprint on their familiars and must have this scent-placing contact. Mike had claimed that gualareps can throw their thoughts. Perhaps like the blue macaw, they embodied ancestral spirits who offered guidance. That was unlikely, though, since the reptiles were imported from Cicero.

Kyle Rula and I went into the fortress where she moistened a cloth with spring water and washed Ralph's saliva streaks from her face and arms. "It's a blessing that Ralph honors me. He has ruined more than one skirt with stains, however."

She led me to the big table in the library room. "Dr. Beecham, if I may show you a thing." Laid out there were several masks and ceremonial garments decorated with bright parrot feathers of red, yellow, and green. I also saw stark-white egret feathers and the long, black-tipped wing feathers of cranes arranged in delicate and celebratory patterns on Mekucoo suede. There was even a Siibabean headdress that was a shoulder-to-shoulder halo of murmurey feathers, most unique. I picked it up to test the weight. The backside where the feathers were secured showed excellent workmanship.

"These are marvelous," I said.

"Do you think there might be an offworld market for them?"

"Surely, for all Dolviet goods. On Earth, these are considered exotic because they traveled through the wormhole. Can more be made?"

"A Cylahi skill, nearly lost to us now. Cylahi cannot afford the materials. I may know a couple older women, however, who can perhaps be coerced into teaching the methods if there's a market."

"None of these designs use blue feathers."

"Dolvia veils Herself in blue; it's not a good color for commercial items."

"These should bring a good profit," I said confidently. "I can talk with Colonel Hartley, if you want. And the furniture?"

"We have a local market for more than we can produce."

"How fortunate."

That evening after we checked Dr. Greenboro's condition – I mean Mrs. Shaw's condition – Kyle Rula and I settled in for a lovely conversation. Outside her fortress entrance, the families of Arrivi furniture makers had gathered around a communal fire and were chanting in their familiar humor.

> "Sheeks-Cylom knows many men
> There's Karl and Ralph and Mike
> But Ralph prefers a sister of Arim

Who even his two mates do not bite"

Kyle Rula chuckled and quietly closed the wooden door. "We had not seen one such as Sheeks-Cylom," she shrugged. "When she first arrived, we thought perhaps she was … I believe your English word is disabled."

"You thought Mrs. Shaw was a cripple?"

"Kecouroo wondered at Sheeks-Cylom's thoughtlessness." She flashed a mischievous smile. "Mrs. Shaw, as you call her, seldom looked up and then made instant decisions on long-painful matters."

"Kecouroo takes exception with her treatment of Karlyhi?" I guessed.

"Her action was breathtaking," Kyle Le said.

"I was told that Karlyhi was mistreating Brianna."

She nodded absently. "Kecouroo feels grateful for Mrs. Shaw's interest in the girl students. We were just surprised."

"You would not have intervened?"

"Usually we don't correct the warriors."

"Karlyhi knew the academy was responsible," I summarized. "He had no rights over Brianna. He acted wrongly."

Kyle Le shook her head as Hakulupe Le often did. "Softcheeks are a delight, truly. Mrs. Shaw often voices three objections in such a rhythm."

"She's is a delightful cripple?"

"This is difficult to explain," Kyle Le said with an open palm. "Within our seeing, women from Earth have no distinctive aura features, just an egg shape with a concave receptacle. Softcheeks men are often divided into three planes. You have labels for these divisions such as heart, mind, and soul. Or the id, the … uh, I don't remember the other two."

"The ego and the super-ego."

"Yes, of course. But Mrs. Shaw was different. Can I use that title for acts from before she was married?"

I only nodded.

"Fine, then," Kyle Le agreed. "How to make a picture for you?" She drew on the table with a child's chalk. "The three planes for Softcheeks men form a pyramid. The largest lower tier is for the base instincts. The second tier is for the interpersonal, what the Mekucoo call chikiocahi or chi. And the upper tier is for, uh, thinking."

"The chi?"

Kyle Le drew on the tabletop. "Sheeks-Cylom also has three planes, most unusual for a Softcheeks woman, which is why she appears non-feminine. But the planes shape into an inverted pyramid."

"Uh-huh," I said.

"Her physical self-discipline is apparent in that she drives herself without mercy. Her chi is faint; Kecouroo says because she shared spirit with the wounded warriors when she labored at the hospital. But Sheeks-Cylom's top tier is active and broiling. This would be the mind. She's cera … cere—"

"Cerebral. From the name for a large brain cortex called the cerebellum."

"Cer-e-bell-um," Kyle Le repeated. "Cerebellum, a delightful word. Mrs. Shaw is the Sheeks-Cerebellum." She flashed that engaging smile. I warmed up to her then, despite her more-than-honest assessment of Mrs. Shaw's chi.

"We have bountiful netta while the savannah blooms," Kyle Le said. "We must insist to newcomers that the savannah is a desert and does not have the … what is your Softcheeks phrase? Carrying capacity. The savannah is a desert and cannot carry new groups of Uburu."

"I heard the Uburu were pressured to grow a cash crop. What should I watch for?"

"At the hospital?" she said. "River blindness, caused when colonies of mites infest the body. Their larvae are planted internally. In advanced stages the eyes cloud over, similar to cataracts."

I caught my breath. "You mean onchocerciasis."

Her eyebrows bunched. "That is a made-up word, I'm guessing."

"We have a few cases now. There's no cure."

"Arrivi know it's best to stay indoors during the rains. Dolvia blesses each group in its season. But newcomers won't understand this. They will sicken and die."

"You mean the Uburu families?"

"Many newcomers belong to the next cycle. Many more than three Softcheeks doctors and two Hardhand teenagers."

I tried to keep my expression neutral. "Are you saying you knew I would come before I arrived?"

"It was seen."

"What else is seen about me?"

"You will not have ground-born children," she said warmly as if giving a blessing, "but you will greatly serve the students."

"It was you," I said with sudden insight. "You said the students will talk back to warriors! That was your insight."

"Anybody could see that coming, even Captain Shaw."

"And what is seen about Mike Shaw?"

"Much." She hesitated with a faraway look. "Much is seen."

I teased Kyle Le about her status as Dolvia's foremost authority on Earth's religious thought and philosophy. She glanced around at her book collection with affection. "Once I was accused of seeking contingent clauses, which is funny when you consider it. At the time I did not know what those words meant."

"Which philosopher do you like best?"

"Spinoza, I think."

"Spinoza? But he is awful!" I stood and went to the shelf that held volumes by philosophers from many Earth traditions. "Spinoza thinks categorically, each urge sliced and diced separate from the whole."

"Yes, he thinks like Softcheeks." She said from her seat. "Very informative."

"No, no. Spinoza is not the man. You must read Aristotle, Descartes, and Emanuel Kant."

"In Mekucoo, kant means the lack of kari. No growth, no life force."

"So you skipped Kant?"

Kyle Le shrugged. "He was difficult."

"But what about Aristotle? He was a tutor, you know, to Alexander the Great, who once ruled the known world. Also John Calvin, a simple country preacher, a puritan."

"A purist? I have been called a purist."

I pulled out the slim volume of Calvin's teachings. "You will love John Calvin's works." I handed the book to her and took my seat again.

"I have not tried this one. Melinga."

The blue macaw landed on the long worktable with the market items displayed. He walked up Kyle Le's arm, an act that must have caused her some discomfort. He rubbed his forehead against her cheek. She gently pushed him away, but he repeated his demand for affection.

She showed me that engaging smile. "He's jealous. I have few visitors."

"There are many here."

"But who can discuss philosophy?"

"Braaadt," the macaw said. "Talk phi-lo-so-phy. Who can talk phi-lo-so-phy?"

"Perhaps I shall make a meal of you and sell your tail feathers to Softcheeks."

"Braaadt. Blue tail feathers. Blue is good."

"I made that rule," she said. "I can break it."

"Braaadt." He walked down her arm and over to my side of the table. He walked up my arm and perched on my shoulder, although he did not rub his crest against my face. His grip on my sleeve was light, causing no discomfort at all.

"Dr. Beecham leaves tomorrow," Kyle Le teased. "Perhaps I will have parrot soup then."

"Braaadt," he said and pooped on my sleeve, leaving a messy white streak.

Kyle Le laughed. "That's no way to make a friend." She reached for a cloth to moisten and brush away the filth. The blue macaw flew to a high perch.

"Dr. Beecham, you have been so generous. If I may show you a thing."

"Of course."

She set an earthen bowl on the table and removed the covering cloth to reveal some green and black olives of various sizes. "As you may know, oleastra bushes grow wild all over the savannah. Softcheeks use olives to make oil. Do you know how this oil is produced?"

"I assume by way of a press."

"Like a wine press?" She opened a book printed in English, turning the pages to an illustration for wine making. "Like this?"

"Similar, I'm sure."

"And if we cultivated oleastra to produce a quantity of this oil?"

"For export, you mean?" I thought for a moment. "It would depend in part on your method, and your ability to preserve the olive oil, but I imagine this could be done."

"Is there one on Dolvia, or perhaps a transport resident, who has this knowledge?"

"Have you spoken to Captain Shaw?"

She looked over her shoulder at the room where Mrs. Shaw slept. "I have intended to, but perhaps not now."

"I see," I said. "I can ask Dr. Mitterand. If nothing else, we can secure the technology. We may have to assemble the machinery."

"I may know an Arrivi man—" she began with a furtive gesture.

"Yes, I imagine you do."

I introduced my idea about a bank fund for small business loans to empower resident Arrivi by way of locally suggested improvements to increase their productivity. This was the same idea I had unsuccessfully pitched to Brent Gotskind and Frank Duerr. Kyle Le listened and nodded, but agreed to nothing.

"I will bring this idea to Rabbenu Ely and Orin rabbe Murd," she finally assented. "I am not sure how we can raise the capital."

"You can introduce a tax for the fund, and communal facilities to store grain."

"Rabbenu Ely says taxes are a form of oppression."

"When another group taxes you, perhaps. But if Arrivi instituted their own taxes, you could set aside part of the bounty to dole out during droughts."

She squinted, so I cast about for an example. "You have read the Old Testament. You read the story of Abraham who led his people during good times and bad. The families were required to tithe ten percent, and received the stored grain for their animals when crops failed."

"Abraham was not a good person," she stated flatly. "He would have killed his son except for the goat."

"God provided the goat. It was a test of the purity of Abraham's faith."

"Just the same," she shrugged. "Except for the goat—"

"Perhaps Abraham is not the best example. But his act does not dilute the principles of tithing and grain storage."

She sat back and thought about it. "We look at the whole man, not just at the good. Not just in glory days. We don't embrace your Abraham. We don't like him."

"Well, perhaps I can recommend the story of Moses. He also led."

"I shall read again about Moses and give it some thought. You have brought much for me to consider. John Calvin and Moses."

"Well," I said, "Mrs. Shaw will wake tomorrow. You must release the pressure on her chin brace every few hours, and tighten it again. Her splints can come off after several days."

It was late by then. Kyle Rula led me to a cot next to Mrs. Shaw and brought some linens. "This has been a good mercy seat. I hope we can talk again soon."

"Braaadt, mercy seat," the macaw mimicked.

TEN

ONE FRIDAY WHEN THE RAINS WERE CONSTANT, PIERRE MITTER-
and and I met at the Somule hotel's Executive Club where several Consortium officers whiled away the afternoon with drinks and snooker, part of Colonel Hartley's plan for more tribal contact. The talk was about the barracks officer who had married a research doctor in a civil ceremony, and now she rejected him to live with the tribes.

I didn't add to their speculation. I knew that Captain Shaw had arrived by helicopter at the fortress to a cold welcome. Kyle Rula had met him on the flats and listened to his explanations but shook her head. Captain Shaw gained no access to his wife. He returned to Cylay and his work as Director of Natural Disasters Control.

Dr. Mitterand visited the bush clinic after his duty with the peacekeeper maneuvers. In the warriors' ritual building, Mekucoo men and boys managed snakes and frogs. This task, as Kecouroo called it, was to gather enough venom for offworld tests. Pierre had lingered several days before he sent the specimens and his notes to the Cicero biosphere laboratory for anti-venom development.

At the Somule Executive Club, Pierre lit a long cigarette and sat back to cross his legs. "The Mekucoo did not understand," Pierre said, "the Sheeks-Cylom's sudden departure. Cara was defensive, but showed me some illustrations torn from a medical book. We joked about how the size of reproductive organs belied their use. To Cara's mind, the spider's tiny venom sacs were analogous to their manhood. One stored death, the other stored life. Powerful things come in small packages, huh?

"Cara's a great hero within their rubric, you should know," Pierre added. "Handling snakes touches on sacred things such as courage and hallucinations and bite recovery. Dr. Greensboro would never have been allowed to participate."

"Mrs. Shaw," I corrected.

"Mrs. Greensboro-Shaw, maybe," he grinned. "Her doctor's reputation will show on the patent papers when we finish."

Pierre had provided Cara with an HGEAM, assembled in the former female enclosure next to the ritual building. The place took on the mystique of a shrine. Whenever Pierre booted the machine, tribesmen gathered and stared. Pierre restricted his, well, his public talks to Colonel Hartley and the transport librarian so no pantheon of offworlders appeared within the light. Mekucoo called Colonel Hartley Hanthudilciage, meaning floating head. Somehow that got shortened to Hamilcar, easier to pronounce.

At the Officer's Club, Pierre finished his cigarette and his drink. "Did you hear that Lieutenant Manenowski was sent to the clinic school to instruct students in accounting lessons? Perhaps Captain Shaw hopes for his sudden demise from snakebite."

Dr. Mitterand and I braved the rain to cross to the doctor's office where we planned to boot the HGEAM and check for Cicero lab results for anti-venom test. Dacupitte was on the covered sidewalk with two warriors in uniform and carrying karkars. He was easy to recognize with red dreadlocks streaming down his back. "Dr. Beecham," he said. "You should have an escort tonight."

"What's going on?" I asked.

"Uburu families," Pete said. "Many are gathered near the railhead, but there's not enough room to bed down. Not enough Consortium officers to contain them. Some families have entered the street of shop to find shelter for the night."

"They seem docile, though," I offered to be positive. "No fighting."

"Some cooking fires. Some petty theft."

"What do you see is coming?"

"In Cylay, a Bryant warehouse was cleared for the refugees," Pete said. "The Consortium sent rations. But more arrive every day."

"Well, we're just crossing to the doctor's office. We're in no danger."

"Melinga," Pete said and turned back to his companions.

Once we climbed the steps to the platform sidewalk that ran along the street of shops, we were stopped by two Arrivi women, very unusual on the open street.

"Dr. Beecham, don't you know me?" one asked.

To my surprise, it was Mrs. Shaw, dressed in the traditional Arrivi skirt with the burka on her shoulders as a shawl. She and Hakulupe

Le strolled from the bazaar in soiled Arrivi sandals under long and generous skirts. Her injuries were healing, although she appeared thin from having her jaw immobilized. Her blondish hair was drawn back and stained, no doubt with the gummy paste Dolviets used as insect repellent.

"Mrs. Shaw," I said. "You look Arrivi."

She shook my hand and Pierre's hand. "I read your reports, Pierre. Congratulations on your progress with Cara and the Mekucoo."

"How generous," he returned in his intimate way.

"And what brings you to Somule?" I asked.

"There's a student exchange with some Consortium graduates from the transport, a Carl and Heather Hartley. Hakulupe Le asked me to oversee the welcome."

"Yes, I heard they were coming."

"They are arriving at the hotel," Mrs. Shaw said. "Won't you help us greet them?"

We four ducked our heads against the drizzle and headed back to the hotel. While we walked, Mrs. Shaw quietly spoke to Pierre. "Brianna believes you plan to take her to Earth."

His look was neutral like he was just caught in a lie. "Perhaps I will."

"As what?" Mrs. Shaw could be most direct.

Pierre only blinked. "As Brian Miller's daughter."

"That's no answer," she said. "Brianna is just a little girl."

At my elbow, Hakulupe Le said, "I am told you have been in talks with Kyle Rula concerning certain prophets in the Bible."

"We talked one evening about some Bible principles," I hedged.

She nailed me with those gimlet-like eyes. "There's a prophet whose life I also would like to discuss. Solomon."

I groaned. I did not feel equal to the epistemological dialogue.

"'To everything there is a season'," she quoted. "'A time for each thing under the sun.' Isn't that how it goes?"

"If memory serves."

"I wanted to ask, if Solomon had everything, why was he so sad?"

"Perhaps from living in the shadow of a famous father. David was God's favorite."

"Yes, well, I wanted to ask about him, too."

I groaned again.

An ECCAV was just stopping outside the hotel entrance. From its cool interior emerged the Consortium students, Carl and Heather Hartley. She wore a large-brimmed hat against the rain. They looked around at the drizzle, but recognized us and stepped under the hotel awning for handshakes.

"Dr. Beecham," Carl said. "We didn't expect you would be available for the welcome. Dr. Mitterand, you remember my sister Heather?" She wore a tan skirt and jacket, and sturdy shoes. Wisps of dark hair framed her face.

"Of course," Pierre said with a winning smile. "This is Mrs. Shaw, just in from the flats of Arim. You may know her as Dr. Greensboro. And may I introduce the school administrator, Hakulupe Le."

"Hiki, Carl Hartley," Hakulupe Le said, holding her palm high. "Melinga."

And then for some unknown reason, across the way Dacupitte handed off his karkar and munitions belt to his compatriots and joined us. Carl stared at Pete's decorated suede tunic over dunga-rees. Dr. Mitterand and I each shook Pete's hand.

Mrs. Shaw introduced Heather Hartley. "This is Dacupitte who we call Pete." Heather smiled and murmured hello before she ducked her head, obscuring her profile by the hat's brim. Pete deeply blushed. He sacrificed none of his warrior aura, but under the sunburn and body oils, it was apparent that he experienced exci-tation from contact with the visitors.

Carl put a hand on Heather's shoulder and defensively led her into the hotel lobby. Pete glanced around at our nonplused faces before he rejoined the warriors without explanation.

When we reached the lobby, Carl was shaking hands with Con-sortium officers he knew from the transport. Pierre joined in that talk. Heather hung back, removing her big hat and glancing out the big windows. "Who was that?" she asked.

"A transport officer's son," I said. "Dacupitte is a leader here, but Softcheeks by blood."

"He is ground-born then?" Heather asked.

"His mother was Heather Osborn," Mrs. Shaw said with humor in her voice, "after whom you were named, Heather."

"My mother told us stories about Heather on the transport and about the famous trial," Heather said. "We expected to meet Joey Osborn and Carline Bryant. But this … this warrior is not in contact with, um, with transport personnel."

"Perhaps we should invite him to tea," Mrs. Shaw suggested. She sucked in her cheeks to control her delight at the prospect.

"But that hair," Heather said. "Does he ever wash it?"

Carl and Heather Hartley remained in Somule for several days, and even attended church services with Joey and Karen Osborn. There were outings for entertainment so the Hardhands and the tribal young people could spend time together. I was present at more than one gathering, and Pierre told me about some others.

I attended the tea Mrs. Shaw had suggested, held on the second day of the visit at the Somule doctor's office. The unused hospital branch office included a large back verandah for the needed seating, and maybe dancing. So Heather's culture shock was addressed, Mrs. Shaw arrived dressed in a western skirt with a linen jacket. She submitted to my examination of her fading accident injuries.

"How's the head?" I asked.

"Perhaps something was jolted loose," she offered with humor. "I have swimming dreams now. In some, I migrate upstream against the current with a school of breeding kariom, and we sing an ancient song in unison. In other dreams, I'm exploring a cave, diving deeper than I could ever go. I see tunnels with luminous jellyfish and glowing algae, all in dark blue and red. Then I emerge from the water and walk close to the ground with my nails clicking and my tail swinging left and right behind me."

"You have no sedatives at the fortress?"

"Not helpful with a concussion."

Joey and Karen Osborn arrived before the afternoon heat had passed. Dressed for Sunday services, Karen looked like a frumpy housewife. Brianna wore a western-style drop-waist linen dress for her first dress-up party. Her hair was pulled back and secured with a ribbon. She looked provincial and yearning.

Heather arrived on the arm of her brother and was dressed similarly to Dr. Greensboro. Carl shook my hand and Dr. Mitterand's hand. The shock was Pete's looks. He joined us wearing a Western suit and tie. His dreadlocks had been washed and combed out, and the thick orange hair secured in a tail at his neck. Polished western shoes pinched his feet.

We sat on the cane chairs on the back verandah near a table set for service. Pete fumbled with the tiny teacup and saucer and said nothing. He waited and was apparently waiting. Whenever Heather glanced his way, Pete blushed, a raging purple flush not concealed on his freshly scrubbed and freckled cheeks, an awkward posture for a 27-year-old warrior.

Counting Hakulupe Le, there were five women and five men. From a tray the hotel restaurant had catered we sampled fruit and small sandwiches with the crusts removed. Pierre opened two bottles of white wine and served some along with the bitter tea. Soon the tense atmosphere relaxed, mostly a function of the expensive spirits. Even Brianna was allowed a taste. She frowned and stuck out her tongue before she set aside the wineglass.

"So, Hakulupe Le," I began while the day waned and the young people talked among themselves. "How many students will graduate after the rainy season this year?"

"We have five students in our first graduating class," she said proudly. "I meant to ask, could you give the convocation speech?"

"I would be honored." The wine was too strong for afternoon, causing me to flush.

"And these students," Carl asked diplomatically. "Will any go to university?"

"Two have passed," Lupe grinned, "the translated entrance exams from the transport library, but they speak no offworld languages."

"They could take immersion courses," he suggested.

Hakulupe Le shrugged. "They cannot afford tuition, at any rate."

"But they become," I added, "the most educated members of family groups and will conduct business with cartel Hardhands."

"The next generations of civic leaders, no doubt," Carl added.

"Next term," Lupe said, "fourteen more students graduate. And next year, twice that many with Brianna among them. Dolviet-trained teachers can serve remote family groups."

"Time spent with books is a luxury," Pete interjected. "The students will find work as herders and warriors."

"We can have commerce," Lupe countered, "without dependence on the Bryant cartel."

Joey shook his head. "Arrivi have no licenses to sell offworld and no entry-level commodity in sufficient quantity. Artifacts and one-of-a-kind curios are not competitive." I only nodded and kept mum about what I had seen for industry at the fortress of Arim. I didn't trust Joey any more than his sister Carline.

In the office with French doors open to the back verandah, Mrs. Shaw and Heather inspected some old CDs left over from Abercrombie's estate. Pierre took from his suit coat a small case that held a new CD with recent ditties. He gently spoke to Heather, an act that made Pete frown, and inserted the bright disc into the player.

They came out onto the uneven verandah floor. Mrs. Shaw and Lupe pushed back the cane chairs. Pierre held out a hand to

Heather. They stepped forward and began a light dance to the music. Joey attempted some steps with his wife Karen who stumbled and giggled.

Carl Hartley offered a hand to Mrs. Shaw. She shot a mirthful glance at a sullen Pete before she danced around the long platform in Carl's arms.

Pierre asked Brianna to dance. She glowed under his attention, enamored with the day and the event as only a 15-year-old could be. Joey danced with Heather, while in the grassy yard Karen and Lupe grasped each other's forearms and circled together. Behind the tall back fence, curious Somule children giggled and pointed, attracted by the music.

A sly smile played on Mrs. Shaw's lips when she approached Pete. "Allow me to show you these dance steps." She drew him out onto the floor.

"This is foolish." Pete was aware, I think, of the staring kids in the alley.

"It's easy." Mrs. Shaw showed him where to put his hands and how to move. She encouraged him to count the steps and to relax, have some fun. Then she changed places with Heather, and danced off in Joey's arms.

Pete and Heather stood in the middle of the verandah platform. She was gracious and waiting. He was stiff and unsure. She encouraged him to try, so he put his hand on her waist, and held her other hand while they moved from side to side.

Pete's face betrayed delight and hunger along with the fear of looking foolish. He had chosen to tolerate the day to get close to a bright-faced Hardhand girl with dark hair. Here was his reward.

Mrs. Shaw watched their display with a sly smile but saw me and sobered somewhat. She came to my side. "Do you think the Bryants will make an offer to Carl Hartley to join their businesses after university?"

Where did that idea come from? I wondered. "They would be foolish not to," was all I could muster.

Mrs. Shaw went inside to change the CD. When the music stopped, Heather flirtatiously smiled and put her hand on Pete's cheek. He reflexively drew back but tolerated the touch. I was glad Mrs. Shaw had missed that painful moment. My response was petty, I know, but I was glad anyhow.

Carl asked Heather to dance and the siblings swung off in a rolling step that was obviously practiced. Pete was left standing in the middle of the group with empty hands. He frowned and stepped back.

While dancing with her brother, with each turn Heather boldly glanced into Pete's face, encouraging and confident. Pete averted his eyes and stepped into the office where Mrs. Shaw was turning on the lamps in the twilight. I loitered by the door. I ached to hear their words.

"Why does Heather do that?" Pete asked.

"What?" Mrs. Shaw asked too brightly and bit her lip.

"Grin like that? Why does Heather grin like that?"

"She likes you."

"Her brother covers her," Pete reasoned. "He should know how disgraceful that looks."

"In their world, her gestures are proper and charming."

"It looks bad."

"Still, she holds your attention."

Pete looked at Mrs. Shaw, maybe seeing her in a new light. "How many women are present today?"

"Our customs are not so straightforward."

Pete heavily sighed.

"Get used to these events," Mrs. Shaw added. "If you truly wish to know Heather, there will be many more." When she saw my face, Mrs. Shaw shrugged her shoulders with her palms spread as if to say her hands were clean.

The next day Carline Bryant visited Somule, staying at her brother's house and was seen about town with Carl and Heather Hartley. Braving the daily rains, they journeyed to Haku rabbe Murd's land for a formal tea with Karima Le. Brianna served there and told me about it later. We were in the office where dancing had taken place, and where Brianna was too energized to sit. "A high privilege for a goulep like me, Dr. Beecham," she chattered, "to serve the veiled sisters of Arim."

"They wore burkas?" I asked.

"May and Kyle Le wore the famous sky-blue burkas," Brianna reported, "with the square facial panel. Lupe had hers as a shawl. Mrs. Bryant wanted to know what she had done to sacrifice the honor of viewing the spirit in their faces."

I chuckled at the old tribal phrases and lit my pipe. With ground duty, I had taken up smoking again using a combination of stale tobacco stripped from cigarettes and kari root. I waited for an delayed order for Columbian tobacco to travel through the wormhole. Pierre had claimed that request was a small extravagance considering our service.

"Carline Bryant demanded to know where was Marcy," Brianna added, moving her shoulders to pantomime. "Was she not Marcy's equal? Were they not seated together at the trial where Brian Miller argued for the tribes?"

"Did Marcy join them?" I asked.

Brianna made a face. "Nnoooo. And then … Heather touched Kyle Le's burka. She asked to wear one, just to try it."

"And Kyle Le gave her one?"

"Carline got in the way with her talk," Brianna said, "claiming the burka was for Arrivi only. Why is she so bitter?"

I slightly shook my head. "There's some history there."

"Somebody should tell Heather about history," Brianna said. "She asked to meet Kecouroo."

My mouth fell open. "Really?"

Brianna nodded, too bright. "A courtesy call on the sister of Dacupitte. What is that to us, a courtesy call?"

"What did Karima Le say?"

"That Kecouroo was gleaning herbs on the savannah. Heather was free to seek her there." Brianna chuckled. "Like that's going to happen."

In Cylay I visited the Bryant warehouse that housed the displaced Uburu and where Louise Bilesketchum had been tasked with establishing a first aid station. The noise reverberated in the rafters. The odor was sweat and human offal and desperation. The few wash-rooms were overwhelmed and not cleaned. Women and children sat in family groups on the hard concrete floor while men stood along the walls, suspicious of any new arrival.

"They ran out of the food they brought with them," Louise said, "maybe three days ago. The Consortium provided rations, but mothers don't recognize packaged food like canned peaches. Warriors punctured the cans with beltknives. Kids jumped back when the sticky syrup sprayed out. They drank the liquid and left the peaches in the can."

Louise was a big woman, or maybe because I viewed her in com-parison to Mrs. Shaw. Her blonde hair was coarse and pushed back in a surgical mask. Her features were ruddy, and the doctor's coat was no longer crisp. "A shipment of taro and okiioc came from the Siibabean," Louise reported. "The Consortium supplied millet, dried milk, and some flour. Uburu didn't know what to do with these supplies.

"The Arrivi slaughterhouse," she continued, "sent over some cuts of meat. Of course, now the mothers have cooking fires on the floor. I told them to start a communal kitchen in the backyard, but the Uburu families don't know each other and hoard the food."

"Maybe we can demonstrate how to use a grill to provide meat on paddies."

"Captain Shaw tried that yesterday," Louise said showing her frustration. "The Uburu men took control of distribution and wanted to charge families for cooked meat. Two fights broke out and the grill was turned over."

I nodded. "For now we'll have to prepare some meals off site and distribute them when the families queue up for handouts. We can organize–"

"More Uburu arrive each day," Louise said without listening. "These ones will escape to the savannah soon. We cannot contain them."

"I'll ask around for more support," I said. "I appreciate the efforts you're making here."

I accompanied Dacupitte that night to one of Carline Bryant's dinner parties. Pete wore a Western suit with his hair tied back in an orange tail. He explained his reasoning while we rode in the hotel taxi to Carline's house.

"Uburu are already in Somule and trying to settle on the savannah," Pete said. "Exhausted, hungry, and willing to take insult. We have to provide services or be ready for an armed conflict."

"What does Rabbenu Ely say?"

Pete shook his head. "Ely just wants to write more laws. There's already an ordinance against cutting firewood, and one for squatting. Now he wants to charge a fee for hunting the wild birds. How is he going to enforce that? His Putuki police won't venture out while the plain is flooded."

I packed my pipe from a pouch of old tobacco and kari root mix, and lit it with a utility match. "But you're in Cylay in time for dinner with the Bryants."

"There's no other game in town."

I exhaled with relish. "You don't care about the game. You just want to know the girl."

"You think I look ridiculous," Pete said. "Beyond help. When I look at the sky, I think that it is the blue of Heather's eyes. The apricot sunset imitates her cheeks. Odors of the savannah are in contrast to her perfume. The sounds of bush creatures, even the motor of this car, they come to me now in Heather's voice. What can I do, huh?"

When we entered the house, Frank Duerr shook Pete's hand and introduced him to Brent Gotskind. "Oh, yes," Pete said, comfortable in his leadership role. "You brought rice farming to the Southeast Arrivi."

"The village we visited should have a bumper crop."

"A crop you can unload at Stargate Junction for six times their sale price," Pete added. Gotskind stretched his face into a brittle smile. "Then you overcharge them," Pete continued, also smiling, "at the Bryant seed stores for needed supplies."

Before Brent Gotskind could form a reply, Carline led Pete into the gathering. Carl and Heather Hartley greeted the Mekucoo warrior who blushed. And blushed again.

Carline sat Pete at her side for endless courses with white sauces. Carline spoke to Heather Hartley during dinner, assuming the role of a mentor. "Commerce is different from farming," she said. "Dolviets need to get a perishable product to local markets. But storage for distribution, exchange rates, and franchise rights? They just don't understand the underlying principles.

"I am looking after tribal interests," Carline added. "My brother Joey and I protect them from the Chinese Company that would steal their wealth and leave them with nothing."

"And Dolviets have secured so many civil rights in the Bryant sweatshops?" I asked.

Carline frowned, her face bloated from alcohol intake. "Dr. Beecham, the tribesmen and especially the women, are not properly grateful for our efforts, by any measure. My managers complain about it constantly. They invest the time to give simple instructions but get only hard stares and resentful grunts.

"Even Brian Miller in his time," she added, "complained about the uneven labor force. Workers mosey along without thought of deadlines or uniform product. To change habitual patterns sometimes takes a little coercion."

She showed a wide smile to Heather. "We have good people as overseers. Hardworking Hardhands, some even married to Dolviet women, the clean ones. Allow me to represent you and your parents for trade with the tribes. I can get the best deal. And I'm fair, across the board. Everybody says Carline Bryant is fair in her dealings."

Pete only nodded and stole a glance at Heather Hartley. I wondered if the sounds of knives and forks against plates came to him in Heather's voice.

Frank Duerr watched from under an arched eyebrow. "You sit on the tribal council, don't you, Pete?"

"Yes, with Mekucoo."

Heather sweetly smiled at him, her most important suitor. "This new ordinance that the rabbenu is proposing," Frank said. "I doubt the move is in your best interest." He explained for Carl Hartley, "A law where land deeds must be publicly offered to full-bloods before they can be traded to offworld merchants."

Frank turned his attention toward Pete. "The move leaves the council open to charges of influence peddling. I mean, how many full-blooded workers can afford to own more than their family farms?"

"When we don't insist on tribal rights of first refusal," Pete said, "your cartel buys up the foreclosed land the same day that the bank decides. Dolvia for Dolviets is Rabbenu Ely's motto."

"But Ely wants to restrict the offering to tribal Dolviets, mostly Putuki," Brent said. "Even Carline is ineligible to buy the deeds."

Pete showed a blank look. "Carline is part of the cartel."

"She's ground-born," Brent countered, "and your half-sister."

"She is a Bryant." Pete grinned at his hostess. She falsely smiled.

"You know, Pete," Frank pressed him, "the census you completed during the erriv vaccination was good administration. The register of households can serve as a basis for taxation and for granting voting privileges. One household, one vote, perhaps."

"Governance has the rabbenu structure," Pete said. "Each leader knows his people and their needs. The local rabbenu speaks for them at council meetings."

"One day," Frank returned, "perhaps Dolviets will elect leaders by ballot in open democratic elections and for limited terms. Then the register can manage the voting process."

"You could limit the right to vote to property ownership," Brent added.

"If we tie voting to property rights," Pete said, "we must include the women. Among Mekucoo, for example, the men own nothing."

"Women are not asked to fight or sit at council," Frank said. "They are not educated or initiated as warriors. The right to vote would make them equal to the men in certain respects."

"They raise crops," Pete shrugged. "They build the villages. They manage household finances. I dwell in the home of my sister Kecouroo, for example."

"But she is not your real sister," Heather asked for reassurance. "Like Carline."

"I'm closer to Kecouroo than any soul in the universe. To dwell in her house means we lend covering to each other through our tribal acts."

"And when you marry," I asked, since this was a subject I had long wanted to broach, "your wife will also live in Kecouroo's house?"

"Until she has constructed her own hut in the same village."

"Women do construction?" I asked.

"Women do everything."

"Everything?" Heather incredulously asked.

"So the men can hunt and defend the land."

"Mekucoo women," I asked, "butcher game and plant crops and grind barley? They do beadwork on the warriors' tunics and shields?"

"Yes," Pete shrugged. "Everything."

With saucer eyes, Heather glanced at her brother before she stared at her dinner plate.

Later, I was taking a post-prandial cordial on the verandah. Brittle leaves provided a rustling melody in the breeze. Dolvia's two moons hovered above the blooming acacias. The high moon was Nettom, and the minor one was named Nettki.

I was just about to light my pipe when Heather stepped outside with Pete. They stood between me and the interior lights, so although I could not escape my eavesdropping, I was concealed in the shadows. I lowered the pipe, unwilling to announce my presence.

"Heather," Pete whispered as though he enjoyed pronouncing her name. "Meet me tomorrow."

Heather stood in the amber light. "Will you travel to the transport?" she whispered. "You can meet my father."

"I must return to my warrior duties."

"But you have—"

"I came to Cylay to . . . I mean, I have other—"

"With the Mekucoo?" she asked. "And no place for me in Kecouroo's village?"

"You could stay in Somule like Karen Osborn."

"She has only a house in that outback town," Heather objected. "I want adventure. I want safari, to see undiscovered lands and meet strange people."

"There is no unknown land here," Pete said.

"Come to the transport. Take up work with my father, something important."

"As a Mekucoo warrior, I'm responsible for what I am as much as–"

She drew close to him. "Just visit the transport. My father will—"

He stepped away from her. "You're not listening to me, Heather. I have a place."

"But don't you want to?" She pouted, touching his jacket lapel. "Don't you want to join my world and be somebody? Somebody I can admire and be seen with? Don't you, Pete? Don't you want it?" Heather turned up her face, offering the long-sought yielding moment, the kiss he would forever remember out of time. Pete's brow wrinkled.

Pete put his hands on her shoulders and set her back at arm's length. He stared into Heather's face for a long moment, his expression changing from hunger to cynicism. "You want a puppet, a trophy to display during your university breaks."

"Pete, we're just getting to know each other. Things can work out."

"This cannot be," he said with Mekucoo succinctness. He stepped around her and strode across the dark yard.

"But, Pete . . . Pete, come back! Can't we talk about it?"

He didn't even glance back. Walking resolutely, he loosened his hair so that it pushed away from his shoulders with each step. With curt gestures, he pulled off his jacket, then the tie and white shirt, dropping each on the ground. By the time he had reached the gate, Pete was barefoot, bare-chested, and Mekucoo. He vanished into the moonlit Dolviet night. Not even the rustle of acacia leaves lingered.

With a frown, Heather went inside. The Hartley teenagers left Dolvia a few days later.

ELEVEN

 the air was fresh, and young creatures ventured from the nests. The air was filled with drifting bird-down while hatchlings gained flight feathers. Lemurs had trooped down from the forest to take advantage of the bounty while adolescents of all kinds with floppy ears and oversized paws explored the overflowing billabongs.

I was at the fortress of Arim to look into extra services for the Uburu crisis. The road below the manufacture buildings was tightly packed with Uburu families. Women walked in brightly patterned sarongs and turbans, caked with road dust. Men wore body wraps of more subdued colors, called baktus that hung from waist to knees. Some Uburu carried their belongings in impossibly heavy bundles balanced on their heads. Some dragged trapezoids piled with poultry cages and young children. Their vacant eyes were neither hungry nor accusing, just numb.

Lines of armed warriors watched the stream from stations on both sides of the road to keep the newcomers bunched. Mekucoo, Arrivi, and Cylahi in various clutch uniforms watched for stragglers or families who wanted to leave the group.

Kyle Rula and Mrs. Shaw left the fortress, carefully securing the door and joined me by the ECCAV. "Hiki, Dr. Beecham. Thanks for the visit," Mrs. Shaw said. She was plumper and the bruises were gone. I wondered why she had not returned to the bush clinic, but maybe she preferred to discuss philosophy with Kyle Rula. Mrs. Shaw wore the Arrivi skirt and paneled tunic, and her hair was bound with a cord. "The buildings here are full of Uburu," Mrs. Shaw said, "and we cannot feed them all. Warriors are threatening to pen up the men to keep them from hunting the wild birds."

"We have to consider the Uburu point of view," Kyle Rula added. "So much fresh water. So much wild life. But they are denied food and water?"

We walked down to the warehouse where Arrivi and Cylahi warriors stood at every entrance like prison guards. Orin rabbe Murd and Joey Osborn were talking and came forward to share their ideas. "The refugee camp stretches from here to the shattered butte," Orin said. "And it's not the only one."

"You were told, Dr. Beecham," Joey Osborn added. "Tuang Cho knows that Arrivi don't store their grain. The Company knows the rabbenu structure is not equipped to handle a crisis."

Dacupitte and Karlyhi came up together, accompanied by Siibabean ambassadors with circular headdresses of Murmurey feathers. Ralph was with them, but the Siibabean seemed comfortable with his presence. Of course, Ralph was in the forest with Karlyhi not long ago.

Siibabean seemed to complain with big gestures about the influx of refugees streaming into the forest. One Siibabean looked past my shoulder. His eyes grew wide and he stepped back a few inches. I realized he was staring at the Sheeks-Cylom, that ghostly Soft-cheeks who gave legs to snakes and entered their bodies at will.

"The Siibabean?" Mrs. Shaw asked behind me. "Why are they included? How many young warriors died on my operating table? How many with a Siibabean spearhead in his side?"

"We have a common problem," Kyle Rula told her.

Tears stood in Mrs. Shaw's eyes. "They killed hundreds. I saw the bodies. You can just shrug that off?"

"We see a greater threat from the outside," Kyle Le said gently.

A Mekucoo man looked to Dacupitte for a signal. Pete slowly nodded. The man handed his karkar and munitions belt to a compatriot and stripped off his tunic. He stepped forward, too close to the Sheeks-Cylom. He raised his arms to display his muscled and rib-textured sides. He pointed at three long scars that were battle wounds expertly knitted together using a maser. He stepped back.

Two more Mekucoo repeated his same action while several Arrivi struggled out of their sleeveless tunics. The stouter Arrivi also approached Mrs. Shaw but with less pride in their bodies, lifting their arms to show battle wounds that Mrs. Shaw had tended. She looked away. "Tell them to stop," she whispered to Kyle Rula.

"These you have saved. With whom you shared chi."

"Make them stop," she repeated.

Kyle Rula nodded to the men with an open hand gesture, and they ceased their provocative display. A Siibabean stepped forward from his tribal group. Mrs. Shaw reacted with disgust, but Kyle

Rula gently steadied her. The dark and handsome man dropped his weapon on the ground before he stripped his headdress and also let it fall. With obvious pride in his body, he raised one arm only, displaying a long jagged scar that was a healed battle wound. Mrs. Shaw had saved more than Arrivi. She had attempted to save each bleeding man who had crossed her operating table. She was the Sheeks-Cylom.

"Berkensii," he said in his barking dialect. "Fullemah. Sheeks-Cylom."

"He said," Kyle Rula said, "I live to fight again because of Sheeks-Cylom. This is a great honor for you."

Beads of sweat were obvious on Mrs. Shaw's upper lip. "I need to sit down now."

"Nu delaya," Kyle Rula said to the warrior. "Melinga." The warrior picked up his gear and returned to his tribal group. Mrs. Shaw watched him leave.

"I can't do this," she complained and stepped backward toward the fortress.

"But you have time for dancing with Carl Hartley," I said to her back. I disliked my accusing tone, but the crisis was so great.

"Maybe tomorrow, Dr. Beecham," Kyle Rula said to me and followed Sheeks-Cylom to the locked fortress door. Ralph went with them.

"Let's review the camp," I said to Joey Osborn and went to the ECCAV.

Near the swollen stream in the butte's shadow, we instructed warriors for where to construct sanitation facilities and the need to establish lanes for traffic through the refugee camp. Whispers soon became group confessions about rapes and executions in the yard, and the Company's scorched-earth policy. Rumors circulated about finding charred bodies on the road, the heads and feet and genitals severed with machetes. Chests had been laid open and the hearts cut out. Women and children were beheaded and their skin stripped away.

The stressed women talked about Blackshirts, but also native enforcers from the Gora clan who carried out much of the abuse. We didn't know what to believe. "These are terror tactics to prevent Uburu from moving back to their land at night," Joey Osborn repeated. I was glad when he was called away to oversee some new dispute.

The Director of Natural Disasters Control arrived with two helicopters loaded with supplies. Desperate Uburu women rushed the landing space, but peacekeepers with blue tam stepped in front of them to maintain order. Captain Shaw instructed his detachment to parcel out the tents and cooking staples. Four officers even spoke Uburu, just as though a crisis had been anticipated.

Armed officers in crisp uniforms and blue tams entered the stream of exhausted Uburu and labored to separate mothers with sick children. They gathered angry warriors for questioning and reassured the frightened women that the men would return, that the men were not being taken for massacre. It seemed odd, though, to see the wondering Mekucoo and Arrivi standing on the side, whispering in tight groups, while these Consortium troops labored among the refugees.

Captain Shaw joined us but looked around, straining to see beyond the aid workers.

"Maybe tomorrow," I told him. "Mrs. Shaw may join the aid station tomorrow."

He squinted with his lips drawn in a straight line. "Will you travel with me to review damage to Uburu land?"

"You mean now?" I said. "There's so much–"

"Now is when the helicopter is available," Captain Shaw said. "My officers will establish a structured camp and separate the sick people. I'll bring you back before dark."

We strapped in and the choppers lifted while Captain Shaw slammed the door. The whoop-whoop-whoop of the blades had a slight echoing sound when the chamber was empty. Mike Shaw drew a package from under his seat. "Colonel Hartley sent this to me. Dr. Mitterand at the hospital told Eugene that you were doing fieldwork."

"Eugene?"

"Colonel Hartley."

The shipping box held a new pipe with a tamper, and a two-liter pouch of Virginia tobacco. I opened the sealed pouch and deeply inhaled, reveling in the rich aroma that made me think of better times.

We stopped in Somule to refuel and pack the chopper interior with Consortium provisions. We were delayed by a sudden downpour, so I stepped back to fill the pipe and indulge in a smoke. To my surprise we picked up two more passengers. Rabbenu Ely went to the chopper and took a seat with a grunt. Captain Shaw introduced me to Simon Sumuki, a Putuki man with a stunted arm and malformed hand. "Dr. Beecham, well met," Simon Sumuki said while he watched me stow the pipe and pouch. "We can discuss the tribal contributions to the Cylay refugees."

"Refugees all over the savannah at this point," I said.

Simon launched into his ideas about who should pay. I listened and nodded, but was glad when we boarded and the chopper lifted again. The engine noise was too loud for talk. The second leg of our trip skirted the Canyon of Buttes that we viewed from maybe two kilometers. We followed the Iamida River toward the Uburu mesas and saw more streams of families trudging toward Arrivi land with all their goods.

"So many more," I said to Captain Shaw. He only shrugged, so I returned to staring out the window. Tall mida trees followed the river's path, with tamarind and acacias in the exposed areas. I had never seen the mesas that were lit by intermittent sunlight breaking through the high and fat clouds. Several squat plateaus were grouped with deep gulches between and family homes clustered on the shady side. The mesa tops were carefully manicured by Uburu and tilled for raising maize, barley, and some pecan shrubs. Except many areas showed abuse from conflict. We flew over the scorched land, following a corridor of family farms where freshly planted crops had been set aflame. Dead goats were in the yard, troubled by predator birds and insects.

"The Uburu are good farmers," Captain Shaw said to Rabbenu Ely over the engine noise. "The Company knew when to strike. If we opened a safe corridor today, Uburu have little reason to return before the next planting season."

Rabbenu Ely nodded and stared, but had little to say.

"The Company was careful to leave the roads intact," Mike Shaw added, "and the irrigation system. Tuang Cho is reshaping the population to better serve their substitute crop choices."

"Will coffee grow here?" Rabbenu Ely asked.

"It's untested," Mike said. "There's an obscene exchange rate for coffee, you understand, at Stargate Junction. But coffee does not yield a crop for several years."

"What leverage?" Ely asked.

"We can guarantee a market for Uburu endemic crops," Captain Shaw suggested, "and supply seed for the next cycle. We must place a warrior presence between here and the Company's forces."

"An expensive undertaking," Ely shouted over the noise.

"Less expensive than maintaining the refugees," I said to add my voice. "Rabbenu can secure an offworld capital loan through Colonel Hartley."

"At eighteen percent interest."

"If the charity funds continue through the rains," Mike Shaw said. "If the pox doesn't break out … If the Uburu agree to farm again using seed grain that we supply … And if we have another season of bountiful netta, then this crisis will pass."

After a long silence, Rabbenu Ely asked. "And the Company's next move?"

"Household registration," I said, "that leads to forced labor relocation. A forty percent crop tax."

Ely seemed serious. "So we must act, even if it's wrong."

Mike Shaw nodded. "The Company created this vacuum so they can fill it."

"What about negotiation?" Rabbenu Ely asked.

"You cannot afford their price," Captain Shaw said darkly.

To my surprise, Rabbenu Ely and Simon Sumuki stayed with the chopper while we returned to the refugee camp near the butte. It was late afternoon by then, but the pair stepped down from the chopper and waded into the sea of needy people. Captain Shaw hung back with instructions for how to unload and deploy provisions. I followed Ely wondering what was next. We strolled down a narrow lane with warriors posted at defensive positions. We reached a communal fire where Dacupitte and Karlyhi were already talking with Uburu leaders. They stepped back while introductions were undertaken. Arrivi introductions could take twenty minutes.

I took out my pipe and packed the bowl from the pouch, lightly tamping the real tobacco. I lit a utility match, and heads turned while I inhaled the rich smoke. Mrs. Shaw was suddenly at my side. "The smoke reminds me of my grandfather," she said using the open hand gesture of greeting.

"Supplies just arrived through the wormhole," I said. "I couldn't resist a taste."

She glanced at Ely talking with the Uburu leader named Metobak. "I know you're angry with me," she whispered to me. "But like Kyle Rula says, we have to consider the other's point of view."

"You're needed at the aid station for–"

"My research is trashed," she continued without listening, "or shifted to Dr. Mitterand. My suggestions for better methods are pushed aside. I feel, um, separate from this trouble."

"It's a crisis," I said, not more than a whisper. "Your energy runs hot and cold, serving your ideas for research more than today's crisis."

She crossed her arms as if in defense of my accusation. "I won't exhaust myself again like with the erriv vaccine. There's no premium in it."

Karlyhi turned slightly and gave us a sinister squint. Mrs. Shaw fell quiet. I shrugged and gave my attention to the meeting.

Metobak's potbelly hung over his baktu. Gold rings set with peridot gems squeezed his fat fingers. Behind him stood several old and dry men who reinforced his word. Their man who spoke Arrivi was Mabe Jo who was missing three front teeth. His spittle sprayed whenever he pronounced the word Arrivi. Rabbenu Ely's man was Lt. Manenowski who understood only some phrases, but his presence intimidated the Uburu.

"All this is desert," Rabbenu Ely claimed with a wide gesture while Manenowski translated.

Metobak looked around at the verdant wetlands and squinted.

"Birds and kariom are just resting here," Ely added. "Soon the plants will all die. Tunanin will blow sand dunes across the land." When Mabe Jo translated, Metobak sardonically smirked. "And after it is a desert," Lt. Manenowski said, "the rains wash everything downstream."

Mabe Jo spoke only three words in translation, probably something to the effect of, "Too dry then too wet."

Metobak spoke, and Mabe Jo translated. "Arrivi have no heart. And what is this gruel you expect us to eat? Warriors crave meat. Give us erriv to slaughter."

Arrivi men drew back with alarm. Erriv were not slaughtered in the season of birthing.

"Arrivi withhold erriv," Mabe Jo spat out, "so our warriors grow weak. Arrivi are selfish." Mabe Jo's spittle specks showed on Rabbenu Ely's round glasses.

"The council will discuss what resources to give," Simon Sumuki said over Ely's irritation. The two turned to retraced their steps and the meeting ended. As Rabbenu Ely passed by me, he angrily whispered, "And you want us to save them."

Mrs. Shaw had melted into the crowd, probably avoiding her husband's notice. I stowed the pipe and returned to the aid station where Uburu children were dehydrated with cramps and diarrhea. It was painful to see vacant eyes in their starved craniums. Food was available, but the condition of some children was so advanced that we started IVs in a stifling tent where the weakest refugees were gathered. Mothers accepted each death with resignation, blaming themselves rather than the Company that had pushed Uburu off their land.

But then Marcy, wife of Rabbenu Ely, came to have words with me. I was spoon-feeding an emaciated child who had brittle bones and an oversized head. Marcy stood over me and watched for a few minutes. "River blindness is not a result of coming here," Marcy said without trying to make me look at her. "The larvae must mature in the victim's body over time. Uburu bring their ailments to the savannah."

"Is there a native cure?" I asked while I held a spoon to his lips.

"The insect repellent prevents nesting," Marcy said. "But once you have an internal colony, only netta can save you."

"I can order netta from the transport."

"It must be natural netta. Sun-dried netta."

I was grasping for solutions, repeating suggestions that the leadership group had rejected out-of-hand. "Perhaps we can get Captain Shaw's men to crop dust Uburu ravines with pesticide to destroy the mites."

"Spread chemicals on the land?" Marcy asked with a squint. "This will not be allowed. The warriors will not agree."

She left, but within the hour Rabbenu Ely entered the children's tent. Marcy must have related to her husband my idea for crop dusting. I was mixing another bowl to offer nourishment to an orphan who laid on a single piece of cloth. He weighed less than a newborn lamb. I was exhausted, but it was mostly from my heartstone.

Rabbenu stood in the tent entrance. "You must stop this now," he insisted, his face twisted in anger behind the round-rimmed glasses. He stomped to my side. "Will this Uburu child be alive tomorrow?" he asked. "Will he survive the journey back to Uburu land?"

I offered another spoonful to the listless child. "I can help."

"Allow him to die today," Ely said. "You prolong his suffering with your help."

"I cannot stand by and watch."

"You think rabbenu is cruel," Ely said, "when it's Softcheeks who are cruel. Spill chemicals over the savannah. But that's no solution. Uburu must be made to understand; the savannah is a desert, and will return to desert next season or the next."

I set down the work and sighed. In truth, I looked forward to returning to the hospital where I would not have to watch children die.

"You must learn to see what we see," Ely said. "If it takes a few hundred deaths to convince the refugees, then let it be so. Several hundred others will leave here and learn to survive on Uburu land. This is how Dolvia would have it.

"So you are wrong, Dr. Beecham," he articulated precisely from behind his round glasses. "Wrong with your misplaced compassion. And I am right with my tribal logic. Cease these efforts or you will be forcibly returned to the hospital where you belong."

Rabbenu Ely left and I waited. The Uburu women stared with blank faces. I picked up the bowl and returned to spoon-feeding. Marcy entered the tent. Brianna came to my side and took the bowl from my hand.

"Don't share chi with these ones," Brianna said. "When they die, a part of you is lost."

"You exhaust yourself with your compassion," Marcy added. "Rabbenu Ely is correct. Some must die today so they don't all die tomorrow."

Brianna helped me from my seat. She walked with me through the camp to a waiting lorry that Karlyhi drove in his pell-mell manner toward the hospital. During the ride, I looked into the truck bed, expecting to see automatics and ammo crates. But the back was crowded with mixed-tribe warriors, each cradling a karkar. We passed more armed warriors on the open road.

"Who are all these people?" I asked.

"Arrivi guard the refugee camp," Karlyhi said.

"But this is an army."

Karlyhi concentrated on his driving. "Some have argued that now is the time to kill Uburu warriors while they're under our power."

"A massacre?"

"This is a tribal matter to be decided in its own time. By tribal logic, not by Softcheeks."

"You mean, like the assassination of Dr. Abercrombie?" Karlyhi turned his implacable face my way, but said nothing more.

I slept several hours in my own bed. I dreamed of swimming in a grotto. I dreamed that I glided through the water, deeper and deeper, where I viewed the deep walls and rock formations. I could see in the dark, distinguishing shapes in hues of red and blue. I swam through more chambers in the aquifer, effortlessly propelled by my swishing tail. I surfaced and languished without fear or discomfort while water splashed against my always-open eyes.

I dove under the waterfall and reveled in the pounding weight and rich spray. I emerged from the grotto and sought sunlight. My view was low to the ground. Hyrax and salamanders scurried away from my approach. I basked in the afternoon sun with my mouth open, enjoying its replenishing warmth on my marbled hide. *Ka, ka, ka, ka, ka,* Edna sang in my dream.

I felt refreshed when I awoke the next day. Dr. Mitterand didn't ask me to share hospital rounds, claiming that we had mostly Arrivi cases, not refugees. He reported that refugees gleaned the savannah for food and fuel. They netted parrots and kikis. They trapped snakes and kariom. They gathered erriv dung for their cooking fires. "A trade in parrot feathers," Pierre added, "has sprung up here. Refugees get a good price in oblu for the red, yellow, and green tail feathers. Cylahi refuse to purchase feathers from the blue macaw, though."

Unfortunately, there was also commerce for karkars and munitions. We heard that Karlyhi had complained to Cara who ordered Mekucoo warriors to search the tents. Uburu women sat on the weapons and denied they had seen any. Warriors were forced to manhandle the matrons in efforts to disarm the increasingly resentful Uburu men.

Since I withdrew from the aid stations, I had moments of regret for my attitude toward Mrs. Shaw. I heard that she completed some shifts with the suffering refugees, mostly to establish procedure with aid workers and lecture the nurses about better hygiene. As the minister of the grant structure, I still received reports of how the crisis progressed. I often left the unopened manila envelopes on my desk.

Some good did come from the turmoil. Through council maneuvering, the savannah was deeded to the men of property who herded erriv. The right of first refusal for any sale of family land was secured for Arrivi, meaning the four tribes, disposition. Tithing of ten percent from all property owners and from workers' wages was collected for grain storage and disaster relief. Rabbenu Ely appointed teams of magistrates called welfare ministers to visit local residents and mediate disputes, to collect the tithe amount, and to dole out relief supplies.

The Arrivi and Putuki men who sat in council challenged Ely's authority to levy taxes. Ely argued that he collected no taxes. Taxes and tithing were different, since tithing was voluntary. Also, those families who displayed generosity could offer sons and brothers to serve as welfare ministers, thereby safeguarding their considerable contributions. Angry arguments broke out concerning Rabbenu Ely's elitism. But Orin rabbe Murd assented to his leadership, and Cara lent him influence.

Apparently, some tribesmen approached Dacupitte who they remembered from when he visited their family land during the vaccine task. Landowners and workers petitioned Pete to challenge Rabbenu Ely in the council meetings. Pete reached out to Kyle Rula concerning what was seen. She only reported back that Rabbenu Ely led during this cycle.

At the hospital, the council members gathered again. Before the meeting started, Pete and Karlyhi stood smoking kari root at the hospital entrance. "Metobak's power has tripled since they arrived here," I heard Karlyhi confide to Pete. "He does not want to go home where he is just another maize farmer."

Haku rabbe Murd made the trip to sit in the desk chair in my office and add his opinion, backed by his considerable wealth. I was allowed to attend, I think, so Ely could demonstrate that he was right and I was wrong. Haku hoisted his obese self from the seat and stood before the others, the old napalm burns obvious on his face. His clouded eyes surveyed the group.

"Uburu have known a hard time," Haku rabbe Murd began. "Our sympathy is with them, and we have offered a helping hand. Uburu must return to their farms now. If they stay, two things will happen. Their condition will worsen as the savannah heats. Blame will be placed on the four Arrivi tribes for not supplying more from our resources.

"Secondly, Uburu will migrate to high grazing land while we are bringing the erriv down from there. This contact must be prevented at all costs. This foreign tribe will poach our herds. They will spread their diseases and despoil the pasture.

"Uburu must be encouraged to return home now," Haku added. "Not after the savannah suffers. Not after the grazing land suffers. Whatever trouble the Company has brought to their farms, Uburu must stand and fight in the mesa land. In the days of Cyrus the keti-whelp killer, savannah tribes stood against the Company in a struggle of overwhelming odds. Uburu must attempt the same for their own land. Our warriors may volunteer to support the struggle for home rule. And that is my word on it."

Haku rabbe Murd's words were published in three dialects and distributed on a flyer. The tract was also published in Uburu and distributed in the tent city. An Uburu-language flyer was presented to Metobak. He crumpled the paper and let it drop to the ground. His Uburu warriors, whose families received the best of the rationed food, stood behind him.

Then the offworld media arrived.

One Consortium newsman named John Milan approached me in the hospital corridor after I had tallied the daily list of dead Uburu children. He spoke into a handheld microphone while he walked along with me. Another man with a shoulder camcorder walked backward with his glaring lights focused on us.

"Isn't it true," John Milan demanded, "that Consortium aid is tardy for the refugees? Isn't it true that Arrivi militia keep them bottled up under desperate conditions?"

"Arrivi did not invite the Uburu here," I said. "There was no warning." Tears came to my eyes. I felt my throat constrict.

"But isn't it true—"

Dr. Mitterand got between the camera and me. "We have a considerable relief operation here on the savannah," he said, facing John Milan and the bright lights. "Everything that can be done is undertaken.

"An unfortunate situation," Dr. Mitterand added with a wry smile into the camera lens, "that will escalate unless the Company allows Uburu safe passage back to their land. The Company has created this crisis by burning Uburu crops and by executing the people."

"But isn't it true that more Uburu are dying each day?" John Milan asked.

"Unfortunately, the refugees brought tribal diseases with them," Dr. Mitterand said, at ease in front of the camera. "Arrivi leaders have been most generous, providing aid and comfort. Uburu children will continue to die until they are allowed, by the Company that threatens their land, to peaceably return home."

Over the next several days, Dr. Mitterand was often solicited by the media for his opinion of events. He was viewed as neutral, being Softcheeks and a doctor. Soon the distant Company felt the heat of his statements concerning their degree of guilt. It was made known that the Company would welcome back any Uburu family that agreed to take up the cultivation of coffee as a cash crop.

Pierre was a solace to me in that time with his ever-cheerful manner. He spent one sunny afternoon with a camera at the camp by the butte. He selected a few six and eight-year-olds, mostly big-eyed girls, and photographed them standing near something intrinsically Uburu. He journeyed to the Somule academy on Friday, anticipating a long weekend spent at the hotel. He showed the photos to Hakulupe Le and requested that her students write letters. Nothing long or revealing since the recipients could not read Arrivi, but different sentences in different handwritings. He matched the letters with certain photos and forwarded them to the Softcheeks relief organizations that solicited charity dollars from suburban Americans beyond the wormhole.

When I asked Pierre about this less-than-honest endeavor, he just smiled. "If not here, the same charity dollar will go to some other Westend charity. What harm if Uburu get a share?"

As we had feared, pox broke out in the tent city. Uburu warriors craved meat instead of rice gruel and taro soup. How it was explained to me, some Uburu bartered for erriv with an Arrivi family that was sick with open sores on their arms and faces. Uburu slaughtered the heifers while still in the company of the pox-ridden Arrivi and smuggled the meat into camp. Their families sickened the next day. Weakened Uburu warriors silently stood with compatriots, but women brought their feverish and splotchy-cheeked children to Sheeks-Cylom at the aid station. It was apparent within a few minutes what they had.

Mrs. Shaw wore a surgical mask and instructed aid workers to use separate containers for Uburu food and water rations. They must burn the refugees' colorful clothes and issue disposable hospital gowns. Mrs. Shaw blamed herself. "If only I had developed a pox vaccine," she said over the EAM while we discussed precautions. "If only I had stayed with my research instead of retiring to the fortress of Arim."

Similar procedures were imposed at the Cylay refugee camp. Uburu warriors were gathered by Louise Bilesketchum to receive medicine and sit like truant schoolchildren in the quarantine section wearing the green gowns. Some ran away, carrying the infection with them.

With the news of the spread of disease, the media no longer visited the hospital or the tent city. Pierre told me that reporters preferred a Cylay hotel where they filed stories packed with rumor and aching prose. He chuckled bitterly. "Reporters stand in front of their stationary cameras on the hotel balconies and point left. 'There live the Arrivi.' Then they point right. 'There live the Uburu.' Very informative."

One day Captain Mike Shaw arrived by helicopter at the hospital. He introduced his seconds who were Hardhands by birth, Lt. Taylor and Lt. Milo Sector. "Just call me Milo," the big man said with a grin under his black mustache. What was it about these Consortium officers with their strong chins and square shoulders? They were authoritative and appealing like leading men in old cowboy movies. I was glad to cede management of the crisis to them.

Captain Shaw flew to the tent city. He walked with resolution through the dank alleyways, flanked by his seconds, and entered the quarantine station. Mrs. Shaw labored there wearing a hospital smock. She pulled the surgical mask to below her chin and just stared at Mike. He took a step toward her. She took a step back. He glanced back at his men, but then grabbed her arm before she could get away. With square shoulders and stoic faces, Mike's lieutenants blocked the entrance when staring tribespeople and refugees crowded the tent.

Mrs. Shaw cursed Mike and struggled. They bumped a table that overturned, and medical equipment fell to the ground with a clatter. Captain Shaw carried Mrs. Shaw fireman-style, kicking

and complaining, out of the tent to the waiting chopper. His officers followed, screwing up their faces to hide their grins.

Mike ignored his wife's slaps and angry words and strapped her
into the chopper seat. He jumped in also and signaled to the pilot
who took off. Once their superior was out of sight, Lieutenants
Taylor and Sector bent double, releasing their laughter with great
booming sounds.

We heard later that Mrs. Shaw was resting comfortably in a Cylay
hotel. I rather wished that Captain Shaw had carried me off to feath-
erbeds and room service. All I had as defense against my heartstone
were my tobacco pipe and my grotto dreams.

TWELVE

THE WEEKS WORE ON. THE BILLABONGS RECEDED AND DRY WINDS troubled the tent cities. The Uburu families that were able began deserting the camp near the flats to walk north toward the high grazing land just like Haku rabbe Murd had predicted. The first groups trudging north were turned away by the peacekeeping contingent under Lieutenant Taylor's command. But then came a steady stream of families, carrying their few possessions on their heads and cradling children.

Lieutenant Taylor's men could not contain the flow. Only three officers spoke Uburu. With poised guns and barked commands, the blue-helmeted men stopped some groups and turned them back. They forced others off the road. But people walked around the mechanized forces in a wide and resolute front. Lieutenant Taylor's men were at a loss. What action could the Hardhands take? Fire on them?

The first herds of erriv were returning to the savannah. Families from the southeast near Cylay had hereditary rights to lead the return. Pregnant heifers must reach family villages early or lose their burdens. Arrivi families depended on the increase. Southeast Arrivi had little refugee involvement and resented being restrained by Consortium soldiers. Rabbenu Ely, Orin rabbe Murd, and Dacupitte went among the families with explanations and suggestions for alternate herding paths among the billabongs.

There were more council meetings and more angry arguments. I was told that Pete suggested a certain number of erriv could be selected for slaughter and delivered to Uburu families in the tent city, along with better sanitary conditions. If their condition improved, the Uburu would have less incentive to migrate further into Arrivi land. Orin rabbe Murd asked in the meeting that, with such improvements, wouldn't the Uburu have less incentive to go home? How many erriv must be sacrificed for the uncounted thousands? And for how long?

Apparently Karlyhi suggested at the council meeting that armed warriors surround the migrating families and execute a few as an example to the others. Many council members had nodded in agreement.

I accompanied Dacupitte for a ride to Cylay on the mail run. Brianna went with us to visit Mrs. Shaw, accustomed now to helicopter flights. We flew over the refugee camp near the Cylay warehouse district that was bigger and more desperate than the camp by the butte. I stared out the side window to view the suffering to the sound of whoop-whoop-whoop of the chopper blades. In Cylay, the infant mortality rate had dipped, but rose sharply again when the pox spread. Predictably, a disease that only scarred Arrivi swiftly killed Uburu and infected offworlders. Karlyhi had dubbed the pox the silent hand.

At the hotel suite, Brianna washed out Pete's mud-caked braids and secured his lush hair into the long tail at his neck. He dressed in the Western suit and tight shoes ready to visit Sean Bryant's office at the former bank building. "Make no concessions to the Bryants," I told Pete. "They will leverage their advantage for provisions to grab the export licenses."

"Come with me," he suggested. "You have talked with them before."

Since one Bryant warehouse was used for distribution of supplies to refugees, the Bryants had consolidated operations in a manufacture building closer to the business district. The offices had a temporary feeling with exposed brick walls and overhead ducting. The Bryant receptionist asked if Pete had an appointment, but soon directed him to the stairwell leading to the fourth floor.

We stepped onto a catwalk in the windowless building and looked down on a sweatshop operation where Hardhand managers wore side-arms and carried leather batons called billy clubs. Behind them sat long rows of young Cylahi and Arrivi women, each laboring over a workbench where she hand-stitched the tough sole leather for sport shoes that bore a Dolvia-Made tag.

We waited again near a group of tribal women chained together at the ankle who assembled volleyballs with quick stitching. The closest women stopped working. They sat with eyes averted and hands folded in their laps as was correct when in the presence of a Mekucoo warrior. One manager noticed their rest and slapped the long bench with his baton. "Get back to work!" The women glanced at Dacupitte who squinted at the manager. With frightened eyes the women took up their labor.

The manager scowled. "Stand across the way," he told Pete.

Presently we were shown into Daniel Bryant's office on the fourth floor, where Daniel and Patrick puffed on kari root cigarettes and looked down through smoked acrylic windows onto a crowded factory floor.

"Dr. Beecham, how are you?" Daniel said. "We have been missing you, Pete, at Carline's dinner parties. You haven't attended since Heather Hartley's visit."

"I have tribal business."

"Of course," Patrick said. "A great warrior like yourself cannot spend all his time pursuing teenage Hardhand girls."

Pete expression was neutral, but his color was high. "We came to Cylay," Pete said evenly, "to find solutions for the refugee crisis."

"Sean left for the transport yesterday," Daniel said. "The shuttle returns in ten days. Can I answer your questions?"

Pete and I accepted Daniel's invitation to sit. The chairs were cracked leather with deep cushions. "As you know," Pete said, "Arrivi resources are strained. We know the Bryants have a reserve of stored grain. We ask that you take part in the charitable aid effort."

"The uninvited guests took over one warehouse already," Daniel said. "The Consortium makes demands for better sanitation."

Patrick looked at Daniel before he asked, "And our return for this generous gesture?"

"The satisfaction of knowing that you have saved lives," I said.

"Satisfaction is an intangible," Patrick claimed. "We need something we can put on the company balance sheet."

"What did you have in mind?" Pete asked.

"There is one named Kyle Rula, an in-law of yours, I believe," Patrick said. "She holds certain offworld trading licenses that operate in competition to ours."

Pete glanced at me before he dropped his chin. "It's open commerce," Pete said.

"Yes, of course," Daniel agreed. "We're not trying to shut her down. However, to gain Bryant generosity in this crisis, we need points, a certain percent of her profits, into perpetuity, as a premium for participating."

"You negotiate commerce rights for relief provisions?"

"That's our price." Daniel sat back in the big leather chair.

"People are dying," I said. "Relief supplies are essential for their recovery."

"We sympathize. However, ours is a business, not a charitable foundation."

"All groups including Dolviet businesses," Pete said, "have made sacrifices in this crisis. None other has demanded a kickback."

"Kickback is an ugly term," Patrick said. "We must see a return."

"This will never be agreed," I said.

"Think it over," Daniel said while he lit a new cigarette. "I imagine you will be back before the harvest. Then perhaps our price will increase. Late capital is expensive capital."

"Capital?" Pete asked. "As in investment?"

"We must look to the future." Patrick stood to show us the door.

Outside the office, Brent Gotskind was just coming up the steps to keep his Bryant appointment. Pete had stared into his face. "You know about this place?" Pete asked.

"The Bryants manufacture quality products," Gotskind said as a practiced answer, "with a strong end-market. The Bryant export capability is essential for building market advantage."

"Essential for whom?" Pete pushed past him and we left the sweatshop's stifling atmosphere. Once we had reach the street, Pete asked me in a hard whisper, "Did you know about the sweatshops?"

"I didn't know the conditions were–"

"They chain the women to work stations," he said hotly. "Next they'll add Uburu to their labor force."

I shook my head. "They want the refugees to be our burden. To expose cracks in tribal unity."

"The Company needs no cracks," Pete said. "They have the Bryants in their pocket."

The desiccated body of an Arrivi boy who labored with his father's herd was found near an erriv-poaching site. He was not reported as missing, and was not covered against carrion eaters. His remains were unfit for his mother to view.

We felt an immediate tribal outcry. The hearts of warriors who surrounded the tent city quickly changed from charitable to resentful. More Uburu families slipped away at night to reappear in the forbidden north grazing land.

Pete and Karlyhi were in my hospital office conferring with Orin rabbe Murd who had supplied erriv for the refugees. Pete's orange hair spread wide on his shoulders, as he had recently returned from Cylay and his meeting with the Bryants. Pete claimed that the heinous murder of a child was perhaps planned to inflame emotions. Orin was inclined to agree.

"Arrivi complained to Lieutenant Taylor," I added, "that his peacekeeping force was not effective. But what can he do? Shoot them all? Lieutenant Taylor contacted Captain Shaw, who told him to stand pat."

"Will you go with us to the refugee camp?" Pete asked me. "As a neutral presence."

"Whatever is needed," I said.

The tent city was showing wear. Garbage was piled high and the lanes were rutted by foot traffic. The smell of urine was pervasive because women were afraid to use the public latrines after stories of assault and rape had circulated. Several tents were abandoned, emptied of personal belongings, their tattered flaps banging against tent poles. Ralph came with us into the camp, just because he was often with Karlyhi, and women pulled their children into the family circle. Their first view of a male gualarep.

We sought the one Metobak who was hiding behind his fat wife and numerous children. Mabe Jo was also rooted out. Uburu warriors no longer stood with these two.

Pete requested through Mabe Jo to know what Metobak proposed in response to the death of the Arrivi boy. The sputtering man complained in his dialect. Mabe Jo translated, "Uburu are divided now. Warriors are sick with the pox. Arrivi provide no beef."

"Pull it together, man," Pete said. "What is your best plan of action?"

Metobak shrugged.

Two Cylahi under Karlyhi's command entered the meeting, dragging with them a young Uburu man. They forced him onto his knees before Pete and Karlyhi, claiming he was caught smuggling beef into the camp. Ralph baked twice but assumed the muscles-down posture when Karlyhi gave him a sharp look.

"He was carrying this." The Cylahi soldier threw a fistful of Cicero-made coins into the sandy yard. The groveling prisoner gathered each shiny piece of silver into his palm while he spoke a long lament in Uburu.

"This man's wife is held hostage by the Company," Mabe Jo translated. "Maybe she is turned out in a Company brothel if he does not produce results, if Arrivi and Uburu don't take to fighting. He is newly married. He loves his wife. He felt compelled to kill the Arrivi boy to save her virtue."

"And if you killed Arrivi for virtue's sake," Pete asked, "then why these coins?"

The prisoner looked up with terror on his gritty and tear-streaked face. His eyes wandered to Ralph as he hunched his shoulders.

"Stand him up," Karlyhi instructed. His seconds pulled the groveling man to his feet.

Before judgment could be pronounced, however, a knife came hurling out of the crowd and pierced the prisoner's ribs from behind. He slumped between the warriors and coughed twice. Blood dripped from his mouth.

The Cylahi dropped their prisoner who was dead before he hit the ground. With karkars poised, they took defensive stances in front of their leaders. Ralph joined them while facing the surprised Uburu.

Mabe Jo quickly explained, "His heart was pierced by his father's knife."

A weeping woman, his mother, fell to her knees near the body, loudly wailing. She was joined by other Uburu women. Crowding Uburu stepped back to reveal an older and bent man with a tragic face. The elder did not move, his piercing glare focused on Dacupitte.

"Hold these two," Pete instructed, indicating Metobak and Mabe Jo. The warriors quickly complied. Pete showed an open palm at elbow height to the elder who had sacrificed his son for peace, and proclaimed before the gathered refugees, "Search out your instigators to be judged by this man. Starting with Metobak."

Mabe Jo, who was translating, stumbled over the words.

Pete spoke directly to the elder. "Mekucoo warriors will provide a safe corridor for return to your farms. Two days of atonement and ritual cleansing will precede the trek homeward."

And so, two days later, the Uburu began walking home. Only the sick remained, and they were escorted by Arrivi who were resistant to the pox to a new aid station on high ground where the quarantine lasted until the next erriv drive.

When word spread that disease was contained, the media spilled out from the Cylay hotel. Offworld journalists with their camcorders and intrusive microphones followed the trudging Uburu. Their reports were broadcast repeatedly on the comtechs, so I followed the events during doctor rounds.

A woman reporter named Regan Villines asked a passing Uburu, "Do you feel you have been well treated by the savannah tribes? What is your reason for returning at this time when your crops are sacrificed? Has the original threat that forced you off the land in some way lessened? Is there a new agreement with the Arrivi who were enforcers to you?"

It was fortunate that few reporters understood the Uburu dialect. Answers from the refugees, when they chose to answer, did not fit the questions. So reporters lined up the ones dressed in colorful traditional clothes or carrying impossibly heavy head baggage and ran stock footage on them.

The reporter John Milan bumped into Mabe Jo who had been spared by his elder. Mabe Jo claimed to understand Arrivi words, and puffed up under the flood of camcorder lights. "I was present at the tent city meetings," he explained through his tooth gap. "I was a player." John Milan and Regan Villines immediately thrust their microphones toward him. But Mabe Jo saw Karlyhi's implacable face in the crowd and suddenly could understand none of their questions posed in Arrivi.

As the worst of the crisis passed, warriors returned to the hospital for one more council meeting. Haku rabbe Murd came in with Orin and again spoke before the gathered men. His presence provided a certain gravitas. Pete told me later that Haku was satisfied with the outcome of the meeting. "The council can leave the hospital now. We appreciate your hospitality and the use of your office as a gathering place."

Apparently, at the meeting Haku rabbe Murd cited the Uburu origins of their former holy woman Oriika. Tribesmen had acted honorably in this current crisis. The rabbenu structure was secure. Welfare ministers would continue to collect the ten percent tithe as insurance against future intertribal crises. And warriors would establish a presence along with Hardhand peace-keeping forces among the Uburu mesas.

"Will you return to Mekucoo land?" I asked Pete.

"I'm slated to work with Captain Shaw," Pete said, "to secure the corridor for returning Uburu. But we can keep in touch."

Rabbenu Ely, however, was steamed that his authority was bypassed with Pete's promise of safe passage. Dr. Mitterand told me that Ely held a private meeting with the upstart Dacupitte. They had harsh words, but Pete assured Ely that in the tent city after the death of the elder's son, Pete had offered only Mekucoo assistance, which was his to offer. Arrivi need not participate, on rabbenu's word, in the mesa police duties.

But of course, they must.

And those were the events, as near as I can relate them, that led to the end of the refugee crisis. I had kept my head down, unwilling to face my heartstone, but was cut low by events just the same. Soon I was coughing and diagnosed with tuberculosis. Can you believe it? I contracted the very disease we came to Westend to prevent.

PART THREE

Uburu from their own land walked
Onto the savannah verdant
But tunanin and heat and pox
Did make their exit urgent
Them and their goats also

Rabbenu Ely and Dacupitte
Wrote deeds still good in om
The oldest son in charge shall be
While younger sons leave home

To learn the weapons parceled
Karlyhi's service warriors honored
For food and shoes and pensions
Against the Borabean they gathered
Big and loud and girded,
While heifers overran the garden.

THIRTEEN

from Brianna Miller

NO, IT'S NOT BRIANNA LE, JUST BRIANNA. DON'T WORRY ABOUT
me, though. I understood what you said. I have many English words.
Sheeks-Cylom taught me at the clinic after my academy classes and
when I brought her tea.

I rode in helicopters before, you know, with Dr. Beecham. I rode
in the lorry and in military trucks. None of it was new to me. I'll
travel to Earth one day, too. Dr. Mitterand promised. He said that
when he jumps back through the wormhole, he'll take me on a tour
of Earth's capitals; skyscrapers, Disneyworld, everything.

I went to Cylay in their helicopter along with the Hardhand
officers. They dropped me off at the hotel after a ride in the back of
their jeep. Kyle Rula had said it was correct that I should join Dr.
Greensboro, that I should leave my duties with Dr. Beecham at the
aid station and travel to the Cylay hotel.

I learned plenty during those weeks in Cylay. I felt I could learn from anybody. People's life stories, their rich experience, and what they chose to relate. That was important. Each person's story was important. Even mine, Brianna's. My story also carries weight.

One should keep a channel open, that was Captain Shaw's phrase. He took Dr. Greensboro to Cylay, rescuing her from work in the quarantine tent. But things were not good between them. Early in my stay there, he said, "One should keep a channel open."

When I climbed the stairs to the seventh floor that first day, I saw Captain Shaw in the corridor. I was leaning against the wall with my rucksack dropped on the floor, panting after the difficult climb. Captain Shaw was dressed in fatigues and a blue tam. He was a big person, you know, with big hands. He smiled at me and nodded, and waited near some doors while I entered Dr. Greensboro's rooms. I later learned those doors were the elevator. Ha, that was something.

When I opened the suite door, perhaps Dr. Greensboro thought it was Captain Shaw returning, like he forgot something. "And don't think these orchids mean anything to me either," she called out. "Because they don't!"

She saw me then. "Oh, it's you, Brianna."

"Hiki, Sheeks-Cylom," I said with a palm held high. "Melinga."

She was still in bed, languishing on satin sheets against the big pillows. She wore something lacy and had the insect repellent washed out of her hair. A breakfast tray with an untouched meal and a bowl of orchids rested on the plump comforter next to her.

She leaned back and stretched her arms over her head. It seemed odd to see Dr. Greensboro in that setting. I mean, at the clinic she allowed herself no luxuries. She took no personal comfort over what the tribeswomen could secure.

In Cylay, she lived as Mrs. Captain Michael Peter Shaw and was told to rest and regain her strength. They were registered at the hotel as husband and wife, and she appeared in public with him. At functions and all. During the whole time I served her there, we traveled in military vehicles with a military driver, even for shopping. "We're being bullied," she whispered to me more than once.

But it was my impression that Mike Shaw slept on the suite floor. He was not forgiven.

That first day she slipped out of bed and pulled on a silken robe. She carried the breakfast tray to the balcony. The view was not great, overlooking the crooked alleyways and smoking stovepipes. But the morning air was cool, and the planted vines were daily watered.

"Here," she said. "Eat this."

"But it's for you."

"Captain Shaw prefers hefty women. He wants to fatten me up so I resemble Louise Bilesketchum." She spat out the name like venom. "You eat it. I'm taking a shower."

So I ate the breakfast and drank some tea. Presently Mrs. Shaw returned from the other room. Her hair was wet. She wore a shimmering blouse and tan skirt over low-heeled canvas shoes. There was a jacket and scarf laid out. She sat in the morning shade and put up her feet. She drank from the cup I poured.

Mrs. Shaw could be demanding sometimes. She didn't see it, though. She got started on one subject or another, and she could not be distracted. Like with the English lessons, "*i* before *e* except after *c*." I had that drilled into my head.

And when I complained, she just had my heart. "Demanding?" she said. "I'm never demanding. What do you mean, demanding? Just give me one instance, one time when I was demanding. Just one."

Like that.

It didn't bother me, though. I told myself that Dolvia blessed Sheeks-Cylom. The blessing spilled over onto me because of my service. I mean, there were good parts too. She made a place for me. She included me when she talked with the men. At the clinic, one day we even rode into Somule; we just took off. That was something.

Edna had nearly recovered from her goring by then. The rains had passed. Dr. Greensboro was supposed to be studying spiders with Cara in the new ritual building. She up and decided she wanted to go. We piled into the lorry and left, just like the men would have, just like Karlyhi.

What a grand trip. Edwina joined us before we reached the savannah, overcrowded with nesting birds. Edwina had earlier kept her distance, you know, since the day Edna was gored. She knew Mrs. Shaw's unforgiving heart.

But who could resist Edwina with her calming spirit? I shared many grotto dreams with her. I asked her to help Dr. Beecham when his heartstone became a burden at the aid station. Edwina did not care for the idea so much, with Dr. Beecham being an outsider. In her own way, she could be as unforgiving as Sheeks-Cylom. That's why it was so special, how they reconciled on the savannah. That was a moment.

On the hotel balcony, Dr. Greensboro fingered the orchid she had claimed she did not want. "So what are Hakulupe Le's homilies this week?"

"Time is a loop," I quoted from what I remembered lettered on the academy blackboard. "Sometimes we are through events before we know their meaning in our lives."

Mrs. Shaw chuckled. "I wondered how long it would take before Lupe stopped using Softcheeks sayings. What's another one?"

"Only the law stands between us and forces Dolvia allows."

"Who is that from?"

"Oriika, I think," I said. "The holy woman from the time of the resistance."

"Ah, yes. People remember she was Uburu by birth. Let's hear more. Lupe usually writes six or seven on the blackboard."

"You cannot avoid war by yielding, nor achieve peace by disarming."

"That's Softcheeks," she said. "Some Chinese guy. So Kyle Rula still studies her enemies. She would like to use their words against them."

These mental exercises were a game for her, priming the pump before she started that day's research, except there was no research. Mrs. Shaw had no equipment or biopsy cultures in the hotel suite. There was only me to pester.

"And what new words do you have? Anything English?"

"Ah, there is tarmac."

"Good word."

"Discretion. Oh, and sub-ter-fuge."

"A French derivative. Did you get that from Dr. Mitterand?"

"From Lieutenant Milo Sector, the supply officer."

She squinted and put her feet down to sit forward. "Milo? There's a supply officer named Milo?"

"What is wrong with that?"

She laughed to herself. "Nothing. It's perfect." Mrs. Shaw had many private jokes. And many she and Dr. Mitterand shared without explanations. It was from being Softcheeks, I think.

She wanted me to take a shower, but I did not know what that was. She led me into the other room that had a washbasin and a water closet and a water trough for erriv that seemed out of place. She turned some knobs in the tub and water sprayed down. She pulled a curtain so we would not get wet.

"Now undress and get under the spray. Here's soap and a wash-cloth and a towel. When you are done, we can go shopping. You can buy some Softcheeks clothes."

Mrs. Shaw left then. I closed the lid and sat on the water closet. I was not getting under any spray. Presently she knocked on the door. "Brianna, are you decent?"

Mrs. Shaw entered and stared with her eyebrows raised. Steam settled on the big mirror behind the basin. "You may have your own room here at the hotel and room service. But you get none of these until you learn to take showers."

I moved the curtain slightly and watched the spray. "I'll strip you myself if I must," she added. "And I will know if you're cheating. So get wet, and do it now." She closed the door again.

It wasn't too bad. I learned to like showers after a while. Mostly I liked the feeling when the shower was over. You know, when your skin is all soft and spongy.

Shopping was all right too. We rode to the stores in the Consortium jeep even though it was just a few blocks. She insisted the driver wait on the heated street while we lingered in the air-conditioned boutiques.

That is a French word too. Boutique.

The clothes were very strange. We tried on layers of them: panties and camisoles and hose and blouses and jackets and scarves and hats. And perfume and lotion. The lotion was for after the showers, to fight the destructive effect of getting wet each day.

We returned to the hotel and had our packages carried upstairs by Putuki men in red jackets while Mrs. Shaw dismissed the military driver. He was greatly relieved.

In the hotel restaurant, we sat at a window table and held up these huge folded plastic things. Mrs. Shaw called them menus. I could not see around mine.

Perhaps that was how I missed Carline Bryant's entrance. Apparently, she snubbed Mrs. Shaw when she came in. Carline sat at a prominent table with two brothers of her husband. She glanced our way once, so she could start to ignore us.

"Brianna, aren't you related to Carline?" Mrs. Shaw asked.

"Not by blood," I said. "Carline is the second child of my father's wife. By Carl Osborn, Heather's first husband. They disembarked together as colonists. Carline is half-sister to Dacupitte, whose father was Hamish Nordhagen. But Heather and Hamish did not marry. Heather and Brian Miller married. Then after Heather died, Brian was with my mother, Klistina Le of Arim. Before they could marry, Brian Miller was killed during the assault on the refinery."

Mrs. Shaw's eyes glassed over. She always struggled with understanding relationships. She signaled the waiter who rushed to her side. "What is that room?"

"For private dinner parties, up to sixteen people."

"And does Carline Bryant hold dinner parties there?"

"No, ma'am. At her home."

"Does she have them catered?"

"No, ma'am. Mrs. Bryant hires a French chef from the transport."

"A French chef?" She eyeballed me. "A French chef."

That was funny, hearing him call her ma'am. I put my hand over my mouth, though, to hide my grin, with Mrs. Shaw being so unforgiving.

Later, I was assigned a room near hers. Not a suite, but a room with its own bathroom and small balcony a ways down from their balcony. The packages were piled in there, and I hung up the clothes as much as I could figure. Mrs. Shaw fussed around my room, and then told me to follow her back to the suite for English lessons. I thought maybe she did not want to, you know, to be there alone when her husband came in.

Mrs. Shaw made two lists of names and studied a monthly calendar. She dug out the room service menu and flipped through the pages. Her mind wandered off, but she looked back at me and wanted more paragraphs recited. I only hoped that all of our days would not be so long. Captain Shaw arrived late, close to midnight. I was still catching up on English lessons. Who said they could add in those silent letters? Softcheeks were something.

So anyhow, Mike Shaw came in brooding and vague. He hung up his uniform jacket and placed his polished shoes together in the closet. I had never seen a grown man, you know, do that for himself. He sent me with the ice bucket down the hall and poured a drink when I returned. They were already having words.

"We need Hakulupe Le at the dinner to provide an equal number of men and women," Mrs. Shaw claimed. "And the Hartleys should join us for the second event."

He rattled the ice in the drink glass. "Why are you doing this? What do you care who Carline Bryant invites to dinner?"

"You made me into Mrs. Shaw," she shot back. "This puts Carline on notice; her colonist salon is not the only game in town."

"Of all your projects, this is the most unseemly."

"Unseemly?" she asked hotly. "Who are you to talk about unseemly? Will you have your office send out the invitations or not?"

He noticed me. "Why don't you go to your room now, Brianna? It's late."

I bolted.

Over the next days Dr. Greensboro made plans, talked with pur-veyors about delivery, and compared prices. She had an EAM delivered to the suite and tagged the transport concerning china and flat-ware and ingredients for exotic foods she wanted prepared. What was Oysters Rockefeller, anyhow?

She rented the private dining room and had the china delivered. China turned out to be thin and brittle dishes with garden scenes painted on them. She talked with the hotel chef and insisted he make several entrees for her to taste. Entrees is French. She had dinner delivered to the suite, but when Captain Shaw was late in arriving, the entrees went untouched while they argued.

"So I'm supposed to put the refugee crisis on hold," he asked, "so you aren't embarrassed in front of the bellhop?" He lifted the silver cover from one entree on the cart and squinted at the sight of something with white sauce, which was brown sauce by then.

Later I was in my room, glad to be alone for a moment. I could hear them arguing on the balcony that was just across the way from my small balcony. "Why dress Brianna like a mannequin?" Captain

Shaw asked his wife. "She cannot wear those at the academy, or any-where without you. Just let her be a little girl."

Mrs. Shaw shot back. "What do you know about little girls? Except to deflower them. I wasn't your first virgin, was I? Or your last!"

Later it grew quiet. I smelled kari root smoke, so I peeked over at their balcony. Captain Shaw stood alone, smoking before he settled in on the suite floor. He sheepishly smiled at me. "One should keep a channel open."

I attended the Cylay academy on weekdays wearing my Arrivi gown and sandals. I had been a student by then at each academy loca-tion, but Cylay was different. The instructors were not so helpful as Hakulupe Le. They didn't demand correct answers each time like Kecouroo did. I learned more at the hotel. I rested in class, though, and thought about events.

Not all the students understood Arrivi, so we were taught in dif-ferent groups. There was some hair pulling among the girls. Tribal boys were cruel. They did not bother me much, though. I think it was the implied presence of Dacupitte, my adoptive brother.

One day the teacher chastised me for daydreaming. She required that I recite before the class. We Arrivi girls never displayed our-selves like that, you know, in front of everybody so our measure can be taken. The girl who sat next to me named Vera spoke up. "It's unseemly. Brianna is a sister of Arim."

"I am goulep," I whispered. "No honor is due." Later in the girls' bathroom, Vera and I compared answers on the pop quiz. She seemed bright.

Karlyhi was waiting outside the academy one day when classes let out. I saw the lorry first, then Karlyhi and his two followers carrying karkars. His seconds were simple, thoughtless men with no … well, no backbone. They hung around Karlyhi for privileges and to partake in his aura. They swaggered as if they reinforced him. Without his presence, they were cowards and bullies. True heartless bullies, not like what Mrs. Shaw said about her husband.

Karlyhi watched me walk down the steps with Vera and the other schoolgirls. When we passed, he made a smacking noise with his lips, imitating a Softcheeks gesture called kissing. Tribesmen knew little of kissing or about Softcheeks' mating customs. Not that those customs were so special, judging by what happened at the hotel. But on the street, throwing a kiss was rude toward a woman.

Karlyhi sent me another kiss. His friends snickered.

Academy students came and went, depending on their family situations. Some, especially the girls, were absent after a certain age. They were taken for the sweatshops, most of them unwillingly. The families were in debt to Bryant Inc. from buying seed or household goods in the shops. The public household register listed the idle workers who were schoolchildren. Hardhands with clubs waited outside the academy building and grabbed the tribal girls by the arms when they tried to enter. We did not see them again after that.

One weekend afternoon I was out with Mrs. Shaw who was doing her Lady Bountiful thing. That was what Captain Shaw called her errands that she ran as Mrs. Shaw. I should not have repeated his words.

Anyhow, we waited in the jeep while a semi-truck backed out through the gate of a high fence. The roll-up door of a loading dock was open, and we could see into the building there. Several women sat together, chained at the ankles, and jumped up when somebody barked a command. They were led around the building's side and huddled together, obviously afraid of the manager. One of them was Vera. Her feet were bare by the ankle chain. She had fresh lacerations on her face and limped a little. She saw me but ducked her head in shame.

I came to understand what was heartstone.

There were other currents. Tribal leaders visited. First was Dacupitte who asked me to groom his dreadlocks. I showed him the shower in my room and he just laughed. We used the washbasin.

When Pete returned from his talk with Daniel Bryant, however, he was in a foul mood. We ate some whitefish with parsley in the suite with Mrs. Shaw. The entree was nothing like kariom. "I don't know which is worse," Pete claimed. "Displaced Uburu or chained sweatshop workers."

She spoke in a tone she never used with Captain Shaw. "Aren't there laws against taking workers for the sweatshops?"

"The family register we assembled during the vaccine task," Pete said, "exposed the numbers of idle workers in family groups. Bryants use the excuse of family debt, but the loan amount never lessens. It just makes me sick."

"Then enact a child labor law. And a truancy law."

"They work on family farms."

"Make that the exception. That's how it's done among Soft-cheeks."

"Sweatshops are from Softcheeks too," Pete said.

"White sauce is Softcheeks," I added. Mrs. Shaw squinted at me. Pete's presence had not relieved the tension.

Later that night, she and her husband had harsh words. Captain Shaw made the mistake of asking about Pete's visit. A real blow up ensued. I heard the arguing from my room's balcony. I thought maybe she had compared him to Pete and found Mike Shaw wanting.

She started in about the sweatshops. Couldn't his men confront the Bryants and clean out that area? Or did he only care about young girls who were sexually available to him?

"To me?" he asked. "What about your favorite, Dacupitte? He has been with all the tribal women, married and single." They broke some china and slammed some doors.

I was proud for Captain Shaw, though. He was beginning to fight back. I imagined that she wanted him to fight back, even kept up the pressure until he blew. I thought she wanted him to grab her and smother her complaints with his kisses.

He stepped out onto the balcony and smoked kari root. Maybe his reluctance was because he was so much bigger than her. You know, it was unseemly to fight back.

I arrived at the suite too early the following morning and found Captain Shaw still there. He was pulling on his uniform shirt over a green sleeveless t-shirt. She was watching him. I figured that was marriage, what marriage was all about. How she tortured him every minute but watched him like that when he was not aware. I mean, they lived together. How could you live with such a man and not have thoughts?

And I figured that was the deal with the hotel. She lingered there when she could have returned to the aid station or to the clinic, or to the fortress of Arim. She wore lacy things and perfume and languished about. She spent too much money, created fights, and made him crazy with her revealing clothes.

Mrs. Shaw couldn't ask, you know. She could not forgive, always with her chin stuck out. And there was nobody on Dolvia bigger than her who would engage the fight, only Michael Peter Shaw. He loved her so much that he just took the abuse. He had a high threshold of anger. I did not realize how high until Rabbenu Ely visited.

We had this friendship by then, Captain Shaw and me, from sharing in the torture and sharing in the secret. He never touched me or, how to say, signified on me like Karlyhi did. Captain Shaw did not need the trouble from his wife about deflowering young girls. But sometimes when she got, you know, around the bend with her anger, we left together. He let me tag along on some errands.

We went to the command center with Rabbenu Ely that day. Traveling with Marcy's husband was deemed safe, even though Ely had grabbed me for a beating more than once. The office was cool with wall maps and many EAM monitors. The uniformed men barked answers with crisp salutes. Lieutenant Milo Sector said hello to me. I liked his mustache.

We boarded a helicopter, and I rode with them while Captain Shaw went fact-finding with Rabbenu Ely. They were talking about the Company and who had out-figured who. Or whom, I guess. I stared down at the Cylay refugee camp that was sprawling place and dirty.

We followed the Iamida River into the mesas. Captain Shaw pointed left before he pointed right. That was Arrivi. That was Uburu. He had an idea of boundaries, like an overlaid matrix on the mesas. I saw terraced green plateaus with torturous footpaths along the side of the mesa. Orderly clusters of adobe houses had slate roofs. We saw contoured fields of barley and multi-colored maize. I shared images with Edwina. She liked images of the savannah gained from the viewpoint of the chopper.

But then, some of the houses were burned out. Captain Shaw and Rabbenu Ely pointed and talked, intent on what they could decide. I sent out images to Ralph, but got no response. I try to do my part, you know. We flew back to Cylay with the constant swoop-swoop-swoop of the chopper blades. Mike Shaw smiled at me. It was a grand time. It made my heart sing.

When we exited the helicopter, my hair was tangled and standing up, and my arms were gritty. I was glad for my shower that night.

I sat in class the next day and thought about how Captain Shaw led the soldiers all day, how he studied maps and laid plans. He knew the daily tally of Uburu dead. He knew the quantity of stored supplies. He knew about the Company's next maneuver. Then he came home after a day of making decisions for everybody and greeted Mrs. Shaw who spat poison at him for his infidelities. It was a wonder that there were not more infidelities. But I did not tell her that, and neither did he.

And so that night was the first dinner party. The plan was to have a very public and high-class event to make Carline Bryant grind her teeth. Later Mrs. Shaw would hold a second dinner and send Carline an invitation to rub her face in it. Colonel Hartley and his wife, parents to Carl and Heather, had agreed to disembark and attend the second dinner. That was considered a major social triumph. Carl and Heather were away at university, however.

Colonel Hartley was the talking head known by Cara and the Mekucoo as Hamilcar. I asked Mrs. Shaw one day, "If he leads the Consortium, why does he have a woman's name, Hart Le?" She just stared. I had distracted her from something.

I was expected to attend both events and wear the store-bought clothes. Captain and Mrs. Shaw argued about her insisting on including single women, you know, the same number as the men. He thought including me might appear to the tribesmen as a form of turning me out, that the officers might get thoughts. She insisted that Mike should lecture his men. These were nice women, not brothel women.

They argued about everything, or at least she did.

In the rented dining room with the china and flatware set out, Dr. Beecham came in with Marcy. He seemed rested, and I wondered if Edna still sent him grotto dreams. We talked for a moment about my lessons and the Cylay academy. He asked what books I had read. He seemed to really care.

For the meal, I was seated between Hakulupe Le and Dr. Beecham. I was safe enough. Lupe asked me about the entrees served there, but Mrs. Shaw answered each of her questions before I could speak.

Dr. Beecham talked with Lt. Sector about the new helicopters. Milo Sector, seated across the way, winked at me. He took up a discussion with Hakulupe Le about prophets of the Bible. "What was Solomon's problem that made him so sad?" Lupe asked, her vivid-green eyes flashing. Milo pursed his lips under the black mustache. He enjoyed their talk, even though their quiet exchange made Mrs. Shaw frown.

Brent Gotskind was there with his wife. I had not realized he had a wife. She was thin and dry, and her eyes were too close together. She drank a lot.

Rabbenu Ely asked Mr. Gotskind about the sweatshops. Did he understand the deplorable conditions the tribeswomen endured? What about city ordinances? What were their options for zoning laws?

Mrs. Shaw directed a triumphant look toward her husband.

Then they discussed the bumper crop of rice the Southeast Arrivi may achieve. It was all kind of tedious, especially the food. Did Softcheeks everywhere continue to stuff themselves long after their hunger was gone?

I overheard Captain Shaw with Dr. Beecham; this was later, while they stood apart and Mike smoked kari root. "Tribesmen have no perspective," Captain Shaw claimed. "A distant enemy counts for less than thousands of invading refugees. A neighboring tribe appears more foreign than . . . than Softcheeks even."

"Uburu women at the aid station," Dr. Beecham added, "blame themselves for each child's death. There's no righteous anger at the Company. What forum do they know for resistance to Blackshirts?"

"Blackshirts?" Captain Shaw asked. "The Company won't enter the savannah with military personnel. They tried that, decades ago. They use the Gora fighters as enforcers. They assume Rabbenu Ely cannot muster warriors into a unified force."

"There's no solution that favors the tribes?" Dr. Beecham asked.

"Arrivi could offer aid in competition to the Company."

"The four tribes see Uburu as the enemy," Dr. Beecham shrugged.

"We should labor against that attitude. The tribes must band together."

During my time in Cylay and within my viewing, Captain Shaw had many such discussions with each leader. He was stalwart. That's an English word, stalwart.

The next day, Marcy and Hakulupe Le visited the academy. They came into the classroom and chatted with the teacher before they went with her out to the hallway. Lupe came to the door and signaled that I should join them. The boys snickered, so I figured Lupe wanted to ask me about daydreaming while in class.

But it wasn't anything. Marcy and Lupe wanted me to go with them for lunch. To spend the afternoon like they missed me or something. I asked if Mrs. Shaw would be there.

"Just us tribal girls," Marcy said.

I was surprised at what I saw on the streets of Cylay. Captain Shaw only went to the Consortium compound when I was out with him. Mrs. Shaw kept mostly to the business areas and malls for shopping. I had never been in the distressed areas that smelled of urine and slaughtered animals. While we walked along a Cylay street a couple blocks from the school, I saw free-ranging pigs and chickens, filthy toddlers dressed only in rags, and women huddled in the entrances of buildings to claim an hour's worth of shade.

Tribeswomen near the bazaar who claimed to be holy women used cards and charms and wanted money for their visions, calling out their willingness to read our fortunes. In one palm, the filthy and ragged woman held a few stones gleaned from the desert, meteor stones called tektite and silicide. "This vision stone will boost second sight so you can know what's coming for you and loved ones," she called out through cracked lips. "This crystal amplifies light. Spend the deep night on the desert, and the crystal will light your way."

I was staring at the poor woman and her few stones, maybe with my mouth open. Lupe led me away shaking her head. "Imagine trying to sell the gifts of Dolvia."

We stopped at a street vendor and bought dried kariom on a salted patty. I greedily chewed the best food I had tasted in weeks, licking my fingers. "So Dr. Greensboro still works with you for English?" Marcy asked while we munched and walked along.

"Sure," I shrugged.

"And you go shopping?"

"Sometimes."

"Your visit to Cylay has not been so great, huh?" Lupe asked.

"Well, you know." I shrugged. "It's Sheeks-Cylom."

Marcy stopped and turned me toward her. "We know you have been unhappy."

I heavily sighed. I had not felt bad, so much, until she said it out loud. "Captain Shaw has been kind."

"And you have been a solace to him." They smiled together.

"What?" I asked.

"You must learn to exercise some discipline with mental pictures," Marcy said. "How can we get any work done with you sending this anxious stream?"

"Is Edwina angry?"

"Edwina?" Lupe asked. "I was preparing new lessons one weekend, and received this image of a young girl in a sweatshop."

"That's Vera. I have heartstone for her."

"Brianna, you don't know your gift," Lupe said gently.

"But I get no answers from Ralph or from you."

"We should encourage you to talk all day?" Marcy asked. "Ralph is losing teeth about it."

"Sorry, but I did not realize. What should I do?"

"When something upsets you, some image," Marcy said, "try thinking about something else. Do multiplication tables or English exercises in your head."

"The only time we have peace is while you're in class," Lupe said. "Are you tired of school?"

"Classes are different in Cylay. I learn more at the hotel."

Hakulupe Le laughed out loud, showing her teeth.

"We know that," Marcy said. "Perhaps now is a good time for the talk about privacy."

"Before Ralph petitions to be returned to Cicero," Lupe added.

I rolled my eyes, wondering why they kept secrets from me. I needed instruction so I stopped making so many mistakes. I sighed and thought I would just go back to the classroom. Marcy gave me a quick hug. "Mixed blood is not so bad," she said. "I am Lucy's kid, also of mixed blood. Have I done so badly?"

We walked to Captain Shaw's command center where Marcy was to meet her husband for the helicopter flight back to the refugee camp. Rabbenu Ely stood in a tight circle with Mike Shaw and his officers. Milo Sector winked at me. I liked him best.

Lt. Sector left their circle and joined us. "Hiki, Marcy," he said. "Hakulupe Le." She only nodded. "I'm assigned to pilot you back to the savannah. Have you enjoyed your visit to Cylay?"

"Business, you know," Lupe said. She looked down, averting her rich-green eyes from his hot look.

"Listen, about your school," Lt. Sector ventured. "Perhaps the students would value an officer's visit. You know, the pep talk about staying in school. Apply yourself by working toward the future."

I suddenly looked up. Captain Shaw broke off his conversation and looked over at me. We each knew that the other knew, all the confirmation he needed. "The situation has changed," Captain Shaw told the others. The officers and tribesmen waited.

Marcy and Hakulupe Le stared at me. Within remote viewing sent by Ralph, I had seen an Uburu man brought before Pete and Karlyhi in the tent city near the butte. I saw this man jolt and look at Pete with confusion while blood poured from his mouth. I saw Pete speak to an elder who was the man's father.

"Milo!" Captain Shaw barked.

Lt. Sector nodded to Lupe and rejoined the officers. Captain Shaw spread out a map and indicated boundaries. "Do a projection with these parameters," he instructed. "What if Arrivi, Siibabean, and Uburu were allies and presented a united front to the Company?"

"We can pool resources and move the equipment south," Lt. Sector postulated. "And the command center."

"But . . . but—" Rabbenu Ely sputtered.

"Uburu refugees," Captain Shaw firmly informed him, "will start the journey home in two days. The refugee crisis is over."

Rabbenu Ely stepped back. His look darkened, and he glanced my way. Marcy and Lupe actually stepped in front of me, masking their move with the bustle about preparing to board the chopper. "Brianna, do you have my pack?" Lupe asked even though she carried it on her shoulder.

The officers began addressing the new challenge with maps and EAM calls about munitions and availability of trucks. They maneuvered around Ely with indifference to his presence. Ely looked left, and he looked right. Marcy stepped to his side so he wasn't isolated in the command center. Lupe quickly guided me out of the room.

At the helicopter, Lt. Sector helped Hakulupe Le step up and demonstrated how the shoulder strap worked. He devoted some moments to the instruction.

After they lifted off for the trip to Somule, I saw Captain Shaw smoking kari root and waiting for me. That seemed unusual considering the sudden bustle among the officers. We rode in his jeep back to the hotel, and all the time he watched me with his studious indifference. "Ralph was present with Pete today," he finally said. "Ralph and you share mental pictures?"

"Well, Pete is my brother. And, you know, the man died."

"Perhaps you are blessed by Dolvia."

I shrugged. "No honor is due."

"You need to stop hiding behind that now. Goulep does not carry the same meaning as when Marcy was your age."

"Then what should I hide behind?"

"You have many friends," Captain Shaw gently said.

"Even Ralph?"

Smile lines showed by his eyes. It was good to see Captain Shaw smile for once.

When we went upstairs to the suite, Mrs. Shaw started in on him about if he had so much power to command these idle soldiers, then why couldn't he close down the sweatshops like any decent human being would?

Mike was busy changing his uniform shirt as if he was going back to the command center. He answered that if she was Sheeks-Cylom, why didn't she stop lying around the hotel and find a cure for the pox? Or was she dependent on Edwina to supply all her medical discoveries?

I retreated to my room and did multiplication tables in my head.

The next afternoon I was riding in the elevator with Mrs. Shaw and saw her chikiocahi brightly glowing; or I thought I did, you know, from what Kyle Rula had described.

"Mrs. Shaw? Are you all right?"

She looked at me with unfocused eyes. "My husband is correct. I should take up some useful work."

"You worked plenty at the clinic and at the aid station."

"It's feast or famine with me, huh?"

"I don't know what that means."

"Come sit at the EAM. We can assemble a few supplies."

We tagged Kecouroo on the clinic EAM, and talked with Haku-lupe Le at the Somule academy too. We ordered books, equipment, and cultures to be delivered to the hotel by Captain Shaw's men during their regular supply stops. We hung up the clothes and cleared the table of perfume bottles and lotions.

We accessed the flora encyclopedia and did a cursory search. She sat back and thought about it. Her eyes glowed while she concentrated on the question of the pox cure. Here was the Dr. Greensboro we all knew and loved.

I asked Edwina if she had a suggestion. *Pox?* she asked. That was a tough one.

So I tagged Kecouroo on the EAM and asked if she could demonstrate for Edwina what Dr. Greensboro was seeking. Kecouroo's return note wondered if Sheeks-Cylom could find the answer herself. I did not tell Sheeks-Cylom that, though. I was enjoying the peace.

Captain Shaw was also relieved that his wife had taken up some work. He was gone more days with the new situation for the Uburu who were beginning to return to their mesa homes. When he was in the suite, he smiled at me, you know, in our secret way. But he still slept on the floor.

Then the Blue Angels visited. This is how the new arrival was explained to me, and I may not have all the words right. The squadron was de-com-mis-sioned on Earth because of new technology. A better plane did the same maneuvers but was also ex-tra-at-mosphere. The new plane was not a long-distance transport, like to Earth's moons, but could orbit out of sight.

Anyhow, these aging fighters were dis-as-sem-bled, brought through the wormhole, and re-as-sem-bled on each planet for a goodwill tour, along with their pilots and ground crews.

Lieutenant Milo Sector in his regular talks with Hamilcar had mentioned that Uburu warriors trusted Hardhand settlers, especially Bryant Inc., more than the peacekeeping forces or Softcheeks. Did Colonel Hartley have an idea for a goodwill gesture that could win over the suspicious tribes?

Goodwill, did you say?

So six Blue Angels jets landed on the tarmac one day and prepared for a low-flying air show past a grandstand constructed there. Tribespeople gathered early to walk around the narrow planes and kick the tires. Certain dignitaries including Captain Shaw were allowed short joyrides. Later the Softcheeks pilots would sign au-to-graphs and speak at academy locations concerning the value of a good education.

The squadron commander greeted Captain Shaw at the command center. With Lt. Sector translating the commander's Southern drawl, they discussed what Mike should expect during his participation in the short flight; something about gripping the armrests and bearing down at the right moment.

While we rode in his jeep to the tarmac event, Mike Shaw repeated the instructions with a big laugh like he was nervous or something. Mrs. Shaw and I wore our best store-bought clothes, and she sported a low-brimmed hat that she donned only after we arrived at the hangars.

Lt. Sector joined us as interpreter. Captain Shaw shook hands with each pilot. They were so handsome, strong jawed and brash. Without hesitation they shared chi from some deep reserve. They created joy in me; not the same as Edwina but similar.

"These officers are from America," Mrs. Shaw whispered to me. I was seized again with the desire to visit the land of my father.

Mrs. Shaw shook hands and spoke in English to each pilot. One was Commander Guy Gibson. "Guy Gibson?" she asked, and turned to the next pilot. "And I suppose you're Alan Sheppard."

"No, ma'am. Commander Bud Hall here."

"And where do you hail from, Bud?"

"From Indiana, ma'am. And you?"

"I was an Army brat," Mrs. Shaw said, "so we lived anywhere there was an Army base, mostly in the South."

"Yes, ma'am. Army's a good corps, ma'am."

"But it's not the Air Force," she returned.

"No, ma'am," Bud Hall claimed with a big grin. "Army's not the Air Force."

"It is reassuring, somehow," she said, graciously including all the pilots, "that some things never change." The offworlders laughed together. Captain Shaw beamed.

We walked around to the lead plane. They were all exactly alike with sleek noses and wings that looked partly folded back like when the murmurey dives on prey. Lt. Sector winked at me and asked what I thought. "They're blue," was all I could muster. He explained to Commander Bud Hall in English that blue was sacred to Arrivi.

While we headed for the viewing stands, I heard Mrs. Shaw ask her husband, "Let me get this straight. You're saying these jets plus their crews and fuel traveled through the wormhole to be reassembled here for an air show and academy lectures, just so Milo Sector has an excuse to enter Lupe's classroom?"

Captain Shaw nodded.

"At least Milo lives up to his name."

I stood with Hakulupe Le and Marcy while Mrs. Shaw and the Consortium officers gathered on the dignitaries' stand. The American pilots and crew made a big show of marching in unison across the tarmac and saluting each other. With giggles, Marcy and I marched around imitating their quick turns and straight-backed posture. From her place on the stand, Mrs. Shaw made a hissing noise with a sharp frown silhouetted by the hat's wide brim. I saluted her.

The air show was grand, with jellyrolls and starbursts. That's what they called the maneuvers. Mostly the sonic booms impressed tribespeople, and the white smoke trails.

Commander Bud Hall was the pilot who visited my Cylay classroom the next day. He did not say the word ma'am one time during his talk. "I was rejected the first time I applied for entry into the squadron," he told the class. "Rejection was a crushing blow. I thought about quitting, and just working as a farmer like my dad. But I studied and went back to take the examinations again. And again. I was determined to be a Blue Angels pilot. And applying myself to classroom lessons paid off. I have adventure and good buddies. I meet new people and get to learn about your lives.

"So stay in school," he added. "Do your homework. Mind your parents. And one day you can realize your dreams."

I happened to be on Mrs. Shaw's hotel balcony when the Blue Angels left the savannah for demonstrations in other parts of Dolvia. I felt the sonic boom and looked up. I glimpsed their fire-spewing back ends, called afterburners, just before they disappeared into the sun's glare.

Then came the time for the second dinner party Mrs. Shaw had arranged. She was deep into her research by then with the cultures and the microscope. I think she was actually sorry she had sent out the invitations. But we dressed and went downstairs with Captain Shaw to make Carline Bryant eat crow, whatever that means.

Colonel Hartley was there with his wife. I liked Billie right away. She had a big laugh, and I wanted to sit next to her for the meal. "Brianna?" she asked. "That would make you Brian Miller's daughter. We knew Brian Miller. He was a good man. He believed in the cause."

You could see her teenagers in her, you know, in her face. Billie talked with Mrs. Shaw about university and how no news was good news. She showed photos of her youngest, a girl named Jesse who lived on the transport. I was kind of jealous. What a great life, huh?

Captain Shaw had a good laugh with Colonel Hartley about how I had been so impressed with the HGEAM when they had first booted it at the bush clinic. How Colonel Hartley's image had appeared within the cycling cube. On that day, I had dubbed him the talking head. I blushed and turned away. I was no longer that rural schoolgirl. I was something else now.

Captain Shaw described in detail, for Colonel Hartley's edification, his ride in the Blue Angels' lead plane.

Joey and Karen Osborn arrived. Carline came in with her husband. Sean Bryant was smaller than her, stringy kind of. He had a piercing stare. He was not happy about the evening's event. Sean stood on the side with drink in hand and talked in low tones to a Steve Swanweil, a man I had never seen before.

Frank Duerr arrived with his wife. She had white hair. That was something.

Pete was there, of course, being half-brother to Carline Bryant. He did not even react when Carl and Heather Hartley were mentioned.

Marcy and Hakulupe Le were present, you know, to supply enough women for the seating arrangement. Mrs. Shaw wanted to seat Lupe at the other end of the table from Lieutenant Sector. At the last moment, Milo switched name cards with me, and I got to sit next to Billie Hartley. I did not even care about Mrs. Shaw's frown.

That night was very different from the first event. Captain Shaw and Colonel Hartley posed casual questions to the Dolvia civil authorities about offworld trading rights and exchange rates. They drew out Sean Bryant and Steve Swanweil in a boasting way about their many contract negotiations with the networked banking interests.

Steve Swanweil was fascinating. His aura was all colors, but none of them mixed together. And he seemed to shimmer like I was seeing him through a clear pool of undulating water. When he spoke, words left his mouth and fell to the ground. But I did not see the three levels Kyle Rula had described. Maybe that was for Soft-cheeks only. Steve Swanweil was Hardhand.

I saw events swirl around like a dance. Pete complimented the Bryants on their business presence in Cylay that employed the tribespeople. And he smiled, you know, right in their faces. I glanced at Colonel Hartley who glanced at Captain Shaw. There was stuff going on here. Mrs. Shaw had put this evening together for a wrong reason, but like I said before, Dolvia blessed her, maybe more so when she was wrong.

She even left Lt. Sector alone. Milo talked with Lupe and touched her arm. She blushed and agreed and asked a quiet question. They seemed to be separate, like a glowing cocoon had settled over them. Mrs. Shaw disapproved of them; I could tell by the way she looked at her husband before she looked away. The long knives were no longer out.

Marcy asked me, "Do you still want to visit the transport?"

I looked up, trying not to jump out of my seat. Marcy spoke to Billie Hartley. "Brianna is one of our academy students. She has been learning English."

"Soon you will be qualified to teach other students," Billie said in whole tones.

"The academy is small potatoes to Brianna," Mrs. Shaw corrected. "She wants to jump back to Earth."

Billie turned to me. "A big ambition. At this table, only Mrs. Shaw knows about Earth."

Carline squinted. That was funny to me. All this had been engineered to make Carline feel small. But once dinner got underway, nobody cared to pursue that angle. "Dr. Beecham and Dr. Mitterand are from Earth," I said to Billie. "But they're not here tonight because that would mean there are too many men."

Billie sucked in her cheeks to hide her smile. Mrs. Shaw let it pass.

The dishes were cleared away by Putuki servants, and brandy and coffee were served. Coffee looked like dark tea and tasted like old sandals. And this was what Uburu were encouraged to grow? I felt sorry for them. How could they subsist on coffee instead of barley and maize? What would their livestock eat?

I was proud for Captain Shaw that night. When the guests milled about before leaving, Mrs. Shaw stood at his side while they talked with Colonel and Mrs. Hartley. She even allowed Mike's hand to rest at her waist. I figured maybe he would not be sleeping on the floor much longer.

Dacupitte finished his glad-handling of Sean Bryant and sent him out, along with Steve Swanweil. Pete and Marcy came to me. "Tell me about the day you knew Uburu would go home," Pete said in a distrustful tone.

"Captain Shaw saw Ralph's images too."

"Perhaps because you saw them," Marcy whispered.

"Mental pictures began with Mike Shaw and Ralph," I hedged.

Marcy considered that. "Brianna has been here a full turn of Nettom, and lonely," she reasoned with Pete. "She was raised with you, and you had just visited. The man was killed, a traumatic image."

"We can wait, then," Pete concluded. "This remote viewing may be unique."

I did not like that they talked about me as if I was not there, like I was a pox culture that needed watching within an experiment. I wanted to visit the transport and spend time with Billie Hartley and Jesse who was not much younger than me. And I wanted to visit Earth where the men were like Commander Bud Hall. Yes, ma'am. No, thank you, ma'am.

Later after we went upstairs, Captain Shaw smoked kari root while he stood alone on their balcony. Mrs. Shaw came out to him wearing one of those lacy things. He snubbed out the cigarette and they went inside together. Nobody said anything. It's hard to kiss and talk, I guess. Also, there had been plenty of words between them already.

The next day Mike Shaw seemed uplifted. I was not sure from which success.

Rularim visited soon after that, arriving by the train from Somule. I don't know if she had ever been to Cylay before. She came up to the suite and had tea with Mrs. Shaw.

Kyle Rula displayed some hand-stitched Arrivi gowns that she hoped to sell offworld. Could Mrs. Shaw explore secure channels for her offworld resale licenses that were dormant?

I told Kyle Rula about the dinner party and how Steve Swanweil had appeared to me. That I had not seen the three planes of Soft-cheeks, but his words fell to the ground. She seemed pained for a moment. "Be careful what you wish for, Brianna. Dolvia may bless you with it."

They discussed the pox and how a culture from a resistant Arrivi held the key for an Uburu vaccine. Kyle Rula allowed Mrs. Shaw to draw a sample of her blood. As a salve sort of, for treating her like a specimen, Mrs. Shaw admired Kyle Rula's shawl that was a lightweight Arrivi burka. Kyle Rula unfolded the length of cloth and offered that Mrs. Shaw should try it on. She snapped the ends so the square cloth fluttered in the air. Mrs. Shaw stood under it like a wedding veil, and pulled the material until she could see through the facial panel. They giggled together. That was a grand moment, full of light and color. I sent the image to Edwina. I figured that my gesture would not violate anybody's privacy.

There was a knock at the door, and the bellhop delivered something. Mrs. Shaw removed the veil and sheepishly looked around, embarrassed before strangers. "I should have been working this whole time."

"Much work is accomplished during this mercy seat," Kyle Rula claimed. "You begin more new work than you know."

Even if Mrs. Shaw wasn't merciful. No mercy was in this mercy seat.

Kyle Rula made a gift of the shawl. Mrs. Shaw in turn offered a perfume bottle that Kyle Le had admired. And that was the whole event. Rularim had journeyed to Cylay for that only.

FOURTEEN

was not something a tribeswoman would confess, you know, even in private. But Kyle Rula said it was correct that I should tell my experience so the same does not happen to others.

I was taken.

When school ended one day, the men with leather batons were there and grabbed two younger girls, too young for sweatshop work. I rushed them, loudly complaining, and placed a few blows. The Hardhands who worked for Bryant, Inc. got me between them and forced me into the back of the truck along with the two girls. They gagged me and bound our hands behind our backs, using a lot of physical contact—especially upper body—like they enjoyed it.

They secured a black hood over my head and delivered a blow against my temple so fierce that I saw stars. I guess I was fighting back too hard.

I woke up alone in some room, but it was not the Bryant manufacturing building where I had seen Vera that one day. The floor smelled of treated wood and fuel oil. I was certain the building was close to the shuttle launch pad. My hands were still bound behind my back and tingled from the lack of blood flow. I worked the gag out of my mouth, but I couldn't see through the hood. I stumbled around. There were a desk, a couple of chairs, and a cot.

I heard someone's footfalls in boots come down a wooden hallway. He used a key in the door. He dropped a heavy key ring onto the desk, and added his baton and sidearm holster. He grabbed my arm and stood me up. He roughly massaged my breasts with his palm and ripped my gown. He put his hand under my skirt and fingered me there. He was breathing heavily. I thought I smelled liquor.

He turned me away from him and leaned me over the desk. He hiked my skirt and well, you know. While he pumped me, I tasted my salt tears inside the hood. But I did not whimper, and I did not beg.

When he was done, two other men entered. They whispered and laughed. The first man picked up his gear and left. The others did what he had done, only more so.

Then I was dragged down the hallway and forced through a door. I fell onto the wooden floor and heard the rustle of ankle chains. I felt a hand on my shoulder and pulled away. "It's all right," a woman whispered. "It's me, Vera." She pulled my gown onto my shoulders and straightened the skirt hem past my knees. She untied the hood and pulled it off.

The room was completely dark. Even when my eyes adjusted, I could barely make out shapes. "I saw you in the light when they opened the door," Vera whispered. "I recognized your clothes."

I heard them move around when chains scraped the floor. There were maybe eight women of various ages. "Were others taken with you?" a woman asked from the dark.

"Two girls."

"Younger?"

"Yes."

There was complete silence. Someone sighed. "What?" I asked.

"We don't see the little ones again," Vera whispered. "We assume they have robbed the desert of some." My heart pulled down in my chest. I sent out mental pictures of where I thought I was, of how many were trapped here, and of the manager's firepower.

"Are you brought here each night?" I asked.

"Most nights." Shame was apparent in Vera's voice. There was a place more harrowing than this dark room. "Just rest," Vera whispered. "There is nothing more." I sent out more images. I did not care about privacy. I hoped I irritated the piss out of Ralph.

It was daytime when the warriors came for us. We heard men running up the hallway, followed by gunfire and explosives. We huddled together as well as the chains allowed.

Someone unlocked the door and sunlight streamed in from the hallway. Karlyhi stood there holding a karkar. He saw me and curtly gestured that I should come to him. I stood and helped Vera to stand while the other women struggled to their feet. Karlyhi gestured again that I should walk out, but I stepped back with the women who were the same as me, setting my jaw to meet his harsh look. I would not leave until they could leave.

A warrior entered and used a big key ring to unlock the chains. The women pulled the links through their ankle braces and waited. I took Vera's arm and moved forward. She limped markedly and stumbled when we reached the light.

Karlyhi held out a helping hand. I jerked away. "She's with me."

"Have it your way. She's with you." He looked at his men as if to claim he was the hero here. On the way out, we passed the bloodied bodies of the two schoolgirls I had tried to defend. One prisoner began wailing; others openly cried.

I helped the others into the back of a waiting lorry and pushed away the warriors' outstretched hands. "No hospital," I said to Karlyhi in a voice I did not recognize. "No soldiers. No reports."

He shrugged, his face actually showing emotion. "It is a tribal matter."

During the ride, I began to shudder. Wind whipped through the open truck, but the disturbance was not cold. The women and girls only stared ahead and said nothing. Perhaps they barely believed they were free, or more likely, they were considering the shame they had brought to their families.

We were driven to the council building. We piled out and entered the wide meeting room. I sat there and tried to think of what to do. I could not muster the will to make a plan. Mrs. Shaw came to my side. Her face was splotchy, and her eyes rimmed with red.

"I fought them," I said. "I did not beg."

She controlled her face. "You have some shock. I can give you a hypo before we bathe you and change your clothes. You must allow me to complete an examination."

Somebody put a blanket on my shoulders. I saw his hand and drew away. "Tell the men to leave, please," she instructed. "Thank them and say that we appreciate what they did. But they cannot be here now."

She bathed me using a big sponge and examined the mark on my forehead. She gently spread my legs and looked there. She helped me into an Arrivi gown that was from Kyle Rula's delivery before she pulled the blanket over my shoulders. She showed me a big pill and a cup of water. "We call this the morning after pill. There's no pain."

I swallowed it without energy.

Mrs. Shaw quickly took stock, as she often said. "I must see to the others."

She moved to Vera who shivered under the blanket. She administered a hypo to Vera's arm. "What is your name?" She showed Vera the wet sponge and pulled at her ragged clothes. "So I can notify your family. Can you tell me your name?"

I stirred myself and approached them. I pinched Mrs. Shaw's upper arm, as I had once seen Lupe do. "Ouch!" she complained and pulled away. That gave me more pleasure than it should have.

"Their families won't come," I said in that voice I had heard myself use with Karlyhi. "These ones are goulep now. Your questions only increase their shame." I took the sponge from her hand.

"What can I do?" she asked.

"Perhaps some tallow. Turn out the lights."

The victims relaxed when the lights were cut. Mrs. Shaw began examinations by tallow light. At my insistence, Vera was first. She was bruised all over and her ankle tendons had been severed. "My god," Mrs. Shaw said. "I have seen such wounds, but only on warriors brought in from battle."

"Vera spoke up for me once in class," I said. "Perhaps she spoke up once too often at the sweatshop."

I bathed and dressed each goulep myself, using Rularim's Arrivi gowns that were finely worked in anticipation of their export value. I held the victims' hands while Mrs. Shaw looked for open cuts, broken bones, and infectious diseases. Each was given that special pill, except the three who were obviously pregnant. The ten girls and women vacantly stared ahead and cringed at every touch, but they did not resist. The fight had gone out of them.

Some had whip marks on their backs. Some had bruises from the leather batons on their thighs and buttocks. A couple of the girls had broken ribs from body blows. Their ankles were raw where we removed the chain braces. We did not ask them what had happened. The physical evidence was enough. Why make them talk?

"It's all right," Mrs. Shaw said to one. "It's over now."

"Their ordeal is just beginning," I corrected her.

Mrs. Shaw made each girl drink from a silver canister when we finished with her, so they slipped into sleep. I refused the canister in my turn. "I was there only a few hours. My suffering was not as deep."

Karlyhi stood at the doorway. Mrs. Shaw joined him for some whispered talk, but soon returned to me. "These ones must leave Cylay. The lorry waits to take them to Somule."

Karlyhi's men carried out each sleeping woman wrapped in a blanket. "They can stay in the Hardhand church for now," Mrs. Shaw explained. "The pastor has agreed to open a convent there."

"There are others."

She nodded. "Fewer now. You should come with me back to the hotel."

"I will go with Vera."

"She's going to be all right."

"Just the same."

I pushed past Karlyhi and climbed into the lorry. He offered me the canister, but I shook my head. He looked at me for a long moment, apparently angry. He tossed the canister into the truck bed before he pushed his men aside and took the driver's seat.

I saw Mrs. Shaw sigh and turn away.

During the ride, I stowed the canister so it would not roll around. I straightened their skirts and pulled each woman's blanket to her chin. I took Vera's head onto my lap and closed my eyes against the bright day. I did not want to know about the day.

The sun was setting when Karen Osborn met us at the Somule church entrance. The victims were coming awake. Hardhand women led them into the basement where soup and cots were laid out for them.

"You can stay at the fortress of Arim," Karen said to me only. "Kyle Rula sent word."

"I will stay with Vera."

Karen looked at Karlyhi who rolled his eyes. "Don't make me defy Rularim," she whispered. I only waited. "Perhaps Vera could stay at the fortress as well," was Karen's best suggestion. Vera limped back to the lorry and climbed to her former seat where I joined her. I saw Karen's concerned face recede when Karlyhi drove away with us riding in the back.

I looked at Vera and attempted a smile. I did not know her except for a few days of class. I did not know why her companionship was so important to me. I just knew that if she was protected, then my life was better. I could face them off; I could go on if I knew Vera was no longer abused. If Vera was okay, then I was okay.

We were told later that five sweatshop managers were made to stand in a line, and their hands were nailed to their batons. The skin was stripped from their chests and backs. Ankle chains were tightly wrapped around their torsos and dug into the raw flesh. Their genitals were cut off and stuffed into their mouths. Some had broken jaws from the struggle. Then they were allowed to bleed to death.

The sweatshop managers had kidnapped the wrong tribal girl on that day.

Other Bryant Inc. forced laborers were released and ferried out of Cylay. The Somule church filled with goulep tribal women. The overspill was housed at the Somule council building until a location could be determined for the convent.

When Sean Bryant and his brothers complained to the Cylay authorities, the bodies of two little girls, naked and sexually abused, were displayed outside the Cylay council building. The Bryants declared a moratorium and closed shop. They claimed to have no knowledge of the managers' abusive treatment of workers.

At the fortress of Arim, Kyle Rula made a place for Vera and me in the most recessed room. She allowed me to mind Vera's needs and burn only tallow for light. Later while I rested, Kyle Rula sat beside me at the cot's edge. "Dacupitte went to Carline Bryant's house for the keys and locations of more holding areas. Carline asked why he cared; you were not blood to him. She accused him of thinking he was better than her. And why had he deserted his pursuit of Heather Hartley? Because he was too good for Hard-hands? Carline asked Pete straight out, what was one orphan of mixed blood to him?

"Pete pushed Carline against the wall and put his knife to her throat," Kyle Le continued. "He made her swear on the soul of their mother that she would never speak your name again, that she was unworthy to articulate the syllables of Brianna Miller of Arim.

"Carline finally gave Pete the locations of more holding areas. Warriors broke down doors and released the captive women. Punishment was administered before Karlyhi left for the eastern fighting. Pete and Karlyhi labored for their adoptive sister Brianna Miller."

I looked away. Kyle Rula waited.

"Rularim?"

"Hummm?"

"Can we journey to the Canyon of Buttes? Like my mother when she returned from the transport?"

"If you would like."

"All of us. The gouleps."

"Whomever cares to participate."

"And we should walk the whole way as part of the cleansing ritual."

"We can set out from here," she reassured me.

"Rularim?"

"Hummm?"

"Why did the warriors wait until it was me?" I whispered. "Why didn't they break down the doors for Vera and for the other women who suffered?"

There was a long silence. Finally, Kyle Rula said, "That's a good question."

When I awoke the following day, Edwina was in the room with us. She fingered my face with her big tongue. She waited while I sat with Vera and calmed her new fears, explaining that Edwina was there to help. But joy was not created in our hearts. After a while Edwina left, and Vera was visibly relieved.

Dr. Mitterand visited, so Kyle Rula guided me into the library to greet him. I did not look at Pierre's face. The blue macaw sat on his shoulder and pooped down his sleeve. Kyle Rula hid her smile and brushed away the filth with a wet cloth.

"Dr. Beecham has taken ill," Pierre said. "He blames himself. If he had not allowed you to journey to Cylay, then … He sent this." Dr. Mitterand held out a large book. It was the collection of Irish folktales that I had once thumbed through at Dr. Beecham's office. "Henry says every little girl should have a dream, however whimsical."

Pierre placed the book under my arm. When he touched me, I shuddered and drew away. That was a big surprise to Pierre, that he was included in my revulsion of men. Having not committed the crime, he assumed he was exempt from the condemnation. But however charming, Pierre had not prevented the crime, and today he offered no covering.

I went back to my place next to Vera. I did not want to know about the academy or English lessons or soldiers with mustaches. In the other room, Kyle Rula articulated loudly so I was sure to hear, "As with Karlyhi when his Cylahi mother failed to return, Brianna Miller's childhood has ended now. She is prepared for the future Dolvia holds. Brianna Miller is a woman of high honor."

That night I had grotto dreams. I tried to block them, but they came to me again. I swam deeper and deeper through the tunnels glowing in hues of blue. I came up under the waterfall spray with the foam tickling my marbled hide. I languished in the water while its surface splashed against my always-open eyes. I emerged into the sunlight, my nails clicking against the rocky path. It was days later that I realized the grotto dreams were from Ralph and not sent by Edwina. Ralph was the only male who could break through my pain.

Provisions were piled onto Kyle Rula's two-wheeled cart drawn by a floppy-eared erriv heifer. I made a place for Vera to ride so she could wield the whip and guide the beast's steps. I went to our cots in the fortress and reached to help her stand.

Vera wore the sleeveless Arrivi gown with its lightweight full skirt. She sat cross-legged on the cot and turned her face away. "I must not travel with you. I am unworthy to commune with Dolvia."

"And will Dolvia join me at the mercy seat if I leave my friends behind?"

"You are not beholden to me."

"We are free to choose. We must learn to exercise that right."

When we exited the fortress, the blue macaw also flew out. I had never seen him on the flats and thought we should shoo him back inside. He came to rest on the cart and, tucking in his wings and tail feathers, gingerly walked to the place that was Vera's.

Rabbenu Ely, Cara, and Pete stood with Kyle Rula while she loaded the last of our provisions on the cart and tested the binding ropes. All carried weapons except Cara who wore a long necklace of ketiwhelp claws. I was impressed that Cara was there, as though his presence might change our minds.

"We have no time for this," Rabbenu Ely complained from behind his round-rimmed glasses. "We have the ranching season and the western fighting."

Kyle Rula answered with a sly smile, "There is always time for Dolvia."

We joined them and I helped Vera onto the cart. I shooed away the macaw that circled our gathered group on the wing before he rested again on the piled pallets.

"Braaadt," he said. "A time of gouleps."

Vera ignored the men and took up the reins and whip. She easily gathered the long end and held the whip's stiff base like a queen's scepter.

"We cannot spare the warriors to accompany you," Pete insisted to me, actually leaning forward to enter my line of vision. "I have not decided you can go."

"I have decided."

"How will you manage the cart?"

"Vera," I stated, "the warriors say you cannot drive the cart."

Vera did not look at them. She cracked the whip and the heifer stepped forward. The cart began moving. Vera swung the long and braided end over her head so it snapped near Pete's face. He stepped back while Cara hid his smile.

"What are you expecting here?" Rabbenu Ely asked Kyle Rula. "Three women and a bird on the savannah."

"We are going first to Somule," she told him. "Twenty-seven women will journey to the Canyon of Buttes accompanied by the female gualareps."

"This is foolish!" Ely said.

Pete caught my arm. "You cannot go, Brianna."

I jerked away. "What are you going to do? Chain us together?"

"It's a thought!"

I left then, walking beside the cart. Pete spoke to Rularim. "I'm trying to help here!"

She spoke over her shoulder while she brought up the rear of our procession. "Your help is tardy."

"Braaadt," the macaw called from his perch. "A time of gouleps now."

Rabbenu Ely spoke to Pete. "And you want us to give them the vote." He brushed against Pete's shoulder and strode in the other direction. Pete rolled his eyes. Cara spoke to his frustrated kinsman, "Only Cyrus could ever control Kyle Le."

"Soon there will be twenty-six more just like her."

We reached Somule early that afternoon and stopped by the Hardhand church. It was at the end of the long street, so our stroll had led us along the main street and under the view of shop owners and customers. The cart waited in the heat while some gouleps joined us to ask questions and to commit to the adventure. Karen Osborn had asked to join our trek and had even argued with her loitering husband about participating. She came to the cart and looked over our piled provisions. "Will this be enough?"

"Joey," Kyle Rula said. "Will you please take the macaw to Dr. Beecham at the hospital?"

"He cannot fly there?"

"Braaadt," the bird complained. "Murmurey bird. Murmurey above." He flew to perch on Joey's shoulder and pooped down his sleeve. Kyle Rula laughed out loud, showing her teeth. Joey sourly walked away with the bird bobbing along on his soiled shirt.

Not all women who had suffered in the Bryant sweatshops cared to traverse the savannah for a cleansing ritual. Some who chose to remain behind waited inside the church door, and their faces crowded its front windows.

"Now is the time," Kyle Rula spoke in a clear voice, standing there in the middle of the street. "Those who feel so moved may journey with us to the Canyon of Buttes. The others will remain here and begin plans for the new convent. Each act brings honor; neither brings shame."

Twenty women were gathered into the sunlight, each wearing her Arrivi gown supplied by Kyle Rula by way of Mrs. Shaw and carrying some supplies. They stepped with Karen to stand behind the cart. Kyle Rula nodded to Vera who cracked the whip over the heifer's head.

We passed the Somule academy. The day's classes had recessed, so Hakulupe Le stood on the verandah talking with a young Cylahi student. She sent him on his way and reached inside for her small pack. She pulled the door closed before she came down the steps and fell in beside Kyle Rula. Nothing was said. Words were not needed.

I ran up the academy steps and peered into the window. The homilies written on the blackboard were these:

"What is twisted cannot be straightened; what is lacking cannot be counted."

"Raise up the child in the way he should go, and he won't waver from that path."

"Sow your seed in the morning and in the evening let not your hands be idle, for you don't know which will succeed."

I ran to join the others, uplifted by Lupe's listed sentiments.

Some tribespeople and garrison soldiers paused during their afternoon work to watch as we left the town and entered the heated savannah. Some shook their heads at our foolishness during the hot weeks. Others dryly smiled.

It had been a big-wet year. There was no drought, even that late in the season. Oleastra shrubs displayed rich foliage. Vining hyacinth, now bare of blossoms but crowded with succulent leaves, extended tendrils along the path. The clear air was heated with dry talc in the late afternoon. The sun lingered well above the horizon and at our backs when Kyle Rula pointed left. A swirling column of gritty air erratically twisted in the same general direction we traveled.

"Tunanin," Kyle Rula called out. "Our ancestors accompany us."

A murmurey bird flew above, his big shadow passing over Vera's form. He cried out that aching call of portent and circled our small band. "A good sign," Lupe said to Kyle Rula.

"Not to the macaws," she returned with a big smile.

While the shadows grew long, Kyle Rula and Hakulupe Le walked left, away from the group. Lupe sought my eye and indicated that I should join them. "Vera, you're in charge," I instructed and saw Karen Osborn's frown. I strode forward to catch up with the women in leadership. I knew what the problem must be.

Edna and Edwina waited for us near an outcropping with several shrubs showing new growth. "Ka, ka, ka, ka," Edna said at Lupe's side.

"I am glad to see you, too," I said with a grin. I sat on the ground and Edwina fingered me with her long and moist tongue. "Quit now," I said. "Enough of that."

She was golden with swirling accents of ivy-green. Her marbled hide was warm and yielding, and she was in peak health and weight, ready to breed. She strongly rubbed her flanks across my front. I lost my balance and rolled onto my back. She stepped over me as though she would, you know, place her scent on me.

"Edwina!" Kyle Rula said. She backed off and cocked that noble head as if her intent was to tease. She treated me like the little girl she had known, playful and ungainly. I sat up and hugged her neck.

"Will the women accept them?" Lupe asked.

"You accepted them," Kyle Rula said. "Why should gouleps do less?"

I stood and brushed the sandy grit from my skirt. I walked back to the group accompanied by Edwina. The gouleps whispered and pointed, crowding together. Edwina and I took positions on the right of Vera's cart. The heifer snorted and tossed her head but continued her steady pace.

Lupe walked toward the group, accompanied by Edna. She took up her place on the cart's left and Edna came alongside, laterally swinging her golden body with each pigeon-toed step.

Kyle Rula remained separate from us, perhaps twenty yards. She donned a sky-blue burka and strolled along as if in the company of a suitor. The gouleps took a signal from her and fanned out behind the cart. Those with burkas pulled them on, perhaps for protection against the cooling afternoon. All walked in determined silence for several hours.

We bypassed a deserted Uburu refugee camp. Discarded plastic and tin containers, broken tent poles, and misplaced personal belongings littered the ground. Tramped alleyways and the communal laundry were discernible on the open land. All would be washed away in another season, replaced by a teeming billabong overrun with transient birds.

We saw an erriv drive coming our way from the north. I grabbed the heifer's halter and guided her up a rise beyond their path to avoid the trail dust. Gouleps gathered around the cart and watched.

Tribesmen walking beside the slow-moving herd cracked their whips and called out commands. The adolescent males were made responsible for this herding work of returning the erriv to the drying savannah. Warriors, especially those from the southeast families most vulnerable to Company invasion, were east serving as militia for the Uburu.

Kyle Rula's sons Lynus and Rufus, caked with trail grit, broke away from their herd duties and joined her at a place somewhat down from us. They gladly accepted the fruit and bread patties she offered. Both young men had their straight hair tied at the neck. Rufus was barely fourteen with narrow features. His too-white skin was obscured by oils and dirt.

Lynus and Rufus were tolerant under Kyle Rula's obvious gestures of pride. They waved to her and walked down the rise to rejoin their herding duties. Vera cracked her whip. The cart and gouleps began moving away from the erriv drive.

Much later, Dolvia's sibling moons lit the dry ground where we stopped for a night's rest. Nettom was high and staring down, while Nettki hovered teasingly just above the horizon. "There's no escaping the men," Vera whispered while I helped her from the high seat onto moonlit ground.

Two gouleps stepped forward to feed and water the unharnessed heifer. Karen grudgingly helped Vera pass out the pallets and water canisters. Dried kariom on a salted patty was provided. Several women still wore their burkas. Those who had gone uncovered gingerly rubbed aloe onto their tender arms and foreheads.

Hakulupe Le stood apart with Rularim. The female gualareps were absent but not far removed. We posted no guards. The savannah held no predator more lethal than the gualareps. Gouleps quietly settled in and rested for the few hours until dawn. We needed to cover considerable ground the next day in order to reach our destination.

In the dawn, I smelled brewing tea and heard the crackling fire. Ah, to awake on the savannah; to gain one's rest lying back to back with Dolvia. I sat up and realized I was one of the last to come around. Women smiled and ducked their heads. One named Sarah brought a shallow bowl of spring water and a cloth. She offered a wide leaf laden with aloe for my arms and forehead. She bowed slightly and backed away. Another girl brought fruit and tea.

"Please," I objected. "No honor is due."

Kyle Rula and Hakulupe Le stood outside the camp. Karen was with them, talking in a tight group. I stretched and joined Vera who agreed to rub the aloe onto the back of my neck and shoulders. I covered her neck and soft arms with the same.

"Would you like to walk part of the day?" I asked.

"Very much."

"You can lean on me."

She sadly smiled. "Later perhaps, when I need to."

I nodded and joined those who were in leadership. "Karen, will you manage the cart this morning while Vera walks?" Kyle Rula and Hakulupe Le controlled their faces when Karen looked sharply at me.

"Whatever is needed," she finally said. She walked past me with long strides.

"Thank you," I said to her back. "A great service."

"Karen thinks the women avoid her because she is married," Lupe said. "Sleeping with the enemy."

"Many of these women will marry," Kyle Rula added. "When it's their time."

"Karen must become Vera's ally," I said. "Not me so much."

"Why not you?" Kyle Rula asked.

"I have no heartstone for Karen."

Kyle Rula moved her gaze to the horizon. "We must get underway."

We walked east into the morning sun. We took up our determined, sure-footed pace, anticipating silent hours of ritual cleansing. Vera limped along for ninety minutes or so, but gladly leaned on my arm when I offered.

"My cleansing will be deeper," she breathlessly claimed. "I sweat more."

I hoped her cleansing drained every bit of dross from her spirit so she no longer shrank away with shame.

The female reps came up before the heat of the day. Vera released her grip on my arm. "It's all right," she whispered. "I want to walk awhile in silence."

Lupe and I joined the girls. They jerked around with quick flashes and hopped in jubilation before scurrying off across the dry land. "But where are you going?" I called after Edwina.

"Sa-a-a-va-a-a-a-na-a-a-aah," Edwina cooed. Her burst of speed was astonishing. Their bodies did not swing laterally while they raced out of sight.

Hakulupe Le looked at me with saucer eyes. "Edwina articulated to you."

"She likes the savannah," I shrugged. "Besides, the blue macaw talks, a lot."

"And Ralph?" Lupe gently asked.

"I don't think Ralph likes me."

"He sent Karlyhi."

"Ralph did?"

"How did the warriors know which doors to break down, huh?"

My heart pulled down in my chest. "I don't want to talk about that."

Hakulupe Le put her hand on my shoulder. "Time enough for talk."

"Lupe?"

"Hummm?"

"Who is the woman who walks with Kyle Rula?"

"You see her?"

She was veiled and not tall, walking at Kyle Rula's other side.

Her sky-blue burka was the very same as Rularim's, so I had first assumed that she was a reflection in the shimmering heat. "There with Rularim. She was not in Somule. Did her family bring her up when we passed the erriv drive?"

"She's a cousin of yours named Katelupe Le after her aunt, but called Kat."

I had heard of Kat, Karima Le's youngest, who was near Lupe's age but who had vanished before my mother's death. "But she's gone."

"You see her no longer?"

"I see somebody near Rularim."

"Then she's not gone, is she?"

I scowled at Lupe. I had expected to confront certain mysteries during our journey; I even desired it, but not such blatant ironies. "She's there or she's not?"

Hakulupe Le looked their way. "Kat is there."

"And she's the second Katelupe Le, Karima Le's daughter?"

"Yes, the holy woman."

I watched Lupe with distrust, but she only smiled, innocently blinking her lids over those lambent-green eyes. I went back to Vera and walked at her side for a time.

"Vera, do you see Rularim with somebody?"

Vera looked left, her head bobbing with each limping step. "With Kat."

"How long has Kat been in our company?"

"All our lives."

We stopped for a short repast and to rest the heifer. The one named Sarah petted the heifer's long and fleshy snout while it reached for a treat, snorting and blowing dust from its wide nostrils. Sarah seemed a rather serious person and seldom smiled. Vera and Karen doled out water and salted bread. Others shared fruit and sweets from their personal packs.

I reached to help Vera onto the cart's seat for her afternoon duties guiding the heifer. Others, including Karen, grasped Vera's arms ahead of me. They lifted her while she pulled the long and soiled skirt around her dangling legs. I saw the angry scars on her ankles where the tendons had been severed.

Vera scrambled to her seat and grinned down at me. That was enough.

I took up my station on the right side of the cart. While we moved along again, I was troubled by the presence of Kat, and I often strained to glimpse her veiled movements while she walked across the way next to veiled Rularim. Perhaps I was a little jealous.

I walked away from the group twenty paces, as far distant on the right as the daughters of Arim were on the left. Karen and Sarah walked forward and filled my station near the cart. They chatted with Vera while they walked along, chummy and smiling.

I was glad for the heat and sun that overlaid my stirring emotions and muted my senses. I had no veil and would not have donned it anyway. Too imitative, I thought and shrugged.

I broke away from the group but kept them in sight to my left. I sought to commune with Dolvia and feel Her purifying heat sear recent memories from my heart. Dolvia was large and accommodating. She was patient and murmuring. Dolvia did not judge me or push me away. She did not chain me to one place. She was my ideal.

I was raised by Karima Le after my mother died. I was a biracial orphan with no mantel. My father was Softcheeks and long dead. I had been sent to study at the clinic academy where only Kecouroo took an interest in my progress. Hakulupe Le, goulep herself, was my cousin, but she spoke to me only for correction and service. Kat was my cousin who I had not been allowed to know.

Karlyhi had put hands on me to whip and to use. Pete had spoken kindly under Kecouroo's direction, more to please her than to instruct me. The only men who noticed me were Hardhand and Softcheeks. I was exotic to them, an object of fantasy. They had thoughts.

Perhaps that was not, you know, fair. Dr. Beecham was a kindly old guy who treated all women the same with his formal manners. He did seem to care the few times I was in his charge. But the refugee crisis had robbed his energy and his health.

Dr. Mitterand was encouraging, but that was just a diversion to make the day more fun. Pierre would use me as quickly as Karlyhi would.

Then there was Captain Shaw with whom I played a different game. He wished me well in part because he wanted to appear righteous before the tribespeople. He kept a lookout for the orphan who served his wife, no more than that.

The rabbenu structure was for men only. Warrior training was closed to me. Except for domestic chores and academy classes, I was taught nothing. Open enrollment was an ideal Mrs. Shaw had implemented. Our studies did not mean there would be a place in civil service for the trained women. There was not; there never would be. Sending tribal girls to the academy was gratuitous, a privilege quickly withdrawn at the first sign of hard times.

Academy boys herded their fathers' erriv. They learned their fathers' trades. They could inherit land, except the Mekucoo. They were initiated as warriors and embraced in the structure to defend the land. But tribal girls had none of these options. We worked with our mothers until it was time to work for our husbands. That was all.

I journeyed now with gouleps who could not return to parents and family farms. And no husbands. They were goulep. No honorable trade or guild waited for them. They had nothing but their shame from having been taken and used. I saw prostitution for some and convent work for others. The mark of shame dragged on our hearts because we had no worth.

Tribesmen had not defended them. Their fathers and brothers, and husbands in some cases, did not rise up in righteous anger when the girls were taken. Families closed their doors and mourned in silence. We were alone. We had only each other.

The girls I had known at the academy were the best students. They learned quickly, associated ideas, and remembered the lessons to apply to their daily activities. They were prompt, willing, bright, and effective. But they were devalued because no station with pension waited to utilize their academy skills. Learning would make us better mothers, it was said. Wouldn't work with dignity make us better people? Why couldn't we work the same as tribal boys?

We worked in the sweatshops.

I was hooded when the Hardhands abused me. They didn't know it was me, and they did not care. I was nothing to them, just an object.

Why was it necessary to dehumanize us before we had value in the marketplace? What was it about a young girl that threatened them so that open competition for work was disallowed? How had I offended them to bring on this oppression?

I had not, and that was the truth of it.

Sweatshop managers captured and abused tribal girls for two reasons. First, they could not otherwise get sex; not from their own women, and not without paying for it. Second, our families had not fought back. After the managers abused and destroyed one girl without consequence, where was the deterrent for taking another and the next and a younger one? The way was open. Their appetites had been whetted.

Nobody complained. Nobody came to our rescue except Ralph who had sent Karlyhi. Karlyhi had accomplished much to hold onto Ralph's respect. Not mine but Ralph's.

I was goulep. Vera and the others too—we were all goulep.

I needed to embrace it. I needed to repeat my new place to myself and face the future. I needed to toughen myself for what I must do, for what I must become in order to survive, in order to help Vera and the others survive. There was no other help, only us banded together.

I was mulatto and goulep.

Marcy had asked, was mixed-blood so bad? Look at her, had she done so badly? She had found a place with Rabbenu Ely.

Kyle Rula was goulep and Hakulupe Le. They had each found a place. Kyle Rula held Kecouroo's respect. But she had been Kecouroo's father's wife; Cyrus's wife.

Hakulupe Le had a suitor, a Hardhand lieutenant who commanded military resources to put on an impressive display. He labored to impress her, his efforts for Hakulupe Le, a goulep by birth. But why? It was because Milo Sector had thoughts.

Why must we be associated with a man to gain place? Why not my own place? Me alone, Brianna Miller of Arim. Not Karlyhi's competitor. Not Pete's adoptive sister. Not Captain Shaw's servant. Just me. Just Brianna.

Nobody asked who Karlyhi submitted to.

I sighed and looked around. Fata morgana shimmered on the horizon. My skin was tender. I wondered if there was any more of the protective aloe for communal use. I looked back toward the cart but could see nothing through the rising thermals. I was alone with Dolvia. I felt abandoned and unsupported. Nobody cared. Nobody came looking for me.

"Ka," I heard behind me and nearly jumped out of my skin. It was Edwina. She cocked her head while she considered me with question. I must have been sending her a steady stream of mental pictures without realizing it.

"Sorry," I said. "I have things on my mind."

"Ka, ka, ka, ka."

"That is not the answer for everything, you know."

Water? she said in their special way.

"Ah, I am not carrying some with me. I should get back to the group."

Take you, she said. *Water.*

"You can take me to water? To the grotto?"

Pool, she told me.

"A savannah pool? One I don't know about?"

Edwina walked right on a path that diverged from the gouleps' trek. I could catch up later with Vera, I told myself. Swimming with Edwina was too tempting.

"Will you tell Lupe?" I asked while we walked along. "So I don't receive a pinch on my arm for worrying her."

"Ka."

We came upon a low rise of red sandstone. Oleastra bushes flourished there, a sure sign of subterranean water. Edwina stopped, tense and listening. Presently I heard a slight digging noise. Ralph came out from behind the boulders and hesitated several feet away.

He was considerably larger than Edwina, displaying sandstone red and oleastra green in swirling patterns on his marbled hide. His head was overlarge with a square jaw. Behind each jaw hinge were new decorations, round protrusions as if he held softballs in the back of his mouth. They were the musk glands that a male gualarep develops late in his second decade announcing his sexual maturity.

Then it came to me. They had a nest here with eggs that Ralph tended. "Soon there will be little Ralphs to care for," I postulated to Edwina.

Water, she said and then moved off to the left, away from him.

"See you, Papa Ralph," I called out and followed her. He watched with that noble head raised and did not leave his guard duties until I was out of range.

There was a wide cleft in the savannah floor and a depression as tall as a man. Edwina slid into the opening without hesitation and sidled over the sandy bank below. I dropped in behind her, fearless in her company.

It was cavern water. Kyle Rula had spoken of the artesian flavor and how it was not deadly, unlike heated netta water.

Yellow butterflies with black-tipped wings fluttered on the water's edge. A low mist hung on the cold surface, brilliant blue and at the same time transparent. The glassy water receded deep into the fissure, looking piled overhead rather than carved by time, as though if one removed the correct stone, the ceiling would collapse.

"Is it safe?" I asked Edwina. I scooped a handful of water that was aromatic and cold, perhaps feeling colder to my sun-warmed hand. Edwina gently slid into the pool and dove under. The water swished closed behind her. Smaller and smaller she became through the clear ripples. She flicked her tail and was gone.

Presently a great bulge appeared several yards ahead, followed by a white froth. Displaying the colors of Softcheeks flesh on her marbled hide, creamy with vein-blue flecks, Edwina breached the surface and fell on her side, sending a wave rushing to my feet.

I laughed and tied up my skirt into tight pantaloons. I dove in and swam to where she had surfaced. She came alongside and I grabbed her shoulder. Edwina dove deep with her undulating motion, dragging me through a narrow sandstone passageway. I released my hold and surfaced, gasping for air.

The sound of my violating the water's surface reverberated through a broad, low-ceiling cave that was underlit by the penetrating sunlight from our entryway. Edwina swam into the darker regions, celebrating and rambunctious. I hesitated because I could not see in the dark.

She came back to me and called, "Ka, ka, ka, ka." She swam away again, expecting me to follow. I treaded water near the entryway. I thought if she did not return, I could hold my breath long enough to get back.

She was absent several minutes. I looked around the ceiling and walls, and realized there were faint drawings on the sandstone near a narrow ledge. I remained in the water while I inspected the stylized murmurey bird and hunting ketiwhelp pack followed by men with spears.

Edwina must have been under me. She released air bubbles in a big circle that tickled my legs and gave me a fright. She surfaced and swam around as if checking my progress.

"I am turning blue, Edwina. We should get back."

I grabbed her shoulder, and she guided me deep and fast through the passageway. We swam to the sandy beach and scrambled through the boulder cleft.

In oleastra shade, I lay against Edwina's broad side while she basked with her mouth open to regain blood flow after our chilly adventure. "I was feeling unwanted, Edwina. You and Dolvia have cheered me up. I don't know what the future will bring, but none of that matters for now. Today I have friends and adventure and sunlight. It is enough."

"Ka," she said.

FIFTEEN

EDWINA AND I WALKED WITH OUR BACKS TO THE SINKING SUN, returning to the gouleps. On the horizon the canyon wall reflected diffused light. We reached the camp in the apricot sunset. Swirls of fine dust filled the air refracting light in accents of pink and mauve.

Edwina greeted Edna with an open mouth and lolling tongue. They jerked around in a mock fight and scurried away. "Where were you?" Vera asked while she handed me kariom on a salted patty.

"With Edwina."

"There's a celebration tonight," she eagerly whispered.

"For what?"

"Anticipating the canyon. Many secrets are revealed."

I forced a smile. I had sought the journey and hoped for revelations, but my heart was no longer yearning.

"Did you walk again this afternoon?" I asked to have something to say.

"For a while. Karen helped me, and Sarah."

"You and Karen have become friends, then?"

She gestured to indicate the murmuring women who sat in tight groups and shared their provisions. "Many have become friends, as you planned."

"I had no plan, just my heartstone."

Hakulupe Le signaled that I should join her standing on the right with Kyle Rula. I left Vera's side, but I was hoping she would hold a place open for me so I would not be isolated during the event.

"And where were you?" Lupe asked.

"Edwina sent you images."

"You prefer the old water pool to the company of your sisters?" Kyle Rula asked.

"I felt . . . I don't feel—"

"Come along," Kyle Rula said. We walked right, away from the group. In the gathering dark I saw Karen Osborn standing with the one Kat, holding a piece of black stone call tektite. She was showing it to Kat but was rebuffed. That seemed odd to me since Kat was the younger of the two. Karen noticed our approach. She bowed to Kat and moved away, passing us to walk back into camp. Kyle Rula guided me to this cousin I never knew.

"Hiki, Brianna Miller of Arim," Kat said. "Melinga." She was demure but rock steady with gimlet-like eyes. Her long hair was coiled at her neck in traditional fashion and her earbobs were peridot. She wore a hand-stitched gown with a long skirt, but the sky-blue burka was laid aside.

"Hiki, Katelupe Le."

"We are proud of our sister who serves Softcheeks as Kyle Rula and Marcy served your father in their youth."

I said nothing. I did not know what was coming.

"Plus Ralph likes you," Kyle Rula added. The three women smiled together. I only ducked my head with embarrassment. Ralph had not been so friendly that afternoon.

"We wanted to thank you for suggesting this journey," Kat said. "And for defending your tribal sisters. And now you have a few questions."

"I don't know what you mean."

"I told you," Lupe added to Kat as though that settled an earlier argument.

"You may ask your questions," Kyle Rula encouraged, "of the holy woman."

I sourly shrugged. "If we are cousins, why wasn't I allowed to know you before?"

Kat graciously smiled. In spite of myself, I warmed up to her. "It is as Dolvia would have it," she said. "You are for outsiders. I am held close to the land. Our paths did not cross until today."

"It's so simple?"

"Dolvia covers those who serve as holy women," Kyle Rula said. "One can be standing beside you and, unless Dolvia wills it, you would not know."

"But I know you."

"I was never a holy woman," Kyle Rula said, "just troubled with second sight. I was for marriage and children."

"You won't marry?" I asked Kat. She shook her head no.

"And these ones?"

"Your heartstone for the gouleps honors you," Kat said. "Many will marry, later when it's their time."

"Why is marriage so important?" I asked. "Why can't each stand in her own light, one alone?"

"They don't have your strength. They don't desire it."

I made a sour face. I had no more questions.

"You will marry," Kat prompted.

I looked left, not interested in this topic of discussion.

"You are destined for Dacupitte."

"Ha! Pete has an army of descendants." The words were out of my mouth before I could bite them back. The women smiled together.

"But he has no wife," Kat corrected.

"Nor will he if I must."

They laughed, showing their teeth. "You were right," Kat said to Kyle Rula. "She's his match. I look forward to the contest."

I was ready for a different subject, any other subject. "Was that tektite Karen had? Does it boost seeing like they say it does?"

"Why do you ask?"

"Kecouroo wears a necklace with those stones. Is she increasing her powers?"

Kat gave me a level look. They loved to keep secrets, this group. "Each person is gifted as Dolvia provides. Kecouroo has some jealousy about Kyle Le's gift of second sight."

Kyle Rula raised a hand of impatience. "I would gladly pass the burden to her."

"Kecouroo is friends with Edwina," Kat said.

"You mean Edwina talks to her." They looked at me, so I added, "Edwina chooses who she shares with, not the other way around. Is it true what they say? The tektite necklace boosts Kecouroo's ability?"

Kat turned green eyes my way, very like Lupe's look. They were sisters, after all. "We are more interested in stones with real properties that can be measured, like sufferstone that causes radiation burns. Or silicide that amplifies light." Kat held out a strand of her necklace that included long pieces of the clear crystal-like stone.

"I have seen these on the necklaces of Mekucoo women."

"Silicide is also a meteor stone, but we think that it may have liquefied and dropped to the ground before the meteor fragments hit. These pieces formed in the absence of oxygen and so they are heavy and have few impurities."

"Does it boost second sight?" I asked.

"Its special property is that it amplifies light," Kat said. "Since it's not a crystal, but rather a liquid in solid form, under the right circumstances silicide can be softened and spun into long strands that guide light better that other conductors."

"Why are you telling me?"

"You need to know about certain principles so you can use our goulep knowledge to better serve the women of the savannah. Have you harvested gum arabic, for example?"

"The sap of the acacias?" I asked. "I saw it done on the land of Murd, but I lived in the towns or at the clinic for school, so I never gleaned the savannah."

Kat sighed. "There's too much. How can we impart in such a short time—"

"And whose fault is that?" Lupe asked.

I looked from one face to the next. "What? What is seen?"

"Finally," Lupe complained. She saw my look. "The others ask daily, but you never come forward. Your actions are more like Sheeks-Cylom than a tribeswoman."

"I did not realize I was being watched."

"More than watched," Kat said. "Embraced." My eyes itched with tears. I set my jaw and held my head high. "The gouleps look up to you," she added, "and you must join the celebration tonight."

"I can sit with Vera."

"Good," Kat nodded. "That is good."

I looked around at them. "Go on then," Kyle Rula said.

I walked back to camp alone. I saw them whispering and knew they had made some decision about me. I did not care what it was.

A big campfire was lit, and the women gathered into the friendly groups they had formed during our two-day trek. Vera sat next to Karen and the one named Sarah. Vera looked up at my approach and moved aside so I could crowd in.

Kyle Rula and Hakulupe Le came to the circle's center, but Kat hung back at the firelight's edge where Edna joined her. I felt the pang of jealousy again. I had spent my day with Edwina, but I could not, you know, be glad for Kat's friendship with Edna. My heart was not pure. I felt separate from the gouleps' mounting joy.

"Now is a time of gouleps," Kyle Rula called out in clear tones, "and we are anticipating a new season of kari. Urges spring forth like kariom from the mud with the first rains. We embrace a new energy and a new venture. We must prepare ourselves.

"We are the women of the savannah. We journey here to receive Dolvia's blessing and to glimpse our place in the whole. Many things are seen. Many more shall be revealed.

"Some in our group seek purification," Kyle Le continued. "Some journey for companionship. Some have come to escape prying eyes. But one among us journeys to serve her sisters. We embrace this motive as worthy. We are glad for the mercy seat she has requested. She asks nothing for herself, even when questioned. She acts in leadership without demanding honor. She trusts her future to Dolvia. I call forward Brianna Miller of Arim who has led you out of suffering."

The women loudly clucked and slapped their thighs as they would in a tribal chant. Vera grinned and nudged me. I was pushed forward. Kyle Rula took my arm and formally guided me in a wide circle around the fire while the gouleps raised a jubilant noise. She stopped finally and put her palm against my cheek. "Always remember, you are the daughter of my sister Klistina Le and Brian Miller."

I suddenly realized her interest in me. "You loved him."

"I greatly miss Brian Miller. I see more of him in you each day."

"I never knew him."

She turned me toward the gouleps. I did not know what was required. Their faces swam before my eyes while they called my name and raised a ruckus with clucking and chanting. I nodded to them again and again and made my way back to my seat.

> Brianna Miller of the sisters of Arim
> Raised in service to Sheeks-Cylom
> Fought back in anger and saved our lives
> Along with Karlyhi and Pete and Ralph

And now our cleansing at the Canyon of Buttes

After the noise quieted, I found I was trembling. Tears came to my eyes when Vera put an arm around my shoulders.

Hakulupe Le was honored in the circle, followed by kind words for Kat. Karen was allowed to speak of the day when the gouleps had arrived at the Hardhand church and what to expect from convent life.

Kyle Rula spoke again. "We can provide work for those with skills or who want to learn. Who has an idea for industry?"

Vera called out. "I can sew together volleyballs." The women cynically smirked. They had been taught certain skills in the sweatshops.

"Sarah is good with numbers. She kept the count."

"And Vera is a good manager," Sarah said in her turn. "She spoke up for us."

"My mother taught me to fashion gold jewelry," an older Cylahi girl hesitantly offered, "before she went to a Cylay brothel."

"Perhaps we shall call on her," Kyle Rula said, "and offer an alternate trade." The girl shyly nodded.

Kyle Rula spoke to the group. "There's also furniture making and agriculture, especially oleastra planting. Who has gleaned the savannah for herbs and the resin of acacia trees?" They all grinned. Every tribeswoman gleaned gum arabic. This was a skill?

"We can talk more over the next couple days," Kyle Rula said. "We want to hear your ideas. Nothing is wrong. All must be voiced. But for now, let's celebrate!"

We made a game of calling out the homilies that Kecouroo and Hakulupe Le had drilled into our heads.

"Duty first and honor above all!"

"There's more to heaven and earth than is dreamed of in your philosophy."

"A fools' work wearies him, and he does not know the way to town."

"Sometimes to save something precious, you must walk away."

And my favorite, "Time is a loop. We are often through events before we know their meaning in our lives."

We sang chants, danced in a circle, laughed, and hugged each other. Later I fell into a dreamless sleep lying next to Vera by the cart.

Again, I was one of the last to wake, which was awkward since the women could not pack the cart without disturbing me. "Sorry," I groggily claimed. They shyly stepped around me. I realized they had been quiet to serve my need for rest.

Sarah brought tea. "Please," I tried to refuse.

"I gain honor by serving you. Why do you withhold honor from me?"

I took the cup and sipped. I yawned and looked around to see them all waiting. I stood and stepped out of the way so the cart could be loaded and the heifer harnessed. Karen was prepared to ride and crack the whip.

Vera limped to me. "Is it all right to enter together?"

"It's perfect."

I had seen photographs of the Canyon of Buttes on the EAM. Aerial photos revealed that it was three miles in length and oblong with tall structures randomly grouped together. The granite and flint butte walls, now worn by time and the elements, had not given way when the mantle sank under geyser activity centuries ago.

But the EAM photos could not capture our sense of anticipation. We approached from the sunlit plain to enter the high protective canyon, greeted by a sentinel butte that stood just inside the opening. We walked perhaps twenty minutes to bypass its granite majesty. Before we turned the last corner, we felt cool air similar to a closed and unused building. Mist swirled at our feet as if to invite us into its home. We reached the canyon's heart and stared at the many tall columns grouped like celebrants at a wedding.

To the left were four crumbling red sandstone buttes. It was said that these were friends of Heather Osborn. Karen and Hakulupe Le walked there to give reverence. Vera limped after them. Karen stopped and waited for her to catch up.

Kyle Rula stood to the side with Kat. They pulled off their sky-blue burkas and carefully folded them. I had the feeling they were waiting for me to ask to join them. I thought this one time I would take the chance.

Kyle Rula smiled when I came forward, just as though she knew I would. That gave me a new foreboding feeling, but I shrugged it off. These were the women of the savannah, and I was counted among their number. "I will show you a thing," Kyle Le whispered.

I walked with them to a center butte that was tall with sheer gray walls that would soon be bathed in the noonday sun. "This one has always reminded me of Martin Sumuki, Martina's father, whose aura was bright and unwavering, unaffected by those around him. Now it makes me think of you, Brianna, and your independent strength."

I only shrugged.

"Come along."

They led me farther back into the canyon to a mineral pool bubbling with orange and green sediment. Laid out in the shallows there was some burlap. "This is netta water?"

"You must know it, to learn what to avoid."

I knelt by the stream and handled some. "But it's just heated water."

"It has aroma and color," Kat corrected. "And weight. Netta water is most often present by the heated pools with green and orange showing. It makes netta during the weeks before the rain."

I nodded and dried my hands while Kat drew near. I recognized Karima Le's features in her face. "Your way will be difficult," she said. "A time is coming when we cannot reach you even for mental pictures. But you are not separate from us. We are always connected."

She took two stones from her pocket, one sandstone and one granite. "These are the textures of the savannah," she whispered as though it was a fun joke. "This one is you, the unyielding granite that shaped the land. This one is me, sandstone that crumbles and is remolded by the geo-thermal mantle."

She knelt and buried the stones together in the soft earth banking the mineral pool. "Now we are planted forever in the Canyon of Buttes. Now we are protected from evil by the force of netta. Now we cannot be separated."

"You were never separate," Kyle Rula corrected.

"But I will be absent?" I asked.

"For a time."

"And now I have one more homily for you," Kyle Rula added. She turned me toward her and recited. "The race is not to the swift, nor the battle to the strong … But time and chance happen to us all."

"But what does it mean?"

"You will know, on the appropriate day."

"You have seen my fate," I guessed. "You grieve for me."

"It is no matter. You will have ground-born children."

"Pete's children?"

"Yes." I scowled at that idea. They smiled together.

The former sweatshop workers prayed and chanted and whispered together. We made promises of friendship and discussed ideas for commerce. We were cleansed and refreshed, and we faced our lives anew. The rest was goulep knowledge and not to be reported here.

Before the day waned, we climbed the ridge of the far wall. We looked back at the big columns below and beside us like guests at a wedding. We walked single file along the ridge to descend and spend the night in a new savannah camp as a new people.

The following day we walked with the morning sun at our backs. Vera limped along at my side while Karen showed Sarah how to manage the whip and drive the cart. We were gritty, dehydrated, and sunburned. But we were bound together and making plans for the future.

Before the sun began to beat down in earnest, we saw Captain Shaw's transport helicopter approach from Cylay. Kyle Rula and Hakulupe Le joined Vera and me. The others hung back while the chopper landed and its blades kicked up a biting dust swirl. The vehicle powered down. Mrs. Shaw opened the hatch and stepped out wearing her tan skirt and jacket and topee. She hesitated and asked Sarah which goulep was Kyle Le. Sarah pointed at the veiled sister of Arim.

Mrs. Shaw approached Rularim and held an open palm at elbow height. "Hiki, Kyle Rula. Melinga."

Kyle Rula waited a moment before she pulled off her sky-blue burka. "Melinga, Sheeks-Cylom. You honor us."

Mrs. Shaw wheezed slightly. "I'm sorry to interrupt your time of reverence. My errand is for Brianna." Vera stepped back slightly, but I took her arm. I still wanted her support, the companionship of one who was the same as me.

"Dr. Beecham has taken ill," Mrs. Shaw said. "He will be evacuated to the transport. He asks that you accompany him."

"He cannot protect me from what Dolvia offers," I demurred.

"Perhaps Dolvia offers this task," Kyle Rula said.

Mrs. Shaw showed Rularim the evil eye, so rude. "You wanted to visit the transport," she said to me. "You can stay with Colonel Hartley and his wife. It's just for a short time."

"With Billie?" I asked, suddenly eager.

Mrs. Shaw's breathing was shallow and noisy. She turned back to Kyle Rula. "Ah, we need to make connections for the shuttle."

"If you will give us a minute."

Mrs. Shaw glanced around but received no response, even from Hakulupe Le. "Melinga." She walked back to the chopper.

Vera sadly smiled and offered a hug. "We can chat on the EAM," I offered. "Once you learn the convent's code."

"Melinga," she said, and limped back to Karen who waited with the gouleps.

Kyle Rula turned me toward her. She kindly peered into my face. "I wish we had more time."

"One thing," I said, feeling the need to direct their actions in my absence. "The convent's location."

"You mean, over the savannah pool?"

"You might want to wait to break ground until—"

"Until Ralph and Edwina are done nesting there?"

I hesitated. "Are you sending me because you have seen I will leave?"

"I would keep you with me if I could," she said. "But Dolvia has set this task for you. We cannot know Her ways. It is only for us to obey."

"You should put that on the blackboard as a homily."

She tapped me twice on the chest with her index finger, resolute but teasing. "Perhaps I will." She walked away, shaking her head. And that was the last time I ever saw Kyle Rula. I often thought about it, about how I would be glad to greet her again with her quick and promising smile.

I scrambled into the helicopter that lifted off with a dust swirl. I waved wildly to the gouleps while we flew over their position. The pilot took off his goggles and leaned back into our compartment. "Hey, girl."

It was Lt. Milo Sector. I should have known him from his big mustache. "Hiki, Lieutenant Sector." I must be healed of my sweat-shop scars, I thought as I worked the shoulder strap. I was glad once more to greet a man.

Mrs. Shaw breathed from her inhaler. "Kyle Rula thinks she's so much better than us. And what's with that burka?"

Sheeks-Cylom had not changed much.

Presently the chopper set down in the Cylay hospital yard. We climbed out while Lt. Sector powered down the motor. It felt odd to move so quickly from one part of the savannah to the next. The air here was moist and the oleastras planted in the yard were heavy with blossoms. Few people were about, though, just three convalescing patients in white trousers and using crutches. "You should get cleaned up," Mrs. Shaw said.

"May I see Dr. Beecham first?"

"This way."

The blue macaw, which properly belonged at the fortress of Arim, lifted from a nearby tree and swooped down near our heads. Mrs. Shaw ducked and waved her arms in irritation. "He has claimed the entire complex as his and destroyed the bird nests."

I gave out a big peal of laughter, which felt good—better than good. On the wing, the macaw imitated my voice with exact tones. Milo and I looked up with big grins. Mrs. Shaw frowned in her special way, her face all a-pucker.

"He will return to the fortress when Kyle Rula arrives there," I said.

"Let's keep a good thought."

The macaw came to rest on the verandah rail and tucked in his wings. His lush tail feathers hung down. He walked to where we came up the steps. Mrs. Shaw shot him a hateful look. "Braaadt," he said. "Gualareps on the savannah."

"Gouleps," she corrected.

"Gualareps on the savannah," he repeated.

She walked ahead with resolute steps. I put a finger over my lips to indicate that it was our secret that Ralph and Edwina had a nest full of eggs. Milo and I followed Sheeks-Cylom inside. We entered a long dormitory where rows of empty patient cots were made up in white sheets with draped mosquito netting overhead. Dr. Beecham lay in the far cot, asleep and ashen. His mouth was covered by the stiff plastic cup of an oxygen mask. Wisps of gray hair fell away from his emaciated skull.

"He's sedated for the flight," Mrs. Shaw whispered. "I have some medicine you can give him, if need be." I nodded and received from her hand the medical bag along with a small traveling case.

"I packed some clothes in there," she continued. "You should shower while we load the stretcher. There will be no time at the launch pad. And here, you must have this." She grabbed my arm and pressed an injection gun against it.

"Ooohh!" The bite was more surprising than painful.

"Signed inoculation papers are in the bag. You would not want me to perpetuate a lie, would you?" Her expression did not change. Sheeks-Cylom shared no chi, maybe appearing extra-cold to me after the camaraderie among gouleps.

I was led by an attendant to a patient bathroom where I undressed and got under the spray. I wanted to remain there, enjoying its soothing effect on my tender skin, but I knew they waited for me. I dressed in the store-bought clothes Mrs. Shaw had thoughtfully brought, fumbling with the buttons, before I hurried to the helicopter.

Lt. Sector helped me on board where Mrs. Shaw was already sitting next to Dr. Beecham on the stretcher. The ride to the launchpad was short. The chopper provided a constant swoop-swoop-swoop rhythm, too loud for conversation. I felt native and sunburned in my Softcheeks clothes, and my arm ached near the inoculation shot. I wished for the lotion Mrs. Shaw had once insisted that I use. I searched my pack and found the remaining aloe on a big leaf. I smeared some on my nose and forehead.

I tried to smile at her watching me but then looked away. I missed Vera.

Milo Sector set down the helicopter on a painted circle at the shuttle launch pad. Mrs. Shaw and I entered the low metal building to escape the blades' disturbance. People looked up at our entrance, and a few stared at my sunburned face. Some were seated with three or more pieces of luggage, inspecting the travel ticket or checking a packed case. The air was dry and distasteful, recycled to remove the humidity. Through the revolving door, I saw Lt. Sector talking with a Consortium official to direct the stretcher unloading.

Outside the far window stood the shuttle rocket in an upright position, spewing exhaust plumes and underlit by ready lights. I would soon enter its wingless embrace and leave Dolvia.

"So what is wrong with Dr. Beecham?" I asked Mrs. Shaw.

"Tuberculosis, a Softcheeks disease we seldom see anymore. We should have caught it earlier, but who knew? It's treatable."

"But he can travel?"

"We don't know how vulnerable Dolviets are. The Consortium can provide the best care in this case."

"And if I catch it?"

She blinked twice. "It would have to be airborne from his lungs. We took precautions."

"You mean, the mask and all?"

"He will go into isolation on the transport." She shrugged with a furtive gesture. "He's older. He's been working too hard. The Uburu children—" her voice trailed off.

"It's not your fault."

"If I had not lingered in Cylay—"

"Rularim claimed that it was a needed mercy seat."

Mrs. Shaw vaguely smiled. She went to talk with the suited attendant and pointed at me, probably requesting extra attention as this was my first flight, goulep aborigine orphan girl that I was. She walked back to where I waited with the medical bag and the small pack.

"My husband wanted to be here for the departure," she offered. "But the fighting in the Uburu mesas demands his attention."

I only nodded.

"I'm returning to the clinic," she continued. "We can keep in touch via EAM."

"The clinic? Truly?" I felt a rush of affection. I had pleasant memories of my time there and especially of Kecouroo's classroom guidance.

"This transport visit will give you a chance to practice your English, huh?"

"Do the Hartleys know about my ... I mean, did you tell them that I was—"

"Only that you were on the savannah with the gouleps," she answered. "Share what you feel comfortable telling, nothing more."

"Thank you for arranging everything and for fetching me."

"I will send a message to Billie Hartley," she added, very auntie-like, "with a collagen prescription for your burn."

"How long will Dr. Beecham have to stay on the transport?"

"That depends on how he responds to treatment. The shuttle returns every ten days, so you will be back soon, I am sure."

Two squads of Consortium soldiers with their duffel bags and shouldered weapons boarded first. A few others, mostly Hardhand businessmen, showed their tickets and passed the attendant to walk down the causeway, struggling to manage the many pieces of luggage. Two Consortium corporals passed with Dr. Beecham's stretcher on wheels. Milo Sector stood on the side, no doubt waiting to ferry Mrs. Shaw to her bush clinic.

The uniformed attendant signaled that I should come forward.

Mrs. Shaw hesitated. "My husband wanted to be here."

"You said that."

"Yes, of course. Go on then."

I seemed to be forever saying good-bye to people. I waved to Lt. Sector who signified on me with a lopsided grin under his mustache. I walked down the causeway and looked back. Mrs. Shaw showed me a worried face.

In the shuttle's passenger section I settled into a bucket seat, strapped on the wide belt, closed my eyes, and waited for the torque-loaded shuttle rocket to propel me into the black sky.

SIXTEEN

WHEN WE DISEMBARKED ONTO THE TRANSPORT, THE SAME CON-
sortium corporals managed the stretcher on wheels while Dr.
Beecham slept, breathing into the mask. We walked down the
causeway toward midship, an open mall with neon accent light-
ing. Overhead comtechs with lowered volumes provided vacillat-
ing blue tones. People in brown uniforms milled about. The cold
rush of air-conditioning reached our place, causing me to cough
shallowly from the distasteful recycled air.

The customs officials were Consortium, all wearing similar uniforms. I was struck at how confined people were here, all dressed
the same as if there was a ceremony to attend. Two Company men
loitered behind the barrier. I knew they were Company executives
from photos I had seen at Captain Shaw's command center. These
men wore dark blue suits that buttoned down the side. Their breast
pockets sported an emblem of a panda in a yellow circle with a

purple rim. Round white collars against their blanched skin lent a formal look.

Billie Hartley waited past the customs barrier and waved to me. When the stretcher approached the counter in our turn, the executives stepped forward. One spoke to the customs official who checked Dr. Beecham's papers. The Chinese man approached the stretcher, and Billie joined us. "This Softcheeks doctor has contracted TB," she said in bright tones in English.

The Company executive frowned.

"He is slated for isolation to prevent its spread."

The two men exchanged glances and glared at me. "This child serves as his attendant from the Dolviet hospital," Billie added. "Hiki, Brianna."

"Hiki, Billie Hartley. Melinga," I said with a palm held high. I coughed shallowly, and the Chinese men recoiled. Disdainful looks crossed their faces. One signaled that we should pass through customs. The corporals wheeled the stretcher while Mrs. Hartley and I followed, quickly walking down the corridor.

Billie put a motherly arm around my shoulders. "Good move."

Midship was all about corridors and who had access to certain work areas. The continuous overhead light fixture made the channeled activity uniform in color. More men in uniforms stood guard than actually worked. Colonel Hartley was waiting for us at the infirmary entrance wearing a blue uniform with many brass buttons and bars of honor. Soldiers dressed in the same blue stopped the corporals and took control of the stretcher, which they wheeled through a door at the right. We followed while two guards stepped to flank the door.

Inside a brightly lit room with medical equipment at the ready, one lieutenant searched under the thin mattress of the stretcher and extracted a manila envelope. Another took film canisters from the stiff pillow under Dr. Beecham's head. They nodded to Colonel Hartley and left by another door.

He turned to me. "Welcome, Brianna," he said in English, which was the transport's universal language and by default the Consortium's language. "We are glad you came to visit."

"Is Dr. Beecham really sick?"

"His condition is serious," the colonel said. "We're just being opportunistic."

"Op-por-tu-nis-tic," I slowly repeated.

"I speak some Arrivi," he said. "Your visit will give me a chance to increase my skills." While we talked, he rooted through my pack. First he pulled out the soiled Arrivi gown I had worn on the savannah. He glanced at Billie.

"There was no time," I said and reached for it, rolling its folds into a gritty wad. He searched through the pack's pockets. He found another small square envelope and quickly stowed it in his uniform tunic. Then he zipped my pack and handed it to his wife.

Colonel Hartley surprised me with a quick hug. He smelled wonderful. "Welcome to midship," he said, and then left with the corporals from Cylay.

"I can show you the room now," Mrs. Hartley offered. "Also, I have a prescription for your burn." How odd I must have appeared to them with my sunburned face and my wide-eyed wonder. Billie walked with me down another narrow corridor at a more relaxed pace. "You can take meals with us and attend classes if the English is not too difficult. Also, there's the possibility of more student exchanges, but we can discuss that later."

She stopped outside a door, one of several doors all the same. "This is your place," she said and handed me a key. "You cannot get lost. See, this number on the key is the same as outside the door. The rooms are numbered consecutively, even numbers on this side, odd number across the way."

I grinned, very relieved. I would never have figured that out. "Con-se-cu-tive-ly," I repeated.

"We'll just drop off your pack for now. Then I can show you how to get around." My place was one room with a bunk, a table with chair, and a bathroom. I was glad to find a shower there.

The Hartleys had a five-room suite, well lit and homey. Pictures on the wall were of Carl and Heather in school uniforms and one of Colonel Hartley holding a large fish in both hands. A table defined a kitchen area and beyond was a living area with a tired couch and two easy chairs.

Billie's younger daughter Jesse was ten-years-old with cultured manners surprising for one of her age. She took her meal early and was sent with a nanny to bed before the adults sat down at the table. I was included as an adult.

We dined with Steve Swanweil who had also just arrived on the shuttle. I had set the table with plates Billie gave me. She dished up big bowls of vegetables and a steaming meat platter that I brought to the table. We passed the food around and served ourselves using oversized spoons. My day had been full, but all was forgotten with Swanweil's presence in the private apartment. He was ingratiating with the Hartleys, very different from on Dolvia. He counted them as allies working against the resistant tribes.

Colonel Hartley winked at me while he listened to Steve Swanweil's casual reasoning. "Other Consortium planets are developed with working governments and stock exchanges. Schools and hospitals, good roads and industry. But Dolvia, what a headache. I mean, I can see opportunity there. But there's no infrastructure, no set rate of exchange. The tribes negotiate everything separately. Their leaders are ignorant, arbitrary, and xenophobic."

I wondered what xe-no-pho-bic was. Perhaps it was a French word.

"Like with Sean Bryant's operation," he continued. Billie glanced my way. Colonel Hartley only poured more wine for his guest.

"The Bryants were forced," Mr. Swanweil said, "to shut down one whole section of their enterprise from this worker scandal. Nothing was proven. There was no inquiry, no right of redress. Just rumors and hate mongering.

"When the Bryants lodged a formal complaint," he added, "tribal leaders displayed two dead girls and asserted that their fate was the fault of the shop's managers. That was justification for the brutal torture and deaths of five trained Hardhands? It's barbaric."

My heart pulled down in my chest, and I felt chilled through. I looked at the gooseflesh on my arms. Why not speak up? Why not offer the truth in answer to this man's twisted words? I had sought the right to speak. I had asked Dolvia for an opportunity. But now my throat constricted, and I could barely draw a breath.

Billie put her napkin next to her plate. "Yes, well," she said. "Perhaps I shall escort our sunburned guest to her room while you men take brandy and coffee. Brianna?"

I put my napkin next to my plate, nodded to Colonel Hartley, and followed her out. While we walked through the corridors Billie offered, "Tomorrow you can visit Dr. Beecham. Would you like that?"

I only nodded.

"Get some rest," she said when we reached my door. "We can talk tomorrow."

What good was talk, I wondered, in the face of Mr. Swanweil's reasoning? I entered the blank room and threw myself onto the bed. My arm throbbed near the inoculation.

Colonel and Mrs. Hartley's marriage was very different from Captain and Mrs. Shaw. Nobody yelled or broke china. He managed the scrambled eggs the following morning, as well as Jesse's pre-school needs. It was odd to see the uniformed officer pour orange juice from a pitcher painted with teddy bears and unicorns.

"Will you be at school?" Jesse asked while she assembled her books.

"Maybe later," I said. "I want to visit Dr. Beecham."

"Honey!" Colonel Hartley called out. "We are going now!" He and Jesse left.

Billie entered with a big yawn, wearing a cotton dress and low-heeled shoes. "Hi," she said and went to the coffee pot.

She sat with me at the table and sipped from the steaming mug. She booted a comtech screen there and watched for a moment. A Chinese woman stared out, talking in crisp accents. Soon I was lost in the colorful display. I looked up, glassy-eyed, when Billie stood at the door and spoke my name. "Brianna, let's go."

I looked around. The dishes were absent and the kitchen spotless. I must have been staring at the comtech for twenty minutes without knowing it. "Sorry," I said.

Dr. Beecham had been moved to another room where his bed was covered by an acrylic box. I know because I had experience with acrylic from Dr. Greensboro's bush clinic. Inside the box, Dr. Beecham sat under a sheet with a book and reading glasses. He had some personal items laid out on the nightstand there.

I was led to a straight-backed chair on the box's right side, and the nurse flipped a switch by an imbedded microphone above a double-door compartment. "Brianna?" Dr. Beecham said. His voice sounded thin and scratchy. "How do you like the transport?"

"The Hartleys are very kind people. How are you feeling?"

"It was thoughtless of me to endanger everybody. But things will be better now."

"How long will you stay in this box?"

"For a while. You can attend classes, though. In two weeks Carl and Heather will visit on university holiday from the biosphere."

"Two weeks?" I didn't know how long that was.

"Yes, well. There's much to absorb before you are acclimated to the transport."

"Ac-cli-ma-ted," I repeated to myself. English was hard.

Later Mrs. Hartley introduced me around in many departments. I did not catch all the crewmembers' names. We came to the command center in the military ship. Colonel Hartley signaled through the big glass window that we should enter. Several screens displayed different types of information, including the comtech channel and an orbiting view of Dolvia. Men in blue uniforms talked into headsets or spoke with bench mates. They didn't acknowledge me.

The two Dolviet corporals who had accompanied the stretcher stood with the colonel by an EAM screen that displayed aerial photos of Uburu land taken from a helicopter. "I was there," I volunteered. "I accompanied Captain Shaw when he took Rabbenu Ely fact-finding."

The men glanced up at the big windows. The corridor was empty. "How much did you see?" Colonel Hartley asked. "Do you understand these photos?"

"That's just north of the Iamida River, before you get to the burned-out area," I said. "I sometimes visited the command center with Captain Shaw."

"Actually, that would be Major Shaw now," Colonel Hartley corrected.

"Really?" I grinned. The corporals hid their smirks.

"She's familiar with the savannah," Billie added.

"So we see." Hartley touched my nose, peeling from sunburn, with his thumb. I glanced at the corporals and ducked my head from embarrassment. Colonel Hartley thought about it for a moment. "You can spend some afternoons with us, after your classes. Come directly here and ask for me. There's no need to discuss our arrangement with the other students."

"I understand."

Billie and I had our talk over lunch in their suite. We made the sandwiches ourselves. The bread was soft and the butter was hard because it was kept cold. That was something. Billie showed me how to cut thin shavings of butter for each slice of bread. Everything in their apartment revolved around groceries and the kitchen table. "We were thinking that more students should visit the transport," Billie said. "Who do you suggest?"

"Well, there's Tom, the Cylahi who did the drawings for the flora encyclopedia. He learned some English when we assembled the pages for Hakulupe Le. And there's Rufus, Kyle Rula's younger son. He's good with numbers. He likes the EAM."

"Good," she said. "Who else? Any girls?"

"Vera, please."

I went to school with Jesse each morning, my fourth school situation in a short season. The room was smaller than any schoolroom on Dolvia, and the books about tribal canon from which Hakulupe Le taught were missing. Again, I was impressed with how compressed facilities were on the transport. English was the teacher's language for lecture, although she spoke a strange language from Cicero to specific students.

I joined Colonel Hartley some afternoons, and Billie accompanied me to visit Dr. Beecham. She called him Hank. What a great word, Hank.

Dr. Beecham asked me to read sometimes. And he wanted to talk, to reminisce about the Uburu refugee crisis; about what had really happened and in what sequence. And about who was responsible. He went over it and over it. He was divided then, within my viewing, onto the three planes of Softcheeks. That was the first time I was certain I understood Kyle Rula's description of their aura.

I took meals with the Hartley family. They played a game similar to Mrs. Shaw, you know, wherein Jesse and I were required to speak out our lessons for the day. Afterward I wandered down the hall to my sterile room to sleep.

Oh, I forgot to say. Their showers were air baths. Ha! That was something.

When I was in the command center they called Ops, Colonel Hartley talked over my head with his officers. He encouraged me to speak up when I felt they got something wrong. More than once during their discussions he saw me frown and made some excuse so he and I could talk on the side. He was careful with me, you know?

They booted the HGEAM and talked with Major Shaw in the Cylay command center. Colonel Hartley had me sit next to him so that my image was also projected within the cycling cube on Dolvia. I became one of the floating heads. Major Shaw and Lt. Sector said hiki. Milo brushed his mustache with two fingers and grinned.

Mostly we stared at the photos and compared them to long-distance transport photos until Colonel Hartley understood the topical map that the light and dark splotches represented. He was gentle and patient but worried. He always smelled great.

The officers monitored troop and armament deployment under Major Shaw's direction, as well as the Company's response. They discussed Uburu mesa passes that created supply bottlenecks and helicopter flight paths that could avoid detection. They were concerned about possible surprise attacks from the Company and their Gora enforcers on the savannah railway and on the shuttle launch pad in Cylay. It was all con-cep-tu-al and well reasoned.

The Consortium officers' concerns were so very different from Pete and Karlyhi's methods, unemotional and reasoned outside of warrior agreement. Colonel Hartley simply ordered the men, called de-tach-ments, to this place or that place without explanation. And the men and officers journeyed there because they were told to go there. You would never, you know, get Mekucoo to act thus. What honor was in that?

One day Colonel Hartley showed me another photo taken from the ground. It was a stone totem, a big carved face with a menacing frown; it was covered with vines and undergrowth. "What is it?" I asked.

"You don't know?"

"Well, it's on Uburu land. See the moss and the okiioc stems? They get more year-round rain. But this totem is old and hidden. I did not see this image among their jewelry or sewn designs when they were refugees. Is there another tribe?"

"Very observant. Uburu never enter this volcanic area. Monsters live there," he whispered with mock seriousness.

"Perhaps monsters do live there," I said. "And now you will send a de-tach-ment."

"Yes, to discover its strategic advantage. Mrs. Shaw wants to go along."

I laughed, showing my teeth.

"Why is that funny?"

"You'll find out."

One night I had swimming dreams from the savannah pool; Edwina sent them. I was surprised she could reach the transport with images. It occurred to me that I might be sending mental pictures from loneliness, like when I had first attended school in Cylay. I resolved to exercise more discipline so I would not, you know, violate anybody's privacy or make Ralph angry.

Another day, the officers in Ops were tense and watchful. "What is it?" I asked.

"The Company shuttle arrives today. There may be increased customs inspections."

"From Company men? You never invite them to dinner, only Hardhands."

"Company executives are not naive. We would give away more than we would learn."

I found the word naive in the classroom dictionary. As I suspected, it was originally French. French was better than English, I thought. You could hide more meaning in fewer words. French was like Earth's Mekucoo. I mentioned that to Billie while we washed dinner dishes one night. We only rinsed them and loaded a contraption called a dishwasher that made a lot of noise and made the kitchen area hotter.

"Latin would be Mekucoo," she demurred.

"What is La-tin?" I asked.

"It's a dead language now, used only for religious ritual. But it's the root of the romance languages; French, Spanish, and Italian. Only Greek is stronger for root words because math and medical terms come from Greek."

I shook my head. Softcheeks were something; there was no getting around that.

Two shuttles had come and gone by the time I waited with Billie in customs for Vera to disembark with Tom and Rufus. Midship was loaded with Blackshirts, and the whole ambiance had changed. Each Company man had the panda logo emblazoned on his sleeve. Rufus stared down the Company executive who rifled through his pack, but they were blithely unaware of his Mekucoo challenge. Finally, the Dolviet students were released into midship, and Vera limped to me. "Hiki, Vera," I said with an open palm gesture. "Melinga."

I was so glad to see Vera, I gave her a big hug. That was a surprise to her, you know, there in public. "That's how it's done here," I boasted. She rubbed her arm where she had been inoculated. I imagined Mrs. Shaw and her injection gun and the struggle when Rufus's turn came for the hypo. I wished I'd been there to see that.

Tom and Rufus bowed shortly to Mrs. Hartley. "We're sorry to drag you away from the erriv drive," I said to Rufus.

"Erriv returned to the savannah," he returned in a harsh tone. "Haku's heifers have all delivered twins."

I didn't believe him.

Then I stopped short. Across the way in midship, Colonel Hartley stood with Steve Swanweil and a squad of Chinese Blackshirts. One Blackshirt displayed his crop, an ornamental sidearm that many carried on their belts; the crops were originally used to discipline horses. Colonel Hartley admired the tooled leather handle, easily sharing chi with this group.

"What is it?" Vera asked at my shoulder.

"Nothing. Let's go."

We visited Dr. Beecham who was glad for the company. I had neglected him for several days. His soft cheeks had color again. Tom and Rufus tapped the acrylic box and scowled at each other.

They held their counsel, though, making me admire their warriors' reserve.

Vera was assigned a room next to mine. The tribal boys were given similar rooms on a lower deck. That was to keep us from having sexual thoughts while separated from our parents. Rufus thought that was funny.

He and Tom argued about the need to take air baths.

The Hartleys had enveloped me into their family routine. But where one tribal girl was an oddity, four aboriginal teenagers were a delegation. We were assigned a lunchroom for our communal meals and after-class gatherings. There was a kitchen area with a re-fridge-ra-tor that was stocked with fruit drinks and cut vegetables. Two posters displayed instructions for how to wash hands and how to help a person who was choking. Over the next days, other students sometimes joined us to learn Arrivi and sit for caricatures that Tom drew. Students wanted to practice the tribal chants Vera taught. I had not grown close to any of the students, not even Jesse. It felt odd to me that the transport young people were so eager to share.

Soon Rufus took my place with Colonel Hartley in Ops while they poured over the aerial photos. Rufus's knowledge was not better than mine was, Billie had explained, just of a different sort. I was not jealous, really. I was glad for the break so I could sort out the motives behind Colonel Hartley's intimate manner.

Besides, I had Vera. We sat in my room where I had only slept before. We talked and talked about the gouleps and their new skills and how Kyle Rula had provided for everybody. Vera drew from her skirt a packet with a cover letter written in English. "I was told you should give this to Colonel Hartley, if that's appropriate."

The packet contained photos and samples of ceremonial gowns decorated with parrot feathers, as well as some high-quality olive oil. The letter asked Colonel Hartley to look into activating long-dormant import and export licenses, and perhaps instruct Vera concerning their EAM management.

"Rularim said you would know when the time was right," Vera whispered.

"You will need to master English. Also their technical terms," I said, sounding very much like Mrs. Shaw. "And how they add the columns of numbers. You will have to apply yourself, you know, in the transport classroom, more than in the Cylay academy."

"I will do whatever is required," she promised.

"You will like working with Colonel Hartley."

She waited.

"What?" I asked.

"There's a campfire chant about you."

"Among the gouleps?"

"A Mekucoo chant."

"Mekucoo?"

"Rularim said that Kecouroo keeps you in Pete's mind this way."

"I don't want to hear it." There was a lengthy pause. "All right, what is it?"

Vera shrugged. "I can tell you later."

When she left to sleep in her own room, I lay back and thought about how transport experience was so different with several Dolviet teenagers here. I realized that I must be a loner, the same as Mrs. Shaw, except I had not been alone, really. Rather, I had been accepted as a member of the Hartley family. Anything to not be like Mrs. Shaw.

Perhaps the Hartleys were just being polite in taking the edge off my solitary ways. I had felt friendship, but maybe from my own need. They were overfriendly with Steve Swanweil also. He had not seen a double-faced meaning. Perhaps Colonel Hartley was relieved that he no longer needed to listen to a willful and superstitious tribal girl but could commune with a warrior, the son of Cyrus. Perhaps I was only tolerated.

I drifted into sleep. I had swimming dreams, but not from the grotto. I was propelled along a swift current in murky waters with tangled vegetation and ever-changing shafts of sunlight. Schools of kariom accompanied me, and I detoured to protected pools where I lingered under broad and tough lily pads. Then I hovered on the water's edge, stalking the long-legged flamingoes gorging themselves on kariom fry and tadpoles. I lunged from the pool and clamped down on a feathery treat while hundreds of transient birds took to wing in flashes of pink and white. I sank back into the water and swallowed my prey whole, feathers and all.

The next morning I went to see Dr. Beecham by myself. Inside the box, he sat like a holy man under the crisp sheets. He looked over his reading glasses and considered my face, but I looked away. I did not have anything to say. I did not have a case to make.

"Carl and Heather will arrive on the Company shuttle from Cicero," he offered. "Then you will have more cosmopolitan companionship."

"Cos-mo-po-li-tan," I repeated under my breath.

"Would you like to visit Cicero?"

"The Hartleys are so kind," I shrugged. "Are they just being polite?"

"Billie likes you."

"And Colonel Hartley?"

"He thinks you're sharp, but perhaps too sensitive. He is unsure about the need to be careful with your feelings. I did not tell him why."

I frowned. I had put my recent Dolviet experience out of my mind. The sweatshop events need not enter my relationship with my Consortium hosts. "Dr. Beecham, am I more sensitive than I was during the refugee crisis?"

He smiled. "Perhaps I am more sensitive." That was no answer.

Later, though, I was invited back to Ops where Colonel Hartley was ready with explanations. "Rufus is suspicious and too reserved. You're more malleable."

"Mal-le-a-ble," I whispered under my breath.

"Besides, he has little English and tests the limits of my skill in Arrivi."

I only smiled. My sympathy was with Rufus. English was hard.

SEVENTEEN

I DREAMED ONE NIGHT OF EGGS HATCHING. THE INFANT GUALA-
reps, wet with filmy eyes, called each other forward with unsteady barks. They poked their heads from the collapsed leathery shells, and scurried to the freshly turned dirt Ralph had provided. They scampered to his leg, there in the burrow, flicking their tongues to identify his scent.

They crawled over Ralph like he was a boulder. He gently nudged one that had ventured toward that noble head. Then he moved. That must have been something to them. He led the infant reps out into the sunlight.

The next day while I sat in class, I thought of sending out mental pictures. But I decided my idea was silly. Ralph must have shared with Kyle Rula and Major Shaw. Surely Edwina had provided images for Mrs. Shaw. The birth announcement. The proud parents. I was glad for them. I missed the savannah and swimming with Edwina.

As it turned out, by remaining on the transport I had missed much more than the new season of kari. When I looked back on it later, I wondered how I had survived my days in such a state of ignorance. Perhaps the trouble was being severed from Dolvia.

Perhaps I was, you know, the naive and petulant loner people took me for. Perhaps a native girl was as superfluous as people believed.

First Dr. Mitterand visited on his way to Cicero to test the pox cure. He came to dinner at the Hartleys. I was included for the event seated with Jesse. "We found a possible vaccine compound from the cultures Dr. Greensboro was studying at the Cylay hotel," Pierre said.

"From Kyle Rula's blood?" I asked.

"Ah, I cannot say whose blood."

I was certain that secret was extracted from Rularim's blood taken on the day she had so thoughtfully provided the gowns that were later used to cover the sweatshop gouleps. Such a leader was Rularim.

Colonel Hartley and Dr. Mitterand moved to the deep chairs and talked with their heads together. Billie Hartley was kind as ever, allowing me to help with the dinner dishes. "We tested the olive oil you provided," she offered. "Excellent quality. There may be a Consortium market."

"Separate from the Bryant cartel?"

"Through the dormant licenses that Kyle Rula of Arim supplied. Do you have an idea of what quantity they can produce?"

"After the big-wet season, there's plenty. Another rainy season may be different."

"So, Brianna, are you ready to return to Dolvia?"

I shrugged.

"Vera should remain and learn the needed inventory menus for Kyle Rula's licenses."

"Then I will stay."

"Vera is a goulep?"

I hesitated. I knew the next question. "My suffering was different from theirs." I stared at the floor. "I was not chained to a station or made to work."

Billie blinked several times like she was resisting tears. "We don't have to talk about this, unless you want to."

I set my jaw. I could not cry in front of Billie, not after all she had done for me. "Vera will do a good job for you," I said. "She wants the position so her sisters have work."

"I'm confident she will do fine. Nobody blames you. You may remain on the transport until you and Vera are ready to go home."

I nodded. I saw no double-faced motive. "Dr. Beecham said Carl and Heather will visit."

"They are on university break and will arrive in a couple days. Then you will have some company your own age, huh?"

"Yes, ma'am."

"Hey, I'm Billie. When did I become ma'am?"

"Sorry. Thank you, Billie."

She gave me a hug then, pressing me to her ample bosom. The Hartleys were big on hugs. She smelled of dishwashing soap.

I joined Dr. Mitterand the following morning when he went to visit Dr. Beecham. Pierre whispered with a wink. "So ... we're together again, just like at the bush hospital."

Dr. Beecham sat in the acrylic box looking ashen and thin. He wore reading glasses and had several medical books open on the bed. His white gown and white sheets reinforced the wispy hair against his transparent skin. He looked like an expensive orchid corsage I had seen at the transport mall's florist. His books provided supporting greenery, all presented in a clear, stiff box. Only a red bow and card were missing.

Dr. Beecham was serious, though. He wanted to know the full report, as well as what Pierre thought new events could mean. Hank liked to structure the talk in terms of lists. There were three of such-and-such, or three reasons for that. He spoke always in lists of three. They talked about Dolviet power centers and perceived threats and how the net was closing.

"Young warriors travel to Uburu land as volunteers," Pierre said, "mostly to escape their herding duties. The young men are suddenly rich with issued shoes and uniforms. None will wear Mekucoo leather again.

"In part it's Rabbenu Ely's fault," he continued. "Ely saved the land from Hardhands and Softcheeks by registering deeds. By going public with inheritance rights, however, he created a landed society wherein the oldest son inherits everything.

"Erriv are secondary property now, valued for their price per kilo, but no longer as family members. Essentially, the family farm as a city-state ruled by committee has vanished. Landless younger sons unwilling to serve their brothers have gone off to war."

"So there will be war?"

"A standing division of regulars are bivouacked on Uburu land," Dr. Mitterand said. "They operate separately from sane voices like

Haku rabbe Murd. The warriors carry automatics and are trained how to fire the wagon-mounted ordnance by Lieutenants Taylor and Sector."

Dr. Beecham shook his head. "They have police duties only. The distribution of relief supplies and seed grain."

Pierre shrugged. "Warriors are told to stand and wait. They must hold their fire when challenged. How long will that last?"

"When the rains come, they will return to their Arrivi herds."

"They are regulars now and draw a monthly paycheck. No more hoplites, those warrior-farmers who planted crops one season and fought during another. Some warriors have settled in with Uburu and Gora women. I am telling you, it's a regular army, and it grows every day."

"Under Rabbenu Ely's command?"

"Ely's a politician. These ones follow Karlyhi."

"Karlyhi?" I asked. They looked at me, surprised at my interruption. I bit my lip.

"Brianna's right," Dr. Beecham said. "Karlyhi is just a couple years older than her. He was at the academy maybe two seasons."

"He controls the weapons arsenal," Pierre shrugged. "Men old enough to be his father follow him."

"He's from the Cylahi tribe."

"Karlyhi is the man. Mark my word."

I left with Dr. Mitterand. In the corridor, he invited me back to his rooms. I thought that was strange, and I just shook my head in the negative. "You remember when we talked about visiting Earth?" he asked. "How eager you were to see the land of your father's birth?"

I only smiled and stepped back a bit.

"I'm leaving for the biosphere on Cicero. You could travel with me."

"I intend to stay with Vera."

"The pox vaccine may turn a considerable profit, if we can synthesize it," Pierre said. "It's possible I won't be back this way." I only shrugged. "Well, consider it," he said. "You could view the wonders of another planet. And Cicero is one step closer to Earth."

He knew what I loved. "But what would I do on Cicero?"

"We can visit Two Forks. Go to museums and movies, and the zoo." Pierre winked and slyly added, "And their gaming parlors."

"They would not allow me to enter even."

"You would be with me. I'll buy clothes to flatter your looks, not that schoolgirl stuff that Dr. Greensboro prefers."

"And that is enough?"

"Well," he whispered, "you know what I want. We would be together as a couple."

"Oh. I see."

"It's not like you're a virgin. Not anymore."

"No, it's not like that."

"Give us a kiss to seal our bargain."

I pulled away. "I intend to stay with Vera."

Pierre watched me for a long moment. "Well, keep me in mind. That door is always open." He did not seem too upset that I turned him down.

I went to find Vera who was doing her homework in the lunchroom set aside for us tribal students; she was hunched over a tablet and laboriously writing. "You can do all that on the EAM."

"This is a letter to Kyle Rula."

"That can also be accomplished on the EAM."

She shrugged. "I guess I'm afraid of the keyboard. I mean what if I hit the wrong key and shut it down? Or shut down the transport?"

"Or end the time-space continuum?"

Vera turned a cold shoulder to me. "I don't know what that means."

I sat next to her, seeking the warm feeling from when we were on the savannah together. "I am sorry. I did not mean to make you feel small."

"You're so far ahead of me, of us all."

"We're the same."

"We are not the same," Vera said. "You always claim that, but it's not so."

"Whoever notices us sees two of the same."

"So brave you are. You easily meet people. Dr. Mitterand likes you."

"That's a mixed blessing. You voiced three objections, you know. Soon you will think just like Softcheeks."

She sadly smiled and looked away. "I could never do that."

"Come on. We can sit at the EAM and learn the codes and menus." Vera gathered her pen and pad. She had much to learn before I could leave her alone.

Dr. Mitterand left on the same shuttle that delivered Carl and Heather Hartley from Cicero. Pierre casually signified on me with a wink and walked up the causeway. I thought that perhaps I would not see him again. My heart pulled down in my chest at the lost opportunity.

The Hartleys invited all four tribal teenagers to dinner that night in celebration for their own teenagers' return. Carl was twenty, but that was not mentioned. Jesse and I pulled on the kitchen table so it separated in the middle, and we added an extra wood panel to spread a clean tablecloth over the extra length. We included a centerpiece of cut flowers from the florist Billie liked to visit in midship. There were extra glasses and extra forks to make a formal setting.

Rufus sat next to Tom, silent and watchful. Tom was a favorite in the transport classroom; I had seen how he in-ter-act-ed with them. He daily completed drawings and tolerated their teasing about his poor English. He was the model scholarship boy, humble and grinning. Rufus was Mekucoo; the students had all learned that. He was not the kidding-around type.

That evening Heather glanced at the tribal delegation and sent a hard look at Vera in her hand-stitched Arrivi gown. "Did you have to invite everybody to the homecoming?" Heather asked her mother.

I remembered Heather as an eager high school senior, freshly disembarked on Dolvia and ready for adventure. She had giggled with Pete and danced on the back verandah with Carl. But her pursuit of an exotic suitor of Softcheeks descent did not include camaraderie with his adoptive tribal sister. When Heather looked at me, she saw a servant. Vera was a crippled servant.

Colonel Hartley was as diplomatic as ever. He asked Rufus about warrior initiation. "I supposed you would rather serve with the militia detachment than attend class."

"Uburu land is a steep climb," Rufus said with a shrug.

"You have been there before?" Colonel Hartley asked with new interest.

Rufus looked around at their faces. I came to understand Colonel Hartley's complaint that he was too reserved. Plus Rufus did not drink wine like Steve Swanweil had.

"Oriika was Uburu," Rufus said. "The holy woman from before the season of netta. Her brother dwelled for a season in my father's house, during the time of Cyrus's first wife. Kecouroo served this man named Moab."

Tom grinned while Rufus warmed up to the story. "Moab led the resistance against Company control of the gold mines that border Uburu land. The effort failed, and Moab was later killed by Siibabean. His death was a great loss, although he died well. Kecouroo visited his family for a time, out of respect."

"Thank you, Rufus," Colonel Hartley said, "for a well-told story. Carl, you could learn much from Rufus. No extra images, and each sentence is full of motivation to push the story along. This same attribute resides in Mekucoo reports I have read. A valuable talent."

Carl frowned and glanced at his sister, waiting his turn for his father's attention.

"I was wondering, Rufus," the colonel continued. "Are there many Mekucoo of mixed blood? Your tribe seems to have more contact with the northern tribes."

"Mekucoo women prefer warriors. There is only Cyrus."

"Cyrus?" I asked.

Rufus shot me a hateful look. Colonel Hartley was ever-gentle with me. "Didn't you ever wonder, Brianna, why Cyrus's hair was long and straight, not like Cara's? It's very like his father's hair, like Borabean hair."

"Borabean?" I incredulously repeated. Rufus showed Tom a look of disdain. Tom put his hand on his chin to control the humor in his face.

"Many Mekucoo chants exist about my father," Rufus said with steel in his voice. "Some speak of his mother Kyros and the circumstances of his birth."

"Tell us," Colonel Hartley suggested in whole tones.

"Do we have to do this now?" Carl asked.

"Yes, now," his father shortly returned.

"But I wanted to tell you about—"

"Later, son." Carl glanced at Heather who sourly frowned.

"Rufus has a family story you will like, Carl," Colonel Hartley added.

Tom sat back, ready to enjoy a chant from his culture. But Rufus chose to relate the story in English without lyrical cadence or repeated refrains. "There was an Abydian king," he began, "rich and renowned for his wisdom. With the support of his powerful army, he demanded tribute from surrounding tribes. He needed the resources for his building projects near the ocean.

"Uburu sent warriors," Rufus continued, "to treat with this king, as did Siibabean. These ones told stories of Mekucoo as ketiwhelp killers, and of the beauty of our women. So this Abydian king also demanded tribute from us. Kyros was sent as a young woman, a diplomat of no importance. Kyros was armed with a set of riddles to test this supposed wise man, as well as eight wide wagons loaded with pelts and beadwork.

"When Kyros arrived at the ocean-side city, she was received as a queen. She was quite taken with this wise king and toured his ambitious building projects. He was taken with her beauty and virtue. Several times Kyros remained on Abydian land after the times of departure passed with no movement. Finally, she had to leave and told King Abyd that her advisors would carry her back to Mekucoo land. He begged Kyros to remain one more night and called for a banquet. He ordered the cooks to add generous spices to the food, and he also provided music late into the night. Then he suggested that the Mekucoo sleep at the palace.

"The king set up a chamber where Kyros would rest on a pallet, and he would sleep on a nearby mattress. Being a virtuous woman, she tried to refuse the arrangement. The king said he would not take anything that was hers if she took nothing of his.

"But later, Kyros awoke thirsty from the spicy meal. Even though it was only a sip of water she took, King Abyd claimed she had broken her promise and therefore he was under no obligation to keep his. They spent the night together as lovers, and she left for Mekucoo land the next day.

"At the time of her departure," Rufus said evenly, "the amorous king gave Kyros a signet ring as a token of their peoples' treaties and of his great regard. He did not know that from their single night of love was born Cyrus the ketiwhelp killer who, it is said, ate the beating hearts of his enemies."

"He did not eat the hearts of his enemies," Carl interjected.

Vera drew in her breath. Nobody countered the claims of Mekucoo.

"Cyrus was a great warrior," Colonel Hartley said. "He deserves our respect."

"He did not—" Carl began.

Billie placed her hand on his forearm resting on the table, and Carl fell silent. Colonel Hartley turned his attention to Rufus. "And Cyrus never met his father?"

"Cyrus visited the ocean-side city," Rufus said, "after he was initiated as a warrior. He showed the signet ring and was received as a lost son. He remained for several seasons.

"The Borabean king was an old man by then," Rufus continued, "and his building projects had been ruinous. The people were rebellious. For their return, the king loaded Cyrus and his companions with riches and ambassadors, handmaids, and wranglers. Many of these later settled on Mekucoo land and never walked home to the ocean-side city, not even for the great king's funeral."

"And is that how Kecouroo learned the languages?"

"Many can communicate with our eastern neighbors."

"Thank you, Rufus, for a marvelous story. Wasn't it grand, Carl?"

"Yeah, sure. A good story."

After coffee, Rufus and Tom bowed and left. Colonel Hartley stepped away with his son who eagerly related his university experiences to the attentive officer. While Jesse and Vera fooled around on the EAM, I helped wash dishes with Billie. That was when Heather also lost her patience. "Mother, please," she said with hands on her hips.

"It's all right," I said. "I can finish here before I help Vera and Jesse on the EAM."

Billie placed her palm on my cheek. "You're a sweet girl, and malleable." They left arm-in-arm for a good mother-daughter chat.

I felt like the servant Heather took me for. I started the dishwasher before I stood behind Vera and Jesse drying my hands.

Jesse shared chi as easily as her parents did. She explained a certain EAM dialogue box where Vera had struggled to understand the next step. "It's easy," Jesse claimed, turning up her round, jolly face. "Like one-two-three."

"I get it now," Vera nodded. "I just didn't know its use before. Thanks."

"We should go," I said. "Will you be all right, Jesse?"

"Sure. I live here."

Vera and I walked through the quiet corridors to our rooms. "The Hartleys are so generous, don't you think, Brianna? I'm so glad you invited me to join you here."

"You don't see a double-faced motive?"

"No. Should I?" We had reached her door. "It's correct, the chant about you."

"Kecouroo's chant? There I do see two-faced motives."

"What do you mean?"

"You never wondered?" I asked. "Pete has offworld blood, yet he's offered as their leader. Kecouroo consolidates her power without offending her aunts from other factions, the ones who would offer forward their sons to lead."

"If Kecouroo were a man," Vera said, "there would be no need for Pete."

"So you have to wonder," I returned. "Will Pete lead because it is seen? Or is it said to be seen so he can lead in her stead? Perhaps Karlyhi is Dolvia's true choice."

"It is seen, that's all. Kyle Rula saw it."

"Kyle Rula was married to Kecouroo's father. Her sons are for a later cycle."

Vera whispered, "Don't you want to know the chant about you? Brianna Miller of Arim has delivered us."

"Delivered you into their hands, you mean."

Vera frowned, unhappy that I did not share her high spirits. "You're too suspicious."

"You're right, of course. I don't know when I became so cynical." I sighed. "One thing, though. There is a custom here. If you don't mind, a hug?"

"Oh, Brianna!" She gladly hugged me. "You're the best. Surely you are." She went into her own room then. Vera never knew how much that moment of warmth meant, or how glad it made me that she could be so giving. She never knew.

I could not sleep, so I went down to the tribal lunchroom. I rooted around in the refrigerator and munched on some carrots. I heard the door open, the one to the seating area. Carl Hartley and Tom entered. He had Tom by the arm and a kerchief secured over Tom's mouth.

"You think you are so much better than us, huh? 'That's a good story. Wasn't it a good story, Carl?'" he sourly mimicked his father. "Well, it seems you need a reminder of who's in charge here. And I'm the one to show you."

I sank down behind the kitchen counter and tightly closed my eyes. I heard Carl slap Tom and punch him twice. I screwed up my courage and silently peered over the countertop. Carl had turned Tom away from him and pulled down his pants. Carl undid his own clothes and committed on Tom the same crime I had known.

"I tell a good story too, don't I, little scholarship boy?" he demanded while he pumped Tom from behind. "Huh? Don't I? You will remember this story-telling long after the other is forgotten. How's this for a good story?"

Carl pushed Tom so he fell. I sank to the kitchen floor again, hiding and stifling my sobs. I heard the scrapping of chairs pushed aside while Carl punched and kicked the scholarship boy.

Carl left. Tom sniffled and pulled up his clothes. From where I huddled, barely breathing, I heard him gently set each chair in place before he left. He would say nothing to Rufus, I was certain.

How was it that the Hartleys, who were so generous and had bright-faced Jesse, had also spawned Carl and his unforgiving sister Heather? Did offworlders all grow into something less? After all, the serpent egg was pure white, but the blue macaw egg was speckled.

That coward bastard Carl could not face the Mekucoo warrior Rufus, so he used the weaker Cylahi student to humiliate him. That was what sex was for; to make you feel small. And Tom had to take it. He had been oppressed. I knew; I had been oppressed too.

I had endeavored to set aside my sweatshop experiences. I had displaced them by giving my time to Vera, and by leaning on her for acceptance. But memories washed over me then, reminding me of how I had been abused, and that I could not even see my assailants through the hood. How they had not cared who I was because they knew what I was: worthless, uncovered, and not defended by the men of my culture.

I dried my face and wandered back to my room. I heard myself recite excuses for not speaking up, for not making some noise to interrupt that cowardly bastard Carl. I told myself that when I had tried to defend oppressed Dolviets before, the two girls were found naked and dead the next day. My efforts had yielded nothing.

I heard myself reason that if I had cried out to Carl, I would have increased his abuse and Tom's shame. If I had made a noise, I would have put Tom's life in jeopardy. I had every slimy, sniveling, cowardly excuse for my silence, just as Dolviet families had every excuse for not defending the gouleps. I understood their inertia. Fear was a numbing emotion.

Self-loathing carried fear forward into each of life's moments. I had no courage, no warrior's will. I was worthless, a worthless orphan goulep. I might as well have left with Dr. Mitterand as his mistress. I had no honor. Malleable was just the Hardhand word for something that gets used up and oppressed.

I did not leave my room the next day. By afternoon Billie Hartley arrived, worried and carrying a medical kit. "Is your stomach upset? Do you have a fever?" She checked me all over and found no organic reason for my listlessness.

It was painful to gaze into her face. Unsuspecting, worried, naive. Billie was naive.

Rufus and Tom stood at the doorway, and Vera showed me her furled brow. I glanced at Tom. He had attended morning classes, I was sure. He had told nobody about what happened last night.

Vera sat with me for several hours, but after that, she came for less time each day. She and Jesse came into my room and played games together. Vera talked about how she had mastered the EAM screens and talked daily with Kyle Rula and with the gouleps in their new convent.

"The buildings have red sandstone brick," Vera said, "with wide hallways and round arches. There's a room called a sanc-too-air-ry that they enter only one morning a week to sing songs and pray. And the gouleps have work; oleastra planting plus bead and feather work on Mekucoo suede. They glean the resin of acacias on the savannah.

"There will be a ded-di-ca-tion ceremony soon," Vera eagerly added. "Kecouroo and all the leaders will be there. So will the Consortium officers. Sheeks-Cylom is coming in from her research on Uburu land. The scientists she travels with will be there to honor the day. Won't it be marvelous?"

I said nothing.

"Don't you want to send a message to Kyle Rula?" she asked. "Don't you want to sit at the EAM, Brianna?"

I shook my head and turned my face to the wall. Vera and Jesse left then, easily sharing chi together. Vera would thrive in her new position of managing Kyle Rula's business licenses. At least that was accomplished.

After a few days, I was made to resume my duties. I sat in class and did the math exercises, but they meant nothing to me. What did I care what the value of x was? The teacher took me aside. "We had been told of your taste for daydreaming, but that wasn't my experience until now. Has something happened? Something you want to talk about?"

I shook my head no.

"You need to apply yourself, Brianna. I know you can. You have in the past."

To what purpose? I wondered. So I could learn the past great deeds of my oppressors, related in English?

Later that day, Billie led me to sit with Dr. Beecham, but I could not bring myself to smile at his encouragements. Confined in his florist's box, what could he know? What had Dr. Beecham ever known about tribal logic, about our ways that honored Dolvia? His understanding was the oppressor's knowledge. It was not the same as goulep knowledge, not even close.

Carl and Heather had left that very morning to resume their university studies at the biosphere. Carl had visited Dr. Beecham to say good-bye, doing his heir-apparent tour.

"Such a fine young man Carl Hartley is," Hank dreamily claimed during our visit. "Don't you think so, Brianna? The intelligent brow, his fair looks. Such promise. He will go far, mark my words. He's the transport's favorite son, you shall see." Hank never waxed eloquent concerning Karlyhi's promise or his intelligent brow. Dr. Beecham never called Carl Hartley malleable, either.

I must have been sending out disconcerting mental pictures. I dreamed of the infant reps again. Ralph was trying to soothe my loneliness or interrupt my complaining prater perhaps.

On a misty morning, the billabong was calm with a swirling vapor on the blue surface. The air was the same color as the glassy surface for that quiet hour before the savannah wakes. A splash came from the right. Ralph glimpsed a green terrapin sidling into the pool. The infant reps joined Ralph, softly cooing, ready for the day's lessons. Ralph flicked his tail and glided through the glacial blue. The infant reps raced to keep up, undulating their unmarbled bodies. I thought I heard them softly singing—celebrating life and their home pool.

I felt a loud clap and the picture went dark. I woke with a start and sat up in the bed.

A few days later, Colonel Hartley invited me into Ops. He sat facing me with his intimate manner. "You should hear this from me, Brianna. Ralph was killed. It was an unfortunate misunderstanding. A member of Mrs. Shaw's research team named George Villa saw Ralph hunting in the stream there and mistook him for an alligator, a common predator on Earth."

"He shot Ralph?"

"A single forty-five gauge to the back of the head. George Villa had no idea of Ralph's value. He saw other gualareps there; apparently they have been breeding on Dolvia. He did not know."

"He did not want to know."

"The practical result is that the balance among tribes has shifted," the colonel said. "Forces loyal to Karlyhi ambushed and captured the researchers. Karlyhi would have executed them except for Major Shaw's intervention. The Softcheeks are to be evacuated here, the entire research team."

"Mrs. Shaw will arrive here?"

"Tomorrow. But there's more." He watched my face. I offered only what little tribal discipline I could muster. "It seems this George Villa was unrepentant, even after being questioned. Ralph's death was a simple mistake, he claimed. Karlyhi's men have gone ballistic. There's no reasoning with them."

"Bal-lis-tic," I repeated under my breath.

"Consortium detachments have been forced out of Somule," he added. "Offworlders are forced off the savannah. Joey Osborn had to move his family to Consortium protection on Uburu land. Karlyhi is mounting a militia advance on Cylay. He's coming against us, his allies. He wants all Softcheeks and Hardhands to leave the savannah.

"The tribes are behind him," the colonel continued. "We see more than militia regulars; this represents a fanatical grassroots movement. There's even a police initiative that women must return to wearing the burka or be incarcerated."

"In-car-cer-rated," I whispered with a smile. Colonel Hartley hesitated. He had not thought I would react with delight. "Can you give us some insight here? What to anticipate?"

"Close shop and go home. Leave Dolvia to Dolviets."

He sighed and sat back. I had always been honest with him. He had no reason to suspect my words. "It's not that simple," he said. "We have strategic alliances, infrastructure investment, and businesses. The Bryant cartel alone—"

"The Bryants should be deported first."

"I know they had the sweatshops," the colonel said, "but they implemented certain positive advances for the tribes. The Bryants' success brought commerce to Dolviet cities."

"And that justifies their acts?"

"These concerns are not black and white."

"They deposit their riches in Consortium banks, do they?"

He showed me a blank face. "The Bryants are integral to maintaining our wormhole supply routes with the Company."

I heavily sighed. Ralph was gone; there was no changing that. My opinion on current events meant little. "Dolviets have learned much from the presence of offworlders, especially Hardhands. We share this solar system. We have learned about the galaxy and gained knowledge from the first colony of Softcheeks. But . . . but ours has been a painful lesson. Much was swept away.

"Warriors desert the land," I added. "Women turn to prostitution just to eat. Children grow without hearing the chants of their ancestors. Perhaps Hardhands should leave now and allow us time to heal."

"You mean, withdraw our peacekeeping detachments?"

"Or be forced out."

"Karlyhi would not go that far."

"Armed warriors are not submitted even to Karlyhi. Your safety cannot be guaranteed. Besides, Karlyhi knows there's no forgiving."

"You mean, there's no going back?"

"Back to erriv herding?"

Cicero's shuttle delivered the Consortium media, those intrepid journalists who traveled at great personal risk to Westend's hotspots for prize-winning reporting of breaking news. They wore khaki and corduroy and carried camcorders and duffel bags full of film and collapsible satellite dishes. They were in transit to Dolvia. The Somule hotel, with its Chinese-style restaurant, would soon enjoy a windfall.

The shuttle from Dolvia docked later that same afternoon. Midship bustled with talk, mostly last minute changes and de-brief-ing interviews. The media corps was going in one direction, and the arriving researchers headed for a different destination. Reporters labored to gain advantage of the moment. I saw George Villa, the scientist who had murdered Ralph, relaxed and talking within the media spotlight. His facial wounds received when Karlyhi had questioned him were healing.

This great white hunter easily shared chi with reporters, as if he had single-handedly ridded the world of Godzilla. The reporter Regan Villines talked fast with him, smiling and nodding. She did not question the moral problem of George Villa's act. Ralph was not indigenous to Dolvia, after all, but imported as a garrison officer's exotic pet. Gualareps were common on Cicero, even displayed in their zoos.

Mrs. Shaw joined me there while I watched the interview with George Villa. "It's all right," she claimed. "Nobody's fault."

Tears came to my eyes. How could she say the murder of Ralph carried no weight? It was everybody's fault.

Major Shaw was there with her, but he was much changed. The way it ran was that everybody had been present for the convent's dedication ceremony at the end of the rains. George Villa had gone great white hunting on the flooded savannah the following morning. He wanted to get in some recreation before the scientists traveled to the research digs. That was when he murdered Ralph. The research-ers later set out for an Uburu fossil site, unaware of George Villa's sportsmanship. The subsequent tribal ambush of the research team was aborted only because of Major Shaw's presence. Casualties occurred on both sides.

In midship that day, Major Shaw had butterfly stitches over one eye and his arm was in a sling; wounds acquired while defending Softcheeks against warriors he had personally trained. "Hiki, Brianna," he said with an open palm gesture.

I reached up and hugged him. I remembered how much a corridor hug had meant to me. He seemed surprised. "That's how it's done here," I said. Mrs. Shaw led him away then, heading for the infirmary to visit Dr. Beecham.

The Dolvia shuttle was doing double duty with civilian evacuations from Dolvia in anticipation of Karlyhi's advance on Cylay. It was refueled and primed to disembark again. Rufus and Tom came up to midship with their packs, along with Vera.

Billie and I had discussed how I should stay and accompany Mrs. Shaw to Cicero as a helpmate to Major Shaw during his healing. Dr. Beecham would take the same shuttle to Cicero. Given a clean bill of health, Hank would be released from quarantine.

Vera chose to go home, to her new convent home and her goulep sisters. Rufus and Tom were slated to rejoin the warriors. Class time was over. A new attitude prevailed.

Billie had asked what I wanted claiming that I had many options, but I did not see them. All I knew was that I could not return to Dolvia. I could not face the gouleps who had applauded me and sang chants about being delivered. Why not continue my adventure with Softcheeks? The holy woman Kat had said I was for outsiders. What difference if I was gone from Dolvia? What difference did it make?

So I hugged Vera one last time. I showed an open palm to Rufus and Tom. I watched them walk down the causeway behind the media advance team, behind John Milan and Regan Villines and their cameramen and portable equipment.

Midship seemed to fill with Blackshirts suddenly, as if they had kept out of sight from Rufus but relaxed when the Mekucoo warrior disembarked. I saw Steve Swanweil greet a Company executive, a small man with almond eyes and no expression on his porcelain face. He was Tuang Cho; I recognized him from photos at Major Shaw's command center.

They walked right past me like I was a bug on the wall. I went back to my room.

Mrs. Shaw came for me when I was late for dinner with the Hartleys. She knocked and entered just as though that was her right. I was made to get ready for a shared dinner.

"I know you miss Vera," she claimed as we traversed the corridor. "But I need your help to handle Major Shaw's needs. My husband never complains, you understand, but things have been bad."

"You mean his arm?"

"Major Shaw has a ruptured spleen, an organ in his back. There's some pain plus the danger of sepsis. We need to watch over him and to mind his diet and activities so he takes no chances." I only shrugged.

"He mourns for Ralph, you know," she added. "He takes on all the blame. The shifting balance of power and everything."

We stopped outside the Hartleys' suite. "You must not mention what I'm about to tell you," Mrs. Shaw said. "Major Shaw cannot return to Dolvia. The spleen is the immune system's last line of defense against infection. Mike's medical condition means he will be planet-bound on Cicero. It's Consortium policy, meant to prevent the spread of infections to other planets, to protect Dolviet and Cicerean people.

"I know you and my husband have a special friendship," she added. "He will listen to you where he fights me. You don't mind, do you? Just spend the time for a short while."

"Sure," I shrugged. She patted my cheek. At least she did not call me malleable.

The Hartleys received the Shaws with cordial manners, just as they did players from each faction of Dolviet politics. Mrs. Shaw held a drink that included ice while she stood by the sink and complained about her lost experiments. Billie filled the serving bowls with steaming vegetables, handing them off to me to carry to the table. I realized finally that much of Colonel Hartley's work was accomplished at the dinner table where guests relaxed and talked more freely than in Ops or in midship.

At dinner, Mrs. Shaw was in her element managing each of Mike's gestures. "Don't eat that. It's too spicy. And only water for you, no wine."

Major Shaw frowned. Billie glanced at me but looked away.

They discussed the Dolviet situation, especially Mrs. Shaw's frustration that her research was interrupted. "We made marvelous finds," she said of the Uburu ruins site. "There were pristine specimens of decorated pottery and gold pieces. I'm certain there's an ancient city there under the vines and moss. And just when we were getting close to some answers, so close … That was when this trouble started." She sat back, outraged that Dolviets put their futures ahead of her broad research goals.

"You mean, when your friend murdered Ralph," I said.

"He did not know it was Ralph."

"He did not care."

"Please," Mrs. Shaw said. "You only make it worse with recriminations."

"So George Villa just waltzes home?" I asked.

"He did not know it was Ralph!"

"And that's good enough for you?" I looked at Major Shaw. "For you?" He was strangely quiet all this time.

"Leave him alone," Mrs. Shaw defended. "Hasn't he suffered enough? Ralph was his, you know."

"His pet?" I asked.

"Brianna," Colonel Hartley said. "Not at the dinner table."

Mrs. Shaw turned to the conflict's most shocking aspect in her view: the call for the return to burkas. She played to Colonel and Mrs. Hartley with her opinions, just as though they felt the same. "In Somule, an unveiled woman cannot walk down the street or barter for produce at the bazaars. Most tribes never wore burkas before. Cylahi women had to scramble to secure the piece of cloth before they were arrested or beaten.

"So nonsensical," she added. "Women do all the work. They always have, so the men are free to herd erriv and to fight. Now commerce has ended, and hoarding is commonplace. The academy is closed and so is the hospital. Cylahi nurses were told to go home, even though they have no home but the hospital."

The colonel spoke calmly. "Brianna applauds the return to burkas."

Sheeks-Cylom showed me the evil eye, so like her. "Surely you can see how that robs women of their rights."

"Offworlders rob the people of their dignity," I said. "People without dignity are not so concerned with a list of rights."

"I harmed nobody," she shot back. "I work for the common good. I funded the academy."

Three objections. Sheeks-Cylom was in rare form. "You funded the academy," I said, "with profits from the catarrh vaccine taken from a Dolviet orchid."

"Which I discovered," she insisted before she could stop. She knew that I knew that Edwina had brought her the flower.

"And now you enter the circle of elites," I said. "You can write newspaper stories about how to handle the resistant aboriginal tribes."

"You insolent little—"

"Me? What about you, with your blood cultures and your murdering colleagues?"

She opened her mouth to let me have it, but Major Shaw intervened. "Transport experience has opened your eyes, Brianna."

"At least she's talking again," Billie added.

I looked around at their faces. Anger had been the key. My irritation with Mrs. Shaw had made me, you know, functional again. "I'm sorry," I said to Colonel Hartley. "You and Billie have been so kind."

"Your impressions of what really happens on Dolvia have served us," the colonel said evenly. "We are sorry to lose you as a consultant."

"Perhaps," Mike added with a wink, "Brianna should join our circle of elites, as she calls it, and go on a lecture tour."

I blushed. I had forgotten how he could see right through me.

During coffee, Mrs. Shaw showed me a lily pad section. I guess she wanted to make up for yelling in front of the others. The fibrous and leathery leaf had lost its vibrancy with dehydration. "It grows at the rate of eight inches a day under the right conditions," she said, her eyes bright with enthusiasm.

The lily pad colonized the billabong after the rains, growing within a few days, providing spongy walkways for transient egrets and cranes. Dolviets knew that. The white flower offered a deep bell that acted as a breeding place for wasps and damselflies. Hard-shell nuts later fell to the muddy pool bottom and were revived during the next rainy season.

"We can extract the growth enzyme," she said, "and synthesize it for burn repair, like a skin overlay to promote pliant cell growth. No more unsightly scar tissue."

I forced a smile. I could not remember being so irritated with Sheeks-Cylom. She absconded Dolvia's secrets without care for Her soul. Her chi had not been diminished, I decided, from her hospital duties during the Siibabean conflict as Kecouroo had claimed. Mrs. Shaw had always been chi-challenged.

We watched the comtechs all the next day, even in class. The Consortium media members had assembled their equipment in Somule and spoke into the cameras with authority. "Tensions in the jungles of Dolvia have risen to the breaking point," the reporter John Milan began.

Jungles of Dolvia? I wondered where that was.

"Rebel forces," he continued, "have taken this village and surrounding area and have imposed martial law. There's minimal looting and gunfire today, but leaders have called for a return to tribal canon including burkas for women."

Rebel forces? Who were they? And why would Karlyhi's men loot Somule? Which was a city, not a village.

"Services have been cut off," John Milan continued. "There's no electricity or fresh produce. Rumors abound, but for now the real fighting seems to be far distant."

No services, huh? What, no pressed duck d'orange at the hotel restaurant?

Colonel Hartley sent word that I should come to Ops. Major Shaw and the duty officers were glued to the comtech screen there. That was a relief. I had wondered if my interest in the news was from the colorful display on the screen. Unfolding ground events, in-country events they were called, held everybody's interest.

"What do you think?" the colonel asked in his solicitous way.

"Reporters have been there one day," I shrugged. "What can they know?"

"They talk to the people."

"Dolvia does not give up Her secrets so easily."

Major Shaw glanced up. Apparently I had reinforced his words. I moved aside, out of their busy routine, not really being one of them.

But later I was called back to the comtech screen. We viewed a Cylay street skirmish between rebel forces: Karlyhi's men in militia uniforms against Bryant managers. Reporters had captured the event with field camcorders that showed parts of the colorless wall when they began to run in the other direction. Rocks and firebombs were thrown. Gunfire was exchanged. Several civilians laid dead in the street.

"Wait a minute," the colonel said. "They will replay the footage." The incident began again, like a rewound movie.

"There," Major Shaw said.

I glimpsed Carline Bryant's face inside the manufacturing building, cautiously staring out a second-story window. Tear gas was fired. A canister broke the panes there, and she stepped back. Smoke wafted out.

At the many windows along the building's front, managers with gas masks and karkars took up defensive positions. Below, a door opened. Gun barrels were apparent, awaiting an assault.

Without warning, Brent Gotskind was pushed forward out the doorway. His face was wet with desperate tears and a bloody nose. His white shirt was sweat stained. He held both hands in the air, begging for mercy. A rain of karkar bullets from Dolviet attackers pelted his chest and the doorjamb. He fell forward. Managers closed the door and retreated from the windows.

"The Bryants sacrificed him," Major Shaw said. "He was not even at fault for anything."

"He was the civil authority," Colonel Hartley said.

"He was their patsy! They orchestrated this event! Didn't you see Carline Bryant checking for cameras?" Mike waited a long moment. "Gotskind's death means our men have to save the Bryants. Get Lieutenant Sector on the EAM. We are not here to cater to their demands."

"Mike," Colonel Hartley said. "Consortium reputation is on the line."

"Let me talk to the media. I can set them straight on who's who."

"It makes no difference what you say," the colonel said. "The Bryants are offworld-born so we must mount a rescue mission to save them."

"Carline Bryant," Major Shaw spat out, "has always played both ends against the middle. Suddenly she's pearly white?"

I looked at his face then. I had not considered this trouble as black against white, or tribal against Consortium. But the comtech screen made no comment. It provided no annotation concerning the players. It was theater. In this case, racial theater.

It was better to live in the physical concrete world, I thought, even to tolerate the burka. The comtech's substitute world displayed none of the conflict's nuances. To the Consortium audience, Carline was a heroine by virtue of her birthright and her skin color. The details of her business practices were not germane. And she had played them. Consortium men would die at the hands of the tribesmen whom they had trained and lived with, by weapons they had supplied, all because Carline Bryant had pushed Brent Gotskind from the sweatshop door.

We watched the news throughout the day, but nothing more happened. Consortium detachments needed to set strategy and undertake an achievable mission with few casualties. Colonel Hartley sent cautious and coded messages via EAM.

So in-country, as it was said, Lt. Sector negotiated behind doors with Karlyhi to deport the Bryants and their managers without shedding blood. The media were not told, of course. Han Chinese Company executives watched the same news channels Colonel Hartley and Major Shaw monitored.

The next day I waited in midship to board the Cicero shuttle and leave Dolvia behind. My desert home would become a blinking blue star in the night sky while events from Dolvia replayed on the comtech's Consortium news reports.

Dr. Beecham came into the holding area with Major Shaw. Both men were diminished by their Dolviet injuries. Damaged lungs for Hank, and a damaged spleen for Mike Shaw. Perhaps disease and fear of disease was Dolvia's way of deporting them, just as the pox was a silent hand for the Uburu.

Mrs. Shaw joined us. She seemed indestructible.

Billie was there, and Colonel Hartley who hugged me. He smelled great.

We settled into the bucket seats of the crowded Cicero shuttle for the six-hour ride. The line-up was Dr. Beecham by the window, then me. Major and Mrs. Shaw sat in the middle aisle seats. Then across the other aisle were two research scientists, one being George Villa.

He tried more than once to strike up a conversation with Mrs. Shaw. But her loyalties had become clear. Ralph had belonged to Major Shaw. George Villa had murdered Ralph. As we drifted away from the conflict's front lines, leaving behind Karlyhi and tribal logic, that reality became more important than pedigree and skin color. She gave George Villa the cold shoulder, as Softcheeks say.

The shuttle's overhead comtechs blared news of Dolviet events, except there wasn't any news in Somule where the media had established their camp. "Rebel leader Karl Wyley keeps out of sight," one reporter said, "but he controls the militia and the roads. His forces are disciplined and vicious. They take no prisoners."

The effete reporter was safe. Warriors would not notice him.

Before we landed, though, there was footage of Louise Bilesketchum riding into Somule on a tractor crowded with the hospital orderlies and Cylahi nurses, having made the trip across the wet savannah.

She easily handled the grinding gears of the oversized machine. Its textured tires under yellow fenders had crushed the reeds and clumps of razor grass on the marshy roadside. Louise wore trousers and no burka. Karlyhi's men had not bothered to impose the law in her case. She halted the behemoth in front of the Somule hotel. What an entrance, like a Viking queen descending from on high. Reporters stationed in Somule were starved for hard news. They crowded Louise, soliciting news about events on the savannah, her opinion about important players, and what would happen next.

She spoke English with a thick German accent. "Tribespeople are intractable," she said into the glaring camera lights. She pushed back matted blond hair, exposing sunburned skin. "Each group has its own motives and methods. A real can of worms."

"Look, dear," Mrs. Shaw pronounced in whole tones while we watched the comtech screen. The entire cabin full of travelers heard her comments. "Our good friend Louise Bilesketchum has escaped the intractable wormy tribespeople riding on a tractor."

Major Shaw groaned and ducked his head.

"I just don't understand," Mrs. Shaw brightly said, "how it is tribespeople don't embrace her. Would you know, dear? Would you know why our Louise is not universally loved?"

I hid my grin when Mike Shaw looked my way.

We disembarked and waited in customs. The room was in a low building with no features, much like any customs station. Cicero reporters approached and spoke with Major Shaw, soliciting his impressions about events on Dolvia's savannah. I did not know his answers; all comments were in a strange language. But the suited businessmen were respectful toward the wounded officer in a starched uniform and with his arm in a sling. Mrs. Shaw stood on the side, posing as the wife, silent for once. That was something.

I had not thought that people on Cicero spoke anything but English. Transport personnel all spoke English. Lieutenants Sector and Taylor spoke English and Arrivi, as did Lieutenant Manenowski. I had not heard Cicero's languages, even from the Hartleys in their family home.

We rode in a taxi with Dr. Beecham to a nearby hotel. The air was cool and the streets were regular and clean. It did not feel like another planet until I looked up at the night sky. Cicero had one moon only. She hung there, reflecting sunlight, bald and undressed, every crater and mountain range discernible, exquisitely lonely for all time.

"There's Dolvia," Dr. Beecham whispered, pointing to just above the horizon. "Isn't She lovely?" I could not make out which star he meant, or which sky object. Dolvia no longer cared for me. I was far from Her embrace.

EIGHTEEN

 named for the river that branched near there. As I rode with Dr. Beecham in a taxi to our appointments, I saw mostly clapboard houses with big front verandahs called porches. Major and Mrs. Shaw rode in a taxi ahead of us, and Hank said our choice of transportation classified us as rich. The residents were white, stout and friendly, very like Billie Hartley. I saw one Putuki woman shepherding some kids that weren't her own, judging from skin color, into a yard away from street bustle.

Sagebrush and cactus dotted the parched landscape. "When is their rainy season?" I asked.

"They don't have one," Dr. Beecham said.

"You mean it's always like this?"

"In a couple months it gets hot."

"Where is the Company biosphere?" I had heard about its wonders many times, how people never went outside and never missed fresh air.

"It's located in a different province beyond our travel."

"Too bad."

On the morning of our second day in Two Forks, Major Shaw was checked into the hospital with something called sepsis. I accompanied Mrs. Shaw to visit him in the sterile white room, one of many rooms along a hallway filled with equipment.

After we sat with Mike Shaw for several hours, we motored with Dr. Beecham in a rented ECCAV out to a small farmhouse on a small rise, the former the home of Major Shaw's parents that he still owned. We would live there along with Dr. Beecham until the Dolvia situation was resolved. This was Sheeks-Cylom's new residence.

The unfurnished interior had large rooms and tall windows that rattled in the wind. There was a staircase that led to some bedrooms and a bathroom. The banister was a single branch of fine wood, a Cicero variety that was rare, or so Hank Beecham said. There was also flowered wallpaper, some of it yellow and brittle. That was something, flowers on the wall. With her usual efficiency, Mrs. Shaw got busy ordering clean-up crews, landscaping crews, and furniture deliveries.

Through the window, I saw falling-down outbuildings that banked a wide barnyard. The kitchen door led to an unkempt backyard with a shaded wooden swing. I pushed open the screen door and joined Dr. Beecham in the overgrown flower and vegetable garden with a stagnant pool. He started a motor there and water came belching up in the pool's center.

"This will do," he said. His wispy white hair fell over his forehead in the dry breeze. "This will do." When he smiled, Dr. Beecham's soft cheeks seemed more prominent. He set about making plans for a new garden. He appeared to me as a hothouse orchid enthused about the prospect of nurturing peonies and snapdragons.

That afternoon we visited Major Shaw before returning to the hotel. His arm was out of the sling, but still bandaged. A battery-powered IV dripped Consortium medicine into his veins. "I feel useless just lying around in bed in the middle of the day, waiting for my spleen to flush the antibodies."

"We'll need to buy two ECCAVs," Mrs. Shaw told him, "so we have freedom to come and go from the farmhouse. I can look for something secondhand." They went around and around about immediate concerns, setting aside the discussion of the savannah conflict.

Mrs. Shaw went into the corridor to complain to the nurses about the lack of cleanliness. Mike and I watched the Consortium news channel on the overhead comtech. There was replayed footage of a confrontation with Hardhands on a littered Cylay street corner. Dolviet youths threw rocks and homemade bombs, followed by the sound of return gunfire. None of the combatants wore militia uniforms.

After Brent Gotskind's death, Milo Sector's men had surrounded the Bryant manufacturing buildings in Cylay and erected street barricades. Milo received a field promotion to captain. In the news reports he looked right smart in his new uniform and blue tam when he spoke to the swarming reporters. The camera focused on his square jaw and black mustache.

"A peaceful solution is being negotiated with the involved parties," he said. "Meanwhile, we need to keep this area clear."

Mike Shaw and I watched the program together. From the glass and steel lobby of a Cylay hotel, the reporter John Milan spoke into his handheld microphone, "The city is full of karkar fire and war chants. There are few casualties, though, and fewer acts of leadership. Services have dried up, and hoarding is commonplace. The real warfare is on the savannah, a hundred kilometers from our location. Here in Cylay, everybody awaits the arrival of rebel leader Karl Wyley for standoff resolution."

I glimpsed Haku rabbe Murd with Orin and two more Arrivi men passing behind the talking man. Something big must be looming for obese and nearly blind Haku to make the train ride from Somule to Cylay. Of course, the reporter did not ask questions of Haku. What could this old and scarred tribesman know?

Our view switched to the air-conditioned command center, the one where I had been a frequent guest of Major Shaw. There, Captain Sector gave a briefing with maps and graphs. The offworld media attended, grateful for an authoritative voice. The daily briefings meant they no longer needed to roam the volatile streets in search of hard news. Rabbenu Ely was also present, waiting on the podium to answer questions. He looked sweaty and put-upon behind his round-rimmed glasses. Captain Sector by comparison was a handsome and buffed matinee idol.

"Brianna, there's something you should know," Major Shaw said. I tore myself away from the screen's colorful images.

"You don't need to tell my wife we spoke about this. She thinks it's best to keep the details quiet. But you must understand what happened and the depth of Karlyhi's rage."

I felt my throat tighten.

"It's about Ralph and when he was killed," Mike confessed. "They, uh … they skinned Ralph and hung up the marbled hide, including the head, as a trophy."

I gasped for breath in the still room. "And they call us savages," was all I could say.

"Then they butchered the body and roasted a section of flank meat for a meal at their campsite. They treated it like a slaughterhouse activity."

"I cannot breathe," I said. I felt hot and itchy and saw stars.

"Sit down here. Put your head between your knees."

I did as I was instructed.

"That's why my wife wants the event kept quiet," he added. "People react."

I sat up, my face red and my throat tight.

"There's no reason why you should," Mike said. "I was just wondering … It's just that … I mean, nobody's at fault here. But could you find it in your heart to—"

"There is no forgiving." I stood and strode out of the room.

"Brianna, wait!" he called after me. "Can't we talk about this?"

I went downstairs to the hospital waiting area and sat on a plastic chair near the nurses' station. The light fixtures hummed a little, and the glare hurt my eyes. The wide doors opened when visitors came and went, filling the area with currents of cool recycled air and hot fresh air. I stood and paced in the overlit hall that led to another ward. I was still angry with flushed cheeks and an itchy back. But there was something more.

It had felt wrong to argue with Major Shaw. It was unseemly to talk back when he had been so generous with me. But my outrage felt righteous too. When I spoke in anger, he understood who I was. Anger enveloped me and gave me identity, shaping a hard shell over me that could not be abused or even bruised. Anger gave me covering, just as warrior's rage was a function of Karlyhi's leadership.

My heartbeat quieted, and I sat again in the plastic chair near the entrance. I overheard the nurses watching a comtech set on the counter of the reception desk. "My Putuki nanny quit last night," one said as they stared at the screen. "She claimed a need to return to Dolvia. I argued with her about why she wanted to go now, when war threatened there."

"More of them leave each day," the other nurse said.

"I don't know how we are going to manage."

"The hospital offers daycare."

"The cost is prohibitive for my twins," the nurse said. "No local woman will commit to the hours as a live-in. And who would she invite into the house? My Putuki woman was here for the children. That was her focus, you know?"

"You could restrict your duty hours here."

"I have to now. Such an inconvenience."

I never pretended to read Hardhands. But if the question was put to me, I would have to report that within my viewing, the competent and helpful nurses at the Cicero hospital resented the amount of time they needed to spend with their own children.

Dr. Mitterand entered through the sliding door. I was surprised because he knew the biosphere and its research laboratory. Perhaps he preferred to work here in Two Forks to be near Mrs. Shaw's research. Pierre had appeared on numerous news talk shows where he expressed heartfelt opinions, peppered with his many anecdotes, concerning the tribal struggle.

He saw me and stopped. "So, Brianna, they left you hanging around. How about that trip to the zoo I once promised? Then maybe we can buy you some real clothes."

I hesitated.

"Perhaps we should get Major Shaw's permission," he added with a sly smile.

"I am my own person," I said, hugging my anger.

Dr. Mitterand spoke to the nurse who agreed to give Major Shaw a message. We left together and Pierre drove a racy ECCAV of a different design to the city zoo. There we saw many exotic animals, mostly birds.

The zoo had curving walkways and bushes cut into funny shapes. Families stopped in front of each display pen and read the words posted there about habitat and en-dan-gered creatures. Mostly the kids ran around to escape a mother's care or begged for a treat from each kiosk they passed. I thought the zoo would be more fun. This was small and crowded and smelly.

People in the crowd recognized Dr. Mitterand from his media appearances. Young people offered their zoo maps, requesting his autograph. In the reptile house, family men asked questions in broken English, especially Pierre's opinion on the relative danger to Cicero civilians stranded on Dolvia's savannah. I stepped away while he shared chi with them.

Along the cool corridor were several square animal cages that reminded me of the transport's acrylic box where Dr. Beecham had been confined while he fought off the TB infection. Except only the fronts of these cages were made of acrylic.

Then I stopped short. In one low cage there, in a puddle of stagnant and stinking water with algae growth edging up the glass, was an adult male gualarep. His tail was curled behind him in the cramped space, and his richly marbled hide was the gray of the corridor floor. Musk glands behind his jaw were sticky with a pungent secretion.

I felt immediate heartstone for him, and once again I gasped for breath. I sank to the floor with my back against the corridor wall and put my head between my knees. I ignored the tramping of feet and parents calling out to kids to stop running. I thought of Ralph and of my swimming dreams. I remembered the time he had hunted in the billabong and had clamped down on a flamingo treat while others took to wing in a pink and white barrage. The caged rep snapped his big mouth closed just as I recalled that image.

I lifted my head. I could breathe somewhat easier. *Saw it?* I asked. He jerked around in the cage. I saw an angry growth of fungus on his back leg.

Perhaps he did not have language, I thought, or English. I sent out more mental pictures of greeting Edwina and swimming in the grotto, and of Ralph when he strongly rubbed Kyle Rula with his flanks. I shared the time Edna and Edwina had joined us on the flooded savannah, and had traumatized one group of nesting birds after another while they traveled fast toward Karima Le's house.

I received swimming pictures of a different sort; of a cold and murky river lined with the big roots of water-seeking mangrove trees. The male gualarep drifted with the current, joyous and singing, and waited in the sun-dappled shadows for schooling channel catfish. Tears came to my eyes. To be trapped in the acrylic cage after living free was a special torture.

Pierre joined me and saw my teary eyes. He glanced at the guala-rep cage. "Perhaps the zoo was not our best choice for an outing." He helped me to my feet and led me away. I sent out more pictures of the savannah and told the gualarep that I would set him free. I did not know how I would get that done, but I was determined the gualarep's days at the zoo were numbered.

Pierre took me shopping for clothes, except his taste was very different from Mrs. Shaw's choices. In the shop, I turned to the young teen section, but Pierre led me into another area for women's clothes. Unconcerned with the need for undergarments, he selected clingy off-the-shoulder dresses. He gave me one to model for him and shooed me into a changing room. He had to encourage me to come out and was soon losing patience with my reserve. When he turned me toward the three-way mirror there, I shamefacedly crossed my arms. I had never seen my form set out like that for any man to view.

Pierre stepped behind me and gently lowered my arms. "No need to hide," he whispered while he ran the backs of three fingers down my arm. "You are your own woman now." He loosened the knot of hair at my neck and fluffed it to rest on my shoulders.

"There, that is better," he said. I glanced red-faced at the salesgirl.

We had dinner at the hotel. The restaurant there was small but had polished edges and many showy statues of naked women, all posed looking down as if they couldn't stay awake or something. There were more waiters than patrons, rushing back and forth or polishing glasses that already sparkled. During the meal, Pierre made me laugh by cracking jokes and imitating the haughty waiters. I was allowed a glass of wine. Before the entree arrived, though, Mrs. Shaw came crashing in.

"What are you trying to pull here?" she demanded of Pierre. "This is a little girl."

"It's only dinner," I defended.

"You look like a Cylahi whore."

"And who made them into whores?" I asked.

"We are not making you into one."

"It's only dinner," Pierre repeated in an innocent tone. Mrs. Shaw dragged me out of the dining room by my arm. People pointed and whispered. I could have died of the humiliation.

I learned a great deal about her that day. Mrs. Shaw had been generous with me, however casually, while in Cylay. But here in Two Forks, her manner was very different. I saw it as a question of identity. She was not an important player here, just the wife of a wounded officer who had started the tribal crisis by importing his exotic pet. She wasn't somebody.

I came to understand Sheeks-Cylom's insistence that she was in charge at the bush clinic and her unwillingness to, you know, join her husband in Cylay. Even her professional association with Dr. Mitterand for the publication of medical papers spoke of the need to establish a reputation in her own name within a society of men.

On Cicero, Mrs. Shaw had no time for generosity. She struggled each day for the very oxygen of identity. Determined as she was, she could not maintain the struggle for us both. It was each woman for herself. I was on my own, even while nominally under her protection.

Time was truly a loop. I was so often through events before I understood their meaning in my life. I puzzled out all this and more while I spent the following weeks at Major Shaw's farmhouse. No effort was made to re-enroll me in school. On Cicero I was seen, by those who bothered to look, as an idle domestic worker. Educating girls had always been, you know, a luxury.

I helped Dr. Beecham in the backyard garden while he dug up the sandy soil, put down mulch, and pressed in rows of flowering plants. He slipped into puttering retirement, his wispy hair catching the hot sun's light. He spoke of his harvest vision of tall sunflowers and red geraniums vining against the fence. Sometimes I sent images of the savannah to the male gualarep I had seen in the zoo at Two Forks, mostly from my loneliness that Hank Beecham called nos-tal-gia.

Major Shaw was brought home from the hospital and was allowed to move around the house in his bathrobe and slippers. His diet was restricted, along with no aggressive physical activity. We played chess some afternoons while Mrs. Shaw traveled to the biosphere and worked alongside Pierre at the R&D lab. She reported that she had dinner with Carl and Heather Hartley at the university there.

There was a resolution, however, to the Bryant hostage crisis in Cylay. The footage was played many times on the comtechs. Sean and Carline Bryant, plus his four brothers and their families, all carrying several weighted suitcases, were escorted under heavy guard away from the besieged Bryant manufacturing buildings. Captain Sector's men stoically withstood the barrage of stones and mud and bad fruit directed at the deported Hardhands.

They reached the military trucks just outside the gated compound, not 24 meters from the building entrance. This was the same building where I had first glimpsed Vera in ankle chains. The Bryants crowded into the back of one truck, stacking their many pieces of luggage. The detachment, in two vehicles, inched through the angry crowd. When their rear lights were visible, tribal men and women of all ages quickly overran the Bryant gate and descended on the buildings for looting and for retribution. I recognized nobody in the crowd.

Later, Captain Sector gave a media briefing at the command center. The Bryants had safely arrived at the shuttle launch pad, he announced, and would leave for Cicero within the hour. That day, Dacupitte, wearing a militia uniform and with his red hair loosely pulled back at his neck, and Rabbenu Ely, stood behind Milo but answered no questions. Karlyhi had not shown his face to the foreign media.

Mrs. Shaw published in the Two Forks Sunday supplement an op-ed piece about savannah eco-lo-gi-cal pressures and the relative guilt of the Bryants and the Cylay business factions. Mrs. Shaw was not invited to speak on the comtech talk shows, however. She was considered too shrill. At the farmhouse, the Shaws discussed in loud voices which paragraphs she should include in the next newspaper opinion piece and what was really underway in Somule. "We should keep our heads down," Major Shaw claimed.

"We cannot skulk around here and do nothing," she said. "Why don't you step forward with your knowledge of tribal players?"

"And risk a house fire?"

Major and Mrs. Shaw had their problems, but it was my impression that their many trials had strengthened their marriage. They were good together.

One day Major Shaw came downstairs wearing his dress uniform. Mrs. Shaw wore a floor-length evening gown and peridot jewelry.

They looked, you know, nice together on their way to the Officers' Club for dinner. I saw little of Major Shaw after that.

While I labored with Dr. Beecham in the sprouting garden with its gurgling pond, I quizzed him on certain subjects. "Hank, is Earth also a pa-tri-ar-chal society?"

"On Earth, as on Dolvia, there are many societies."

"Those societies with English, are they patriarchal?"

"America, the land of your father, is a meritocracy. Any person of any race may be advanced depending on the merit of his or her work."

"You mean, like the field promotion for Captain Sector?"

"Very similar."

"But what if a person's good works are not known, if that person is shy?"

"There's a forum in the media," he said, gesturing with hands covered with mulch, "wherein a colleague speaks well of that person and sets him or her forward."

"Ha! The media only want to know who hates who."

"That's their job in Cylay," he agreed. "To seek out pressure points and anticipate events."

"So would Kyle Rula of Arim be lauded?"

"For her business ventures, most assuredly."

"Would Hakulupe Le?"

"As the academy administrator, she would have a certain status."

"Would Kecouroo?"

"The school teacher? I thought her function was to promote Pete as a future leader."

I fell silent. I suspected the American me-ri-to-cra-cy was run by men. Women there would be as invisible as if they wore burkas.

Dr. Beecham did draw me back to the EAM, though. Some evenings while Major and Mrs. Shaw were in Two Forks, and after Hank and I finished washing dishes from the meal he had prepared, we sat together at the kitchen table. First he quizzed me concerning what I had been thinking about all day, or he asked if I had a homily to share.

"Sometimes to save something precious, you must walk away."

"That is from Major Shaw. What else?"

"Nothing good comes from a false promise."

"Ah, from Pierre. Don't you have one of your own composition?"

I had not realized that I was allowed to create my own. Hakulupe Le had always quoted dead Softcheeks or ancestors. "Anger brings identity," I said with a turned-down mouth.

After a moment Hank replied, "You have grown out of our arms, Brianna." His hazy eyes sadly regarded me. "You have not contacted your family for some time, I'm told. Or Vera. What has she done to sacrifice honor?"

"She tagged you, huh?"

"Vera and many others, even Kecouroo. When did I become so popular?"

I chuckled. Hank Beecham was a good friend of mine.

"Won't you at least contact the convent, Brianna?" he asked. "Construction is finished now. There's an image loaded on the EAM. Let's have a look. What do you say?"

"Under your codes."

"Why not?"

He opened the laptop there in the kitchen and booted the screen. There was a lag time, for communications with Dolvia were monitored by many parties by then. Hank poured us each a glass of red wine.

The convent main page came online and included an image of the sanctuary entrance with its red brick arches and stone fence. A white colonnade on one side shaded a brick walkway. Oleastra bushes provided shade along a winding path. Blue macaws rested on the high eaves, but I decided they had been placed di-gi-tal-ly to add color.

The building had a commanding view from a secure rise above the veld, beyond the pool where Edwina and I had once gone swimming. "And Vera lives there?"

"Also Edna and Edwina and Ralph's progeny. They were each adopted by a goulep and often glean the savannah in pairs. The older gouleps have become welfare ministers while the warriors labor on Uburu land.

"Many stories are told in chants," he continued, "about how a goulep and companion gualarep mysteriously arrived at a trouble spot, offering relief to some struggling family. It's like Katelupe the martyr, except with gualareps instead of ketiwhelps."

"Ketiwhelps don't have mental pictures," I said. We both laughed.

"Would you like to send a message?"

"No."

"Would you like to read their messages to you?"

"No."

"You can go home, you know. You would be welcomed with open arms."

My heart pulled down in my chest. I felt most lonely when I was in contact with Dolviets. "Hank, is my English good enough for America?"

"So your heart is set on that adventure."

"Pierre offered to take me."

"As what?"

"What am I here? What was I in the sweatshop?"

He sighed, his soft cheeks flushed from the wine. "I suppose it was inevitable. Don't go for free, Brianna. Make Pierre secure your future first so you have something to fall back on, something of your own."

"Perhaps I will send a message to Kyle Rula," I said, "if you don't mind. She was seeking an agent to manage her wormhole exports. If my name was added to those licenses, just as a courier, then I could, you know, monitor the activity and report back."

"And you want me to recommend that?"

"Whatever you think is right."

"Mrs. Shaw will say I delivered you up to Pierre."

"Sheeks-Cylom knows there's nothing for me on Cicero."

"I suppose." His cheeks were flushed, but maybe from the strong wine.

"Thank you, Hank," I said and gave him a hug.

He was surprised and struggled to regain his composure, his hazy eyes tearing a little. "This has been a good mercy seat," he concluded.

I took no steps in my plan for several days. I had doubts and maybe some fear. Dr. Beecham called me into the kitchen in the middle of the afternoon one hot day. Through the screen door he shouted, "Brianna, you will want to see this!" I dropped my gardening spade and ran in, mostly because of the tension in his voice.

The kitchen comtech carried a Company news channel. The China-doll announcer spoke with that tone of authority they use during a breaking news story. "Fighting has again erupted in Cylay, the capital city on Dolvia's savannah. But this rebel movement involves neither the peacekeeping group nor the tribal militia. For more we go now to Cylay and investigative reporter John Milan. John, what do you have for us?"

The screen images cut to a Cylay street corner littered with rocks and material from demolished walls nearby. Several young warriors, none in uniform, lingered at the corner. They rushed out to throw flaming gasoline-filled pipe bombs, and rushed back to take cover. Hardhands slinked behind a barricade of tables and a burned-out truck, and fired rifles at retreating youths.

John Milan stepped in front of the camera. "Neither rebel leaders nor rabbenu politicians, nor Consortium officers can keep a lid on the tension that has surfaced in Cylay. Gangs of young warriors roam the streets with automatics, looting and jostling Hardhands and natives alike."

"I told them," I said as we stared at the screen.

"Wait, though," Dr. Beecham said. "There's another piece. They'll rerun it soon."

"High-level talks are underway," John Milan continued, "to set up a meeting between the recently returned civil authority Frank Duerr, Rabbenu Ely and his forces, and Consortium officers. No outcome can be guaranteed, however, without the input of rebel leader Karl Wyley who remains in his savannah stronghold near Somule."

"I hate it when they use that name," I said. "What's wrong with Karlyhi? What's wrong with saying it right?"

Behind John Milan, another barrage of rifle fire was heard. He ducked and jerked around, a most unbecoming posture for the intrepid reporter. The handheld camera focused on the barricade, but nobody showed himself.

The news program cut back to the Consortium anchorman. "Earlier today there was an incident—"

"This could be it," Hank said. The news program ran footage of tribal teens throwing rocks at a Cylay storefront and running away. Two Cylahi boys in the crowd ran toward the camera, laughing and mugging while karkar fire rang out. I recognized one as the scholarship boy Tom. Both boys jolted from being shot in the back. I caught my breath.

With surprised looks on their faces and their arms flying up, the two warriors fell forward onto the littered street. The camera focused on their bloodied shirts while their bodies came to rest face down with their arms in awkward positions.

"Wasn't that the kid who illustrated the flora journal?" Hank asked. "Tom was his name, right?"

I stared at the screen. The anchorman talked about Rabbenu Ely and Captain Sector and Karl Wyley, but I was not taking it in. Tom had been shot in the back in front of the Company cameras, and journalists just went onto the next taped segment. Gentle Tom, the scholarship boy who had taken Carl Hartley's abuse with Mekucoo stoicism. They didn't know it was Tom, just like the great white hunter George Villa didn't know it was Ralph he had murdered.

I sat at the table and drew my breath in short gasps.

"That was Tom," Hank repeated, staring into my face. "He had a real talent with pen and paper. Tom completed what I thought of as a complicated rendition in a single afternoon; that was special. And now he's gone. Such a waste.

"Mrs. Shaw saved you from that," he added. "Whatever the trouble is between you and her, you're not alone and pregnant. And you're not dead in the street."

"I'm going for a walk."

"Brianna."

"I just have to think. Back later."

I walked for a long time on the parched land that surrounded the farmhouse and saw the sun go down. The single moon rose in her lonely vigil, a hovering exposed orb that perfectly reflected my mood.

I don't know why I had assumed that my danger was mine alone, or why I felt the oppression was directed at me only. Tom was nothing to them. I was nothing to them. We were nameless and therefore faceless, uncounted and untaxed, and separate from the land. Nobody protested our abuse or Tom's death. Throw-away people, that was what we were.

If the Consortium reporter John Milan had caught a bullet in his back, you bet there would have been a general outcry.

Good intentions counted for nothing. Kyle Rula had good intentions when she made the fair trade that brought electricity, and therefore Hardhand interest, to Somule. Major Shaw had had good intentions when he taught Karlyhi to drive trucks, thereby nurturing his own nemesis. And Sheeks-Cylom was rife with good intentions, right up until she invited the great white hunter George Villa onto the savannah.

Even the Cicero nurses had good intentions when they had tried to dissuade their Putuki nannies from returning to Dolvia. Who would willingly disembark onto the war-torn desert? It's better to, you know, serve one's betters, right?

Mrs. Shaw was correct about seeking fame as Dr. Greensboro. A most visible reputation in my own name was essential. I must secure my space within the hard shell of anger so when the off-worlders come to murder me, people will be outraged with an absolute uproar against Hardhands and Softcheeks that will be reported on all channels. Angry protests from armed warriors of good name who storm the barricades carrying endless banners with my image printed on them. That would be something.

I must have a name. And it must be my own.

At the next opportunity, I rode with Mrs. Shaw into Two Forks and sought out Dr. Mitterand in his hospital office. It was a room with no windows and many files and reports stacked in unsteady piles. The musky odor was so unlike Pierre's attention to detail. It was as if he was camped in somebody else's office, temporary and yet stuffed with work. Two chairs faced an oversized desk with a computer. A side table had four chairs, and was the only cleared space where an idle HGEAM waited for his personal use. At my entrance, Pierre looked up from some papers he was reading. "Brianna! What a treat. I was just looking over the results from the pox culture study. This could make us very rich, once we synthesize it."

"That offer you once made," I started in a small voice. "Is it still open?"

He put down the papers and came around the desk. "Really? You would go?"

I stepped away. "I have a price. The male gualarep at the zoo. You must get his infections cured and ship him to Dolvia, to Kyle Rula at the fortress of Arim."

"What gualarep?"

"We saw him that day at the zoo."

"That would be an expensive undertaking, Brianna. I don't know if—"

"That is my price. And I travel under my own name. Me, Brianna Miller of Arim."

Pierre drew close. "You trouble me more than you imagine."

He waited for a long moment, you know, counting the cost. "I can pay your price, Brianna. But you must understand, we will travel together as a couple."

"I know."

"Let's have a kiss to seal our bargain."

"After the gualarep is disembarked on Dolvia. And no tricks. I will know when it's accomplished."

"Sure, Brianna. Whatever you say."

"And travel papers in my name."

I spent the next two weeks with Dr. Beecham at Major Shaw's farm. The battling Shaws were sometimes home for dinner. They talked around and around about everything, especially about Carline Bryant's arrival on Cicero and how Mrs. Shaw should not stoop to accepting an invitation to appear opposite Carline on the talk shows.

"The news segment is an opportunity to set things straight," Mrs. Shaw insisted.

Mike Shaw spoke without looking up. "Appearing with you legitimizes Carline Bryant as your equal. The op-ed pieces are more effective."

"You just don't want to see me on the comtechs."

"Look, we have been offworld for months now," Mike reasoned. "The tribal balance has changed. We know nothing about what is on Karlyhi's mind."

"I know what's on Carline Bryant's mind!"

"Why stick out your neck for something we cannot affect from here?"

"You're jealous you were not invited."

It meant nothing, you know, all their opinions and all their good intentions. I felt very distant from them, even from Major Shaw who sometimes sat alone by the window and chewed his thumb. I brought his tea. He looked up with glassy eyes and murmured his thanks. Major Shaw was out of power because of his bad spleen. He had no power. No wonder Rabbenu Ely and the others held on so strongly. What else was there for them after the loss of power?

I remember that time as bittersweet. I knew it would be short.

Late one afternoon Dr. Mitterand came for me. Major Shaw greeted him by the ECCAV and stared at a set of papers Pierre displayed. Mrs. Shaw also stared at the papers and turned to me with anger. "You cannot leave now."

I used words I had rehearsed over the last days. "I have selected this danger." I handed Pierre my small case that he tossed into the back of the ECCAV.

"But you said nothing," she complained. "We had no idea. Brianna, there are other options." Three objections. Sheeks-Cylom stood firm in her arrogance.

"Are you jumping back to Earth?" I asked her. "Is Dr. Beecham?"

"That's not the only way!"

"It's my way."

She breathed in through her nostrils noisily. "Can you stand there and honestly tell me that you love Pierre?"

"I love Pierre."

Hank Beecham came around the side of the house. He removed his garden gloves and tucked them under the bib of his striped apron that was smeared with dark mulch.

"Did you know about this?" Mrs. Shaw pointedly asked him.

"It was inevitable," Hank said, and then gave me an unsteady hug. His soft cheeks were warm and gritty.

"I'm not reconciled to this!" Mrs. Shaw claimed. Major Shaw drew her back onto the lawn. She jerked from him with anger, perhaps to hide her other feelings. She understood the value of anger.

I went around the side of the ECCAV and got in. Pierre took the wheel and we sped away from the farmhouse. I did not look back.

He showed me the papers that the Shaws had inspected. It was permission to jump back, listing a Brianna Miller, American, nineteen years of age, parents deceased.

Pierre showed me a second page that was a bill of lading for the transport of a certain male gualarep, destination the fortress of Arim west of Somule on Dolvia. I did not need to see that paper. I knew the gualarep had left Cicero. We had shared many mental pictures over the weeks.

That night I wore the clingy dress and had dinner with Pierre at the hotel, but I had little appetite for the entrée with white sauce. We went to a Two Forks gambling parlor. The music was loud and the many machines made nonsensical pinging noises. The chilled air smelled like stale beer and kari root smoke. We sat at a gaming table where an attendant who wore a bowtie and white shirt carefully hid his opinion of what we were about; I could see it on his face. The frozen mask moved not a jot while his cynical eyes traveled from me to Pierre and back to me. Pierre showed me how to play a couple games and what to bet. Mostly I was impressed with the bright lights and forced gaiety.

Later we passed a table where somebody called out Pierre's name. It was Steve Swanweil, seated with some Han Chinese businessmen. He and Pierre shook hands, and we sat with them for a drink. One of the Company executives there was Tuang Cho, whose suit coat had the panda logo on the breast pocket. He looked right through me.

Pierre lit a kari root cigarette. Perhaps it was the calming smoke from my own culture, but I saw Mr. Swanweil the same way he had appeared once when I had participated in Mrs. Shaw's Cylay dinners. His aura projected an oily film, like a fluctuating pond image. The words left his mouth and fell to the ground. It all made sense. When Steve Swanweil had attended Mrs. Shaw's event, he had just come from meetings with Company executives. His aura had not yet settled. Time truly was a loop.

"Mr. Chin," Pierre said to the other Chinese man. "May I present one you will be interested to know? This is Brianna Miller of Arim."

Daniel Chin leaned forward from the shadows. A shaft of light fell across his eyes that glistened with interest while he looked over my form. "I knew your father," he said in perfect English. "I knew him very well."

He was small and thin, his hair combed straight back and his face like porcelain. He also smoked, holding the foreign cigarette between his first two fingers like a movie star might. Daniel Chin pursed his thin lips. "I will buy her from you."

"Don't you own enough women?" Pierre asked.

Daniel Chin's slanted eyes never left my face. "But not this woman. Name your price."

Pierre squirmed in his seat, delighted with the turn of affairs. "We're jumping back the day after tomorrow. You will have to count Brianna as the one that got away."

Pierre led me away, and we left the gaming room. In the lobby, he seemed jubilant. He could not stop twisting about, as if he had just been counting his money or something. I can report here that the whole time I was with Pierre, which was not so very long, he never sold me and he never shared me. I firmly believe I have Daniel Chin to thank for that.

In the hotel suite, I sat before a big mirror. Pierre had provided all the trappings a traveling American teenager could want. I puffed powder onto my cheeks and coughed a little. I put on the jangling bracelets and applied rouge to my lips.

I played this fantasy in my mind that I was ensconced at the Cylay hotel and Pierre was my Consortium officer who came home to me each night. Or that I was alone on the savannah and Pierre swooped down in a helicopter to save me from the flood. Or that I was held captive by sweatshop managers and he broke down the doors to snatch me up in the nick of time. Those images carried me through the awkward moments. I was far from Dolvia. What did it matter what I did next? I applied more rouge to my lips.

Later we were in the bed together. When Pierre climbed on top of me, well, there was no fantasy to cover that. I did multiplication tables in my head.

Sex was like showers. After a while, you know, it was not so bad.

At the shuttle launch pad two days later, Pierre and I waited in customs. My stomach was upset and my eyes itched with tears. But I had selected this danger, so I must go through with my plan.

On the overhead comtech that ran Company talk shows, Carline Bryant and Mrs. Shaw were seated as guests with Regan Villines as moderator, arguing in turns about events on another planet. Watching that segment took my mind off my worries. "From any offworld station, we cannot discern the pressures that tribespeople feel," Mrs. Shaw insisted. "Only field men have a chance to offer informed reporting, though their opinions must be shaken out for bias."

"I grew up on Dolvia," Carline Bryant countered, her hair professionally swept back from her heavy features. "I know the Dolviets who fight in rebel forces. My voice carries weight because I was present with the Mekucoo Pete and the rabbenu's wife Marcy at the trial of Katelupe the martyr."

"That was twenty years ago."

"I know them. I can speak for them."

"Then tell us," Mrs. Shaw returned, "what the tribes think about the Bryant sweatshops. Tell us about the depth of their retribution against the managers and against the buildings."

"That has nothing to do with tribal unrest," Carline said quickly. "You tell us, Mrs. Shaw, about your fellow scientist who slaughtered your husband's gualarep."

It was the same everywhere, you know. While the men labored to husband scarce resources, patrician women squabbled for voice. Mrs. Shaw's contained anger served her well against Carline's self-assured prejudice. Sheeks-Cylom had taught me much about the value of anger.

Major Michael Peter Shaw threaded his way through the shuttle crowd and came to my side. "You didn't think I would allow you to leave without saying good-bye, did you?"

"I did not know," I shrugged.

"My wife wanted to be here for the sendoff, but she's detained at—"

I pointed to the comtech. "The program is being aired now."

He glanced up and shamefacedly shrugged. "Yes, well. I brought you these." He handed me a large shopping bag. "Hank packaged them. It's mostly small remembrances from Dolviets you refuse to tag via EAM. Also something from . . . from my wife and me."

"I can open them later."

"Are you afraid you might change your mind?"

"Is that why you came? To make me face my regrets?"

"I came to say that you're always welcome at the farmhouse," Mike said slowly. "I want you to remember that. No matter what happens, no matter what trouble may come. If you need financial help, anything. You can return here and stay with us, for as long as you need to."

I reached up and hugged him. "Thank you."

He blinked several times and looked away. "Oh! I forgot. There was also this." He handed me a telegram from his uniform jacket. "It's from Kyle Rula."

I slipped it into my skirt pocket. "Aren't you going to read it?" he asked.

"Sure. On the shuttle."

Pierre joined us. "Major Shaw," he said and shook hands.

"Dr. Mitterand." Mike turned back to me. "Well … I guess that is all. My wife wanted to be here."

"You said that."

The flight attendant began calling out seat rows for boarding passengers. The crowd moved forward. Pierre glanced at our tickets. "Let's go," he whispered.

"Will you let us know how you're doing?" Major Shaw asked.

"Sure," I said as we walked away. "It's always good to keep a channel open."

Smile lines showed on his worried face.

After we reached the shuttle from the long causeway, Pierre drew me aside. "I have a surprise," he claimed as if he was, you know, competing with Major Shaw's gifts or something. He spoke to the pilot, an American in a crisp blue uniform with many buttons and decorations plus a round hat with a polished bill. The pilot allowed me to look into the plane's cockpit. That is not a French word, cockpit.

A cramped space was filled with dials and luminous displays and two bucket seats. The view from the long windows was pan-o-ram-ic. "How did you get all this equipment crammed in here?" I asked.

"Yankee ingenuity."

"I don't know what that means."

"It means," Pierre interjected, "that they are always thinking, these Americans."

I thanked the friendly man and walked with Pierre to our seats.

We stowed the shopping bag and our carry-ons, and settled into the high-backed seats. I sighed and looked around at the other pas-sengers, all business people or families on holiday. There were no soldiers present. That felt odd.

Some slick magazines were tucked into the seat holder in front of me. I thumbed through one and stopped at a photo of some tall, tall buildings that reflected the sun.

"That's Beijing," Pierre said. "Where we disembark on Earth."

"All that acrylic. What do they store in so many buildings?"

"They're office buildings, and it's glass, not acrylic," Pierre said. "They stand empty at night when the people go home. Behind each pane sits an executive who would rather journey to the Canyon of Buttes."

I grinned at him. "The leaders on Earth must be very powerful to make the people spend their days in glass boxes."

"People want to," he shrugged. "In Beijing, and in Paris, and in New York. They work in skyscrapers for forty, sometimes sixty hours a week."

"That must be the Softcheeks' secret, the reason why they dominate."

"What secret?"

"Well, like the pilot," I said. "He can sit for what, ten hours in that seat, just looking out and checking his dials. No warrior could tolerate that.

"And Dr. Beecham," I continued, "recovered while quarantined in the acrylic box, but the gualarep suffered immensely in a similar box at the zoo. So that must be their secret. Softcheeks thrive even under glass."

"That's an interesting perspective, Brianna."

Pierre snuggled deeper into his seat. "Get some rest if you can. Your body clock will be in a spin for some time now. In a few hours we disembark at Stargate Junction. A few days later we'll arrive on Earth." He crossed his arms and closed his eyes.

I looked around at the other passengers who did not bother to notice me. The gifts were stowed in the overhead compartment, so I could not unwrap them. I settled back and thought about arriving in America, the meritocracy where the always-thinking Yankees chose to spend their days in glass houses.

Then I remembered the telegram in my skirt pocket. Pierre had turned away his face while he tried to nap. I opened the slim page that read, YOUR PACKAGE SAFELY ARRIVED. WE HAVE CHOSEN TO NAME HIM BRIAN. KR.

At least that was accomplished.

EXCERPT

 gesture just as he had accepted the need to wear the Western suit. Rufus was age 28 and light-skinned like his father, with a narrow nose. When our palms met, a battle scar across the back of his wrist was visible. I was certain there were many more.

"Hiki, Rufus. Melinga."

"Melinga. May I present Kyros rabbe Sudl, a cousin to Karen Osborn?"

Kyros hesitantly extended his hand to shake. He was perhaps 35, taller and stouter, with yellow skin that turned golden under the savannah sun. I had to assume Kyros had spent his tender years herding cattle with the Southeast Arrivi, too old to have tolerated attendance in Hakulupe Le's classroom. His wife and academy-trained children most likely participated in rice cultivation. This trip through the wormhole, disembarking in Beijing and onto

Paris, must have been a wonder to him, once he got past the discomfort of inoculation against disease.

I could not resist having a little fun at Kyros rabbe Sudl's expense, maybe because Laura stared with her mouth agape. "Kyros is a woman's name," I said in Arrivi.

"There was a woman named Kyros," Rufus said. She was his grandmother. "There was a man named Brian." Rufus had not changed much, put no strain on my dormant language skills.

"Laura, would you bring tea?" I asked in French. I gestured to the long dining table. "Please, won't you have a seat?" Rufus pulled a chair away from the table so it faced out. He sat with a straight back and hands on his knees spread wide apart. Kyros stood more or less at Rufus's shoulder. Their posture told me everything. Each wore an arm amulet, a glassy topaz stone trapped in a binding cord and tied around the big muscle of the right arm, indicating that they knew a time of mourning. "You will return to the flats now," Rufus said without preamble, "and dwell in the fortress of Arim."

"On your word?"

"You have inherited the fortress by Kyle Rula's hand."

"I robbed you of your birthright?"

"Mekucoo don't require a library."

So Rufus had made peace with Kyle Rula before departing. After a moment I offered, "I had forgotten Mekucoo could be so charming."

His brow wrinkled. He expected resistance, perhaps even a hissy-fit so he could throw me over his shoulder and carry me back to my larger destiny. He glanced around at the apartment's furnishings and exchanged looks with Kyros rabbe Sudl. "Your riches are Dolvia-derived."

"I developed the shipping channels so the convent residents prosper."

"A rich woman is just a target."

I sighed. I had set aside tribal logic, forgetting how numbing and exclusive it could be. I had a life here in Paris, a position and a name, however tainted. Why return to a war-torn desert where women were granted no voice? Where you had to set yourself on fire to be noticed.

"Dacupitte sent this." Rufus drew from his pocket a gold bracelet fashioned into acacia leaves placed side-by-side—the traditional Arrivi engagement bracelet, to be augmented at the wedding celebration by a similar necklace. Dacupitte was called Pete, the 45-year-old father of legions, and my supposed betrothed on Dolvia.

I only chuckled. "Dacupitte assumes much."

"It is seen."

I had never held with tribal prophecy, especially this claim. "That was a convenient vision offered to bolster Pete's leadership status."

Rufus blinked. "You question second sight?"

"I question everything."

Rufus considered that. After a long moment he said, "How sad for you."

GLOSSARY

of character names in The Bush Clinic

NOTE: *listed by last name (where available) and designated by status when first introduced. Locations and terms are listed separately.*

Dr. Leslie Abercrombie – Softcheeks doctor who ran the savannah hospital

Len rabbe Arim – Arrivi who owned the flats of Arim, had four willful daughters

Dr. Henry Beecham – hospital administrator after Dr. Abercrombie

Louise Bilesketchum – pharmacist and dietician, mistress to Mike Shaw

Brian – second adult male Gualarep imported from Cicero

Carline Bryant – sister to Joey Osborn and half-sister to Dacupitte, married to Sean Bryant of the Cylay Bryant cartel

Sean Bryant – a cartel founder and sweatshop operator, husband to Carline Bryant, brothers Daniel and Patrick

Cara – Mekucoo prince and companion to Cyrus

Daniel Chin – Company executive, boss to Tuang Cho and Wan Su

Tuang Cho – Company executive and friend to Daniel Chin

Cyrus – Mekucoo warrior scarred from Company torture

Dacupitte – (pronounced dac-you-pit-tea) Mekucoo for "he who waits with angry eyes", their name for Hamish (Pete), the illegitimate son of Hamish Nordhagen and Heather Osborn, raised by Kecouroo

Frank Duerr – Cicero-born civil authority in Somule and Cylay

Edna – one of two female Gualareps submitted to Dr. Greensboro, later to Hakulupe Le

Edwina – one of two female Gualareps submitted to Dr. Greensboro, later to Kecouroo

Rabbenu Ely – Arrivi leader, a former revolutionary follower of Mula

Brent Gotskind – Cylay civil authority and friend to Frank Duerr

Dr. Edna Edwina Greensboro – bush clinic research doctor, also known as Sheeks-Cylom, later wife to Captain Shaw

Hakulupe Le – daughter of Katelupe Le and Haku rabbe Murd from a union forced on them in the Company prison. Sometimes called Lupe

Hamilcar – common tribal name for Colonel Hartley, taken from Hanthudilciage which means talking-head

Billie Hartley – Colonel Hartley's wife, mother to Carl, Heather, and Jesse

Carl Hartley – son to Colonel and Mrs. Hartley, university student

Heather Hartley – Colonel and Mrs. Hartley's oldest daughter, named after Heather Osborn

Jesse Hartley – youngest child of Colonel and Mrs. Hartley, a transport student

Colonel Eugene Hartley – Consortium officer stationed on the orbiting transport, wife Billie

Karima Le – oldest sister of Arim, sometimes called May, married to Haku rabbe Murd

Karlyhi – Cylahi refugee picked up by Dr. Greensboro, later a militia leader called Karl Wyley

Kat – youngest of Haku rabbe Murd and Karima Le's four children, named for her dead aunt, later a holy woman

Katelupe Le – second oldest sister of Arim, sometimes called Terry, later known as Terry the martyr and unfortunate mother to Hakulupe Le

Kecouroo – daughter to Cyrus by his first wife, raised with Dacupitte, niece to Cara, a bush clinic school teacher

Klistina Le – third-born sister of Arim, sometimes called Tina, Brianna Miller's mother

Kyle Le – youngest sister of Arim, sometimes called Kyle Rula or Rularim, also as a businessperson called Kyle rabbe Arim, a goulep blessed with second sight. Wife of Cyrus and mother to Lynus and Rufus

Kyros – mother to Cyrus, served as ambassador to Urbyd in an earlier season of om

Lynus – son of Cyrus and Kyle Rula, brother to Rufus

Mabe Jo – Uburu translator for Metobak in the refugee camp

Lt. Billy Manenowski – Consortium officer, later an academy teacher of accounting

Marcy – Cylahi mulatto and one of Lucy's kids, wife to Rabbenu Ely

Martina – Martin Sumuki's oldest daughter, scarred on her eye by a former fungus growth, also known as Lula

Metobak – Uburu leader in the refugee camp

John Milan – Softcheeks journalist in the days of the Uburu refugee crisis

Brian Miller – hero of the Company refinery battle, father to Brianna Miller by Klistina Le, a sister of Arim

Brianna Miller – daughter to Brian Miller and Klistina Le of Arim

Dr. Pierre Mitterand – French research doctor completing his residency on Dolvia

Moab – Uburu hero and short-time husband to Kecouroo

Haku rabbe Murd – Arrivi erriv rancher, blind and obese with old napalm burns on his face and neck, husband to Karima Le of Arim, father to Orin

Orin rabbe Murd – oldest son of Haku rabbe Murd and Karima Le of Arim, father of Hakki rabbe Murd

Spindel rabbe Murd – brother to Haku, killed on the road in the days of Martin Sumuki

Hamish Nordhagen – transport crewmember, father of Dacupitte by Heather Osborn

Oria – mythological Arrivi warrior present in many tribal chants

Oroc -- mythological Uburu warrior present in many tribal chants

Oriika – Dolviet holy woman in the days of Martin Sumuki

Heather Osborn – wife to colonist Carl Osborn, mother to Joey and Carline Osborn and Dacupitte (called Pete), later wife to Brian Miller

Joey Osborn – oldest child of Carl and Heather Osborn, brother to Carline, half-brother to Dacupitte (called Pete)

Karen Osborn – Joey's wife and mother to Kelly and Patrick

Pete – nickname for Dacupitte, illegitimate son of Heather Osborn and Hamish Nordhagen

Ralph – Cicero-born male Gualarep, Mike Shaw's pet

Rufus – younger son of Cyrus and Kyle Rula, brother to Lynus

Rularim – latter-day name for Kyle Le

Sarah – sweatshop slave, later a goulep and welfare minister, friend to Vera and Karen

Lt. Milo Sector – Consortium officer under Captain Major Shaw's command

Lt. Michael Peter Shaw – Cicero solider, later Director of Natural Disasters Control

Sheek-Cylom – native name for Dr. Greensboro first given her by Karlyhi, ghostly Softcheeks

Wan Su – Company executive with Tuang Cho

Martin Sumuki – Putuki officer at Tri-City Bank Corp in an earlier season of om

Steve Swanweil – Bryant cartel employee with connections to the Company

Lt. Taylor – Consortium officer in the days of Captain Mike Shaw

Terry the martyr – Katelupe Le, second oldest sister of Arim

Tommy – one of eighteen mulatto Cylahi orphans known as Lucy's kids, cousin to Marcy

Tom – son of Tommy, studied on the transport as a scholarship boy

Vera – school chum of Brianna, a hamstrung sweatshop slave

George Villa – Softcheeks archeologist and murderer of Ralph

GLOSSARY

of locations and terms used in The Bush Clinic

Acclimation pill – Company-issue stimulant for newly disembarking executives who experience difficulty with Dolvia's climate

Airbus – an imported Consortium bus in three sections, the driver's cab, the patient section and a truckbed

Air-lift – elevator in Biosphere and transport

Arrivi – Dolviet tribe who own land and herd erriv. Their women wear full body veils with facial panels

Baktu – male Uburu garment consisting of a colorful wrap-around from waist to knees

Bald – freightate term for a person who live among the tribes without technical support

Blackshirts – Company enforcers, some Han-Chinese and some former conscripts

Biosphere – Company built station on Cicero

Brittany Mill – textile factory owned by Ricardo Menenous and managed by Brian Miller, in the days of Martin Sumuki

Burka – required Arrivi body veil with facial panel

Canyon of Buttes – Dolviet cluster of buttes within a canyon west of the savannah, a sacred area for Arrivi

Catarrh – a sometimes fatal erriv disease that causes boils

Chador – Softcheeks term for the Arrivi burka with facial panel

Chikiocahi – the middle Softcheeks plane, within Dolviet spiritual viewing, which embodies the social self, also called the chi

Cicero – Westend planet nearest Dolvia, a member of the Consortium

Company – Han-Chinese Earth corporation with mining interests in Westend

Company logo – an off-black and eggshell white image of the long extinct Chinese giant panda roundly sitting with one paw on its knee, superimposed over a circle of mandarin yellow rimmed with royal purple

Comtech – linked screens that broadcast Company sanctioned news in public areas throughout the transport system plus at Stargate Junction

Consortium – loosely formed federation of domestic governments on the four inhabitable planets of the tri-star system in Westend which includes Dolvia and Cicero

Cylay – 1) the capital city of Dolvia's savannah region, 2) one of four Mekucoo seasons when forces spread out from the source

Cylahi – poor Dolviet tribe who wear few clothes and fashion gold jewelry for a trade

Dolvia – small planet with two moons, a ring of rain forests at its equator, plus an arid savannah region that includes the cities of Cylay and Somule

EAM – extra-atmosphere modem, a tabletop computer screen for communicating via satellite or directly with the transport. EAM-12 is text only, EAM-50 has video-conferencing

ECCAV – enclosed cross-country air-conditioned vehicle, the Consortium car

Erriv – Arrivi cattle with row of horns along the crest of the skull and neck

Eve of the Hunt – night before the Ketiwhelp hunt

Feast of Oria – Arrivi high holiday that takes place after the rains

Flats of Arim – geo-thermal section of the savannah that includes geysers, bubbling mud pools and mineral springs, originally owned by Len rabbe Arim, Kyle Le's father

Fortress of Arim – manmade cave dug into the caldera wall above the flats and used as a hiding place by Kyle Le and Heather Osborn

Freightate – transport slang

Goulep – persona non grata ostracized by her own tribe

Gualarep – marble-hide reptile originally from Cicero which can regulate it colors, identify by scent, and throw its thoughts

Hai – Arrivi word for yes

Hamstrung – Siibabean war tactic wherein the warrior's ankle tendons are slashed crippling him for life

Han-Chinese – Earth minority group who comprise the elite pool of Company executives

Hardhand – Dolviet term for disembarking colonists who set up small trade businesses in Cylay and Somule

Heartstone – Edna's word for empathetic pain for another's suffering

HGEAM – holographic extra-atmosphere modem that projected a deep-view image of the speaker

Hiki – an Arrivi greeting

Jump back – freightate for the return to Earth through the worm hole

Kam – Mekucoo penny, a copper twist

Kant – a lack of kari, no growth or reinforcement from Dolvia

Kari – one of four Mekucoo seasons when new growth presents itself

Kari root – medicinal herb that Dolviet men smoke as a cigarette

Kariom – Dolviet gray lungfish that hibernates in the riverbank until the ran comes, once worshipped as a god

Karkar – tribal automatic weapon

Karsci – sudden shift of events with a season

Ketiwhelp – four-legged furry omnivores that plague Arrivi cattle

Kiam gin – imported alcoholic drink

Low-fic – short wave communications apparatus

Lucy's kids – eighteen mulatto Cylahi children, including Tommy and Marcy, sired by transport conscripts who Lucy Kempler raises after their mothers die of dysentery

Maser – medicinal laser used for sealing cleansed wounds

Mekucoo – Dolviet tribe renown as Ketiwhelp killers

Melinga – Dolviet greeting, literally "may Dolvia embrace you"

Mercy seat – Mekucoo ideal taken from Earth culture, a peaceful gathering where all parties gain something

Murmurey bird – large flesh eater that nests year-round on the savannah

Netta – 1) a symbiotic balance of sulfur over silica, superheated for decades by subterranean geysers and spewed out the vents before the cooling rains to be captured on natural burlap, most often harvested by Arrivi women, 2) the longest of four Mekucoo seasons when the savannah is dormant, 3) a dry balance

Nettki – female Dolviet moon that never rises to a zenith but hovers continually at the horizon

Nettom – male Dolviet moon that passes overhead before sinking into Nettki's sky

Nu delaya – Mekucoo command to wait

Oblu – Mekucoo quarter, a silver twist

Okiioc – fibrous stalk, a staple in Siibabean diet that helps prevent cataracts and build strong teeth

Oleastra – wild olive shrubs on the savannah

Om – shortest of four Mekucoo seasons when all is made known

Onchocerciasis – river blindness caused when an internal colony of mites breeds and clouds the eyes with larvae

Putuki – Dolviet tribe who are mostly businessmen or domestic workers

Rabbenu – (pronounced ray-ben-you) a title of high honor reserved for the elected Arrivi leader

Regent – Company leader

"Rob the desert of one" – to attempt a foolish act that will kill you before the desert can

Second sight – the ability to discern more than is apparent

Siibabean – traditional Mekucoo enemies, tall and lean with perfect teeth, who wear a halo headdress of Murmurey feathers

Softcheeks – a Dolviet term for Earthlings including Company executives

Somule – the Dolvia savannah city closest to the flats of Arim

Stargate Junction – the space station at Westend's worm hole entrance

Travel number – permission to jump back to Earth by way of Company shipping routes through the worm hole

Treasure of Kyle Rula – a chest containing peridot and topaz gems and Cylahi gold jewelry plus some natural netta that had been offered over time as bribes to Captain Ellis to ensure Katelupe Le's relative health in the Company prison

"Three planes of Softcheeks" – within second sight, how Earthlings but not Hardhands appear to Dolviets

Tunanin – dust columns on the savannah, ancestral spirit who survey the land before the rains

Two Forks – a Cicero city where Mike Shaw's parents had a farm

Tzu – Company-made laser gun

Uburu – a northern mountain tribe forced onto the savannah when their crops are burned

Westend – a space quadrant beyond the wormhole and loosely ruled by the Consortium

Worm hole – the connecting time-compressed space anomaly between Earth's solar system and Westend

ABOUT THE AUTHOR

STELLA ATRIUM IS A CYNICAL SEPTUAGENARIAN. SHE HAS SPENT a lifetime exploring female characters for real world reactions to obstacles. Often pushed into submissive and non-verbal roles, women really live in a world of networking among aunties, cousins, wives of husbands, convenient friends and neighbors. This rich world is largely unexplored.

"I grew up with all brothers, so I knew about women from stories and from school. What I found at school wasn't anything like in the stories, so I set out to learn why."

If you enjoyed *The Bush Clinic,* leave a reader review on Amazon or Goodreads. Visit Stella's website to order book 2, *The Body Politic,* at stellaatrium.com.